"A PHENOMENAL NEW SERIES."
—*Fresh Fiction*

"Alyssa Day works her own brand of sexy sorcery
in this fabulous new paranormal series.
Warriors and witches have never been so hot!"
—*New York Times* bestselling author Teresa Medeiros

"There's nothing more evocative than the
world of Atlantis."
—*New York Times* bestselling author Gena Showalter

Praise for

ATLANTIS AWAKENING

"Fascinating, thrilling, and deeply romantic. The perfect blend
of fabulous world-building and sexy romantic adventure."
—*New York Times* bestselling author Jayne Castle

"Alyssa Day's Atlantis is flat-out amazing—her sexy and
heroic characters make me want to beg for more! I love the
complex world she's created!"
—National bestselling author Alexis Morgan

"The legend comes to life. Alyssa Day's superb writing,
fascinating characters, and edge-of-your-seat story bring the
legend of Atlantis to life. I cannot wait until the next install-
ment." —Award-winning author Colby Hodge

continued . . .

ATLANTIS RISING

ATLANTIS UNMASKED

The Warriors of Poseidon

ALYSSA DAY

BERKLEY SENSATION, NEW YORK

THE BERKLEY PUBLISHING GROUP
Published by the Penguin Group
Penguin Group (USA) Inc.
375 Hudson Street, New York, New York 10014, USA
Penguin Group (Canada), 90 Eglinton Avenue East, Suite 700, Toronto, Ontario M4P 2Y3, Canada
(a division of Pearson Penguin Canada Inc.)
Penguin Books Ltd., 80 Strand, London WC2R 0RL, England
Penguin Group Ireland, 25 St. Stephen's Green, Dublin 2, Ireland (a division of Penguin Books Ltd.)
Penguin Group (Australia), 250 Camberwell Road, Camberwell, Victoria 3124, Australia
(a division of Pearson Australia Group Pty. Ltd.)
Penguin Books India Pvt. Ltd., 11 Community Centre, Panchsheel Park, New Delhi—110 017, India
Penguin Group (NZ), 67 Apollo Drive, Rosedale, North Shore 0632, New Zealand
(a division of Pearson New Zealand Ltd.)
Penguin Books (South Africa) (Pty.) Ltd., 24 Sturdee Avenue, Rosebank, Johannesburg 2196,
South Africa

Penguin Books Ltd., Registered Offices: 80 Strand, London WC2R 0RL, England

This is a work of fiction. Names, characters, places, and incidents either are the product of the author's imagination or are used fictitiously, and any resemblance to actual persons, living or dead, business establishments, events, or locales is entirely coincidental. The publisher does not have any control over and does not assume any responsibility for author or third-party websites or their content.

ATLANTIS UNMASKED

A Berkley Sensation Book / published by arrangement with the author

PRINTING HISTORY
Berkley Sensation mass-market edition / July 2009

Copyright © 2009 by Alesia Holliday.
Excerpt from *Atlantis Redeemed* copyright © 2009 by Alesia Holliday.
Cover art by Phil Heffernan.
Cover design by George Long.
Interior text design by Laura K. Corless.

ISBN: 978-0-425-22322-2

BERKLEY® SENSATION
Berkley Sensation Books are published by The Berkley Publishing Group,
a division of Penguin Group (USA) Inc.,
375 Hudson Street, New York, New York 10014.
BERKLEY® SENSATION and the "B" design are trademarks of Penguin Group (USA) Inc.

PRINTED IN THE UNITED STATES OF AMERICA

10 9 8 7 6 5 4 3 2 1

This one is for the military families everywhere who watch and wait and worry while their loved ones are far away: I hope that reading it offers a little respite, a bit of escape, and perhaps a laugh or two. You deserve it, and I'm right there with you, pacing the floors at 2 A.M. during this deployment. May we all find happily ever after.

And, always, to Judd, Computer Boy, and Princess. My heroes.

Oh, and my apologies to any and all historical societies involved in any way with the city of St. Augustine, Florida, and the Fort Castillo de San Marcos. As far as I know, shape-shifting panthers have never attacked a rebel base there. For everyone else, trust me when I say you're going to want to visit.

It's spectacular.

And when you're there, stop by my friend Pam Cross's restaurant, the Bunnery. You'll be glad you did.

The Warrior's Creed

We will wait. And watch. And protect.
And serve as first warning on the eve of humanity's destruction.
Then, and only then, Atlantis will rise.
For we are the Warriors of Poseidon, and the
   mark of the Trident we bear serves as witness
   to our sacred duty to safeguard mankind.

Chapter 1

St. Louis, leaving regional rebel headquarters

"It's almost impossible to shoot a bow while driving."

Grace Havilland clenched her fingers around the steering wheel of the Jeep and waited for the Atlantean warrior riding shotgun to respond to what she thought had been her very reasonable point.

Waited. Waited a little longer. She'd met Alexios months ago and seen him sporadically since, but she'd never been in such a small space with him. It felt like being trapped in a cage with a lion who'd just eaten a full meal. Deadly, dangerous, and exhilarating, but maybe—just maybe—you'd live through it.

Unless he suddenly felt like a snack.

She wrenched the wheel to the left when she saw the deceptive DEAD END sign appear in the headlights and then took the deserted side street. Alexios finally turned to face her, his golden hair brushing the tops of his shoulders and sweeping forward to hide the scarred left side of his face. Reinforcing the lion imagery so strongly she flinched a little.

He raised a single eyebrow.

"The sign keeps people out," she explained. "HQ escape route and a shortcut to the hospital. Since we're a little behind everyone else, I wanted to catch up."

A weak but warm voice floated up from the backseat. "Shortcut would be good."

"How are you doing, Michelle?" Grace asked, not daring to look over her shoulder at this rate of speed.

"Well enough, considering that nasty vampire nearly ripped my head from my neck. Lucky for me that your dishy Alaric popped in with his magic healing powers. My first mission with you Americans, and the rebel headquarters gets attacked. Bit of a bad penny, me."

Alexios made a strangled snorting sound. "Dishy Alaric. Now there's something I bet he's never heard in his nearly five hundred years. Alaric, the dishy high priest of Poseidon's Temple." In spite of the rich, dark amusement in his voice, he never once quit scanning every inch of the deserted street as they raced through it. Always on guard. Always alert.

A warrior in every facet of his being.

Grace slanted a glance at him. Six feet and a few inches of pure primitive male, all hard lines and curved muscle. He'd fought like an avenging angel back at HQ when their strategy meeting had been viciously destroyed by the wave of vampires and shifters crashing through doors and windows in a multipronged attack. She'd loosed arrow after arrow, each one finding its target, but Alexios and his sword and daggers were everywhere at once, stabbing, slicing, and slashing. All the while, his expression had remained utterly calm and controlled. Even as he'd circled around her, ripping heads from vamps and . . .

A realization seared through the memory. Always around *her*. He'd fought in a perimeter around her, leaving her room to shoot her bow, but never straying far from her side. Anger started a slow burn.

"Were you protecting me in that fight?" she asked, slowly and carefully, trying to keep the lid on her temper. Not good to accuse and attack the fierce warrior ally unless it was true. "Because you know that I don't need protecting. I've been doing this for a long—"

Michelle made a loud shushing noise. "Oh, let's not get our knickers in a twist. So, Alexios. You don't look a day over thirty. But if Alaric is nearly five hundred years old, how about you?"

Alexios's dark gaze touched Grace's face for an instant, hot, predatory, tangible as a caress, before returning to vigilance. She wondered if his eyes were blue or black or one of the many shades of jewellike green, but couldn't tell in the dark vehicle. Atlantean eyes were like mood rings. Unfortunately, they didn't give out the handy decoder chart.

"How about me, what?" he finally answered Michelle.

"How many centuries?"

"A little more than four. Grace, watch that hole in the road."

She swerved to miss the pothole and began to slow for the end of the road and the busy intersection it dumped into. "You're more than four hundred years old? Really?" Okay, maybe a man *that* old had a few preconceived notions about fragile females that could be forgiven.

"Well, you look lovely for your age," Michelle called out. "He's maybe a little old for you, Grace, though. You've only just turned twenty-five, after all."

Heat burned through Grace's cheeks. "What? Michelle, I—"

Before she could stammer out any convincing denials, on the order of, "No, I wasn't casting Alexios in my own personal fantasy," the man himself pointed his gun directly at her head.

She slammed on the brakes, too stunned to react coherently. Alexios and the Atlanteans were *allies* to the rebel cause; they wouldn't . . .

"On the left, Grace. Get down!"

Instinctively, she obeyed the tone of command in his voice and ducked, covering her head with her arms. The explosion of sound and glass tore through the Jeep a split second later, and Michelle screamed.

Over Grace's head, Alexios unloaded the Glock she'd loaned him when he'd realized his daggers and sword wouldn't be of much use in a moving vehicle. He spat forth a stream of words that absolutely had to be Atlantean cursing; she'd fought with warriors for enough years to recognize the cadence. If the Ice King of Calm was swearing, it had to be bad.

The realization brought her to a snap decision of her own. Grace wrenched the parking brake up, released her seat belt, and threw herself underneath his arms in a twisting half turn toward the backseat. Alexios slammed his hard chest down on her back, though, capturing her in a contorted embrace.

"No. If you lift your head, the attacker on the roof of that building is going to shoot you," he breathed in her ear.

"I need to get to Michelle. Now."

"I will not lose you," he said as he slowly pulled away. The words were so quiet that she nearly missed them. She snapped her head to the left and found his face a breath away from her own. Fury rode the high cheekbones and hard angles of his face. "I'm going out there," he said. "When I give the signal, you put this vehicle in gear and get the hells out of here."

He dropped the empty gun on the floorboard and pulled his daggers out of their sheaths. The movement was fluid and oddly slowed by stress-skewed perception, almost encapsulated in a bubble of time. She noticed the hairs on his tanned and muscled forearms were burnished gold, and she even had time to think it an odd observation to make before dying.

Then, in a move that made her wonder if somehow

she'd gotten a head injury in the crash, Alexios simply disappeared. It wasn't sudden. It took maybe three or four seconds. But his body dissolved into a shimmering cascade of sparkling mist, and utterly transparent and nearly without shape, he soared through the open window beside her, leaving Grace with her mouth open in wonder and tiny water drops caught in her eyelashes.

"Oh dear. I think I may have died," Michelle said, moaning. "Either I just saw Alexios turn into an angel, or you and he are going to have some seriously interesting sex."

Stifling her ready retort, Grace resumed her crawl into the backseat to help Michelle, careful to keep her own head down. There was blood everywhere; the gunshot had smashed through the window next to Michelle and hit her shoulder. Glass glittered in her short dark hair, and shallow scratches bled on her forehead and cheeks.

"How bad?"

Michelle tried to smile, but it turned into a grimace. "I won't be wearing any sleeveless dresses for a while."

Grace's eyes burned. If she lost her best friend . . . "Damnit, Michelle, quit with that British stiff-upper-lip crap. How bad?"

In the pale glow reflected from the streetlamp, Michelle's face was whiter than a St. Louis blizzard. "Maybe a little bad. It's just below my shoulder, but I'm starting to have a hard time breathing, and—" As if on cue, Michelle's sentence trailed off into a horrible wheezing gasp.

"It must have punctured your lung, oh, dear Lord and goddess help us, we've got to get out of here," Grace said, offering up prayers to Diana and to the Christian god. She snatched her bow and half-empty quiver from the back and pulled herself into the driver's seat, fitting arrow to bow with an ease born of long practice. She took aim through her open window and waited to deliver silver-tipped death.

She was a descendant of Diana, and her aim was always true.

"I'm going to get you to the hospital," she promised, scanning the area for Alexios or the attackers.

A dark shadow somersaulted through the air toward the Jeep, and she tracked it without thought, acting purely on instinct and natural talent.

"Didn't you have enough back at HQ, you bastards?" she screamed. "A dozen dead shifters and at least a half dozen dead vamps isn't enough? I'll kill every single one of you if she dies."

The shadow moved almost faster than her eye could follow until it materialized into a coalescing shimmer in the pool of light cast by the streetlamp. She eased the pressure of her fingers on the arrow.

Vamps didn't travel as mist. It was Alexios, transformed back into himself.

He bared his teeth and the expression on his face was so utterly feral—so inhumanly predatory—that Grace caught her breath, ice skating down her spine.

"Go. Now," he ordered. "I'll be right above you. Get her to the hospital. Now."

"You got them?"

"They won't hurt anyone else," he said. "Now go!"

Michelle's harsh wheezing fired Grace's urgency to do just that. She slammed the Jeep back into gear and, tires squealing, pulled out into the street and away from the remains of whatever had attacked them in the alley.

"Hang on, baby, hang on, please, please, Michelle, hang on," she pleaded in a constant demand and prayer, as she sped the remaining couple of miles to the hospital. Above the Jeep, matching her pace exactly, a soaring cloud of sparkling darkness watched over them.

She bumped over the curb at the entrance to the emergency room parking lot and pulled the Jeep right up to the door, ignoring signs and the shouts from the ambulance personnel standing around the large double doors. Grace leapt out, shouting for help, and raced around to open the back passenger door. Michelle slumped out into her arms, eyes wide and staring, and Grace instinctively screamed, so loud and long her throat burned, for the one person she needed more than she'd ever needed anyone.

"Alexios!"

"I am here." He lifted Michelle out of Grace's arms and began running for the ER doors. Emergency personnel met him with a gurney. He gently lowered Michelle onto it and backed away as hospital personnel rushed Michelle inside, already snapping out competent-sounding medical speak.

Head lowered, Alexios returned to Grace and lifted her into his arms, holding her to him so tightly she almost felt— *almost*, for a fraction of a second—*safe*.

She saw one of her team approaching from the outside waiting area, and she put her hands flat on Alexios's chest to brace herself and push him away. For an instant, his eyes flared such a hot green that she wondered his gaze didn't burn the skin from her face. But then he slowly, inch by inch, lowered her to the ground and released her, almost as if he, too, were reluctant to break the contact.

"I can move the Jeep, Grace," Spike said. He'd been wounded by the first wave of shifters in the door, but the bandages wrapping both of his arms and the side of his face clearly hadn't slowed him down. "Everybody is already getting treatment. Most all of us are going to be fine. We'll hear about Hawk after surgery."

She nodded, glad to hear it but too drained to comment.

Spike's eyes narrowed, and he shot a suspicious look at Alexios. "We thought that dark-haired guy healed Michelle."

"So he did," Alexios replied, his jaw clenching around the words. "We were ambushed."

Spike was instantly on the balls of his feet, hands hovering near his jacket, underneath which Grace knew he carried at least three guns and several knives. "How many? Do you want us to go after them?"

"They're taken care of," Grace said.

Alexios nodded. "There were only four." Any other man would have been boasting, Alexios merely stated facts.

A flash of respect crossed Spike's face. Grace wasn't the only one who'd seen Alexios in action. She thought maybe Alexios wouldn't want her to mention the mist thing, though. That had been new. Maybe it was meant to be secret.

"Thanks for moving the car. We'll be . . . we'll be inside." She glanced up at Alexios, who started to put an arm around her, then hesitated, as if afraid of being rebuffed. She leaned into him, too tired and afraid for Michelle to force herself to stand alone, yet again.

Just this once, she would lean on someone else. Just this once.

~~~

St. Louis University Hospital, emergency room

Alexios looked around the crowded waiting room, remembering the countless times he or another of his fellow warriors had needed to be healed. Unlike the healing chambers in Atlantis, which were an oasis of serenity—all fresh air and sunlight, soft, silken cushions, and masses of flowers from the palace gardens—this room where desperate and injured humans waited smelled of sweat, blood, antiseptic, and despair.

Grace huddled in an orange plastic chair, strangely diminished without her many weapons strapped to her body. He stood across the room from her, leaning against a battered vending machine, and tried to think of a time he'd seen her without them but came up empty. The bow, knives, and guns were part of her, oddly dissonant to her beauty and her name.

Grace. It suited her. She was grace in motion, in and out of battle. Except now, when she hunched in that ugly chair, arms wrapped around her knees, waiting for the bleakest kind of bad news.

After they'd removed their visible weapons, he'd helped her into the ER, trying not to wonder why something deep in his chest ached at the feel of her in his arms. Then she'd pulled away from him and collapsed into that chair, and she hadn't moved since. Alexios had wasted a good ten minutes convincing various hospital personnel that he didn't need to be treated for a head wound, after they'd caught sight of the apparently alarming amount of blood that remained in his hair and on the side of his face. He'd finally snarled something along the lines of "it's not my blood," and they'd backed off, all wary apprehension with a healthy dose of fear mixed in. Ever since then, he'd waited. And waited.

He despised waiting.

Hospital security was there in force, and the police were on their way. Luckily, Grace had excellent contacts within the local Paranormal Ops unit, and Alexios had met some of the officers before. He wasn't worried about the police. P Ops needed to be told about the attack, at any rate.

However, although he didn't want to examine the reasons *why* too closely, he was worried about Grace.

She'd somehow attached herself to him the first time he'd run a mission with the human rebels in St. Louis, adopting him as a mentor without bothering to ask his opinion of the idea.

He'd snarled at her to leave him alone. Repeatedly. When she'd simply fallen back and quietly continued to shadow him, he'd tried a different tactic and ignored her.

If he were honest with himself, he'd admit that he'd only pretended to ignore her. Grace was a hard woman to ignore. She was fiercely independent, dark eyes burning with quiet intensity and a dagger's-edged intellect. Slender, with firm, toned muscles, she was still an athlete, like she'd been as a child. An Olympic contender in swimming at only fifteen years old, Quinn had told him.

But a decade ago the world had changed, and Grace's world had collapsed beneath her. A band of female vamps, celebrating their newfound freedom when vampires and shifters had declared their presence to the world, had run across Grace's big brother in a bar. He hadn't survived the party.

Grace nearly hadn't survived his death.

They'd been alone in the world, their father gone when they were young and their mother dead from cancer not long before Grace lost her brother. Quinn said Grace had been broken. Lost.

But she'd found a purpose in fighting back. Spent the past ten years training for command in the rebel army. He'd seen her in battle, and she was good. Damn good. Her reflexes and strength were incredible for a human, and she was almost preternaturally lethal with her bow. But she'd been running on rage and adrenaline for a decade, and if Michelle died—Michelle, the only friend she had left from the innocence of her childhood—Grace was going to crash, hard.

Alexios had seen the signs in her. He knew it was coming. The only thing he couldn't figure out was if he wanted to be around when it happened. It was bound to be personal, that kind of emotional overload.

Too personal for an Atlantean warrior, sworn to the service of his prince and the sea god, who'd vowed to live his life free of even the most casual emotional attachments.

A doctor wearing bloodstained scrubs pushed through the doors to the waiting room and looked around expectantly. "Nichols? Michelle Nichols?"

The blood drained out of Grace's face, but she jumped up out of the chair. "Yes, that's me. I mean, I'm her friend. What happened? Is she okay?"

The doctor frowned, and Alexios started across the room. It wasn't news he wanted Grace to hear alone.

"She lost a lot of blood, and she had a collapsed lung,"

the doctor said, wiping his forehead with the back of his hand. "I'm not going to lie to you. We did the best we could, and now we wait and see. If your friend's a fighter, she just might have a chance."

Grace stood frozen, seemingly unable to speak. Alexios put an arm around her and shut down the part of his brain that wanted to think about how right she felt there. She was merely a soldier temporarily in his command, and it was his turn to stand for her.

"Thank you, Doctor," he said. "We'll wait for news."

The doctor nodded, barely glancing at Alexios, and then the man's head snapped up for the customary double take Alexios had grown so bitterly accustomed to over the years. "I hope you don't mind my professional curiosity, but how did you get that facial scarring? And have you ever considered cosmetic surgery?"

Alexios's eyes iced over as he regretted, once again, the fact that he couldn't just stab humans who had balls bigger than their brains. "Your concern is misplaced, Doctor, although I thank you for it," he gritted out, trying not to choke on the words.

Grace turned toward him and rested her head on his chest. It was the first sign of weakness she'd ever shown in his presence, and a wave of fierce protectiveness washed through him.

"I need some air," she murmured. "Please, Alexios, please help me. Get me out of here."

Alexios tightened his arms around her and nodded to the doctor. "Thank you again. We'll wait for any news, as I said."

Losing all interest in Alexios, the doctor started to move off, but then stopped, a trace of sympathy crossing his face. "She's going to be in the ICU for quite some time. You two should go get cleaned up and get some rest."

Nodding again, but not bothering to reply, Alexios steered Grace toward the exit. The doors opened with a hydraulic swishing noise, and the three men outside turned toward them, hands automatically reaching inside jackets. They relaxed slightly when they saw it was Alexios and Grace.

"All clear out here," said the stocky one who'd moved the Jeep for them. Spike, maybe. Or Butch. One of the odd names-that-weren't-names that the rebels used. "Any news?"

Grace shook her head, but didn't speak. Fine tremors shook through her body, and Alexios knew the meltdown was finally on its way.

"Almost everyone is doing well, as you said," Alexios reported tersely. "Michelle was in surgery a long time, though, and the doctor said she lost a lot of blood. He said she'll make it, if she's a fighter, and we all know that she is."

He addressed the words to the man, but they were meant for Grace. She drew in a shuddering breath, and he knew at least part of the meaning had penetrated.

"She's going to make it," he repeated. "But Grace needs some air. We're going to walk a little bit. You're sure the way is clear?"

The taller man, older, with leathery skin and a hawk-like nose, nodded. "We're good. We were sure with dark coming on that the vamps would start showing up, but we ain't seen hide nor hair of 'em. The boys are patrolling all the way around the hospital for the shifters, too."

Alexios nodded. "We won't go far."

He herded Grace down the sidewalk and away from the lights and sounds of the ER. She walked with a jerking, halting gait, like a marionette dancing on the strings of a drunken puppet master. When they reached a low stone wall, partially hidden by some bushes, he guided her to it. Then he sat next to her, his arms around her, and held her while she wept.

The sound of her sobbing—muffled because she tried

to hide it from him—and the feel of her warmth as her body trembled in his arms overwhelmed the rock-solid defenses Alexios had carefully constructed over the past several years. He inhaled deeply, trying for control, but failing miserably when the scent of sunshine and flowers from her hair shuddered through his senses.

She was tough, a warrior woman. She never showed weakness to anyone—ever. And yet here she was, crying in his arms. Needing him to comfort her. The fierce drive to protect and cherish surged through him, and a tsunami of unexpected and unwanted emotion crashed through the barriers around his heart like a tidal wave through a fragile coral reef.

She turned her tear-drenched face up to his when his body shuddered against hers. "Alexios?"

There was only one choice he could make. Only one recourse open to him. He needed to taste her lips more than he had ever needed food or water or even air to breathe.

He kissed her.

He kissed her, and she gasped a little against his mouth, but then she was kissing him back. She was *kissing him back.* She twined her arms around his neck and pulled him closer to her and opened her mouth to his invasion, welcoming and enticing him.

Seducing him with her lips and warmth.

He groaned, or perhaps she did, but either way the sound was swallowed up in the heat between them, and he was tilting her head better to devour her and kissing her and wanting her and needing her . . .

The red flashing light of an emergency vehicle splashed on the side of the building, at the furthest edge of his peripheral vision. A vision but not a vision. A memory but not a memory.

Flames.

The fires. The pain.

The torture.

He wrenched his mouth from Grace's and stared at the flashing light. Heart pumping. Muscles clenching.

Retreat! Escape! Kill them! Escape! Escape!

"Alexios?" She struggled in his arms, and he yanked her even closer, maddened that she would try to escape *him*.

"Alexios," she said, stronger now. "You're hurting me."

Somehow the words sank in past the memories. Past the waking nightmare.

There was no choice. There was only despair, and the death of hope, and an eternity of loneliness stretched out in front of him. They'd twisted him, and now he was broken. Wrong.

Alexios took the only honorable option available to him.

He left her there, bewildered and alone. Walked, then ran, then flew as mist through the air, desperate to escape. He never stopped, not even once, until he'd traveled all the way back to Atlantis. His throat burned with unspoken words; his eyes burned with unshed tears.

He ran, and he made yet another promise: he'd never allow himself to touch Grace again.

Chapter 2

The waters of the Atlantic Ocean,
just off the coast of St. Augustine,
Florida, one month later

Grace cut through the water with long, smooth strokes.
Swimming had always been her refuge. Her solace.

Her escape.

Pool, lake, or ocean, it almost didn't matter. All she
needed was the water, welcoming her, lifting her—buoyant—
above sadness and pain. Water washed her clean of the blood,
the tears, and the grief. It offered comfort, though she didn't
deserve it.

A temporary forgetfulness, though it was her curse always to remember.

She quickened her strokes, slicing cleanly through the
rolling waves. The winter wind was blowing at a fair clip,
tossing swells of deepest blue almost playfully. Nature
watching to see if she could handle the challenge. Chillingly indifferent if she could not. The undercurrents were
a trap for the unwary—stronger swimmers than she had
been towed out to a suffocating death.

Death. Even now, in her ocean refuge, her mind always turned back to death.

Grace slowed her pace, lifted her head out of the water, and shook the droplets from her lashes. Rolled over to float on her back, letting the gentle swell carry her for a while. The cold winter water was too much for most swimmers, but something in her heritage protected her from extremes of hot and cold. The "Diana DNA," she called it. Her hair was a tangle across her body; she should have tied it back. Should really cut it. What kind of self-respecting rebel leader had long hair?

The thought resonated like an echo in her mind, whispering secret refrains to half-buried memories. Robert. *Robbie*. Her brother.

Grace allowed herself to remember. On this, of all days. Once a year, she allowed herself the weakness of memory. Of emotion. And pretended not to notice when salt water of her own making slid down her cheek to join the sea.

"You're going to have to cut it," Robbie said, grabbing playfully for the end of her long braid. "What Olympic swimmer ever has long hair? It's not aerodynamic," he teased.

Grace jerked her hair out of his hand. "That doesn't even make sense. Wouldn't it be aquadynamic *or something? For an older brother, you sure act like you're eight years old sometimes," she loftily informed him. "If—if—I make the Olympic team, I'll cut my hair. But for now—"*

She faltered. Her mom had loved Grace's long hair. Loved brushing it for her and braiding it, ever since Grace had been a little girl. Right up until she'd been too weak and sick to lift the brush.

His grin faded and he pulled her into a one-armed hug, a rarity since she'd turned fifteen and hit what he always called her defiant years. "I know, Gracie. I know. I miss Mom, too."

Before the tears burning in the back of her eyes could

*force their way out, Robbie's phone rang. He checked the
screen. "Gotta go, Baby Sis. You know me, I'm always in
demand. See you tomorrow."*

*As he sauntered off, she almost didn't say it. He didn't
deserve it, always teasing her. But affection won out over
her temporary pout, and she called out to him before he'd
walked out of the poolhouse gate.*

"Happy birthday, Big Brother."

Those had been the last words he'd ever heard her say.
That night, the supernatural creatures everyone had always
believed were only myths had shown up on television and
Internet broadcasts all over the world. They were real;
they'd wanted the world to know. Persecuted minorities.
Time for the world to change and recognize their rights.

But Grace hadn't cared about the world changing back
then. All she'd cared about was that a band of female
vamps, celebrating their newfound freedom to strut their
fangs in public, had run across Grace's big brother in a
bar.

Robbie had been celebrating, too. Twenty-one years old
that very day, time to party. High on a couple of beers and
his first time in a bar, he'd met the most beautiful women
he'd ever seen, according to the witnesses. They'd enthralled him, which was probably easy enough even without vamp mind control.

Twenty-one. Running on all hormones and not a lick of
sense. Most survived it. Robbie hadn't.

Grace dove deep and then slowly floated back to the
surface, still lost in the memories. She'd given up her
Olympic training and given up on life. Turned her face to
the wall and lain in bed, unmoving, all day. Day after day.
Never spoke a single word for a solid month, even to her
aunt who'd raised them after Mom died. Poor Aunt Bonnie
had been at her wits' end, ready to call a shrink.

Then, one month to the day later, she'd gotten out of bed
and gone to the gym. Started working out harder than

she'd ever trained for swimming, but this time with a darker purpose. A killing purpose.

Found a friend of a friend who knew somebody starting up a group. A rebel group. Like-minded humans who wanted to reclaim their lives and country from the vampires and shape-shifters who were slowly and insidiously taking over the United States. Taking over the world, from what she'd heard, but a girl had to start somewhere.

Truly began to live only—finally—on the first day that, curious, she'd picked up a bow. Heard the wood sing through her soul. Spent some time tracking back through her past, on the advice of a shape-shifting shaman. Found the great-grandmother her mother had refused to allow her to know; learned of her heritage. Grace, like her great-grandmother and all the females of her line, was a descendant of Diana, and it was her destiny to protect the world from evil.

Diana, the huntress goddess. Skilled beyond all others with her bows, which were made only of the richest, most magical wood from the heart of an eleven forest. Goddess of the moon and sworn protector of the weak and helpless.

Weak. Helpless. Two things Grace had vowed never, ever to be.

But upon first hearing Gran tell wild stories of unbelievable powers, Grace had privately scoffed, in spite of the faint tingle of recognition that had stirred in her mind. She'd told herself she was humoring the old woman. But finally, when she gave in and took the bow from her great-grandmother's hands the magic had poured into Grace. Changing her. Making her . . . more.

Gran had told her that she'd only held out long enough for Grace to find her, but it was time for her to rest. Kneeling there, watching the life fade from her great-grandmother's eyes, Grace had sworn to use the bow and trust Gran had placed in her, and make something of them both. Make something of herself.

Finally, when she was twenty-one, she'd met one of the rebel leaders so far up the chain of command that everybody said her name with a certain hushed awe. Not that Quinn looked tough. More like a character in a manga novel—tiny, with dark, raggedy hair. But it had only taken one look into Quinn's eyes to know the truth, because the dark gaze held a bottomless well of pain and rage and deep, black knowledge.

Grace had gazed long and hard into those eyes and never looked back. Only a teenager—a girl—she'd honed herself into a warrior. And these days she avoided mirrors and only occasionally wondered if, when others looked into her own eyes, they saw the same thing she'd once seen in Quinn's.

It didn't matter. None of it mattered. She blew the air out of her lungs and sank down beneath the waves again, letting the water swallow her body and her tears. She almost allowed the forbidden thought to enter her mind. The thought that came more and more frequently these days.

The thought of how pleasant death by drowning would be, compared to the alternatives.

But not today. Not on Robert's birthday. A decade since that final birthday—ten long years since he was murdered. It would profane his death and, more important, his life if she were to choose to die on this of all days.

She pushed her body back up through the strong current and gasped in the oxygen she needed. She'd live to fight another day. For Robert.

But the vision of another face superimposed itself over Robert's in her mind as she struck out for shore. A scarred face, with eyes haunted by unimaginable pain and sadness. A face surrounded by a lion's mane of gloriously golden hair.

Alexios. *Alexios.* The Atlantean warrior whose fighting skills were already legendary among the rebels. The man whose face—half ruined by vicious scarring, half sculpted into impossible beauty—appeared more and more frequently in Grace's most sensual and disturbing dreams.

Half of the women in her command had a schoolgirl crush on him. Some sort of Phantom of the Opera thing. He could have slept with any of them. All of them.

But he never, ever had. Or at least not a whisper of it had reached her ears, and a rebel squadron was a very close-knit group. No secrets were ever kept, no matter how minor. Secrets caused failure.

Failure caused death.

No, Alexios wasn't involved with any of the women, or men for that matter, in her command. But maybe he had a girlfriend in Atlantis. Maybe even a wife.

Not that it was any of her business. And the strange, empty ache in her stomach was only hunger. It had nothing to do with regret. Nothing to do with that kiss that had shaken her to her core.

Just before he'd vanished. A girl could take that sort of thing personally.

She reached the shallows and stood to walk the rest of the way, squeezing water from her hair and pushing it back away from her face, scanning the beach as she did. Forget Alexios. Clearly he'd forgotten her. Constant vigilance, even here. *Especially* here. Especially any time or place she might be tempted to let her guard down.

The glimmer of moonlit sand appeared empty, but vampires often rode silken shadows in the night. The only thing truly known about their powers was that the full extent of them was a closely guarded secret. Grace double-checked the sheaths strapped to her legs and then started toward shore.

The voice came out of nowhere, deep, lyrical, and drenched with magic. Forest magic, if she had to guess, since a certain tonal quality resonated through her body like the hands of a virtuoso caressing a violin. "There is something oddly compelling about a woman wearing nothing but a silver dagger and a wooden stake strapped to very lovely thighs. If I had not other, darker business to discuss, I would be pleased to play with you for many hours this night."

As if his voice had opened a window in her senses, she could see him. Fae, of course, as his voice had told her. Tall and lean. Waist-length hair of purest silvery white lifting away from his face in the gentle breeze. Dressed in simple dark clothes that gave no hint as to his identity.

But he didn't need a cloak or crown to announce his rank. The moonlight focused a spotlight on him as if Nature herself preened and flirted in his presence. Fae royalty. Only they had the power to glamour even her from this distance.

She took another step, then stopped. Considered drawing the dagger, but realized the uselessness of the gesture. Clenched her hands into fists slightly behind her back, so he could not see the effort it cost her, then *pushed* at the glamour. Narrowed her eyes and opened her Sight.

Damn. He was still glowing.

"This is not naked. It's a very conservative swimsuit. If you can't tell the difference, you've been out of touch for a few decades. Not to mention the fact that I only play when I choose to do so. But of course you're not just royalty, you're Seelie Court, so you're probably not used to rejection," she called out, after inclining her head in acknowledgment of his position, his royalty, and the fact that he could squash her like a bug.

Still, she wasn't going to curl up in a ball, either. "I think you're in the wrong place, Your Lordship."

"I am never in the wrong place, lovely Grace, descendant of Diana," he replied, inclining his head to her as if to an equal.

Damn, damn, double damn. He knew who she was. *What* she was. And it's not like she could bring her bow with her when she swam, or one of the iron-tipped arrows she kept in her quiver for the occasional rogue Fae. Why would he be here, now? Why her? The Fae were chillingly indifferent to the sorrows and concerns of the rest of the world. They still harbored a certain animosity over being outed by the vampires, but they considered themselves to be far, far above the hustle and flow of the concerns of humanity. If asked to anticipate a visitor, Grace sure as heck wouldn't have guessed elf. In fact, despite the rumors that the Fae had a special connection to her family line, she'd never spoken face-to-face with an elf in her life.

She wouldn't have picked tonight to start, if it were up to her, either.

As if her thoughts were the goad to his actions, he lifted one hand and her bow—that had been in the trunk of her car—suddenly hung from his fingers.

He was holding her bow, and it wasn't hurting him.

"It is a beautiful bow, but of course you knew that." He caressed the curve of the wood, and his mouth slowly tilted into a smile of such terrible, dangerous beauty that she imagined women by the thousands had thrown their naked bodies at his feet just from the sight of it.

Strangely, she was unmoved.

"How can you touch my bow?" she demanded.

"Its wood is from the glades in my forest, willingly gifted to Diana's kin for their use. Of course I can touch it. It responds to my hand and to my call."

He lifted his gaze from the bow and pinned her in place with his stare. "I offer truce and parlay, Grace, daughter of Diana, on my word as Rhys na Garanwyn, High Prince of the High House of the Seelie Court. Please come to shore and let us talk of enemies, alliances, and how we might be of service to each other."

High prince, High House. Yeah. She was seriously outmatched. In a split second, Grace weighed her options and found herself with only one choice. She headed toward shore.

As she stepped onto dry sand a cautious ten feet or so

away from him, he bowed deeply and, rising, held out to her a pile of green-and-gold silk. "Permit me to offer you this cloak so you do not catch a chill, lovely huntress." His voice was heat and light and music, inviting her to dance closer and closer to the flames, and the contradiction of his icy blue eyes offered her everything she'd ever wanted or needed.

Except she didn't want or need any of it. Not love, not passion. Only revenge. Only justice. Now he was ticking her off, but she knew enough not to let him see it.

"Your offer is far too generous, Your Highness. You know of course that I cannot accept gifts of any kind from you without incurring a debt I may not be able or willing to pay. It seems a little unfair that you'd start off a conversation under truce and parlay by trying to trick me."

His seductive smile vanished, turning into a friendly grin. Both expressions deceptive, no doubt. "Well, as you humans say, it was worth a try." He dropped the cloak and it turned to sparkles of light and vanished before it ever touched the sand. "You have my word I will try no other *tricks*."

"Then I must ask for my bow to be returned to me."

He tilted his head to indicate the pile of her clothes that she'd left on the beach. Her bow lay on top of them.

"And the arrows?"

"I had no use for your quiver. It remains in your vehicle."

She strode over to her towel and small pile of clothes and quickly dried off and pulled the dark blue sweatshirt and shorts over her swimsuit, then slung her bow over her shoulder. He, of course, managed to repress any chivalrous tendencies to look away and watched her dress with an expression of sincere appreciation on his elegantly sculpted face.

"You're an athlete, of course. The daughters of Diana always have been. I do love the play of finely toned muscles under silken skin," he mused, almost to himself.

"I'm a fighter," she said flatly. "I'm assuming that's why you wanted to talk about alliances? Although I thought you Fae were like Switzerland."

"Neutral. Yes. We always have been. Yet the vampires have encroached upon and are near to breaking ancient treaties. If they succeed in this quest to enslave both shapeshifters and humans, we of the Fae will be . . . unhappy."

"Outnumbered, you mean."

"Perhaps. Surely at least . . . disadvantaged. We prefer to keep numbers in balance, as Nature herself prefers balance in all things."

She thought about that for a moment. Nodded. "Makes sense. What do you want from us? I thought humans were beneath your notice, no offense."

"Surely you yourself do not claim to be strictly human?" He pointedly glanced out at the cold water and then down at her bow.

She shrugged. "I think of it as human *plus*." She gestured toward the path to the public parking lot at the far end of the beach. She'd feel at least somewhat better in reach of her arrows, regardless of their uselessness against him. It was a comfort thing.

Steel-tipped arrows as safety blanket. She needed a shrink. The laugh tried to escape and came out as a strangled chuckle. She shook her head and started walking.

The Fae prince fell in beside her, his long legs easily matching her stride. He glanced at her, lifting one eyebrow. "This situation amuses you?"

Suddenly she stumbled as the memory of Robert's face flashed into her mind. His smile as he'd walked away from her on that terrible day. As he'd walked toward his death. She shook her head. "Your Highness, *nothing* amuses me anymore."

He was silent for several moments as they crossed the beach. Finally, he nodded to himself, as if reaching some internal decision.

"Then let us talk of unamusing things. Of vampires and shape-shifters. Of alliances and Atlanteans. It is now time for the Fae to assert our place in your world before there is no longer any possibility of so doing."

He stopped walking and was somehow instantly standing in front of her, though she hadn't seen him move. He stood tall and proud, with all the arrogance of his race and his house, and the quality of the light surrounding him changed, deepening and turning to liquid silver as it caressed his moon-silk hair and glittered in the depths of his eyes. The sea grasses whispered their secrets to each other and reached for him with their feathery fronds and even Grace, in spite of her own heritage, was tempted to bow before him.

He finally spoke, and his words held the weight of centuries and the solemnity of a vow. "I am Rhys na Garanwyn, and I offer treaty to Atlantis on behalf of the Seelie Court. I have chosen you, Grace, daughter of Diana, to convey this offer. We will meet on this beach at this very time, one week hence, with the chosen representative of the Seven Isles."

Grace shrugged, which was probably not the response he'd been going for, what with the proclamations and all. "I'll do my best, not that you asked me if I'd be willing to be your messenger girl. But Alexios and the other Atlanteans keep their own schedule."

"Give them the message. They will come." He bowed again and then he leaned closer to her and stared down into her eyes so intently she was afraid he was trying some super-major glamour or something. Before she could retreat, he caught her wrist in his hand and tightened his fingers until her skin burned with the contact. Then he abruptly straightened and released her arm. "You honor your brother with your actions for the cause of freedom, but your death would be the gravest of offenses to his memory."

Ice pierced her chest, as if one of her own arrows had struck home into her heart. "What? How did you—"

But he was gone. Simply gone, as if he'd never been there at all. She rubbed her tingling wrist and absently glanced down at it, and then gasped. There on the inside of her left wrist, glowing in the moonlight, a silver arrow pierced the letter R. She furiously rubbed it with the sleeve of her sweatshirt, but the shining symbol didn't fade or smear.

The Fae prince's voice whispered in the sea-salt air. "A remembrance."

Then even his voice was gone.

Alone again—always, always alone—Grace dropped to her knees in the sand. "As if I could ever forget, damn you," she cried out to the empty night, the ache in her chest threatening to crack her rib cage wide open.

"As if I could ever, ever forget."

Chapter 3

Alexios stood on the snow-covered ground, gazing out over the clear, moonlit waters of the rushing river, and took a deep breath of pure, unpolluted air. The bite of cold made him shiver a little, but he enjoyed the cold. Welcomed the ice and snow.

The opposite of fire.

"It's always the water," he said, almost to himself. "Nature at her most glorious."

Of course his companion heard him. Wolf shifters had excellent hearing.

"Water is life," Lucas replied in his surprisingly quiet voice. The wolf shifters he'd known before he'd met Lucas were more brawn than brain, more muscle than meditation. Yet Lucas continually clawed holes in that stereotype. "Life is beauty. Simple platitudes, perhaps, but still true."

Alexios barked out a bitter laugh, automatically ducking his head so his hair swung forward to cover the scarred left side of his face. "I'm a warrior. What do I know of beauty?"

Unbidden, Grace's face entered his mind. High, proud cheekbones. That glorious honey-gold skin. Masses of dark hair he'd only once—for an instant—seen unbound.

He'd lied.

He knew beauty. And he'd abandoned it. *Her.*

Lucas took a few paces closer to the water's edge. "Great fishing in this river. The trout practically jump into your lap."

"Do you use a fishing pole or just catch them in your teeth?"

It was Lucas's turn to laugh. He turned his head to glance back at Alexios, his smile gleaming in the dark. "I've fished here both ways. I must admit it's a little warmer with fur."

Alexios didn't doubt it. He'd seen Lucas in his wolf form. Three hundred pounds of thickly furred muscle and menacing fangs. Which reminded him.

"How's Honey?"

Lucas's dark face broke into a wide smile at the mention of his mate. "She's huge. Nearly full term with our sons."

"Congratulations, old friend. May the spirits of your ancestors grant Honey a safe delivery and bring you both two healthy boys."

The smile faded from Lucas's face, and he bent to pick up a stone, and then skimmed it over the water's surface. "Healthy. That's the issue. That's why I called for this meeting."

"I didn't think you wanted me out here in the dead of winter, freezing my nuts off, just to blather on about fish and beauty," Alexios said, jamming his hands further into the pockets of his long black leather duster. He'd spent too many years over the centuries basking in the temperature-controlled warmth of Atlantis. He was getting soft.

And the day one of Poseidon's warriors turned soft was usually the day he got killed. Or worse, lost two years of his life.

The scars on his face burned with remembered fire and his gut started to roil. Alexios closed his eyes for a moment, reciting a simple focus chant in his mind.

Not now. Some memories were made to repress.

When Alexios opened his eyes, Lucas was shaking his head. "No, not to blather, as you so elegantly put it. Although a fresh-caught rainbow trout, pan-seared and glistening with lemon and butter, can be truly a thing of beauty—"

"Lucas." The single word hung in the air between them for a long moment.

"I know. I know," Lucas replied, his voice turned to ice whose chill rivaled the delicate sculptures hanging from the tree branches behind them. "But naming a thing gives it power, and I had wished, if only for a short while . . . Still. No matter. We're in trouble."

Alexios felt the internal shift. In the space of a heartbeat, he went from standby alert status to battle ready. Scanning the area with Atlantean senses set to clear, sharp focus, he'd unsheathed his daggers almost without noticing it.

"Where? Now?"

"No. I don't know. Maybe." Lucas ran a hand through his thick, dark brown hair. "It's two things. First, we've got local vamps setting out to enthrall shifters, and that goes against all rules of the Fae accords. You know I'm not much for politics, but even I know *that*. It's here, Alexios." The shifter's voice held real anguish. "It's even here in Yellowstone pack territory. After all the inter-pack cooperation we've developed over the past decade, working together to get the indigenous wolf population back up to non-endangered levels."

"You've done an amazing job. Your animal counterparts

are healthy and thriving throughout the entire three-state region of the park."

"Yeah. Yeah." Lucas started pacing back and forth, an almost tangible hostile energy surrounding him.

Alexios felt the prickly sensation that told him the hair on the back of his neck was standing up. Lucas didn't need a full moon to shift, a boatload of anger would do the trick nicely.

"You said 'first,' which usually implies a 'second.' "

Lucas stopped pacing and clenched his hands into fists, then sucked in a deep breath and stretched his fingers out and back, loosening the tension in his hands. It was an old warrior's trick, useful after too many hours of wielding a sword in one's grasp.

Evidently it helped with claws, too.

"Right. Sorry. The idea of traitors in my own pack damn near sends me into the moon sickness," Lucas said. After another three or four deep breaths, that sizzle of hostile energy around him dampened. "Second, the Fae are suddenly in the game. They're putting out the word that they want to talk to you."

"Me? I haven't run into any of the elf kind for years. Decades, even. What would they want with me?" Alexios resheathed his daggers, but didn't relax his vigilance.

"Not you, particularly. Your kind. Atlanteans. They want to bring a prince gift to Conlan's new heir."

Alexios narrowed his eyes. "The high prince's son or daughter isn't even born yet, though we expect Riley to give birth pretty much any minute. But we've kept this a tightly wrapped secret. How is it the Fae know about the baby?"

Lucas shrugged. "They have their ways and have had for longer than our packs have recorded history. They know all, see all, you know the drill. But the more important question, my friend, is what kind of gift they intend to bring. You know the dangers that come with accepting a gift from any of the Fae—or, worse, of refusing one."

"Depends on the Fae."

"It's Rhys na Garanwyn putting out the word through his brother, Kal'andel."

Alexios whistled long and low. "High court Seelie royalty? Oh, yeah. We're screwed."

He heard them before he saw them, and from the way Lucas lifted his head and sniffed the air, he figured the wolf's sense of smell had warned him. They were Pack, they were in wolf shape, and there were at least a dozen of them. Worse, they were moving in fast and low to surround Alexios and Lucas.

"You mentioned being screwed?" Lucas said, his voice little more than a guttural growl as he prepared for the Change.

"We may be screwed, but we're going down fighting," Alexios said, daggers already in his hands. He whirled so he was standing back to flank with Lucas, who'd completed his shift and transformed fully into wolf form in seconds, as only the most powerful shifters could do.

"Okay, ladies," Alexios called out. "Who wants to dance?"

Before the attackers could charge, two shimmering clouds of mist soared down through the air and coalesced into the shapes of two very welcome allies—Christophe and Brennan.

Christophe shook his hair out of his face and grinned. "Hey, I'm up for it. Just none of that line-dancing crap. Give me a hot, slow song where I can get up close and personal with an armful of warm, willing woman."

Brennan nodded. "I do occasionally miss a good waltz," he mused.

The huge shifter leading the charge, apparently no fan of either dance or witty repartee, snarled and made a gesture to his comrades, who attacked.

Alexios, daggers out, hurled himself up and over the crouching wolf coming at him low, leaving that one for

Brennan, and scored a direct hit on the shifter in the second row, ripping through its jugular with his downward slash. The shifter screamed and fell, blood spouting in a macabre pattern against the stark white of the snow.

The next attacker was more prepared, though, and before Alexios could regain his balance a heavy claw smashed into his head, knocking him to the ground. The ugly ripping sound of his hair being wrenched from his head pissed him off more than the pain.

He flipped over and shot up off the ground, leading with his daggers. Before the shifter could get in another blow, both of Alexios's blades were buried in its abdomen. Alexios kept shoving upward through flesh and muscle until the shifter's eyes went slack, telling him the tips of his daggers had reached its heart. It took a lot to keep a wolf shifter down, and he had no time for do-overs tonight.

"Oh, did the wolfie make you mad when he pulled out your pretty golden hair?" Christophe said, laughing.

"I am so going to kick your ass when we're done here," Alexios said, whirling around, searching for his next target.

Christophe, already calling power, hurled a blue-green energy sphere at a shifter who was charging straight for Alexios. This sphere smashed into the wolf's chest and knocked him through the air a good fifteen feet, slamming him into a tree. There was an audible crack—skull or spinal cord, probably—and the shifter fell into a heap at the base of the tree, head at an unnatural angle.

"That one's not getting up again, Lexi," Christophe gloated.

"Call me Lexi again, and my next dagger is going up your—"

"Incoming!" Brennan shouted, interrupting the very real threat that Alexios had in mind. Alexios spun around to see two shifters charging for him in a coordinated attack.

"It seems rather unfair that all the dance partners prefer you," Brennan said, materializing beside Alexios, throwing stars in his hands.

"Well, I am prettier," Alexios replied, grinning.

Brennan's hands flashed out almost quicker than even an Atlantean eye could see, and two pairs of *shuriken*, made of Atlantean metal instead of the customary silver of Japanese throwing stars, sliced through the air and found their marks, dead center in the foreheads and hearts of each of the two shifters. Momentum carried the shifters forward a few more steps before they dropped.

But by then Alexios had already turned to scan the area and see where the next threat would be coming from. Lucas was caught up in battle with two more of the attackers at the edge of the water, fangs and claws slicing, tearing, and rending. Alexios took off toward them, but some instinct tickled at the edge of his consciousness and, acting purely on instinct, he knelt and drove his daggers straight behind him and up, catching another one of the wolf shifters under its neck on its downward leap. It howled as it died, and the eerie sound shivered ice down Alexios's spine.

He didn't have time for shivers, though. He sprang back up and headed for Lucas again, but by the time he'd reached his friend, the two attackers lay on the ground, dying or dead.

Brennan flashed toward them, scanning the edges of the trees for any further attackers. "I had thought there were more of them, but perhaps they fled."

Alexios shook his head. "I doubt it. They're too intent on this attack, no matter the cost. I'd really like to know what was behind it."

Lucas snarled, the blood dripping from his muzzle underscoring the feral sound.

"I hate wolf shifters nearly as much as cat shifters—no offense, Lucas," Christophe said, walking toward them. "I still can't believe Bastien is going to wed a kitty cat.

Wonder if they'll need a litter box? Oh, and you might want to duck."

Brennan and Alexios hit the ground simultaneously as if choreographed; centuries of fighting together had taught them that hesitation often proved fatal. Lucas snarled again, but crouched low.

Alexios had barely caught sight of the four remaining shifters, lurking at the edge of the tree line, when Christophe's razor-sharp blades of ice arrowed through the air and sliced through their necks.

The Atlantean power over water could be quite deadly when wielded by an expert. Too bad it had to be Christophe.

"That's four at once," Christophe said smugly. "The ale is quite definitely on you three."

"Are there any more of them, Lucas?" Alexios knew the shifter's keen sense of smell would discover any remaining attackers.

Lucas's heavy head lifted as he scented the air. Then he slowly shook his head back and forth, taking a few steps away. The shimmer of the Change hung in the air for a few moments while Lucas returned to human form. The Change had healed the worst measure of his wounds, but what remained showed how badly he'd been hurt in the fight.

Alexios bent to clean his daggers in the rushing waters of the river, then dried and resheathed them, not trusting himself to talk just yet.

Lucas evidently didn't have that problem. "Private meeting. *Private.* I don't quite see how bringing your goons along fulfilled that request," he snarled.

"Goons? Did he just call us goons, Brennan?" Christophe asked. "Listen, doggie boy, I can show you *goons*—"

Alexios sliced a hand through the air, cutting him off. Turned back to Lucas. "Are you freaking kidding me? Did you set me up? What in the nine hells was this?"

Lucas's rage and the shimmer of the incipient Change hung in the air for a moment, but then the shifter visibly forced himself to calm down. "Set you up? Set you up? I called you here to ask for help. Which, as you might guess, wasn't easy for me to do in the first place. Do you really know me so little that you think I would set you up? I was going to ask you to stand as second pack-father to my sons, you damn fool."

Brennan bowed, elegant as always. "Congratulations on the imminent birth, and may the waters of your world serve to nourish your family now and for always."

Lucas's eyes widened at Brennan's formal speak, but he inclined his head. "Thank you. As you may or may not know, the pack-father protects the children as if they were his own—would die for them. The first must be Pack, but there is precedent for naming a second. I've chosen you, Alexios. Maybe that was a mistake."

Alexios ran a hand through his hair, wincing when he hit the part of his scalp still tender from the shifter's attack. "It wasn't a mistake. We've been friends for a very long time, and I am honored beyond the telling of it that you would ask me to serve as second pack-father. I accept, if you still want me." He offered his hand, and with only a moment's hesitation, Lucas grasped it in his own. A shared understanding passed between them, and Alexios knew that he, too, would protect Lucas's children with his life.

"Lovely. Really touching. Maybe we can eat chocolate and watch a chick flick next," Christophe said. "Or maybe we can figure out how in the nine hells they knew we were here? Whatever else that was, it wasn't random. Not only were they here for us but they seemed to be targeting Alexios personally."

"I also had noticed they were focusing on Alexios," but I am not a particular fan of romantic comedy films," Brennan said. "Lucas, did you mention this meeting to anyone else?"

Lucas was already shaking his head. "No. Like I said, I wanted to talk to you about what was going on. Vampires enthralling shifters. Pack acting contrary to our own best interests. Something big is going on—something different. The vamps have found a way to permanently enthrall shifters, Alexios. I don't need to tell you what that means for the survival of Pack—not to mention the survival of the humans."

"Were these members of your pack?" Alexios demanded.

"No. Definitely not. You know we can tell Pack from scent. No way were those from mine. To the best of my knowledge, they weren't from anywhere around here."

"To the best of your knowledge doesn't seem to be worth much, no offense," Christophe sneered. Faint silvery-green power still pulsed at the edges of his fingertips. "It's getting harder and harder to tell who's on our side these days."

Lucas growled deep in his throat, more wolf than man. "You keep saying 'no offense,' and yet you are most certainly offending me. It occurs to me to ask why you felt the need to kill all four of the remaining attackers. We needed one alive to question. Maybe it's an Atlantean who's the traitor," he said, his gaze drilling into Christophe. "*No offense.*"

Alexios stepped between them. "All right, already. Let's compare the lengths of our dicks later. Right now we need to figure out who is behind this attack, and why."

"I would suggest the Primator, Vonos," Brennan said calmly. Of course, Brennan had been calm for longer than anyone really knew, since something about a Roman senator's daughter had gone bad and Poseidon had cursed him never again to feel emotion, forever destroying Brennan's life.

Or maybe not. Maybe having no emotions was a better way to live.

Something in his gut twisted at the thought, but he put it, and any thoughts of Grace, back in a box to be dealt with later. Much later.

"Could be Vonos," Christophe admitted. "But it doesn't smell like him. He's more about power and efficiency than the usual bad-guy evil bwah-ha-ha crap. He and Mussolini were probably buddies."

Ever since vampires, shifters, and other supernatural creatures had openly declared themselves to exist around a decade ago, they'd been rapidly gaining ground in terms of legal rights. The new, all-vampire third house of Congress, the Primus, didn't exactly get staffed by election. Vampires didn't vote. The vamp who was old enough, powerful enough, and ruthless enough to take it was the one who won the coveted position of Primator, ruler of the Primus. Right now, that meant Vonos.

"Vonos is definitely not on our side, and he's bad news. Worse than Barrabas, even," Alexios said. "At least with Barrabas, we could use his hot temper against him. This Vonos is as cold as those ice spears you used, Christophe. Nice job, by the way."

Christophe's grin would have terrified any humans who happened to see it. "Thanks. I've been practicing. I would have thought Vonos was too busy with his new job as Primator to be messing with enthralling shifters in Yellowstone."

"I heard you all had something to do with that. Senator Barnes's disappearance, I mean," Lucas said.

"Senator Barnes." Christophe snorted. "Barrabas, you mean. Damn leech had a lot to answer for."

"Yeah, that was us," Alexios said. "Long story. Vonos is the new big bad and apparently he's trying to blaze a name for himself as being even more powerful than Barrabas."

"We need to investigate this further," Brennan said. "I would suggest we return to Atlantis and see if we've had news from Tiernan and her fellow journalists. The movement to enthrall the shape-shifters is sweeping the country; not only that, but we have recently had news that the same is occurring in Asia and Europe. Maybe even Africa."

Christophe rolled his eyes. "Sure. *That*'s the only reason you want to get in touch with Tiernan. It's not like you went bat-shit crazy and almost dropped her and banged her on the spot when you first met her or anything."

"Christophe—" Alexios began, but Brennan held up a hand.

"As you know, I have no memory of this occurrence. In any event, I would suggest we return to Atlantis immediately and refrain from further pointless discussion on this or other issues until we are in possession of more facts."

"I'll second that," Alexios agreed. "Lucas—"

But Lucas's gaze was turned inward; he stood straining toward the east, his head lifted into the wind. "It's time. Honey is ready to go into labor. I have to get back to her. Now."

"Are you sure? Do you need us? Is there anything we can do?"

Lucas shook his head and grasped Alexios's proffered hand. "No, my friend. This is a time for Pack and celebration. We'll talk again soon. I give you my bond as alpha of the Yellowstone Pack that we will work together on this. The bloodsuckers don't have a chance against the combined might of Pack and Atlantis."

Lucas grinned fiercely, again more wolf than man. He threw back his head and called out a long, undulating howl. "Until then, Alexios. Right now, I'm going to be a father."

With that, Lucas took off running in a blur of speed. Before he hit the tree line he was already fully wolf. Alexios watched him for a moment, silently wishing him well, and then turned back to Brennan and Christophe.

"I think it's time for us to go as well. We can do nothing more here."

"And these?" Brennan said, gesturing toward the fallen

shifters, who had returned to their human forms in death.

"Lucas will take care of them. For us to do anything with their bodies might violate pack law."

"Let's get out of here then," Christophe said. "It's still early enough to find a top-notch ale and a woman with a big, round ass who is willing to do very nasty things to me."

Alexios shook his head. "Seriously, Christophe, you need help. In the worst way."

Christophe laughed. "That's what I'm talking about. The worst way."

Brennan gestured with one hand, and the familiar ovoid shape of the portal began to form in the air. When the iridescent shape had lengthened and widened enough to allow them to pass into Atlantis, their first sight was of half a dozen portal guards crouched at full battle readiness, swords and spears aimed directly at them. The soldiers all wore the silver and cerulean blue of the Atlantean royal guard, and the sight of them was certainly enough to give pause to any who dared to try forcible entry. Not that the portal had ever once opened to an enemy in more than eleven thousand years.

As far as they knew.

Alexios drew his daggers and stepped forward but didn't cross over yet. "Status?"

Captain Marcus bowed and then gestured to his men to stand down. "Lord Alexios. Be welcome."

Alexios sheathed his daggers as the portal guards lowered and sheathed their own weapons. "Status?" he repeated, eyes narrowing.

"Apologies, my lord, but it is happening," the steely-eyed veteran said, breaking into an uncharacteristic grin. "Lady Riley has gone into labor, and the heir to the throne of all Atlantis is even now making his or her way into the world. I believed that increased security at this time would be prudent."

Behind Alexios, Christophe let out a whoop. "It's about

time. Now maybe Conlan can quit walking around with the stick shoved up his—"

"Thank you," Alexios said. "We'd better get to the palace, then."

He waved his arm and first Brennan, then Christophe headed through the portal. As Christophe passed him, Alexios grabbed his arm in a very unfriendly grip. "Say anything like that about our high prince again, and it will be my boot up *your* ass," he growled quietly so that no one else would hear.

Christophe yanked his arm free, eyes flashing a darker green as he drew power to himself. "I'm getting awfully tired of being threatened, Alexios. Know it."

"My lord?" the guard called. "The portal is shrinking."

Alexios crossed through the magical entry into Atlantis behind Christophe, wondering what would happen if the day ever came that he was forced to challenge him. The warrior's ability to channel power was nearly as great as that of High Priest Alaric, and Alexios knew that Alaric could kick his ass in a fight.

Of course, Alexios had learned a trick or two over the centuries, too.

But tonight was not the time for dark thoughts of future betrayals. Tonight was for celebrating. He clapped his hand on the captain's shoulder. "The ale is on me tonight. My friend becomes a father, and Atlantis gains an heir!"

The guards roared out their approval, shaking their spears in the air as they shouted and cheered. Brennan glanced back over his shoulder and raised one eyebrow before he and Christophe shimmered into mist and headed for the palace.

"Please tell the prince and his lady that we are all praying for Poseidon's blessing upon them, my lord," Marcus said.

"I will, and I know he will appreciate it." Alexios took

a running start and leapt into the air, transforming into mist as he did so, then arrowed toward the palace, thoughts whirling.

Finally. An heir to Atlantis. Perhaps he would be the first Atlantean in millennia to grow up knowing the land walkers' world, after Atlantis took its rightful place on the surface

If Atlantis ever took its rightful place on the surface. Because if what Justice's woman, Keely, had said was true, then they had to retrieve the rest of the Trident's missing gems or Atlantis would be destroyed as it tried to rise from the depths of the ocean.

Landing on the balcony of his rooms in the palace, Alexios swiftly returned to human form, dropped his weapons on the bed, and then headed for the throne room, nearly running. Before he made it halfway down the corridor, Brennan appeared at the other end, his face as grim as Alexios had ever seen it.

Alexios slowed to a stop, his heart plummeting. No. It couldn't be. Not the baby. There had been so many problems during her pregnancy—the first Atlantean-human mating in recorded history. He was unable to form the words to ask the question, but Brennan answered him anyway.

"It goes badly. Riley and the baby are both at risk." Brennan's face hardened. "Alexios, they might die."

~~~~~

Thousands of miles away from Atlantis, driving a beat-up old Jeep down a nearly deserted road, Grace felt a wave of anguish slice through her heart like a finely honed *katana*. But she'd never felt a Japanese sword pierce that particular part of her anatomy. Once through the side, sure. A couple of hits on arms and legs. But never a chest wound.

Yanking the steering wheel to the right, Grace pulled off onto the edge of the road and put her head down on the steering wheel, gasping for air until the pain passed. The

Fae. That damn elf must have done something to her. Some sort of delayed reaction spell.

But even as the thought entered her mind, she realized it didn't ring true. The pain hadn't felt like Fae magic.

It had felt like *Alexios*. Wherever he was, he was hurting.

And, warrior woman or not, descendant of Diana or not, there was nothing she could do about it.

Chapter 4

Atlantis, the palace

Alexios followed Brennan through the giant doorway into
the opulent palace throne room, barely noticing the pristine white marble floor inlaid with designs of gold, copper, and sparkling orichalcum, a metal unique to Atlantis.
He strode past the marble columns and never spared a
glance for the ornate golden throne that had fascinated
him so as a child, but simply followed Brennan through yet
another doorway, this one much smaller, into another
room, also much smaller. Prince Conlan's private meeting
room. Conlan had never been much of one for pomp and
circumstance; the formal elegance of the throne room his
father had ruled over had never held much appeal. Most of
the important business of the kingdom was conducted
here, on comfortable chairs and at battered wooden tables.

That is, most of the business of peace. For the rest, Conlan and his elite guard met in the war room. Another refuge, though starkly utilitarian. Another scarred wooden
table. Alexios shook his head to clear it of fancy. The baby

and Riley might be dying, and he was thinking about stupid tables. He was a fool.

Or else his mind was trying to protect him with denial. Alexios had seen more than his share of death over the centuries, but the child's life had never had a chance to begin.

"Please, Poseidon, hear my plea," he whispered urgently, a fist squeezing the place inside his chest where his heart had once been. Now, he was sure that nothing but a blackened husk remained of heart and hope. If the baby died . . . but no. He wouldn't think it.

He couldn't think it.

Entering the room, he saw Justice and Keely first. *Lord* Justice, now that they all knew he was half brother to Prince Conlan and his brother, Ven, the King's Vengeance.

Not that Ven would put up with being called *prince* anything.

Justice had his arms around Keely, like he always did. Ever since both the Atlantean and the Nereid halves of his personality had come together and soul-melded with Keely, the warrior was rarely far from her side.

Alexios ruthlessly squashed the twinge of envy he often felt at the sight of them. They were self-contained. Complete in each other, not needing anyone else. If anyone deserved to have that kind of happiness, it was Justice. He'd fought against a cursed birthright for centuries, unable to claim his own brothers as kin. Now he had a new family: Keely and their adopted daughter, Eleni, a beautiful Guatemalan child who'd lost her parents to vicious vampire attacks.

They deserved to be happy. *All* of them deserved to be happy. It was a sign of his weakness and a flaw in his character that he envied even one moment of it.

Keely looked up at exactly that moment and caught sight of him. "Oh, Alexios," she cried out. "We're so glad you're here."

Pulling away from Justice, she ran across the room and threw herself into Alexios's arms, sobbing. "Did Brennan tell you? It's so awful. Erin is with them, of course, with her gem-singing healing Gift. She's helping Marie do everything they can."

Alexios was so startled by her actions that he almost didn't comprehend her words. His instinct to comfort, rusty with disuse, finally kicked in, and he awkwardly lifted an arm to pat her back, warily watching Justice. Justice returned his gaze steadily, his lips quirking into a flicker of a smile that quickly vanished.

"They will be able to heal Riley and the child," Justice said, not a shadow of doubt in his voice.

Keely lifted her head from Alexios's shoulder and took a shuddering breath. She nodded, scrubbing her face with her hands. Alexios quickly dropped his arms to his sides, releasing her.

"I'm sorry," she said, her voice shaking. "Some tough archaeologist I am, right? I'm just so glad you're all back. Strength in numbers and prayers, you know? Christophe went to help, add his power to Alaric's or something, and it's just—it's just that I've gotten to know Riley so well and if . . . if . . . if something happens to her or the baby—"

Quicker than thought, Justice was beside her, gathering her into his arms. "Hush, *mi amara*, hush. We will not let any part of our family come to harm. Let us continue to offer our prayers to Poseidon, the gods of the Nereid, and your own Christian god. Surely strength in numbers, as you say, cannot hurt with gods."

Alexios stepped away to give them some privacy and crossed the floor toward Denal, who knelt on the floor, his dark head resting against the arm of the chair. As Alexios approached, he realized the youngling was mumbling an ancient Atlantean prayer under his breath. He stopped, not wanting to interrupt, but Denal raised his head, and Alexios got another shock. Denal's eyes were sunken into his skull, and harsh lines had appeared almost from nowhere on the planes and angles of his face.

"She can't die," Denal cried out, his voice a rusty croak. "She can't die, and the baby can't die. I can't bear it if she dies, Alexios. Not again. Not after she sacrificed her life for mine. I've been on my knees for hours praying to Poseidon to let me return the favor. Let him take me and spare her and the baby."

Alexios was a little taken aback at the depth of anguish in the warrior's voice, though on reflection Denal had been smitten with Riley from the first. Had declared himself her champion and protector, and had built up a big case of puppy love, even trying to defend her from Conlan, her chosen mate, over a misunderstanding. But after the vampire attack where he and Brennan had actually died, and Riley had traded her life to Poseidon for theirs . . . well, something in Denal had broken. Some spark of the youth and joy that made them all think of him as an overgrown youngling, though he was man and warrior enough to be part of the Seven, well, that spark had slowly turned to ash and died. Over the course of the past several months, Denal had changed. Become quieter. Less exuberant.

Less . . . Denal.

So maybe Alexios shouldn't have been surprised at the vehemence of Denal's pain at all.

Alexios started to speak, to offer some comfort, but Denal lurched up off the floor and grabbed his arms in a death grip, digging with bruising force into his flesh. "Why won't he take me? Alexios, why won't he take me?"

Alexios shook his head, unable to offer false comfort. "They are gods, Denal. They are gods, and they choose as they will. There is nothing we can do to affect their decisions."

Something dark and deadly gleamed in the back of Denal's eyes. "Nothing? I think you're wrong." He leaned forward as if to embrace Alexios and then, before Alexios could stop him, Denal snatched the daggers out of Alexios's sheaths and jumped back.

"If Poseidon won't take me, then I'll give myself to him," Denal shouted.

Alexios leapt forward, reaching for the blades, but he was too late. Denal plunged both daggers into his own abdomen and screamed loud and long as he fell back to his knees in a grotesque parody of his earlier position, blood streaming down his shirt.

"Two blades for two lives, Poseidon," he cried out. "It's all I have to give. Let it be enough, or I will battle you through all the levels of the nine hells."

Somewhere behind him, Alexios dimly heard Keely screaming. Justice shouting. Even Brennan, calling out for help. But none of it penetrated. None of it mattered. The warrior Alexios had once mentored for half a century had just killed himself in front of his eyes, and Alexios had done nothing. He'd failed him. Like he'd failed Prince Conlan, when Anubisa came for him. Like he failed everyone.

Lost in soul-deep anguish beyond the bearing of it, Alexios threw back his head and roared out his pain and denial.

"Not what I expected to find," a dry, calm voice said over his shoulder. "Bleeding, shouting, and self-inflicted evisceration. What is it about you warriors?"

"Alaric, damn you," Alexios choked out. "You're Poseidon's high priest, so *act like it*. Heal him. *Now*."

Alaric knelt beside Alexios and flicked a sardonic glance his way. "Should I invalidate such a noble sacrifice? Even though Riley and the baby are now doing much better, and the First Maiden told us five minutes ago that a healthy birth is imminent? Perhaps Poseidon would not approve."

"If you don't heal him in the next five seconds, my daggers are going to be digging a hole in *your* belly," Alexios gritted out, knowing the priest was toying with him but not understanding how Alaric could do such a thing while Denal lay dying on the floor in front of them.

Certainly Alaric had grown darker and more silent of late. All of them had noticed it. But to actually let the warrior die when he could help . . . Alexios could not believe it of the priest who'd healed them all, so many times.

Alaric turned his dark gaze to Denal, his face hardening at the grim sight of the warrior sprawled gracelessly in a pool of his own spreading blood. "He's very nearly gone. Get out of my way."

Alexios scrambled backward to give the priest room to work. Alaric called power so swiftly and strongly that Alexios's skin tried to crawl off his bones as the powerful rush of magical energy filled the room. Alaric's hands glowed in the exact center of two pulsing blue-green spheres.

The priest leaned forward and grasped the hilts of the daggers, chanting something under his breath. Yet where Denal had prayed to Poseidon for death, Alaric was praying to the same god for life.

Denal's life.

With one powerful yank, Alaric drew both daggers from Denal's abdomen and tossed them to the floor. Never breaking his chant, he spread his hands over the torn flesh, and the light from the energy spheres sank into Denal's body through his open wounds.

Silently, Alexios added his own prayers. Denal couldn't die this way. Not through a useless, unnecessary sacrifice. Riley was going to be fine—had already turned the corner before Denal had plunged the daggers into his own flesh.

Surely Poseidon would accept the spirit of the sacrifice and release Denal from its finality. But Poseidon had released Denal from death once before . . .

How many miracles would the sea god grant to a single warrior?

Alaric abruptly leaned forward and pushed, his hands pressing deeply into Denal's abdomen. Denal's body arched and then fell back to the floor, and he started choking and coughing, then sucked in huge, gasping breaths.

His eyes snapped open and he stared up at Alaric, an uncomprehending expression on his face.

"Am I dead?" He managed to force those three words from his throat before he began coughing again.

The priest leaned back and held his hands up into the air. The energy spheres burned fiercely for a moment and then disappeared as if they'd never existed, leaving Alaric's hands cleansed of blood. He looked at his hands and smiled, but it was a smile lacking in any trace of warmth or humor.

"If only my soul could be cleansed so easily," Alaric said, so quietly that Alexios knew he hadn't been meant to hear it. Then the priest stood up and stared down at Denal. "No, you're not dead, though you were close. But if you ever act in such a manner again, you may believe that I will leave you to the consequences of your actions."

Without another word, Alaric turned and stalked toward the door. "If you're done with this display, Lady Riley has asked that we be present in her outer chamber so that we can meet the baby immediately after he arrives."

He stopped and glanced back over his shoulder. "I would suggest that you clean up first."

Alexios helped Denal, whose wounds were entirely healed, sit up. All the things he wanted to say tumbled through his mind. Finally, he settled on the simplest. The good news.

"Denal, Riley and the baby are going to be fine. Marie has said so, and she has been First Maiden of the temple dedicated to health in childbirth for many, many years. You know we can trust her instincts. And Erin is there to call the power of gemsong to aid in the healing. All will be well."

Denal just stared straight ahead, his expression blank and frozen. Alexios had seen it before. Hells, he'd felt it before. It was shock. The state of unnatural calm of one who had faced and accepted death. When death relinquished its claim, it took time for the realization of continued life to sink in. The space in between, that gray and featureless limbo, was a cold crossing where sanity hung in the balance. Not everyone came all the way back.

Brennan, Keely, and Justice all gathered around Denal, and Keely put her arms around him, tears still streaming down her face. Belatedly, Alexios realized they'd been right behind him while Alaric had healed Denal. Justice and Brennan each put a hand on Denal's shoulders, offering their own comfort.

Strength in numbers, indeed.

"You Atlanteans," Keely said as she sat back up, mingled fury and relief in her voice. "From the moment I first stepped foot in Atlantis, somebody has been trying to sacrifice himself for somebody else. I've had it. I want to go home where nice, normal people don't go around killing themselves all the time." She batted Justice's arm away when he tried to comfort her, and there was a certain wildness in her eyes. Alexios wondered, not for the first time, how difficult adjusting to life with an Atlantean warrior must be for a human.

Slowly, slowly, Denal's gaze sharpened and focused, and he blinked up at Keely. "Dr. McDermott?"

She smiled through her tears, and in that instant Alexios knew why Justice had kidnapped this woman. Why he'd follow her through all the nine hells to be by her side. She was fierce and beautiful and everything a man could ever desire.

She reminded him of Grace.

"Don't you 'Dr. McDermott' me, Denal. I may be a couple of hundred years younger than you, but I can still kick your butt," she said, wiping her face on her sleeve. "Now let me help you up and we'll get you in a bath."

Fully alert now, Denal stared at Justice in total horror. "Oh, no. She can't—I can't—"

Justice and Alexios shared a glance of complete understanding. "Oh, no worries. My woman is not giving you a bath," Justice said, a wicked smile on his face. "Alexios and I will help you wash your baby-soft ass, youngling."

"I'm not touching his ass," Alexios pointed out.

"Nor do I have any desire to cleanse that part of Denal's anatomy," Brennan said. "Perhaps we should find the palace housekeeper. She did, after all, change his wet clouts upon occasion when he was an infant."

If anything, Denal looked even more horrified. "No! Not Neela! By the gods, I can bathe myself!"

They all started laughing as Denal spluttered protests, but their laughter had a sharp edge to it. Simple joy and relief tempered with the residue of not-yet-vanquished terror.

Denal was *alive*. But he almost hadn't been.

A flash of something unfathomable crossed Denal's expression, and his face hardened. "Then Poseidon did not accept my sacrifice? I was unworthy?"

"You are not unworthy, you fool," Justice said, smacking Denal in the back of the head in a gentle imitation of the action he'd done so many times during the youngling's training. "Your sacrifice, noble though it was, was unnecessary. Riley and the child were out of danger before you—"

"Before you took my daggers from their sheaths," Alexios interrupted, his own smile fading. "I think we will need to come to terms over that, but that's for a later time. For now, get cleaned up and meet us in Conlan's chambers so we can meet our future prince. Maybe you can change some of *his* clouts."

This time, even Denal smiled. Only a little, and it quickly vanished, but it had been a true smile. That was something. It was a start.

Alexios stood and bent to offer Denal his hand, but Denal shook his head, clenching his teeth, and slowly climbed to his feet. As Alexios knew from previous healings, the wounds may have been gone, but the pain from their infliction was very real and stayed around far longer than the healed wounds themselves if Alaric had been in the mood to teach a stubborn warrior a lesson.

The Alaric who had healed Denal would have had no care for pain. Denal would feel the effects for a while. And, judging from the expression on his face, not only the physical effects.

Keely put her hands on her hips and looked at the four Atlantean warriors surrounding her. "Can we go, already? I want to see that baby!"

Alexios nodded. "As do we all."

As they headed back through the doorway he'd entered only a short time—or was it a lifetime?—ago, Alexios offered yet another prayer to the sea god. This time a simpler one.

A prayer of thanks.

Chapter 5

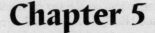

Atlantis, Prince Conlan and Lady Riley's chambers

Marie held open the door and ushered them in. "Please enter, my lord Justice, Brennan, Alexios, Keely. Be welcome and rejoice, for we have a healthy baby to present to you."

Alexios walked forward into the large, airy space filled with sunlight, laughter, and the fresh-garden scent of masses of flowers, clustered in vases all over the room. Christophe leaned against one wall, grinning, and Ven was twirling Lady Erin around and whooping with joy. Erin looked tired, though. The first human they'd ever known to possess the lost art of gem singing, she channeled a great deal of energy when she used her Gift for healing.

"Ven, put me down right now," Erin said, laughing. "You're blocking their view."

Ven caught her in his arms and moved to the side, his face nearly split in two with an enormous grin. "Hey, Uncle Justice. Come meet our new nephew."

Justice's answering smile damn near lit up the room. "Nephew? It's a boy? It's a boy!" He pulled Keely in close to him, pressing a kiss on the top of her flame-red hair. "How does Auntie Keely sound to you?"

"Well, technically speaking, since we're not married yet—"

From the bed, where Alexios could finally see her after Ven and Erin had moved out of the way, Riley laughed. "Oh, quit being such a logical scientist, Keely. Get over here, you two."

Conlan was sitting next to her, his arm around her shoulder, and Alexios could just catch a glimpse of a pink face inside a bulky lump of blanket in Riley's arms. Then the baby yawned, forming a tiny, perfect O with his gaping mouth, and everybody started laughing.

Hesitantly, in that peculiarly awkward way of warriors with newborn babes, Justice knelt beside the bed and touched one tiny fist with his finger. Instantly, the baby opened his eyes and his little hand and clamped his fist around the finger. The look on Justice's face was priceless.

"Clearly our nephew has good taste," Keely said, putting a hand on Justice's shoulder. "He likes his uncle already." She looked up at Riley. "He's absolutely beautiful."

"Thank you. He is, isn't he? It's such a miracle that this tiny person grew inside my body."

Justice started to speak, but nothing but a harsh croaking sound came out. Then he dropped his head for a second and took a deep breath. When he lifted his head again, his eyes were suspiciously shiny, but Alexios was betting nobody in the room was going to tease him about it, since Justice was far from the only one in that condition.

Alexios kind of suspected his own eyes were a little shiny, too.

"We, both the Nereid and Atlantean halves of our soul, are honored to call this child nephew. We will serve and protect him with our very lives, from now until eternity," Justice vowed.

Alexios realized from the pronoun "we" that the melding of the two halves of Justice's heritage had taken an interesting turn. But if Alaric, who leaned against a wall silently watching everything, wasn't worried, it wasn't for Alexios to concern himself with.

"In the name of the prince and heir to the Atlantean throne, we accept that promise," Conlan said. The words were formal but the warmth in his eyes was not. Conlan and Ven had fully accepted Justice into their family as their half brother, and all of them were the better for it.

Riley smiled, and although she looked very tired, she was glowing as though lit from within by a thousand Atlantean sea stars. "Oh, don't get all stuffy and formal, boys. His name," she said, suddenly holding the bundle out toward Justice, "is Aidan. Let's not hang all that prince-and-heir stuff on him just yet when he doesn't even weigh ten pounds. And Aidan wants his uncle Justice to hold him."

Justice looked stunned. "Us? You trust us—me—with your son?"

Keely knelt down next to Justice. "Of course she does. Why wouldn't she?"

"Take your nephew, Justice," Conlan said. "On this day, of all days, my wife gets whatever her heart desires."

Riley smiled at Conlan with such perfect understanding and love that Alexios felt like an intruder on an intimate moment, though the chamber was filled with people.

Slowly and hesitantly, Justice reached for the infant. An expression of complete and utter awe swept over his features as he gently lifted the baby into his arms.

"Support his head, honey," Keely prompted. "Babies can't hold up their own heads for a while."

"He does have an enormous head," Brennan observed, looking bemused. "Perhaps his neck is simply undersized for such a weight?"

Riley, Keely, Erin, and Marie all burst out laughing.

"Brennan, are you calling my baby a bobblehead?" Riley demanded, when she could catch her breath.

"The proportions do seem a little off," Alexios said, stepping closer and winking at Conlan and Riley. He flashed a grin at Erin. "He must take after his mutant uncle Ven."

Ven growled at him, but Erin just shook her head, smiling.

"Don't even go there, pretty boy," Ven said. "At least he doesn't have all that girly golden hair like you do."

"He is quite shockingly bald," Justice said, brow furrowed. "Is that a problem? Is there some—"

The women started laughing again, cutting off whatever Justice had been about to say. "Most babies are born bald or with only a little fuzz. His hair will start growing soon enough," Marie said.

"Not all babies," Keely said, catching the end of Justice's long blue braid in her hand. "Some have a lovely crop of bright blue hair."

"Well, Aidan will have beautiful black hair like his father," Riley said, leaning back against Conlan.

"Or beautiful sunset-gold hair like his mother," Conlan replied.

"I know you're my prince and all, but if you're going to start reciting poetry about her eyes, I'm out of here," Alexios said, pulling an exaggerated grimace. "There's only so much a self-respecting warrior can take."

Conlan burst out laughing, and Riley's lips curved in a tiny, secret smile. "Okay, that does it. Uncle Alexios is holding the baby next."

Alexios held up his hands in protest. "Oh, no. I don't know anything about holding babies." He ducked behind Marie as if to hide.

"I only wish my brother could have been here," Marie said, shaking her head and smiling. "He, Ethan, and Kat are in the middle of land negotiations with the state of Florida over increasing the panther territory, though, and it would have been a breach of courtesy to leave now."

Alexios still couldn't believe Marie had fallen in love with a panther shifter on her very first trip out of Atlantis, but the changes to the old ways were coming quickly and furiously. Little Prince Aidan was living proof of that.

Riley waved an arm toward the masses of flowers lining one entire wall of the room. "I know. Bastien and Kat sent at least a dozen different flower arrangements and enough baby toys to supply half of Atlantis, I think. Aidan will be hopelessly spoiled, if I let all of you have free rein."

Justice, still staring down at Aidan as if entranced, smiled. "Oh, Riley. You have no idea." Then he pinned Keely with a searing glance. "We must have a baby. Now. He will keep Eleni company."

Keely, still kneeling, fell backward and landed on her bottom with a thump. "Wait. What? Baby? What?"

"Give the nice archaeologist time to get used to your ugly face, first," Alexios advised, still safely behind Marie, earning himself a dirty look from Justice and a smile filled with grateful relief from Keely.

"Maybe we should focus on your nephew for a while," Keely said to Justice.

Alexios figured he'd bail out his friend and change the subject. Looking around, he realized who was missing. "Where's Quinn?" Alexios asked, surprised that Riley's sister wasn't present for her nephew's birth.

A shadow crossed Riley's face, and she shook her head. "I don't know. She didn't check in on time from her latest mission. Part of me wishes she was a little less rebel leader and a little more safe and out of danger." Her troubled gaze found Alaric. "Is she—is she okay?"

The priest closed his eyes for a moment, and then

inclined his head. "She is well and in very little danger at the present."

They had a special link, Quinn and Alaric, that none of the rest of them really understood, and nobody wanted to be the first to try to pry into Alaric's personal life. The possibility of ending up as a dark splotch on the marble floor of the palace loomed large when you irritated Alaric.

Riley sighed in obvious relief, but then suddenly looked up and scanned the room. "I know Christophe ran off, but where is Denal?"

Alexios looked around. He hadn't noticed Christophe leave. Then he shot a glance at Alaric, willing him to be silent. "He got himself a little messy, so he wanted to get cleaned up. I'm sure he'll be along soon."

Riley furrowed her brow and Alexios dreaded the next question, but luckily the baby started to make tiny whimpering sounds, restlessly turning his head back and forth. Justice blinked and thrust the baby back at Riley.

"Uh-huh. From the look on your face at the first hint of a whimper, I'm guessing we don't need to talk about babies for a while," Keely said.

Justice apparently thought better of any public protest, so he just took Keely's hand and they stood and moved back from the bed. Riley cuddled Aidan close for a moment then looked up and around the room at all of them.

"Thank you all, so much, for everything you have done for me and for our baby. We wouldn't . . . we wouldn't have survived without your sacrifices on our behalf." She had to stop to compose herself, and then she continued. "We love you all, and as *aknasha* I can feel the depth of emotion from each and every one of you and how much you love us in return. We are so lucky that you are all part of our family. Thank you from the bottom of my heart."

By the end of her speech, the room was completely silent, until a loud and very demanding wail startled them all. Laughing a little, not knowing what to do with the unfamiliar emotion threatening to choke him, Alexios fell back on tradition and ceremony. "All hail Prince Aidan! All hail the heir to Atlantis!"

The room resounded with the shouted replies. "Prince Aidan! Prince Aidan! Prince Aidan!"

Finally, Conlan held up a hand for silence. "Thank you, but my son is very determined that he have his first meal now, so if you'll all excuse us, we're going to let Riley and baby have some much-deserved rest."

Alexios bowed to his friend and comrade the high prince and then turned and ushered the others out of the room. "The ale is quite definitely on me, my friends!"

"Speaking of ale, where is Christophe?" Brennan asked.

"He said that babies make him nervous," Alaric said dryly. "I suspect we'll find him already ensconced with a mug or five of the palace's best brew."

Laughing and chattering, everyone headed for the dining hall to properly celebrate. Alexios hung back to talk to Alaric.

"It's a truly grand day, isn't it?"

"Grand, perhaps, but not yet without danger," Alaric said, his eyes narrowing. "Not all Atlanteans welcome so many changes to the old ways."

"What does it mean, Alaric? The first human-Atlantean prince? What does it mean for tradition and for Atlantis?" Alexios generally tried to stay out of politics, but if something threatened the newborn heir, he intended to be prepared.

"I don't know yet. Poseidon himself approved the match and granted his blessing on the child, so there is no basis for denying him his heritage. But zealots don't always need reasons. We simply need to be ready for them."

"Oh, yes," Alexios said, hands twitching toward the daggers that weren't yet back in their sheaths. "We will be ready."

~~~~

Fort Castillo de San Marcos, St. Augustine, Florida

Even after the sudden thunderstorm struck, Grace continued to pace the long parapets that bordered the top of the fort for nearly an hour in the driving rain. Sometimes walking, sometimes running. Leaping over the gaps. Gazing out at the ocean as if she could see all the way down through the waters to wherever Atlantis continued to hide from the rest of the world.

She paced, trying to outdistance her thoughts and escape the crushing waves of despair that weren't even her own.

It was all wrong. She never formed mental bonds like this—not like this. Not with someone she barely knew.

Never before with a *man*. The memory of their last moment together before he'd disappeared—that kiss—burned across her mind like a wild lightning bolt riding tumultuous clouds.

It shook her up, tossing her nerves into a tempest to match the surf that the winter storm sent slashing toward the shore.

"It won't help, you know."

The deep voice came from nowhere and the shock of it nearly sent her flying over the edge. A strong hand shot out and caught her arm, jerking her back and away from a thirty-five-foot drop.

She tried to wrench her arm free, whirling around with a high kick to smash the intruder's face, but he blocked her kick and lifted her into his arms as easily as if she were a child, smiling down at her. The moonlight shadowed the distinctive bronze hair to black, but there was no way she'd ever mistake that face, even with water dripping from his drenched hair.

Very, very few men could subdue her so easily. But then again, he was a seasoned and powerful warrior, and one of the last of the race of weretigers. More than two hundred fifty pounds of muscle in human form and twice that as a big cat.

"I know it's been a while, Grace, but that's no way to say hello to an old friend," he said, laughing a little. "Also, that old saying about not having enough sense to come in out of the rain comes to mind."

"Jack! I thought you and Quinn were on a mission somewhere in—"

Something in the way he narrowed his eyes stopped her from continuing. "Sorry. It's just—"

He lowered her to her feet and gave her a brief hug. "No details. Not here, Grace. Not out in the open."

Walking to the barrier she'd nearly tumbled over, he stared out at the sea. "I need to join Quinn, but I can't tell even *you* any more about it. We have a lead we think is important regarding the . . . object we . . . lost . . . back in St. Louis."

She nodded. Vonos had stolen the gem the Atlanteans called the Vampire's Bane: a rare yellow diamond that reportedly had the power to kill other vampires without harming the one who wielded it. Vonos already had way too much power as Primator. Now that he possessed a weapon of mass destruction that could kill his own kind, the heavyweight threat was very effectively making him many, many alliances with vamps who'd rather join up than die.

"It may be here?" Vonos quite famously owned a winter home in Florida near Daytona Beach; *Undead People* magazine had done a cover spread on "The Primator at Home." She'd seen it at the checkout stand at the grocery store and promptly lost her appetite.

Jack nodded, a muscle clenching in his jaw. "Apparently it's some vamp macho thing to have a home in the sunniest place around. Shows you're tougher than all the other blood-suckers."

"Would he keep it here, though? Wouldn't the Primus be safer? I heard that the place is a fortress."

He turned his face up to the rain, closing his eyes, for a moment, and then turned back to her, tension evident in the way he held his head and body. "It is. I hear they've beefed up security, too, after we broke in."

Grace blinked. "You broke into the Primus? What? With all those vamps? I heard it's like the undead Fort Knox."

He shrugged. "You heard right. But we had a few advantages. Ask Quinn to tell you about it sometime." But as soon as he said it, his mouth tightened and he shook his head. "On second thought, never mind."

"Come inside, at least," she urged. "Let's find dry clothes, make coffee, and talk. There are only a few of us here until the new group of recruits shows up in the morning."

"I can't. There's no time. I only came to give you a message, so here it is: you can't trust anything the Fae tell you."

She tilted her head, studying his face, but his expression gave nothing away. "The Fae can't lie. You know that."

"The Fae are masters at telling the truth without telling the truth, and *you* know *that*. Masters of misdirection and manipulation."

She nodded slowly. "Of course I know that. I just find it interesting that the same night I had a visit from a high prince of the High House, Seelie Court, you show up to warn me about the Fae."

Interest sharpened his face. "Already? Rhys was here?"

"Not here. At the beach where I swim."

He gave her a quick once-over and grinned. "Naked?"

He'd surprised a laugh out of her. It was rusty, like her sense of humor. "No, not naked, you perv."

"Hey! You've got to watch out for those elves. The whole lot of them are horny, untrustworthy bastards."

She raised an eyebrow. "Didn't you just describe most men?"

Jack clutched his heart. "Ouch. Point and match." But his teasing smile faded and he put a hand on her arm. "Watch out for the Fae. Tell Alexios about it—everything, don't leave anything out—and whatever you do, be careful."

"I'm always careful, tiger," she said, letting a little of the arrogance and power of her birthright flow into her words and stance. "I am a descendant of Diana."

"Yeah. I know," he said flatly, clearly unimpressed. "But your bow's wood is made from their glades. I'm a quarter ton of one of the most powerful predators to walk the face of the earth, and even I'm careful around the Fae. Just do it. For me, and for Quinn, if not for yourself."

She studied him for several seconds and then slowly nodded. "I will. But you be careful, do you hear me? And take care of Quinn, too."

"Always." He hugged her again and then hopped up on the parapet and leapt gracefully over the side before she could scream. She ran to the edge, heart in her throat, expecting to see him huddled and broken at the bottom of the wall. Instead, she caught a glimpse of an orange-and-white shape bounding off into the dark.

"Great. Just what the tourists need to see—a giant tiger roaming through the city," she muttered as she finally headed for the stairs, dry clothes, and a mug of hot tea. "I wonder if we can blame it on escaped circus animals again."

Later, after a hot shower in the temporary facilities set up in a corner of the courtyard, she took a mug of hot, sweet tea with her to bed and wrapped herself in blankets. One the few perks of being in charge: at least she didn't have to share a room. Hers was part of the old officer's quarters. The rest of them were bunking two or more to a room, and the recruits would be sleeping dormitory-style in the old guardrooms where Spanish troops had first slept more than three hundred years before.

Warm and dry, Grace continued to puzzle and poke at the possible meanings and implications of the two extremely odd conversations she'd had that night. Finally, she turned off her lamp, no closer to any answers but content to lie in the dark and listen to the rain and the waves crashing against the shore.

"Ten years, Robbie," she whispered into the dark. "I know it's taken me ten years, but I'm finally getting closer to making a difference. I love you, Big Brother. Happy birthday."

Chapter 6

Atlantis, the war room, the next morning

Alexios shoved his chair back and leapt up from the table. Not even a half dozen mugs of the finest Atlantean ale had kept him from dreaming about Grace, or from thrashing around in the sheets all night long until he'd woken up this morning hard and aching for her.

Now he had to deal with *this*?

"No. No way, no how. You can get somebody else to wipe runny noses for your baby rebels. I've had enough of humans for a while," he said, the words coming out almost in a snarl.

Ven leaned back in his chair and folded his arms across his chest. "You wanna run that by me again? I must not have had enough coffee yet, because I could have sworn I got up out of my very warm bed and left my very warm woman to come down here and give you your marching orders, and you just told me no."

He made a show of rubbing his eyes. "Or wait—maybe

I'm still dreaming," he said, then squinted up at Alexios. "Nah, not with that face. More like a nightmare."

Ven was the only one who'd ever come right out and teased him about his scarred face, but Ven teased everyone about everything. It almost made Alexios feel . . . normal.

"I'm sorry. Maybe I didn't put that very well, *Your Highness*," Alexios gritted out. "I would prefer not to be assigned to the training fort in St. Augustine with Gr . . . with those humans."

"You call me 'your highness' again, and I'll kick your ass," Ven said, but without any heat, as he studied Alexios's face far more closely than was comfortable. "What is this really about? I heard nothing but raves for this commander from Quinn. Grace, what was it, Hanson?"

"Havilland," he corrected automatically. *Too* automatically, if the *aha* gleam in Ven's eyes meant anything.

"Is there a problem between you and this woman?"

Alexios stopped pacing and raised his chin. "There is no problem. I would just rather you assign someone else. Somebody needs to go to Europe and find out what's going on with this vampire claiming to be the long-lost Princess Anastasia. I'll volunteer."

"Erin and I are going. She has some idea about tracking down other gem singers in a part of Switzerland that used to be a Fae stronghold while we're there," Ven said, shaking his head. "I'm still not quite sure how I wind up saying yes to everything she wants."

"Hard to argue with a woman who stopped a bomb from blowing up your thick skull," Alexios said dryly.

Ven laughed. "Yeah, there is that. Anyway, there's more to it than a simple training mission. We hear that Vonos is hiding the Vampire's Bane somewhere near St. Augustine. Evidently he has some kind of super spidey fortress of stupitude or something near there."

Alexios whistled. "Now that *is* a prize. Is it true that the diamond does what the myths claim?"

"Quinn and Alaric saw Vonos use it to wipe out a whole crowd of vamps in seconds. The Bane exploded them clear out of their shoes, which sounds wicked cool. Vonos wasn't hurt at all, either, more's the pity."

Ven stood up, stretched, and yawned. "I think I didn't need that twentieth toast to the baby's health. My head is pounding like there's a room full of hammers in my skull."

"Nobody needed that twentieth toast," Alexios admitted. He'd been trying not to move his own head too quickly ever since he woke up.

"Look, here's the deal. We need you. Denal is in some kind of black funk after that stunt he pulled, and we can't even get him to go see Riley and the baby. Brennan has already gone back to Yellowstone to find out what in the hells is going on with the wolves, because *that's* a big problem, Tiernan is in Florida, and you know she and Brennan can't be anywhere near each other." Ven stopped to take a breath, and then continued. "Conlan's obviously not going anywhere, and would *you* trust Christophe with this? He's as likely just to stab the recruits and be done with it. Also, I don't know why I'm explaining all this to you. I serve as the King's Vengeance, not the damn social secretary."

Defeated, Alexios ignored the jibe and simply nodded. "There was a time when being part of the Seven meant fighting shoulder to shoulder. We are Poseidon's chosen elite—the royal guard to High Prince Conlan. Together, we have battled humanity's oppressors for centuries. Now, it seems as though we are being torn further and further apart."

"Maybe. Or maybe we're finally growing up, my friend. I have a new nephew now, and I intend to make the world as safe as possible for him. Especially since we're almost certainly taking Atlantis to the surface as soon as we find and restore all of the gems of Poseidon's Trident."

"I will do my part, of course. I *will* find that diamond,

and I will do my best to turn these humans into a fighting force worthy to stand at our side."

"I know you will. Now, back to a more fascinating topic. Grace. Did you know the heritage there? She claims to be a descendant of Diana."

"I've seen the bow she carries but only rarely seen her shoot it. She's very good when she does, though. I've never seen her miss," Alexios was forced to admit. "We've fought on the same side often enough for me to know that. I'd trust her to have my back in a bad situation. It's not that she's not a good fighter, it's just—"

"Personal?"

"Yeah."

"Get over it," Ven advised. "We're fighting a war here; we don't have time for personal."

"Is that what you told Erin? Before or after you took her to your bed?" Alexios asked, deliberately crude. He might be going along with this stupid pile of *miertus* plan, but that didn't mean he had to like it.

But Ven didn't take the bait. "Get over it," he repeated. "Or, if it really is that way for you and Grace—like me and Erin—then may the gods help you. Because your life is about to get very complicated, my friend."

Before Alexios could settle on a reply, the prince had left the room, no doubt returning to his warm bed and warm wife.

And maybe the gods *did* need to help him, because suddenly Alexios was picturing a warm and willing Grace in his own bed, and his cock got so hard that it ached. Five years of self-enforced celibacy and strict self-control vanished into the mist at the thought of all that glorious hair spread out on Atlantean silk. Those golden arms and legs reaching to him. Those dark eyes promising delights like none he'd ever known.

Just when he thought he'd go off in his pants like a green youngling, another thought made him laugh and eased some of the pressure: knowing Grace, she was more likely to offer to spar him over who got to be on top.

The gods help him, he may have finally met a woman whose mind intrigued him more than her body. The image in his mind shifted, transformed. Now it was Grace laughing, as she sometimes did with her friend Michelle, those lovely golden brown eyes alight with her generous sense of humor.

Grace serious, offering good counsel on matters of strategy.

Grace stern, arms set like stone as she braced her bow for target practice or battle.

Grace determined—selfless—courageous—as on more than one occasion when he'd seen her throw herself into harm's path to protect another.

Dozens of images whirled through his mind, tumbling around and around like the funnel of a treacherous sea spout.

Grace, Grace, always Grace. And, sadly, not even naked.

It was going to be an interesting mission.

~~~

Fort Castillo de San Marcos, later that morning

"Grace, they're here."

Grace looked up from her computer to see Sam standing in the doorway. Good old Sam. She'd known him for a while; he came and went as needed. Sort of a troubleshooter for rebel groups. He'd gotten in before dawn one day from Georgia, told her Quinn sent him to be Grace's go-to guy. Second in command, she guessed, came closest to a description, not that she even now was used to her new title. Commander. It was almost laughable.

It might have helped if she'd had any military training.

Thank goodness Sam did. Rumor was that a few of the new recruits had been in the army, too, back in the days before all military actions in the United States fell under the direct command of the over-sec def. The over-secretary of defense, appointed by the president but only with the advice and consent of the Primus, was a vampire, by law. The vampires had argued, convincingly enough to carry the vote, that with centuries of experience in military campaigns, it only made sense that their representative was in charge of all matters military.

Plus there was the threat of foreign campaigns conducted by vampires—no human could know how to combat that. Or so they'd claimed. And they'd won that argument, too. Back before any of the rebels had mobilized. Before quiet stirrings of unrest had solidified into fear, and then concern, and finally defiance.

"Grace?" Sam's bushy white eyebrows drew together in a look of concern she'd seen from him far too often lately. "Penny for 'em?"

She smiled and shut the cover of her Dell. Time enough later to figure out encrypted messages about supply chains.

"My thoughts aren't even worth a penny, not that we have one," she said, grimacing as she unbent her long legs from underneath the small desk. "Funny how you never think about revolutions needing money. In the movies, the good guys just seem to have a constant supply of shiny new guns and ammo, and they never actually have to eat."

She walked to the doorway of her cramped office space, part of the officers' quarters of the old fort. When they'd requisitioned the fort for "theater group practice," the city of St. Augustine had been glad enough to turn it over for a monthly fee. Ever since the vampires had shut the fort down as a tourist attraction—apparently it was politically incorrect to celebrate a fort where the Spaniards had once held mass vampire burnings; bet you never saw *that* in your Florida history books—the city had been operating in the red.

Kind of like the rebels.

"They never need to take a dump, either. Didja notice that?" Sam asked as he ambled along beside her. "Nobody in movies ever has to go to the bathroom unless it's some sort of girly bubble-bath thing."

He snorted, whether at the idea of not taking a dump or bubble baths, she didn't know. Probably both. Sam looked and acted like an uneducated redneck when it suited him, but he'd been a colonel in the army Special Forces back before a new "undead bloodsucker of an ass-wipe general" had railroaded Sam out of the service for insubordination.

"Why didn't you ever go into P Ops, Sam?"

He glanced over at her. "What does that have to do with bubble baths, exactly?"

"I'm sorry. I didn't mean to pry. It's just that the Paranormal Ops teams would be thrilled to have somebody of your talents, and I'd think with your background you'd prefer their organization and structure over our raggedy group. For that matter, you should take over this training mission, and I'll be *your* go-to guy."

The sounds of excited voices, unmistakably edged with tension, grew louder as Sam and Grace approached the stairs to the upper deck of the building. All the newbies ended up there, and Grace didn't blame them. The view was spectacular.

The fort sat right at the edge of the entrance to the harbor, strategically positioned to protect the oldest continuously occupied city in America. Grace had had time to learn some of the history of the area, and it was fascinating stuff. The abandoned gift shop was lined with dust-covered bookshelves filled with various books about the fort, the city, and the military history of the area. Cendoya, the

Spanish governor of Florida, had been in charge of building the fort. He broke ground in late 1672, and with a military engineer named Ignacio Daza and labor in the form of
soldiers, Indians, slaves, and skilled craftsmen, the work
on the fort began. Poor Governor Cendoya died only a few
years into the project, though, and the fort wasn't finished
until 1695.

What Grace found most fascinating about the fort itself was the construction of the walls. The beautiful rock,
coquina, was composed of tiny seashells that had literally
been turned into concrete by the sea itself, as if Alexios's
sea god had been playing with building blocks as a child.
The Spaniards had ferried the coquina on an elaborate system of boats from nearby Anastasia Island. The enormous
task had been complicated by pirate attacks and storms, but
they'd persevered, and the fact that the amazing structure
still stood today was a testament to those early builders.

These days, the harbor was often dotted with sailboats
as residents and tourists enjoyed the mild winter weather
and the glorious Florida sunshine. On the other side of the
fort, the historic town was laid out in a wonderful pan-
orama, with so much to see and do that Grace had spent
one day from sunrise to sunset simply strolling from one
end of the old town to the other, stopping at shops, historic
sites, and artisans' studios.

Sometimes, in the midst of training, worry, and planning
for battle, a girl just wanted to watch a glass blower at work.

"You still there?" Sam asked, making her think that
maybe he'd asked before. She grinned and nodded, coming
back from her reverie.

"P Ops wouldn't let me take my dog on patrol," he
drawled. "And Quinn tells me you have special talents that
make you the right one to be in charge of this ball game." He
stopped at the bottom of the stairs and whistled. "Come on,
Blue."

The wrinkliest dog Grace had ever seen lifted his head

from his paws, opened first one eye and then the other, then stood up and stretched in a motion that was about two city blocks away from graceful. Sam had told her Blue was a Georgia bloodhound. "The perfect dog for tracking bad guys and sleeping on porches," he'd said. "Or tracking bad guys who're sleeping on porches. Something like that."

But he'd had that unique Sam grin on his face, the one that told her he was pulling her leg so hard she'd be lucky if it didn't come clear off and leave her with only one, like the "one-legged man in an ass-kicking contest" Sam so often claimed to be busier than.

Working with a Georgia man was definitely an education for a Midwestern girl.

She took a deep breath and rubbed her suddenly damp hands on her jeans, and Sam narrowed his eyes.

"No call to be nervous about this bunch, Grace. They're all in awe of you."

"Of me? Why?"

He ignored her question and answered the one she deliberately hadn't asked. "He's not here yet. Your important trainer fellow."

The nervous butterflies the size of flamingos swarming around in her stomach dialed it down a notch, and she blew out a breath. "Okay. Good. We can focus on meet and greets first. I'm sure Alexios will want to meet them all, too, so we can save the intake interviews for later, when he gets here."

"Fine by me," he agreed, starting up the stairs. "You gonna let me know what it is about this guy that gets you so riled up?"

She didn't bother to deny it; Sam was a bit of a bloodhound himself. "As soon as I figure it out, you'll be the first to know."

~~~

An hour later, Grace made her excuses to the fresh-faced young guy eagerly questioning her and headed to the refreshment table to fill her mug from the thermal carafe filled with hot coffee. An even dozen trainees. It was a pitifully small number, but recruits were down. Ever since the so-called "accidental" fire that had wiped out a training compound in northern California two months ago, during the same week that a "gas leak" had caused an explosion that killed twenty-six rebels at a training compound in Colorado, people had been more and more reluctant to have anything to do with the movement.

Grace couldn't even blame them. Most people had families and friends. Loved ones who would mourn if they died, even for so just a cause as freedom. Unlike her.

She had no one.

She scooped too much sugar and cream into the rich pumpkin spice coffee—one of her few luxuries—and stirred it mindlessly, giving herself pep talk number 67(a), the one in which Our Heroine refused to give in to self-pity. It's not like she was really alone. She had friends. Michelle, Quinn, Jack, and now Sam and—

"Hello, Grace."

She jumped a little at the sound of his voice; the sound she'd been waiting for—and dreading—all morning. Coffee splashed over the rim of the mug, stinging her fingers. "Ouch!"

"Not the greeting I would have expected, but you do have a history of surprising me." The amusement colored his voice until it was as rich and dark as the coffee.

She told herself the shiver snaking down her neck was simply because of the cold. He couldn't possibly be as formidable in reality as he was in her memories. It had been adrenaline-fueled attraction, that was all.

Pasting what she hoped was a friendly but neutral expression on her face, she put the mug down and swung around to face him. "Alexios. Welcome. We're glad you're here. Did you just get in through the magic doorway?"

It hadn't been the adrenaline.

He was tall, broad-shouldered, and lean-hipped with the exact muscular body type she'd always found irresistible, but that wasn't what she saw first. It wasn't what anyone would see first.

In the bright afternoon sunlight that turned his mane of thick hair the color of molten gold, the sight of his scarred face was almost shocking. She'd seen him—seen his face—several times before, but always in the nighttime. Always in the dark. The merciless quality of the winter sunshine cast dark shadows along the jagged edges of the badly healed gouges. The left side of his face was scarred from temple to chin, leaving only his left eye and, oddly enough, his nose, whole and unmarked. But the right side was perfection; both counterpoint and mockery to the damage it mirrored.

The half smile that had quirked at the edges of his lips faded under her perusal and she was suddenly desperately ashamed. How long had Alexios been forced to endure the stares and speculation? And, worse, what torture and unimaginable pain had he suffered that could have caused such scars?

His narrowed eyes, rapidly turning the deep, turbulent blue of a storm-tossed sea at dusk, gave her the answers: far too long and far too much.

"No, I took the tram," he replied to the question she'd almost forgotten asking. "The tour guide was excellent. Did you know St. Augustine is the oldest European city in the United States, first visited by Ponce de León in 1513?"

She smiled, gratefully accepting his unspoken offer of forgiveness. "I did, in fact. I've spent a lot of time exploring the city since we decided to establish this outpost here."

"It still surprises me, when I think of it, to recall just how young your country is. Coffee?"

She blinked. "What? No, I have some, thanks."

"I meant, may I have some? Coffee?"

She felt the heat climb into her cheeks, where it would

probably stay for the rest of the time Alexios was in St. Augustine. She was twenty-five, damnit, and a trained fighter. A commander now, even. Not a giggly teenager with her first crush on a man. No matter that he'd kissed her like a starving man devouring a feast, and she, the feast.

Forget the damn kiss, already.

"Coffee?" he prompted, amusement shimmering in his eyes, as if he could hear her ridiculous thoughts. Oh. God.

"Can you read minds?" she blurted out.

A slow, sexy smile spread over his face and every nerve ending in her body wanted to sing and dance. Even his teeth were gorgeous. Somehow, those sexy eyes and that sinful smile, combined with the sheer virile presence of the man, caused the scars to fade into insignificance.

"If I assure you that I cannot, may I have some of that coffee? It was a late night last night, and my head is not yet recovered."

The blush burned through her cheeks again, so she quickly turned away to find a clean mug. This first encounter was not going at all as planned. She was supposed to be smooth, capable, and in command, and she couldn't even manage to give the poor man a cup of coffee.

"Cream and sugar?"

"No, thank you."

She handed him the mug and their fingers touched as he took it. A shock jolted through her at the contact, and her startled gaze flew up to meet his, but he showed no sign that he'd felt it. Probably just static electricity, not a sign of "someday my prince will come back from wherever he'd *run away to*" nonsense.

Not that she believed in princes.

"Why were you up so late?"

He did a quick scan of the area, empty except for the two of them, then leaned forward. "The prince was born."

Chapter 7

Grace did a peculiar double take at his words. "The prince. Of course the prince was born," she muttered, almost to herself, briefly closing her very expressive eyes.

He ruthlessly stole those moments to drink in the sight of her, from the rich chestnut hair glowing in the sunlight, to the high cheekbones that reminded him of the Native American peoples of the Midwestern states, to her rich golden skin. Just seeing her again, seeing the lovely curves that perfectly balanced her long, lean body, was like a balm to his ravaged nerves.

It terrified him.

He'd been wrong to tell Ven he could handle working closely with Grace. There was nothing about this situation that he was going to be able to handle.

She finally opened her eyes. "Is everybody okay? I felt . . ."

"I'll be fine," he snapped.

"Well, I'm glad," she said, tilting her head and drawing

those lovely dark brows together in puzzlement. "But I meant the baby and his mother. Are *they* well?"

He ground his teeth together at his own stupidity. Ven would be laughing his ass off if he were here to witness this conversation. One sight of her exotically beautiful face and Alexios's mind had turned into sautéed jellyfish. Which almost made sense after the bolt of electricity that had damn near sizzled his insides just from the touch of her fingers on the coffee mug. The exact same electricity that had turned him into a lightning rod when he'd kissed her.

He thought he'd done a good job of hiding that reaction, though. Maybe.

"They are well. Riley, very recently wed to High Prince Conlan, had a difficult pregnancy, but both are well. Prince Aidan has an extremely large head, but they tell us that is normal with newborns."

She laughed, and the sound rang in his ears like Atlantean shell chimes. Liquid, melodious, and so rich in tone that he wanted to instantly become a funnier man so he could make her laugh all the time.

He was in seriously deep trouble.

"Yes, it's very normal. Poor Riley," she said, grinning. "Because of course you came out and told her this, right?"

"No, I did not. However, Brennan may have pointed it out."

"I don't think I've met Brennan. What's he like, other than clearly clueless about babies?"

A sharp, entirely irrational stab of denial plunged into his gut at the idea of her meeting Brennan. Beautiful Grace and Brennan of the unscarred face. "He has no sense of humor. You wouldn't like him one bit," he said firmly.

"Oh, I don't know. So far I like all of you Atlanteans very much. Handy to have around in a pinch. Quinn said—" She broke off and formed a perfect O with her lips, which gave Alexios a mental image that led to a very uncomfortable moment of tightness in his previously loosely fitting jeans.

He wrenched his gaze away from her luscious lips and forced himself to think of calm, non-sexy things. Turnips. Concrete. Greenhouse gases.

"I just made the connection. Quinn's Riley?"

"What? Oh. Yes, Quinn's sister, Riley. I am sure Quinn will be sad to have missed the birth."

"That's too bad, but Jack did tell me she was gone—" She snapped her fingers. "Jack. Right. Jack. The Fae."

Alexios tried to follow the convoluted path of her conversation, but wasn't having much luck. "I beg your pardon? What about Jack and the Fae?"

"Rhys na Garanwyn. The Fae. The meeting. Sorry," she said, shaking her head. "Rhys na Garanwyn, High Prince of the High House, Seelie Court, surprised me when I was swimming last night. He demanded a meeting with you exactly a week from last night."

Alexios's lungs suddenly struggled to take in air. "Why? Why did he come after you? Did he hurt you?" He grasped her arms and offered his precise opinion of skulking Fae lordlings in vivid, virulent Atlantean gutter slang.

"Did. He. Touch. You?"

She shook her head, eyebrows drawing together. "No. He magicked my bow out of my car to show off that he could touch it, and he watched me get dressed, but he didn't touch me."

His fingers tightened convulsively, images of the Fae drooling over her lovely nude body flashing through his mind. "You were naked?"

"No, I wasn't naked," she snapped, yanking her arms out of his grip. "What is it with men and naked? Jack asked me the same thing, for Pete's sake."

Alexios clenched his fists around the hilts of his daggers and imagined himself slowly skinning a certain tiger.

He sucked in a deep breath. "Jack? Jack was here, too? Asking about your nakedness? And who is this Pete?"

Grace's face contorted into a strange grimace, her lips flattening and then twitching, and finally she started to laugh. "There is no Pete. And Jack is an old friend, nothing more, not that it's any of your business. There was no nakedness. Sit down and relax, and I'll tell you all about the Fae. And Pete."

He scowled at her but subsided and leaned against the wall while she recounted the tale of her meeting with the Fae.

"This Rhys na Garanwyn is very persistent, and in oddly connected circles of association," he mused when she'd concluded. "First Lucas, and then you. Both connected to me, in some way."

She raised her chin. "No. Not both connected to you. I have no connection with you other than this training assignment."

He bit back the instant denial and studied her face. Heat swept through her cheeks in a rosy flush, and a tiny bud of contentment unfurled somewhere deep inside his chest.

He stepped on it. Hard.

She wasn't for him. Shouldn't be for him. No matter how much he wanted her. There were so many reasons why he should stay far, far away from her.

He'd always hated reason.

He smiled and lifted a hand to touch her cheek with a single finger; was rewarded when she visibly fought herself to keep from reacting to his touch.

"We need to talk about it," he said. "That kiss. My reasons for leaving, which I thought at the time were valid, but perhaps—"

"What kiss?" She coolly cut him off, eyes narrowed. "I don't seem to recall—"

"Grace!" The shout interrupted whatever Grace had

been about to say. She turned toward the stairs and the man who had called for her. "Grace, is that him? We going to introduce him to these guys now, so we can get them settled in and find some lunch?"

She turned her head while she put her mug back on the table, and Alexios was captivated by the lovely long line of her neck for an instant before he forced himself to snap the hells out of it and move so that she was no longer in his direct line of sight. Maybe he could spend the next few weeks wearing an eye patch. Or two.

"Yes, we'll be right up," she called, then glanced at Alexios. "Is that okay with you? I'd like for you to at least say hi, get any first impressions, then you and I can go get some lunch and discuss plans while Sam takes care of the newbies."

"No!" he said, way too loudly, apparently, considering the way she was looking at him. He didn't trust himself to be alone with her just yet. "I mean, yes, let's meet them and we'll all have lunch together. One often gets a truer opinion of a man at his leisure than when he knows himself to be studied."

She considered that for a second. Nodded. "Makes sense. Except it's at his or *her* leisure."

"I beg your pardon?"

She grinned. "You have to quit doing that. Begging my pardon. Or it's going to be a long few weeks. And I said 'her' because there are five women in the new group."

With that, she bounded up the stairs to meet Sam, who Alexios already didn't like. The man looked shifty. And clearly he was far too old for Grace, so what was she doing hugging him, no matter that it was brief? And what kind of animal was that unnaturally wrinkly pile of fur loping its way down the stairs?

The animal ambled across the grass toward Alexios, who narrowed his eyes. "I was not begging. I am an elite Atlantean warrior, one of the best of the best. I serve the sea god himself, and I do not beg," he told it. Correction. Him.

He barked sharply and then sat down and looked up at Alexios, with his mouth open, tongue hanging out in a doggie grin. Forget Ven. Even the *dog* was laughing at him.

Grace called down to him. "Alexios, are you coming?"

He gave the dog's ears a quick scratch and then headed up the stairs, telling himself to focus on his center. Calm down and immediately cease reacting to the woman in such a way. He needed to meet with the Fae, find the diamond, and spend a few weeks assisting Grace with training. How bad could it be?

~~~~~

The fort, three days later, late afternoon

Alexios paced restlessly through the rooms and grounds of the fort, nodding curtly to the scattered groups of humans who were practicing with various weapons. After years of serving as a tourist attraction to camera-laden visitors and their ice-cream-dripping younglings, the old fort was back to its original use as a first defense against enemies. Of course, the Spaniards who'd built the fort had probably never anticipated that, nearly three hundred forty years later, the enemies would be rogue shape-shifters and vampires. Or, considering the Spanish vamp-killer history that had pissed the vampires off enough to order the fort closed to tourists, maybe they *would* have.

But they probably wouldn't have guessed that an Atlantean warrior would be the one doing the training.

Or that said Atlantean warrior would be failing, miserably.

His foot itched to smash a kick into the coquina walls, but the fragile shell-and-sand limestone was too delicate to take the abuse. Unlike Grace. Who was neither fragile nor delicate, but an enormous pain in his ass. Three days with her had been three days of unrelenting agony. Everywhere he turned, she was there, a living, breathing reminder of what he couldn't have. Couldn't touch.

Couldn't claim.

Even sweaty and dirty from training, she was so sexy she made his teeth hurt from the constant jaw clenching he had to do to keep from yanking her up into his arms and taking her mouth with his own. Worse, she was smart, funny, and generous. Everything he ever would have wanted in a woman—if he'd ever wanted a woman. In that way. That for-a-lifetime kind of way.

Which was crazy. Anyway, she had really annoying quirks that drove him nuts. Like when she was planning strategy or trying to figure out mundane budget issues, she had a habit of chewing on her lower lip and toying with the end of her braid that drove him nuts.

Okay, honesty. Nearly drove him insane with blind lust.

He wanted to play with her hair. *He* wanted to chew on her lips. Taste her. Bite her. Sink his teeth into her.

Sink his *cock* into her . . .

"Alexios!"

As if his churning thoughts had called her name, Grace's voice cut through the muted conversations of the rebels like an electric eel through algae. Somehow, after he discreetly adjusted the fit of his pants for the hundredth time in three days and turned around, she was suddenly only a few paces behind him. The late afternoon sunlight shone on the deep red highlights in her rich dark brown hair, almost mesmerizing him for a moment.

Then she had to go and ruin it.

"Alexios, we need to talk."

He scowled, every muscle in his body tightening in reaction to the musical sound of her voice. He didn't want to *talk* to Grace. He wanted to take her up on the amused speculation in her whiskey-dark eyes. He wanted to unstrap the knives from her thighs, the guns from her hips, and the bow and its quiver of deadly silver-tipped arrows from her back, strip her bare, and put his mouth on every inch of her honeyed skin.

All of it decidedly without talking.

Too bad it would be a cold day in the nine hells before he'd ever tell her that.

Or would it? By Poseidon's balls, his mind was getting a cramp from constantly changing.

"Alexios?" She planted her fists on those lovely curved hips and his mouth went dry, fantasies of what her curves would look like naked conveniently overriding reality. The reality where she stood there, either amused or annoyed or a little of both, her luscious lips pressed tight and her dark brows drawing together in what he'd come to think of as her "time to make Alexios's life a living misery" expression.

If it weren't for centuries of loyalty to his high prince, Alexios would be on a fast portal back to Atlantis. Unfortunately, his present mission was clear: help train this faction of the rebels and find out anything he could about what Vonos had done with the Vampire's Bane.

He'd been having damned little success learning anything about Vonos or the jewel, though, since Grace had scheduled every minute of every day for him and he was finding it impossible to tell her no.

Grace stalked up to him, the only human in the entire fort who wasn't the slightest bit intimidated by him. She was all long, lean lines, but with rounded curves exactly where a woman ought to be rounded, and just watching her walk made his mouth go dry.

"Third time's a charm, my friend. Earth to Atlantean?"

He folded his arms across his chest and glared down at her. Ancient vampires and alpha shape-shifters alike had quailed before the force of that glare.

Grace glared right back and then, unexpectedly, flashed

a grin. "Yeah, yeah, you're scary. I'm quivering in my boots. Now can we talk?"

"I'd like to see you quivering," he growled, then closed his eyes in disbelief as the unintended double entendre struck him. Sex. He had sex on the brain, and it was turning him into a babbling idiot. Of course she'd instantly pick up on it.

Sure enough, she started laughing, and the husky sound of her chuckle tightened something deep in his belly. Only sheer force of will kept his cock from jumping to attention. By all the gods, if he didn't get away from this woman soon, he was going to break every one of the sacred vows he'd made during the rites of purification. Joyfully.

"Honey, you can see me quivering anytime. Just let me know. Sex is a healthy physical outlet for two consenting adults," she said, the amusement clear in her voice. "Or we could spar, or play tennis, which usually works far better for alleviating tension."

His eyelids shot open. "Alleviating tension? Are you kidding me?"

She shrugged. "In my experience, there's not much to recommend one over the other. Although at least sparring is useful. Now if we're done with the small talk, we need to discuss strategy. Also, some of the men would like to know if you'll spar against them. None of them have anywhere near your experience or talent with hand-to-hand fighting, and for close quarters it's essential."

His mind was still back on what she'd said. Tennis and sex. Not much to recommend one over the other. If he had her alone for a single hour, he'd show her . . . He clenched his jaw against the sensual images flooding his brain.

"Right. Sparring. Now," he gritted out, stripping out of his jacket and shirt as he headed for the center of the courtyard. "Any of them. All of them. Tell them to bring it on. I've got some tension to alleviate."

∿‿‿ぬ

Grace knew a little about predators. She'd been training, studying, and fighting for ten long years, ever since she'd surrendered her dream of Olympic gold. She'd faced vampires and all shapes and sizes of shifters, from wolf to panther to bear. She'd even fought alongside Jack, whose ferocity in tiger form was truly stupendous.

But she'd never seen anything like Alexios.

If a poem could dance off the pages of a book and wield daggers and a sword, the sight of it might come close to describing Alexios in motion. His every step was calculated grace and elegance; never a misstep or wasted movement. He'd spent the first hour sparring against every single new recruit they had, leaving them all gasping for breath, battered and bruised, and lost in admiration.

Then he'd started to take on the experienced men and women, egging them into the sparring ring with nothing more than a sardonic glance as challenge. For the past hour, he'd taken them on two and three at a time. Never using any special Atlantean powers or magical tricks, although she was well aware he had those in his arsenal.

Simply fighting with hands and feet and wooden practice weapons, he had taken on and defeated every man and woman under Grace's command, experienced fighters and rank newbies alike. All but Sam, who'd just sat there with his dog, watching. When Alexios had turned to him, Sam had shaken his head, grinning, and refused to play.

She'd stood and watched Alexios for every single minute of those bouts, unable to tear herself away although surely there were plenty of things that needed doing. His shirtless torso gleamed in the reddish-orange glow of sunset, the tanned skin tight over his muscled chest, abs, and arms. Even his back was a work of art, with muscles so defined that she caught herself wondering if her tongue could trace the intriguing curves and dips of delineation.

She'd never seen so many scars on a man, though. Not just his face, although the left side was badly damaged. But the many gouges, slashes, and crookedly healed wounds on his shoulders, chest, stomach, and back told her the story of some of what he'd been through.

An odd tattoo rode high on his left bicep, a circle through a triangle with what looked like an arrow piercing both. She glanced at her own tattoo, forced upon her by the Fae. No, Alexios's wasn't an arrow. A trident, perhaps? It seemed likely.

Alaric, the Atlantean priest, was a healer. Certainly he'd healed Alexios over the years. Probably many times. And she'd seen for herself what happened when Alaric took it in his mind to heal somebody. Look what he'd done for Michelle when that vamp had ripped out her throat. There wasn't a mark left to show that Michelle had nearly died; to hear her talk, Alaric was a cross between David Beckham and Gandhi.

Frankly, the priest nearly scared the pants off Grace. There was something about him. Something so dark and deep that she didn't think any light could ever penetrate far enough to touch it.

Not the point, though. The point was that if Alexios looked like this, even after he'd been healed who knew how many times, what kind of unimaginable battles had he fought in his lifetime? She couldn't even imagine it—couldn't imagine having the courage and endurance to go back to the fight, year after year, decade after decade, century after century, only to suffer so much.

No, she couldn't imagine it. Didn't want to. Because that was the problem, wasn't it? She'd spent most of the past three days trailing after Alexios like a starstruck bimbo, instead of the tough and smart rebel commander she was supposed to be.

Maybe if she just slept with him, she could get him out of her system. That was her new plan, anyway. Yeah, that should do it. Either that or make her so sex-crazed she'd never climb back out of his bed.

Disgusted with herself, she shook her head to clear it of any and all fantasies involving Alexios and caramel syrup. She spun around on her heel to head for her office and smacked headfirst into the chest she'd just been lusting after.

"Damnit! I wish you'd quit sneaking up on me," she snapped, realizing she was being unfair but not really caring.

His laughter rumbled up from his chest, and she caught herself leaning forward, inches away from touching her lips to that lovely, glistening skin. Horrified, she stumbled back a step and probably would've fallen if he hadn't caught her by the arms.

"I was just coming to report in, Commander," he said sardonically. He wasn't even breathing hard. It was completely annoying.

She narrowed her eyes. "You're mocking me. I don't like it. You know you don't have to report in to me. We're allies. Also," she asked, frustrated beyond common sense, "why is it you always make me feel like I have a stick up my butt? I'm not like this with anyone else but you."

She watched in fascination as his beautiful blue eyes darkened to nearly black, but then suddenly realized she'd given far too much away with that comment. "Um, never mind. I didn't mean—it's not important. I have a lot of paperwork to do. Good night."

She tried to pull away, but his grip tightened on her arms.

"Oh, no, you don't," he said, his voice rough. "You wanted me to spar with the troops. I did so. You've got a few good men and women here, a few that will be good with training, and a few who need to take up a different line of work. We can get together with Sam tomorrow, and I'll tell you which are which. But for now, you and me."

"I don't think I need you to tell me—" But her indignation faded away when she realized she was reacting to his high-handed tone and the thoughts—okay, fantasies—she'd just been having about him. The truth was, he could judge this kind of thing far more quickly than she could. "Okay. You're right. Now you can let me go and . . . wait. What?"

Her brain had finally caught up with her ears. "What do you mean, you and me?"

He slowly slid his hands down her arms to her elbows and then released her. But instead of stepping back, he stepped forward until he was most definitely invading her personal space.

There was no way she was backing down. She lifted her chin. "I said, what do you mean, you and me?"

He bent down to the ground, leaning so close to her that his golden hair brushed against her chest. She'd never been so glad of her thick leather jacket that shielded her breasts from the touch of his hair. Or so she told herself.

Standing up, Alexios handed her a wooden practice sword. "Can you handle this, or would you prefer daggers?"

Grace didn't bother to bristle at the question. She'd fought alongside Alexios and had also seen over the past few days that he made no unfair assessments based on gender. He assumed nothing, but watched and surveyed until he had a good idea of the trainees' capabilities. The heavy wooden practice swords they used were too much for most women, who didn't have the arm strength to match a man carrying a sword.

Grace wasn't most women.

"I can handle it just fine. But you've been out here fighting for nearly three hours. It would be a little unfair of me to take advantage of you in your weakened state," she said sweetly.

His face changed, going dark and almost primitive. He stepped forward again, backing her up against the inner wall of the courtyard until nothing but a breath separated them. When he spoke, his voice came out almost in a growl.

"I don't think you understand, Grace, and I'm tired of fighting it. I *want* you to take advantage of me. I want to take advantage of *you*. I want to use the tip of my dagger to slice through your clothing until I have you bare underneath me. I want to put my hands on you, and my mouth on you, and I want to pleasure you until you beg me to take you."

She gasped, the heat from his words sizzling through her body as if he'd actually done the things he'd described, and when he bent his head to her, she lifted her face for his kiss. She wanted him. She needed him. Like he'd just said, why fight it?

But he stopped, an inch away from her lips, so close that she could feel the warmth of his breath. "But I won't. I can't. I've sworn vows. So no matter how much you tempt me, or taunt me, or tell me that sex is no better than tennis, I can't take you," he said savagely. "But I can spar with you. So get that pretty little ass in the ring."

With that, he spun around and strode off toward the practice ring, slashing the wooden sword so fiercely through the air with every step that it made a whooshing, whistling noise; a counterpoint to the fierce beating of her heart in her chest. Only his scent remained, a lingering trace of sea and sandalwood. A sudden crazy longing to find his discarded shirt and carry it away to sleep in swept through her, and her body literally trembled with the force of it.

Three days. She'd had three long days to watch him, study him, try to discover his true self. His hidden self. Three long days of almost constant contact, and she'd learned nothing that she didn't already know, hadn't known within five minutes of meeting him.

He was a warrior.

A true warrior. A man so deeply committed to protecting others that he put his own life on the line as easy barter over and over and over. Fiercely loyal, extremely intelligent, and calm and secure in his own strength. In his own worth. In all the time she'd known him, she'd never seen him lose control.

Until now. Over *her*.

He'd let her see that she held power over him, and the knowledge seared through her on a wave of breathtaking desire. Maybe they could forget the sparring. Maybe if she marched over there and planted a huge kiss right on those sinfully elegant lips, he'd change his mind about whatever "I've sworn vows" meant.

She'd already taken the first step toward him when she reconsidered. Took a deep breath to clear her head. Not yet. For now, he'd thrown down the proverbial gauntlet. She could either pick it up and face him in that ring, or she could run. Back away. Get while the getting was good, if she had any sense at all.

She thought about it. Nope. Guess not.

"Get ready, Atlantean. I'm about to show you what a descendant of Diana is made of."

Chapter 8

Alexios knew it was crazy to jeopardize their working relationship, especially when he was on orders from Conlan and Ven to make this alliance work. Crazy.

Yeah, well, maybe *crazed* was more like it. Ever since he'd first met Grace, fighting with Quinn's team in St. Louis, something about her had stuck under his skin. Beneath his calm control.

That *kiss.*

It wasn't just that she was beautiful, although of course she was. Even now, stalking toward him with fire in her eyes and defiance in every line of her body.

Especially now.

She stood, biting her lip a little, shining in the late afternoon sun like the goddess she claimed as ancestress. The cool sea air whipped at the edges of his hair and he impatiently brushed it back, wanting nothing to interfere with his vision.

Grace's hair was firmly controlled, like every other part

of her. All that long, silky hair was pulled back in a tight braid and coiled around in one of those weird twisty things women did. He wanted to see her hair loose, wild, and unbound. He wanted to see Grace that way, too.

She stripped off her bulky leather jacket and dropped it on the faded winter grass of the courtyard. Without her coat, she wore only a long-sleeved red T-shirt over faded jeans. If anyone had told him a century or two ago that an article of clothing farmers wore to plow fields would become the sexiest thing a woman could put on her body, he would have laughed. But the way that denim hugged the curves of her ass put thoughts in his mind that he had no business thinking.

Ven had been right. Alexios needed the gods to help him, because he was out of his mind to spar with her. He had a terrible feeling that hand-to-hand combat was exactly the wrong way to force himself to quit thinking about Grace, naked.

Grace, in the moonlight up on the parapets. Naked. Gloriously naked, riding him, with her hair unbound and whipping behind her in the night breeze.

Naked.

He shook his head to try to dislodge the thoughts, but she saw him and got the wrong idea. "What's the matter? Did you change your mind?" she taunted. "A little too tired after all, tough guy?"

"I will never be too tired to take you," he said, the impact of his deliberate dual meaning shimmering in the air between them.

She gasped—a small sound he almost missed—and tightened her grip on the practice sword. A rosy red flush tinted her cheeks, catching him off guard. So the warrior woman was a little shy. The contradiction entranced him, and he wondered if she'd blush for him in his bed.

But she entered the ring, so the time had come to focus. Grace would give him no quarter and he knew her to be a very talented fighter. Although he didn't let it show on the surface, he was a little tired from three hours of sparring. With skill and luck, she could land a very hard blow to his head and to his ego.

But he had other plans for Grace, and though they did not—*could* not—include tasting her lovely body just yet, he had plans to do exactly that in the very near future. He and Alaric just had to talk first. About purification and vows and whether five years was long enough to heal a warrior who'd been so defiled he'd prayed for death.

It was time. It was long *past* time. Please, Poseidon, let it be time. Because for the first time in his existence, he may have found a woman he could not live without.

"Are we going to dance around all night, or are we going to do this thing?" Grace asked, slowly circling toward him, sword at the ready. "Is the big, strong Atlantean afraid I'm going to kick his ass?"

He laughed; he couldn't help it. "I've faced far larger and more powerful foes that you, but I've got to admit none of them had quite your gift for sweet words."

"Try to keep up, old man. I know we're not in your century or anything, but we call this trash talk." She grinned, her eyes sparkling. Whatever else may lie between the two of them, Grace really did love the challenge of battle.

He blinked as her words sank in. "Did you just call me *old man*?" He didn't need to fake the outrage. "Old man? I'll show you an old man."

With that, he quit circling and closed on her, raising his sword and feinting left. She blocked him easily and parried right.

"Too easy, *old man*. You have a tendency to feint left, or didn't anybody tell you that over the past few centuries? Maybe you need just a little more practice before you take me on." Then, seamlessly executing a pirouette worthy of a ballerina, she whirled round and shot a high kick directly for the left side of his head.

He ducked and sprang at her, catching her around the waist in mid-leap. Before she could react, he pressed a kiss to her neck, breathing deep to take her unique scent into his lungs. She smelled of wildflowers and sea grasses. No delicate rose, she. He kissed her again, smiling at the rapid pulse beating under his lips, and then he jumped back. "This *old man* has tricks you never dreamed of, woman. Watch yourself, because I claim forfeit for every time I manage to get my hands on you."

She spun around, crouching down into a battle-ready pose, sword held out in front of her. Her color was high, but he didn't know if it were from battle or from his touch. Probably both. This was Grace, after all.

"And what about every time I get my hands on you?" she challenged him.

He smiled and let every single heated thought he'd ever had about her show in his eyes. From the sound of her startled gasp, he figured she'd picked up on his message just fine.

"I thought maybe we could play tennis," he replied, mocking her earlier words. Then he raised his sword to go after her in earnest. He would give no quarter and make no concession for her sex or for her humanity. Right now, right here, she was his, and he was going to take her in the only way not forbidden to him.

"En garde, my lovely Grace," he said. Then he charged.

~~~❧

Grace barely had time to take a breath before he was on her. Wooden swords smashing against each other, she and Alexios battled their way around the ring. With that unbelievably muscled body, deep blue eyes, and the golden hair brushing against his shoulders at every step, he looked like a pillaging Viking come to abduct the village maiden.

Lucky village maiden.

Wait. No. Focus. Resist the Viking, er, Atlantean. Show some pride, girl.

At least part of the time, she felt like she almost had him on the defensive, but whenever it happened she'd catch him watching her, holding back laughter. He was toying with her, and it was driving her nuts.

Worse, whatever crazy plan he had—whatever he was trying to accomplish with the constant touching—it was working. She was distracted beyond any coherent thought of strategy and reduced to hacking away at him like a novice.

Lunge and he would parry, then riposte. Feint, and he would block, circle around, and touch her again. Kiss her neck. Touch her hair.

She was breathing harder than she ever had in a real sword fight, and he wasn't even winded. It was him. All him.

He took advantage of her distraction and feinted left again. She blocked him easily but the feint itself had been a trick. He moved faster than her eyes could track and suddenly he was yanking her up against him, her breasts crushed into his chest, his sword falling to the ground as he used his free hand to unfasten her hair. The heavy braid fell out of its twist and he pulled the tie from the end of it.

"Why do you hide this hair?" He asked, his voice low and husky. A bedroom voice. She tried to answer, but her mouth had gone dry and words weren't coming.

He lowered his other hand to her bottom and pulled her even closer until she felt the unmistakable hardness of his erection pressing against her. She felt him doing something to her hair but it barely registered until he pulled the long length of it, freed from its braid, between them and curled it around his hand.

"Do you know that I have fantasized about your hair? More vividly and more sensually than any fantasies I've ever had? Waking dreams of your hair spread on my pillows, these lovely dark waves silhouetted on Atlantean silk. Of long curls falling on my chest while you straddled my naked body. Of burying my hands in it while I take you from behind. Do you have any idea what you're doing to me?"

He bent his head to the curve of her neck and inhaled deeply, and the feel of his breath on her skin was so arousing that her knees weakened and the sword dropped from her suddenly nerveless fingers.

"You—I—" But she couldn't think. Couldn't form coherent thoughts in order to speak them. All she could do was moan when he opened his mouth and gently bit down right where her neck curved into her shoulder.

Her arms reached up, almost without her own volition, and twined around his neck. She pressed herself even closer to him until there was nothing between his chest and her hard, aching nipples but the thin cloth of her cotton bra and T-shirt.

Even that was too much. She wanted him naked. She wanted *herself* naked.

She finally gave into the secret desire she'd had since she first saw him walk into the room in St. Louis. She put her hands in all that gorgeous golden hair, and the tactile sensations from the silken mass of waves nearly made her moan. His hair was so many colors that simply calling it gold didn't do it justice. It was champagne and sunlight; gold and bronze and copper. It was lush fantasies of a wild jungle cat who only she could tame.

A wild *Atlantean* only she could tame.

If only it were true.

"You're so beautiful," she whispered.

He lifted his head and stared down at her, something dark and forbidding in his expression. For once, he made no attempt to hide the viciously scarred left side of his face. "So I have been told, many times, before this damage was done to me. My appearance meant nothing to me then. A way to divest women of their skirts, perhaps."

His arms tightened around her almost until it hurt, but she said nothing, sensing that he was on the brink of a revelation that she was afraid to hear, but needed to know.

"Then there were those who spoke of beauty to me, but they were talking about pain. My pain. I was captured, Grace," he confessed, the words rough as though she'd ripped them from his throat. "Captured while trying to save my prince, but he was captured, too. They were Algolagnia, the vampire goddess Anubisa's cult of pain worshippers. They only find beauty and sexual release in their own agony and that of others. For so long—so unbearably long—they tortured and defiled and corrupted me until I, too, almost began to believe that beauty was only found in blood, pain, and despair."

A wave of mingled sympathy, rage, and something like terror sliced through her. She started to speak, but he shook his head.

A warning or a denial.

"I ask not for your sympathy—I will not accept your pity. I have never spoken in any detail of the eternity I lived during those two years, and I never will. But you need to know that if you continue to tease me, you're baiting a beast the likes of which you have never encountered. I fear something in me was broken and still lies twisted, with jagged edges, inside the boundaries of what I once experienced as desire."

Grace didn't know what to say. Didn't know what to do. Only knew that she had to say or do something to help dispel the horrible aching loneliness in his eyes.

"I'm tougher than I look," she said, trying to smile. "Despite how little trouble I've given you here in the practice ring. And I'm very good at fixing broken things. I've never tried with a broken person, though."

Abruptly, he released her and stepped back. "And so you should not have to, lovely Grace. I will avoid you as much as possible during this assignment. You have my word. Please accept my deepest apologies for this inappropriate display on my part."

He turned and had begun walking away before she could formulate a response. She wanted to follow him, but she needed to be careful. After all, she didn't know what had happened to him. What was wrong with him. What violence was masked by his undeniably stunning exterior. She'd come to see even the scars as an enhancement, turning classical beauty to rugged. But she needed to be cautious.

She watched him as he walked away from her, his body held rigidly upright, having rejected her before she could reject him. He was protecting her. He was protecting himself.

Her defenses shattered. To hell with cautious. She was going after him.

"Alexios!" She started walking, then running, until she caught up to him. She lifted her hands to cup his face. "Don't. Don't apologize to me. Don't treat me like I'm fragile. Don't run off on me. I think . . . I think there's something between us, and I'm . . . I want to take the time to figure it out. Life is short—"

She broke off, laughing. "Well, okay. Life may not be short for you. But for me, for humans, yes. I learned that brutal lesson ten years ago. Give me a chance to be not just your ally, but . . ."

"But?" he prompted.

She lowered her hands and stepped back, suddenly embarrassed at her own presumption. What was she, a psychologist? How did she think she could offer anything to this man who'd clearly been through so much?

"I'm an idiot," she mumbled, closing her eyes. "Total idiot."

"I seriously doubt that, but why would you say it? Grace?" He caught her arm and stared down into her eyes. His own had turned nearly black, with a peculiar blue-green flame in the exact centers of his pupils. She knew that Atlantean eyes were sort of like mood rings, but this blue flame thing was new.

"Grace?"

She blinked, feeling like she'd just nearly hypnotized herself in his gaze. "Maybe, maybe we could take it slow. Find out . . . discover if there's anything between us worth pursuing. I'm not exactly girlfriend material."

It was his turn to blink, and then a wide grin spread over his face. "Girlfriend material," he repeated slowly. "Oh, may the gods help me. I can't believe I'm going to have to talk to Alaric about this."

"What? What does Alaric have to do with it?"

He bent and kissed her forehead, then bowed deeply. "As you say, we will take it slow. Until tomorrow, *mi amara.*"

With that, he whirled around and started to run across the courtyard, then took a giant leap and dissolved into mist in midair. Grace watched the shimmering cloud that had recently been an Atlantean warrior as it sailed off through the sky.

Well. That was one way to end a conversation.

Show-off.

Chapter 9

Vonos, lord high vampire of the Primus, smoothed out a minuscule wrinkle on the sleeve of his Armani suit jacket and then swept a triumphant glance around the room. He smiled as he signed his name to the document in front of him. *Vonos, Primator in Chief.* That fool Barrabas had been content with the weak title of senator during his term as head of the Primus. But no human appellation would serve to describe Vonos, the most powerful game player that vampire kind had ever known. His first act as newly installed leader of the Primus had been to pay a social call upon the human leaders of the Senate and the House of Representatives.

Each one of them still cringed when they saw him walk by.

Vonos lived for political power. All other pleasures withered with time. As one who had survived centuries' worth of lifetimes, he, more than others, lived for the game. The animalistic lusts and need for violent feeding on both blood and emotion that consumed so many vampires as they aged had somehow passed him by. Perhaps the austerity in which he'd lived his life as a human had followed him through death and beyond. He'd never know; at any rate, it was an intellectual exercise, no more. He had no need to analyze the reasons why he was superior to others of his race and age. He was content merely to accept it.

However, he contemplated with no little nervousness the arrival of one who was beyond analysis. The goddess of Chaos and Night had ordered him to remain in waiting for her, so that they might discuss strategy. Unfortunately, Vonos could think of many, many things he'd rather do than discuss strategy with Anubisa.

Like having his fangs ripped out of his jaw with pliers, for example.

It was not merely that she was emotional, as most women were. Nor that she had the power to force him into an existence of never-ending pain and agony with no more than a thought.

No, the primary problem he had with Anubisa was that she was completely and utterly irrational. She would discard or demolish a decade's worth of careful planning on a moment's whim. The obsession she had with the Atlantean royal family bordered on insanity. Although, perhaps insanity composed the very essence of one who ruled over Chaos, and any other action on her part, indeed any other form of reality, would be counterintuitive.

Dangerous to wonder. Dangerous even to think such thoughts. Especially now.

His only warning of her arrival was the abrupt temperature change in the central chamber of the Primus. Silver-white frost formed on the teak desktop in front of him. So she was making an entrance this time. That, in itself, was information. A clue to her mood. A possible indicator to whether he would survive the encounter or not, the risk he took every single time she came to him.

But reward never arrived without risk, and he had gambled throughout his centuries with political power the scope and breadth of which had toppled kings and crushed dictatorships. He considered Anubisa to be his greatest challenge.

Bowing his head, he waited. It was always difficult to gauge the level of subservience that would appeal to her vanity on any given occasion. If he bowed too low, or fell to the ground prostrating himself, she was as likely to crush him as unworthy of her time as to reward him for his fealty. If, however, he did not show the level of humility that she considered proper . . .

Well. He had heard that one such still hung, skinless and screaming, in a very deep cavern.

Something in the air pressure of the room changed, and he knew she'd arrived. "You wear it well, my Vonos. The evidence of your ascension in power as my right hand," she said. Hers was no ordinary voice, but of course one would not expect *ordinary* from a goddess. Within the tone of it, which rang so melodiously on the surface, the crashing cymbals of cowering death danced and gibbered like a corpse on a hangman's scaffold.

Even he, undead for these thousands of years, felt the flesh rise along his spine as though trying to escape the room from the mere sound of her words.

"Thank you, my lady." He finally dared to raise his head and look at her. Her unearthly beauty far surpassed any that a mere mortal woman had ever known. Hair so black that the reflection of light caressed blue highlights into it curled down to her hips. Her face was perfection as sculpted by dark angels cast into hell for blaspheming their natural talents.

As always, her beauty failed to touch him. His taste had never run to the female, and that had not changed after his death. She knew this, and yet occasionally took his choice as challenge. She seemed to lack the ability to understand why any man or, indeed, any woman would not be drawn to her. It alternately infuriated and amused her, and he supposed sometimes that the puzzle of it was one reason he still survived.

"I have news for you," she said. "I learned enough of the Atlantean's plans, before that fool's mind broke completely and I had to throw him into the Void, to know that we need more of an army to defeat them. You are, of course, among the best at training my blood pride to enthrall the humans. The members of my Apostates have declined since that unfortunate raid by the panther shifters."

A palpable fury swept through the room at her words. Furniture trembled, papers sailed off tables, and light fixtures exploded in a shower of glittering glass. "This is unacceptable," she raged. "I have decided that the bratling princes three will serve me well as bedchamber slaves, when Atlantis rises from the waters currently holding it captive, and I claim it for my own."

Vonos clenched his teeth together to keep from making any comment about the futility and wasted resources involved in Anubisa's obsession with the Atlanteans. Political power was of no use to a pile of dust upon the ground, and dust would be an optimal result in store for one who defied Anubisa.

"Prevacek, too, has some great skill with enthralling humans. He is my second-in-command and is currently in Florida. If you will it, my lady, I shall contact him so that we may plan our strategy together to more effectively serve your needs."

She inclined her head; royalty granting a boon to a peasant. One day, perhaps, she would bow to him, instead . . . but, no. Even to think such thoughts was heresy. Vonos was well trained in suppressing all but the most loyal of thoughts. If she were to learn that he had not yet told her of the diamond, for example . . .

Suddenly Anubisa's eyes flashed deepest scarlet, and

Vonos trembled where he stood. Surely she had not caught such a brief thought? But she was a goddess—

She screamed, a sound of such frustrated rage that the walls themselves shook from the force of it. "No! No, no, ten thousand times, no!"

Blood-colored flames seared forth from her eyes, her mouth, and her nostrils. Flames shot forth out of her fingers and the tips of her toes in their pointed slippers. In seconds, she was surrounded by a conflagration of fire, an inferno that blasted such intense heat he did not know how she could not be consumed by it.

He could do nothing but throw himself to the ground, cowering before her. The scorching heat from the flames scalded the air around him until he realized he would be immolated. His last thought was philosophical, rather than outraged. He'd played the game and taken his chances.

Now he'd take a loser's punishment.

But then, somehow, the fire disappeared. The flames were gone, as if they'd never existed. Only the black and charred scorch marks on the floor of the chamber and the smell of sulfur in the air served as silent witness to Anubisa's tantrum.

A small, delicate hand in his hair yanked him up off the ground and threw him against the wall some twenty feet away. He slid down the wall and crumpled to the floor, afraid to rise. "Have I displeased you, my lady? If you only let me know, I will—"

"Silence, you babbling slug!" she roared. "The heir is born! Conlan's whore of a human female has borne him a healthy son."

He dared to glance at her and saw that she was trembling with a fury that was apparently too great to be contained within the space of her small form. "They do not escape me. I release them, or I destroy them. They do not escape me and breed bastards to carry on their hated line," she raged.

He began to speak, but then trapped the words before they escaped his mouth. In the more than six centuries that she had deigned to recognize his existence, he had never seen Anubisa react like this. Her confidence was always unshakable, her arrogance sublime.

A goddess who showed signs of being vulnerable was a goddess who would destroy any who had seen her weakness. He lowered his face to the ground and shut his eyes tightly.

She laughed, and the sound of it was as razor blades and salt to tender flesh. "So even after all these years, you fear me, Vonos? As you should. As they all should."

She paused for so long he nearly raised his head, but then at last she spoke again, in a more thoughtful voice. "I threw Alexios away, which may have been . . . hasty. But Justice escaped. Yet, in order to cross out of the Void, death magic had to be in play. If Justice killed in order to escape, then he is mine. The stain of death magic upon any soul is enough to consecrate them to the power of Chaos and the dominion of Night. If he killed, then he is mine," she repeated. "And there was no creature living in the Void who would offer self-sacrifice to such a one as he."

Vonos's mind whirled with questions, hypotheses, and more questions. He'd seen the gateway portals to the Void before. What he had never known, and wondered about now, was if a willing sacrifice made from the *other* side of the portal would open the entryway to release a captive. He knew enough about these Atlanteans to know that they were the type to consider such foolish self-sacrifice to be noble. Especially if it had anything to do with the new heir.

However, if the thought hadn't occurred to Anubisa, he would certainly not be the one to bring it to her attention. He shuddered at the memory of the flames as the stench of sulfur still clung to his clothing and body. No, it would definitely not be he who would point out any flaw in her logic.

The question then arose: If her logic could be flawed, was her goddesshood flawed as well? Ruthlessly, he silenced that line of thought as something to consider another day. First and most important was to survive this one.

He finally found the courage to speak. "Then perhaps he is already yours, my lady. You will then be one-third of the distance toward your goal of enslaving the three brothers. Shall I hurry now to find Prevacek and put the rest of your plan in action?"

"Yes. Yes, do so immediately. We have much to plan, and little time in which to do it. If my intelligence is correct, the Atlanteans plan on ascending to the surface very soon. We can ill afford the overzealous techniques that some of our newly turned vampires are using upon the humans and shifters. We need them to be enthralled to do our bidding, not comatose or insane."

He cautiously lifted his head and saw that she was rising into the air, her eyes still blazing a feral red, but with no other sign of the Hellfire she'd called earlier.

"Go now, Vonos. I know I need not tell you the consequences of failure."

"No, my lady, you do not. I will report as soon as I have news."

As he watched her disappear into a whirling tornado of red-and-black smoke that shot through the roof as though it were no barrier, a wash of bitterness swept through him. He wondered, not for the first time, if the idiotic humans who'd coined the phrase "failure is not an option" had any idea how harshly true the concept could actually be.

No matter. He had his orders. First to let Prevacek off his leash, and then a personal matter to attend to, also in Florida. Perhaps the Vampire's Bane had just grown more dangerous than it was worth.

Chapter 10

Alexios had spent most of the night circling the fort; first
on foot, later as mist, soaring through the overcast night
sky, and finally—again in his body—swimming with the
dolphins who played and danced in the windswept waters.
Once it had become clear that all attempts to sleep would
be futile, he'd given up entirely. At first, he'd thought to
return to Atlantis. Sleep in the familiar comfort of his own
bed in his room in the warriors' wing of the palace. But
something in him balked at the thought. It felt like giving
in; as if he were not strong enough to sleep in the vicinity
of Grace without going to her.

If ever he'd wanted to surrender, this had been the
night.

But surrender wasn't in his vocabulary. Unfortunately,
several other words were. Like desperate. Needy. Wanting.

He needed to talk to someone who could help him
untangle the knots he'd damn near strangled himself with.
So, like an idiot, he'd decided on the one person who was

least likely to understand this soul-deep, gut-wrenching, balls-to-the-wall need for one very special woman. If Alaric would ever show up.

He'd been right the night before. He *was* going crazy.

One moment he was sitting all alone, save for the occasional overly bold seagull making an incursion to see if he had food, and the next moment Alaric sat on the wall only a few paces away.

Alexios was fairly proud of himself for keeping most of his startled reaction off his face. "I wish you'd teach me how to do that," he said. "I wouldn't mind learning a few of your other party tricks, either. That energy sphere toss, for example."

Alaric raised one dark eyebrow in that arrogant manner of his. No emotion flickered in his harsh, bleak expression. Of course, if he really was the most powerful high priest in the history of Atlantis, as the elders claimed, Alaric had a right to a little arrogance.

"Is that why you summoned me? For party tricks? If so, then perhaps we need to discuss the duties of Poseidon's high priest." Alaric never looked at him though. Just stared out to sea, his obsidian gaze giving away nothing of his thoughts or mood.

"After all these years, I'm well aware of your duties," Alexios replied. "In fact, that's what I wanted to talk to you about. Nice of you to finally make an appearance."

"Is it the woman then? Grace?"

Alexios should have known. Ven never could keep his mouth shut, unless it was about a mission. Ever since he'd met Erin, he'd been even worse. Alexios muttered a few choice words under his breath.

"I have my doubts that the King's Vengeance will sing 'Feelings' at our next formal dinner, as you so colorfully expressed, but your underlying point is well taken," Alaric said dryly.

"Ven did come to me, but not out of some need for gossip.

He was concerned for you, true. However, it is the mission that is of paramount importance, not your . . . emotions." Alaric spat the word out as if it tasted like sea-slug slime. "You know the value of the Vampire's Bane. If your feelings for this human were to get in the way—"

"They're not feelings," Alexios said, but then he reconsidered. "Well, maybe they're feelings. By Poseidon's balls, I don't know what they are." Alexios was nearly shouting by the end of the sentence. He took a deep breath and continued in a quieter tone. "It doesn't matter, anyway. What's important is another issue entirely. As you know from the message I sent through the portal days ago, High House, Seelie Court, tracked Grace down to get to us. First Lucas, and now Grace. They want to give Prince Aidan a birth gift, and they want to talk to us about an alliance."

A muscle in Alaric's jaw clenched, but he said nothing.

"Did you hear me? I said—"

Alaric held up a single hand, and Alexios desisted, then spent the next few minutes in silence, scowling at an especially persistent seagull. It, like Grace, wasn't intimidated in the least. He must be losing his touch.

"I heard you," the priest finally replied, just when Alexios had been considering the merits of roasted gull. "We have been in council, considering what to do with the information. A Fae birth gift is an enormous honor and must be given in person to its recipient. This holds the weight of millennia of tradition. To deny Rhys na Garanwyn this request would be tantamount to a declaration of war at worst and a slap in the face at best. Even I, who channel the power of Poseidon, would prefer not to slap High House, Seelie Court, in the face."

"We can't let him enter Atlantis," Alexios protested.

Alaric inclined his head. "On that, we are in accord."

"And Conlan's not about to bring the baby to him," Alexios continued.

"Perhaps you could stop offering me your opinions as to what we cannot do and instead listen to my advice."

A seagull flying overhead sounded a harsh caw, as if in agreement. Alexios eyed it suspiciously, not really putting it past Alaric to manipulate even waterfowl to his purpose.

"As I told Conlan, I do not care for this, especially the ultimatum feel of it." Alaric cast a troubled glance at Alexios. "Or that you have been targeted by the Fae to be our emissary, especially in your current condition."

"My condition? What in the nine hells does that mean?"

"You know what I mean. The human. Grace. Less than a year has seen first Conlan, then Ven, then Justice all fall. All three of the Atlantean royal princes. All victim to the soul-meld with humans. Then we have Bastien and his sister, both mated to shape-shifters, unbelievable as that still is to me."

"I see your point, although I doubt they would appreciate the word *victim*. And nobody's talking about soul-melding, here," he hastily added. "It's more of the—more of a—"

"More of a what, exactly? Are you denying that your heart is in danger of becoming involved with this woman?"

"My heart?" Alexios could taste the bitterness like bile in his mouth. "Who knows if I even have a heart? As far as I can tell, it's a useless organ that shriveled up and died years ago. Hells, all I know is I've been twisted up inside since I met Grace. It's just a physical thing."

Then, because he couldn't bring himself to lie to the priest, he tipped over onto the side of blunt honesty. "That's probably not the strict truth. If it was just my cock leading my brain, I would have found another woman and gotten over Grace long before now."

"Then perhaps you should bed her and get it out of your system. Also," Alaric continued, his voice more grim than Alexios had ever heard it, "I cannot believe I am participating in this conversation."

Alexios glanced at Alaric but then quickly faced forward again, gazing out over the waves. "This is not fun for me, either. And the reason you're having *this* conversation is because of one we had more than five years ago."

"Ah." The utterance carried a wealth of meaning. "Your vows during the purification rituals."

"Yes. Are they . . . are they permanent?" Alexios had to force the words past the knot of shame and humiliation in his throat. To have to discuss such things with Alaric was almost more than he could bear, but the priest had saved him from insanity and worse in the days following his release from Anubisa's Apostates. Alaric knew more of the inner workings of Alexios's mind than any other walking the surface or beneath the waves.

Alaric shrugged. "I mean in no way to make light of this, but considering the many enemies who stand lined up against us, the issue of your love life seems rather unimportant."

Alexios jumped up, stung. "Don't belittle the vows I made that day. You know what I suffered. You saw what I feared when you scoured my mind to be sure I was untainted. You can't tell me my concerns were unjustified."

"I am here, am I not?" Alaric's face hardened, and he, too, rose from his seat on the wall. "If there were time, if my own soul were not . . . *No.* There is no time, so there is no point in belaboring it."

He turned to face Alexios and something of understanding was in the deep silver-green of his eyes. "The vows you made that day—the promises you swore—were only to yourself. I merely stood witness, as your priest. Though we were in Poseidon's Temple, they were not vows to the sea god. He would not have asked those particular oaths of you.

"He only demands celibacy of his priests," Alaric continued, his voice rough. "No matter what Keely claims to have seen when she object-read that sapphire, I have found nothing to support her claims that priests once were allowed to wed in Atlantis."

Alexios knew that Alaric was thinking of Quinn, but he didn't know how to offer comfort to a priest. He did, however, know how to offer comfort to a man. To a *friend*. "Your friendship and counsel saved me from taking my own life back then, after two long years of imprisonment. If there is ever any task I can undertake, anything—"

"This is nothing your sword or daggers can solve," Alaric said. "For this matter, I must stand alone. However, I need leave you no such dilemma. You swore those vows of purification for a reason. To protect any who might come to harm at your hands because of the darkness you had endured and taken into your soul. What you must ask yourself now is whether you have defeated that darkness. Or would this woman you hunger for be at risk from those very hungers?"

"I don't know how to answer that," Alexios said, raking a hand through his hair. "I just don't know."

"Well, until you do know, the more prudent course of action is to stay far away from Grace," Alaric advised. "It is, however, true that I can offer you release from your vows, since they were sworn only to yourself." He raised his hands, and a sparkling shimmer of pale silver light shot forward and surrounded Alexios for a brief moment before winking out of existence.

Alexios had to admit he was impressed. For a moment, he'd almost felt . . . different.

"What was that? Some sort of vow-release magic?"

"No. Merely a trick of the light. But I had the impression you were seeking something more formal than 'Okay, go for it,' as Ven would say," Alaric said, a hint of a smile surfacing. "Looked pretty impressive, didn't it? It's a priest thing."

Alexios glared at Alaric, feeling like a damn fool. Then he pointedly stared down at the water lapping at the shore and then back at the priest. "I could pick you up and throw you in that water before you could pull any of your magic tricks, temple rat."

Alaric's eyes widened, just a fraction, and then he tilted his head and laughed. "You know, if anyone could, it probably would be you."

"So basically this is one of those 'the answer is within you, grasshopper,' kind of answers?" Alexios skimmed a rock over the waves.

"Exactly."

"Well, that's a big stinking pile of *miertus*."

Alaric laughed again. "Welcome to my world, warrior. You should stop by sometime when the elders want me to forecast exactly what will happen on each day of the next hundred years or so."

Just then, a skitter of sliding rocks alerted them to someone climbing down the grassy bank, and they turned in unison to see a small dark-haired woman smiling broadly and heading for them. For a moment, Alexios almost thought it was Quinn. But then again, he'd never seen Quinn smile.

Michelle. It was Grace's British friend, Michelle.

Alaric bowed deeply. "It is an honor to see you again, Lady Michelle."

She laughed and held out her arms, her lively blue eyes sparkling in the early morning sunlight. "Don't you Lady Michelle me after you saved my life, you gorgeous thing," she scolded. Her voice held London but also a trace of northern England. Maybe a touch of Wales, too. It had been a very long time since Alexios had traveled in the United Kingdom. Maybe he should go again.

Like now.

Alone.

Michelle's voice broke into his escape fantasies. "Lean down here and give me a hug, then, Alaric. I'm just in from London, and let me tell you there are no direct flights to this gem of a town."

Alexios's jaw dropped as he watched the tiny sprite of a woman gather Alaric to her in a boisterous hug. As if that weren't surprise enough, Alaric returned her hug.

Hello, alternate reality. Clearly, frustrated lust was beginning to melt Alexios's brain cells, if he thought he just saw Alaric hugging a human.

Then she turned toward Alexios, still with that delighted smile. "Hello, Michelle from St. Louis. Welcome. Have you seen Grace?"

She laughed. "Well, Michelle from London, by way of St. Louis. Not, mind you, that I ever want to go back to that nasty town." She shuddered. "Doesn't take a girl getting her throat ripped out by a vampire more than once to want to take leave of a place, I always say."

"But look," she said, lifting her chin high so they could see her unmarked neck. "Alaric healed me completely. Wouldn't be here if it weren't for you, luv." She directed this at Alaric. "So the least you can do is let me buy you breakfast. Both of you, of course. Grace will be along in a moment, as soon as she's done with her important leadership things."

She threaded one of her arms through Alaric's and the other through Alexios's and started walking, herding them along with the sheer force of her personality and chattering on about flights and layovers and terrible mix-ups with tickets, hired cars, and bollixed-up trains that all got sorted in the end. As they walked up the hill toward the gate to the fort, Alaric met Alexios's gaze over the top of Michelle's head and grinned.

Alaric. The mighty and terrible, most powerful, could-melt-your-bones-with-a-glance Alaric. Grinning like a youngling.

Poseidon himself would find it hard to believe.

Chapter 11

Grace kicked the office chair so hard it flew through the air and landed on its side, which accomplished nothing. The loud crashing noise didn't help her headache any, and it sure as heck did nothing to diminish her frustration.

No word from Quinn or Jack. No money had magically appeared in the rapidly dwindling bank account to help her feed or train the new recruits, only about half of whom showed any promise.

Another attack last night, this time in Miami. This one blamed on panther shifters who'd gone rogue and clawed and killed at least a dozen humans. But, as the smarmy news anchor had perkily announced, the humans were suspected to be members of a huge drug cartel.

Translation: nobody cared. Rah-rah for the shifters. P Ops would make a token effort to find them, but nobody would dig too deeply into the reasons and discover that this attack was another piece of the puzzle. The vampires were far too smart to test their new shifter-enthrallment techniques by sending their "experiments" after random humans. They were wiping out the dregs of society. People nobody in law enforcement would miss.

The average Miami resident would probably be indifferent. Happy, even, that some trick of fate had happened to put drug dealers in the path of the crazed killers. After all, it hadn't happened to "good people," so who had time to care?

"At this rate, we'll all be penned up like good little sheep waiting for the slaughter before anybody catches on that we need to do something," Grace shouted, kicking the chair again. A muffled noise caught her attention and she caught Sam leaning against the doorway, chuckling. He wore a plaid flannel shirt and ancient blue jeans, as usual, and his white hair looked like he hadn't combed it in a week. Same old Sam.

"Shouting at the TV again, are we? Does it do any good? And if that chair needs the hell beat out of it, let me know. I'm in," he drawled.

She glared at him, too furious to be embarrassed. "Another one, Sam. Like the attack on that Harley biker bar out West last week by the bear shifters. Another so-called rogue attack that nobody gives a damn about, because they're practicing their technique on the outlaws."

He straightened, all humor vanishing from his face. In that instant he underwent a drastic shift from affable good old boy to the man who'd led teams into and out of almost certain death, over and over, during his Special Forces tenure.

"When? Where? Tell me," he demanded.

She nodded her head toward the newscast playing out on her computer screen, and he reached for the mouse and turned up the volume. Together they watched as an earnest-looking young reporter cornered a big, casually dressed man who was stepping out of the front door of a building.

The label in the corner of the screen told them it was the Big Cypress National Preserve Ranger Station.

"Can we have a moment of your time?"

The man lifted his head and, obviously scanning the camera crew, shrugged. "Apparently so."

The eager-beaver reporter, probably no older than twenty-two, pushed his microphone almost into the man's face. "As the alpha of the Big Cypress Panther Shifter Pride, what do you have to say to those who accuse your pride members of being behind the vicious attack in Miami during the night, Mr. Ethan?"

Something in the man's eyes changed, and Grace inhaled sharply. The reporter was a fool. That man was a predator and he was very much on edge. Maybe a hairsbreadth away from ripping out Junior's throat.

Sam nodded, making a humming sound in his throat that she'd come to associate with approval. "He's a pro, Grace. Watch him. Be a good man to have on our side, this Ethan."

It was true. As she watched, Ethan's face smoothed into an expression of calm composure, his eyes giving away nothing. Anyone watching would think they'd imagined that moment of threat.

Anyone who hadn't trained for battle for ten years.

"We find the incident in Miami to have been extremely regrettable, of course," Ethan said, all but radiating compassion, concern, and a certain gravitas that made her think of politicians or judges.

If this man ran for political office, he'd win by a landslide. What a poker face.

"However, none of my pride brothers or sisters were involved. In fact, we were all at our headquarters, enjoying a very large celebration last night. We're planning a wedding, you see," he confided with a modest grin on his face that won over every woman watching. The man was flat-out gorgeous.

Evidently he won over the reporter, too, who completely

threw his previous line of questioning out the window and practically started bouncing up and down. "A wedding? Is it yours? Who is the lucky woman? We at MDTV will want to cover the social event of the season!"

Just then, a tall, tawny-haired woman dressed in a ranger uniform banged the door open, stormed out, and shoved Ethan. Hard. "If you think I'm wearing white lace on my six-foot-tall body, you're—" Suddenly she broke off, noticing the reporter and camera. "What's going on?"

Sam whistled, nodding his head at the woman on the screen. "That's my kind of woman. Gorgeous. All fire and temper. Bet she's a spitfire in bed."

Grace shushed him. "I want to hear this. Maybe we should meet this Ethan and his ranger fiancée and see what they know."

But the station cut out of the interview into a breaking news update. One of the men killed in the attack had just been identified as Carson Fuller, a "Miami real estate tycoon."

Sam snorted. "Tycoon, my ass. *Typhoon* is more like it. Fuller has a habit of doing dirty land deals and always coming out on top. Word in Georgia is that he'd gone into a new arrangement with a group of vamps. Maybe even Vonos himself."

Grace clicked her computer off and shut the cover, her mind racing. "Wouldn't that be interesting? If Vonos is behind the experiments with the rogue shifters, and this Fuller happened to cross him on some land deal, then how easy it would be to have him murdered. But they said drug dealers. Was Fuller into drugs?"

"Nah, he was all about the real estate. What he sold was clean and legal. It was just his methods that weren't."

Grace felt Alexios before she heard or saw him. A tingling sensation climbed up her spine, and she actually shivered. If she didn't get this under control soon, she was going to embarrass herself even more than she had last night.

"Whose methods?" Alexios asked, standing in the doorway, a forbidding expression on his face. He folded his arms across that broad chest and gave Sam a narrow-eyed glare. "Don't you have work to do?"

Sam grinned at him and casually put an arm around Grace's shoulders. "Oh, me and this li'l gal were just discussing vampires and kitty cats," he said, putting a lot more Georgia than usual in his voice. "Nothing for you to worry your pretty little head about."

Sam had spent most of the past three days poking at Alexios in ways the old soldier clearly found to be very funny, but Grace had no idea why. All she knew was that she was getting tired of it.

Alexios didn't move a muscle but suddenly seemed to loom large over the room. He pointedly stared at Sam's arm as if he'd like to cut it off with one of his daggers. "Perhaps, as your *ally*, I should be involved in strategy discussions."

Grace suddenly, *finally* got it, and she didn't know whether to laugh or cry at her own cluelessness. For some strange reason, Sam was trying to make Alexios jealous and—even more bizarre—it seemed to be working.

She shoved Sam's arm off her shoulder and glared at both of them. "Cut it out. Right now. I don't know what kind of stupid game you're playing, but I'm not in the mood to be the monkey in the middle."

She rounded on Sam. "You're old enough to be my father, for Pete's sake. What are you trying to prove?"

Sam grinned and spread his arms wide in a "who, me?" gesture, then jerked his head toward Alexios. "Hey, he's old enough to be your great-grandpappy three times over, if what he told me about Atlantis is true."

"You—I—" Grace sputtered, but couldn't quite come up with a reply to that before Alexios turned on his heel and left, flinging his last words over his shoulder at her.

"Your friend Michelle is in need of you. I thought I'd

give you the message before my *advanced age* made me incapable of remembering it." Then he stalked off down the hallway toward the courtyard muttering something about monkeys.

Sam burst out laughing, almost doubling over with the force of it. "That boy sure is fun to pester," he gasped, once he could get words out again.

Grace planted her hands on her hips and glared at him. "Why? Why do you want to pester our best trainer and strong ally? Now that you know about Atlantis, you must understand why he's so important to us."

Sam wiped his eyes, still chuckling. "Yes, sweetheart. I know why he's so important to the cause. But I also figured out how important he is to you. I've seen the two of you circling each other like buzzards for three days now."

"Buzzards? Wow." She slapped a hand to her chest. "Be still my heart. When Sam goes for the compliments—"

"Okay. *Horny* buzzards. I saw you in the sparring ring last night before I left for supper, Grace. It's a wonder this old fort didn't burn clear down from the heat of the sparks you two were putting out. I was half afraid I'd find the two of you shacked up in your bedroom this morning."

Heat flamed in her cheeks, and she pushed past him to leave the suddenly way-too-cramped office. "That didn't happen. Not that it's any of your business. And I'd appreciate it if you'd leave poor Alexios alone."

He followed her into the courtyard, chuckling again. "That boy ain't 'poor' anything. He's one of the best fighters—hell, make that one of the best *men*—I've ever met, and that's saying a piece. If anybody deserves you, Grace, it just might be Alexios."

She sped up, leaving his outrageous comment unanswered. There was nothing she could say. Whatever Alexios might deserve wasn't the question. It was more that whatever Grace had to offer, he wasn't interested. Last night's play in the ring hadn't meant anything to him but just that—play. After driving her nearly insane with wanting and need, he'd abruptly disappeared.

Kissed her on the forehead, for Pete's sake. She smiled a little at the thought of "Pete." Anyway, it wasn't, she tried to convince herself—had tried to convince herself all night long—that she'd *wanted* him to kiss her.

She escaped her dark thoughts and raised her face to the bright morning sunshine.

"Grace! Lovely! Let's go have some breakfast with these boys," Michelle said, her arm through Alaric's like the two of them were having a stroll through Buckingham Gardens or something.

Grace had to smile. There was just something about Michelle. Everybody loved her. Even scary Atlantean high priests, judging by the half smile on Alaric's face.

"No time," Alexios snapped. "Grace has training to do, if she's quite done socializing."

Grace clenched her fists, ready to jump right in his face, but then she realized something that made heat rush through her in an entirely different way. He was jealous. He was *jealous.*

She flashed her most dazzling smile, suddenly feeling lighter than she had in months. Men weren't jealous over casual flings, or women they just wanted to play with.

"Alexios is right," she said, still smiling. "Michelle, you and Alaric go. We have so much work to do here. I'll catch up with you afterward, and we'll go to dinner together, okay?"

"I'm disappointed, but I understand," Michelle said, rushing over and giving Grace a hug. "Back soon."

Grace watched Michelle tug a slightly bemused-looking Alaric away, then turned to Alexios, still smiling her biggest smile.

He narrowed his eyes. "What are you up to?"

"Who, me? Up to something?" She batted her eyelashes outrageously. "Don't be silly, Alexios. Now why don't you get your, hmmm. What was the expression? Oh, right. Pretty little ass in the ring, and let's put these guys through their paces." With that, she took off, practically running, toward the recruits standing around the practice ring.

~~~~~

Alexios stood staring after Grace, unable to move. Unable to do anything but stand there like an idiot. She was taunting him.

She was *taunting. Him.*

He'd left her alone, untouched, the night before like he was some kind of damn eunuch, so now she thought she could taunt him with impunity. Either that or she and Sam really did have something between them.

The thought burned through his gut like a slice from a poisoned blade. No. Surely not. Grace had far too much integrity to toy with him if she were involved with the human.

Didn't she?

He realized he was gripping the handles of his daggers so tightly that his fists ached, and he forced himself to relax. To recite the focus chant aloud. Out loud, for the first time in more than a century, because he could chant in his mind all he liked but it didn't help him find his calm center.

Hells, around Grace he didn't *have* a calm center.

But Alaric had freed him. Told him the oaths he'd sworn were only to himself. That Alexios would know if he were ready to relinquish them.

He watched Grace move around the ring, shaking hands with the recruits, offering encouragement. Smiling. Laughing. She'd left her hair down and loose. He wanted to believe she'd done it for him. It floated gently around her with every breath of breeze, with every step she took.

Oh, yeah. He was ready. He could keep her safe from his own black urges. He *would* keep her safe.

"I saw a smile like that once," said Sam, who was

suddenly standing right next to him, though Alexios hadn't heard him approach. "It was on a jungle tiger that was fixin' to pounce on a gazelle."

Alexios deliberately widened his smile, never taking his eyes off Grace. "I know a tiger and am therefore honored to be compared to one."

Sam nodded. "Yep. Except whadaya know? Damn poachers shot the tiger mid-leap, before he could hurt that doe. Craziest thing."

Alexios turned his head and met the man's gaze. "Am I to understand that you are issuing a warning? Be careful how you respond; I am sure that Grace would be unhappy to be compared to a helpless prey animal."

"I'm sure she'd kick my ass for me," Sam replied, unperturbed. "This is between us, though, and you don't strike me as the type to run and tell tales."

"But?"

"But I care about that gal, and she doesn't have any family to stand for her so I thought I'd step up. If she wasn't as tough as she is, I'd be telling you this with a shotgun in my hands."

Alexios inclined his head. "I respect you for that. But you should know that I have no intention of hurting Grace. Not now, not ever."

"Maybe not. But she's a woman who doesn't give her heart or her body lightly. If you just want a fling with some random human gal, go elsewhere."

Alexios finally turned so that he was facing Sam and stared straight into his eyes. "If I wanted a *fling*, I would." Then he bowed to the old reprobate and headed for Grace.

His Grace. Whether she knew it yet or not.

Chapter 12

The Bunnery Restaurant

Alaric stared down at the mug of steaming black tea and the white napkin on the wooden table in front of him and wondered how, exactly, the human had maneuvered him into breakfast.

At a restaurant named the Bunnery.

Ridiculous humans and their need to name everything.

Alexios and the Seven would mock him forever for this one. Not that he, as high priest to Poseidon . . . The unfamiliar laugh worked its way out of his throat, interrupting the disdainful thought. He didn't have room to stand on pomp and ceremony when he was about to eat something called a *cinnamon bun.*

"You smiled again," Michelle said, clearly delighted. "That's twice! We're making some progress here."

"Why, exactly, are my facial expressions of interest to you?" It would never occur to him to care whether another smiled or not.

Except for Quinn, a dark voice whispered in his mind. A smile from her would be a gift beyond price.

"Well, I'm responsible for you now, since you saved my life. Everyone knows that," she said, looking down at her own mug.

"I believe you are misinformed as to the nature of that concept. Would it not be I who am responsible for you? Also, was there not the promise of pancakes?"

"As soon as they call our number." She smiled and pushed elegantly styled dark curls, so different from Quinn's jagged mop of hair, off of her brow. Everything about her, except for her slight form and dark hair, differed so much from Quinn.

Michelle's taste in clothing was clearly fashionable for this time period. Quinn wore items that may as well have been stolen from homeless people. Michelle's nature was open and friendly, where Quinn was dark and distrustful. Cynical and solitary.

Nothing about Quinn, in fact, should have made every thought of her sear her image—her scent—her *taste* into his very soul. He clenched his fingers more tightly around the mug, and the liquid within it began to boil and circle rapidly in a counterclockwise direction.

Suddenly, a delicate hand touched his arm. "You're thinking of her again, aren't you?"

Startled, he released the mug and looked up at Michelle. "Who?"

She smiled, but this time her smile held sadness. "Quinn. I had heard . . . well, never mind, silly gossip. Can't you go to her, work things out?"

He drew his dignity around himself like one of his priestly robes. "You know nothing of my situation," he said, almost sorry for the way she flinched at the arrogance in his tone. Inexplicably, he liked this human and did not care to harm her, but . . . "You presume too much."

"I know. I have a terrible habit of that. Not very British at all, sticking my nose in other people's business, is it? It's just that I'm rather good at getting my friends' situations sorted out, even if I'm total rubbish at doing the same for myself."

A woman at the back pass-through window called out a number, and Michelle popped out of her seat. "That's us." Before he could follow her, she was back with a tray of food. After they'd settled again, something Michelle had said caught at him. "Your friends? You consider us to be friends?"

She blinked, a forkful of pancakes held in midair. "Of course we're friends. Not very many people have saved my life, you know. You're in a very elite group of three. You, Grace, and Alexios."

"I am honored, then, to call you friend, though you owe me no obligation for a simple healing. But I have no need of this sorting you mention."

Michelle took a long sip of her jasmine-scented tea. The delicate aroma was fragrant enough to tease his senses. It suited her.

"Well, of course I could be projecting," she admitted. "I just went through rather a bad breakup in London before I came back here. Frankie wasn't a big fan of me throwing my life in the line of fire again and gave me an ultimatum."

He dedicated his attention to his pancakes, considering her words.

"You chose to leave?"

"I'm here, aren't I?" she said, unknowingly echoing his earlier words to Alexios. She attempted a smile. "I've never been very serious in my many loves, but I think Frankie may have broken my heart."

Alaric leaned forward and caught her hands in his own. "Tell me where this Frankie lives, and I will immediately travel there and end his life for you."

She gasped, then peered up into his eyes and, evidently reassured by what she saw, started laughing. "Oh, you're too evil. No, thank you, I don't need you to end her life for me. She's quite a lovely woman, and we had a grand time together for the past several years. But it's time to move on and let her find someone safer to build a life with."

He'd suddenly had enough of the conversation. Far more than enough. "Safety is an illusion," he pointed out, pushing his chair back and standing. "I must leave now."

She started laughing and reached inside her bag. "That's fine, just let me leave a tip."

Ah. Payment. He tended to forget the mundane realities of life Above. "I am prepared for this. Allow me." He dropped several coins on the table, glad that he'd remembered to bring them.

Michelle glanced down at the coins, then stared up at him with very wide eyes. "We don't exactly leave tips with priceless ancient gold coins, Alaric," she said, retrieving them. "I'll get this one."

She placed a few of the green bills on the table and then walked over and held out his coins. "I thought *I* had a hard time with converting money. Sheesh! Why don't you keep these and we'll get you some proper currency?"

"Please retain those coins for payment for our breakfast," he said, his pride stung a little. "You will be able to convert them into the proper form, I trust?"

She waved to the servant who was rushing over to their table, no doubt to clean the table or count the green papers. It was a strange system.

Alaric followed Michelle onto the sidewalk for the walk back to the fort and shortened his stride enough to keep pace with her. He could not vanish into thin air on a busy street filled with wandering humans without causing her to offer uncomfortable explanations to any passersby.

"Alaric, truly, these coins must be worth a fortune," she said, staring down at them. "Please take them back for important things."

"Your rebel cause is important, is it not?" He narrowed his eyes at a group of loudly singing young men who were approaching them from the opposite direction. The men abruptly quit emitting the horrible noise and stumbled to the edge of the road to allow Alaric and Michelle to pass.

She turned her head right and left, staring at the men, then glanced up at Alaric, grinning. "It's a gift, isn't it? That ability to make the masses of humanity part like the Red Sea before you. And, yes, our cause is very important. Vital. We're so thankful you—"

He strode out into the street to cross to the other sidewalk, contemplating the destruction a well-placed energy sphere could cause to the cretin who squealed to a stop, honking his horn at them.

"I need no thanks. I was merely inquiring. Give the coins to Grace so she may purchase supplies."

She grabbed his arm and pressed closer to his side as the vehicle moved past them with another offensive squealing noise. He contemplated the effect a small tidal wave would have on the fool, but refrained.

"Ah, Alaric, you don't happen to know anything about crosswalks or stoplights, do you?"

He shrugged. "We clearly had the greater need to cross; the imbecile in the vehicle was wasting precious planetary resources by driving that enormous truck."

She sighed. "Red light, green light? Means nothing. Okay, breakfast with you is a life-threatening experience. So noted. Also, thank you for the coins. Grace would puff up with pride and say no, thanks, but I happen to know she's very worried about funds for food and arms. So I'll just accept on her behalf. I know a friend of a friend who's a coin guy. We'll see what we can get."

As they approached the front gates of the fort, she tugged on his arm. "Wait. These aren't some supersecret Atlantean coins that will look like forgeries to a numismatist who doesn't believe in Atlantis, are they?"

He shook his head. "Greek, Roman. Maybe some Spanish. We never really used coins in Atlantis; what few we minted were for ceremonial usage and are never used for currency."

"Oh, naturally," she said, grinning again. "One day I hope to come visit you in Atlantis."

"One day I hope that you shall. Now I must leave. Please give Alexios the message that I go to find Quinn but will return in time for the meeting."

"You bet. Good luck." She held up her arms and hugged him again, then started toward the fort. He leapt into the air, transforming into mist, and focused on connecting with Quinn. West. She was somewhere . . . west. And she was in trouble.

With Quinn, safety wasn't even an illusion. It was an impossibility.

~~⚬~~

Alexios watched Grace circle around the trainee, checking to see that he had the bow properly positioned, helping him hold the arrow just so. He felt his jaw clenching at the sight of her touching the man and forced himself to relax. Simply because he'd come to the momentous decision that he would try to move forward—take that leap out of the darkness—did not mean that the world would magically fall in line.

Besides, the man was prematurely balding and had a soft belly. Grace would never be attracted to him.

Shame followed immediately, crackling in the wake of the smug thought. *Bold words for a man with a face like a monster's.*

Even Alexios, who had never read a child a bedtime story, knew that the original telling of "Beauty and the Beast" ended in the beast's horrible death. Only in modern whitewashed faery tales did the beauty ever end up in the beast's arms.

The trainee laughed and put a hand on Grace's shoulder, interrupting Alexios's morose train of thought. He unsheathed one of his daggers and stalked across the grass. Beasts might die eventually, but in the meantime they were great at slicing a man's nuts off for presumption.

Grace looked up at the sound of his approach, and the smile faded from her face as she studied his expression. She subtly moved so that she was blocking his path.

"That was good. Try that," she said to the man behind her, never taking her eyes off Alexios.

As the recruit rushed off to share his newfound knowledge with his fellow trainees, Alexios sheathed his dagger and scowled at Grace. "He should keep his hands to himself."

"I could say the same of you."

"Those days are over."

She raised her eyebrows and the intriguing rosy flush appeared in her cheeks again, but she said nothing for a long moment. Then she tilted her head and smiled seductively.

Dangerously.

Whatever she had in mind, he had a feeling he was in trouble.

"How about a little target practice?" she said, all but purring. "Winner buys dinner for the entire group."

He folded his arms, trying not to jump on the challenge. Trying to be cautious. Reasonable. "You are a descendant of Diana, goddess of the hunt."

She pulled a long strand of her shining hair over her shoulder and stood twisting it around her finger.

The symbolism was not lost upon him.

"You're a trained warrior, with more than a few battles under your belt," she replied. Her eyes dropped down to his belt, or where a belt would be if he wore one with his blue jeans, and she smiled like a cat lapping particularly fine cream.

That symbolism wasn't lost upon him, either.

He closed his eyes. "Poseidon help me."

"I'm not sure your sea god is going to intervene in target practice, but hey, if prayers help, you be my guest," she said, laughter and challenge in her voice.

"You're on," he said, opening his eyes. "But I choose daggers for my own part."

She shrugged. "Whatever floats your—"

"Continent?"

Her lips twitched, but she couldn't suppress her laughter. As her eyes lit up with amusement, turning honey gold in the sunlight, an epiphany slammed into him with the force of one of her arrows striking its target.

He wanted to hear the sound of her laughter again. And again and again. Every day for the rest of his life.

Definitely in trouble.

Chapter 13

Grace was tired of watching him. Wanting him. Wondering what would happen if they ever managed to push past her wariness and his barricades.

The man had issues.

He'd been captured and tortured badly enough to leave that horrible scarring on his body. A pale reflection of the scarring on his soul. He needed time. Time to heal.

But sometimes healing needed help.

She wanted to be the one to help him. In spite of his warnings and denials. He was a mystery wrapped in an enigma wrapped in a tall, hard-muscled body. His kindness and strength made something sharp and broken inside her yearn toward his heat. Maybe it was time to claim him. To see if sex could be more than fumbling disappointment.

To learn if there were any feelings left in the dark and cavernous hollows of her heart.

Or maybe she should run. Now. She hesitated, her bow

in hand, and watched as Michelle crossed the courtyard toward her. Alaric wasn't with her, probably off to conquer France or squash bunny rabbits or whatever he did for fun.

Retreat was good. Retreat. Safety was usually an excellent strategy, in matters of battle and matters of the heart. Discretion, valor, staying alive to fight the good fight, et cetera, et cetera. No matter what crazy dreams of glory reckless new recruits might have, safety was usually better.

"Safety," she whispered, the word a talisman in her mouth.

"Safety is an illusion," Michelle replied, joining her. "That's what Alaric said, anyway, and he'd have reason to know. That man has seen things that would drive the rest of us over the edge of sanity and right into the nuthouse, I do believe. Blithering idiots drooling on our bedsheets."

She laughed. "Also, there may be a couple of puzzled tourists outside after Alaric turned into mist in broad daylight."

Grace blinked, still caught on the precipice of a decision too vast for making. "What? Drooling? What?"

Michelle glanced up at her, then at Alexios, too perceptive as usual. "He's finally gotten to you, hasn't he? It's worse than just jumping his bones, isn't it? Your heart is involved."

Grace slowly shook her head, watching Alexios as he moved around the training ground from recruit to recruit, adjusting one's grip on a sword, demonstrating proper stance to another. The sunlight turned his hair to vivid gold and her mouth dried out at the sight of the long lines of his body as he bent toward one of the women, Smith or Jones or one of the ridiculous aliases they all used, to show her the proper way to grip the practice sword. Smith turned her unnaturally perky face up to Alexios and flashed a huge smile.

"Oh, no. Oh, *hell* no," Grace muttered, tightening her grip on the bow. "If anybody's going to be smiling the 'come and get me, big boy' smiles at him, it's going to be me."

Michelle started laughing. "Thank goodness. I was beginning to believe you descendants of Diana had some sort of celibacy vow."

Grace glared at her friend. "How can you say that after Cedric?"

"Cedric," Michelle said, managing to say his name and sniff with disdain all at the same time. "He was a wanker, and you knew it. You always pick the idiots so you'll have a great excuse to dump them before you can get anywhere close to being emotionally involved. Have your feelings ever even been touched?"

"I care about you," Grace said hotly, knowing it wasn't Michelle's point.

"Thanks, that's lovely, but you're not my type," Michelle said, grinning. "I think your type is looking for you right now, though. Are you going to go for it or back away like a giant chicken?"

"That's not fair. I've been a little busy over the past few years, you know."

Michelle put her hands over her ears and made quiet clucking noises.

"Oh, right. Great. *That's* really mature." Grace rolled her eyes and threw an elbow, but Michelle jumped out of the way, still clucking.

Across the courtyard, Alexios turned away from Smith, and his gaze zeroed in on Grace. Even across the distance separating them, Grace could see the heat rising in his eyes. An answering flame unfurled somewhere deep inside her body and slowly spread from her core through her limbs to the tips of her fingers and toes and the top of her head, until she felt as though her hair must rise straight into the air from the sheer electrical charge of it.

"He wants you, Grace," Michelle murmured. "Are you going to be brave enough to do something about it?"

"He's four hundred years old," Grace countered, suddenly seeking desperately for some protection—any excuse—from the power he had over her.

"So he's certainly had time to learn a few things in bed," Michelle said, with a wicked grin. "You know, I could use a diversion. If you don't want him—"

"I want him," Grace admitted, to Michelle and to herself. Then, taking a firm grip on her bow in one hand and her courage in the other, she started toward him.

∿∿∿

Alexios watched her walk toward him, all long legs and lean elegance, and his breath rasped in his throat, arid and harsh as the dream of water to a traveler lost in the desert. As she walked, she caught her hair back at the nape of her neck and tied it away from her face. The challenge, then. She'd leave no hair in her eyes to distract her from the target. He'd never seen her miss; but then again he wasn't much for missing, either. It was more than a challenge of daggers and arrows. It was a gauntlet thrown down between the souls of two warriors. She was impossibly young, and yet the knowledge in her eyes was ancient.

Chronological age meant nothing when one had walked voluntarily into the fire.

She didn't stop until she stood right in front of him, close enough that he could see the details of the golden specks in the dark amber of her eyes. She tilted her head, her mouth flat and unsmiling.

"Why do I suddenly feel like this is a bad idea?" Her face gave away nothing, but the tip of her tongue suddenly darted out to moisten her lips. A clue. Tiny but telling.

She felt it, too, then. And it was up to him to keep her from retreat.

"It was your idea," he pointed out. "But I will release you from your challenge if you are afraid."

She lifted her chin, eyes narrowing. "It doesn't work on me, you know. I'm not a child, that a little reverse psychology will pull my strings."

"Human children have strings? Atlantean children do not, to the best of my knowledge." A sudden hunger flared inside him, biting sharply into his control. The idea of strings had led to the thought of silken cords tied around her delicate wrists and around the carved wooden posts of his bed. Pinning her in place so that he could look his fill of her. Touch her. Taste her.

Never let her escape him. Hold her captive . . .

Fantasy trailed off into bitter self-awareness. Hold her captive as he himself had been held captive. Was that truly what he wanted? What he needed? To roll and writhe in the destructive, decadent pleasures of bondage and pain?

Suddenly, he needed to touch her. Needed her strength and purity to infuse the dark and twisted corners that had been seared into his soul.

He caught her face in his hands, wishing they were alone. Wishing he could have captured her startled gasp with his lips. "Grace," he rasped. "I cannot do this. I cannot banter with you as though nothing lies between us; as though this crouching monster of hunger and need and yearning doesn't threaten to burn through my defenses and my self-control. I will play the part you need me to play, but I beg of you, do not toy with me. The mask I always wear slips away with you. I am no tamed and defanged predator you can pet and tease. I'm a man, and I'm a warrior, and for hundreds of years I have taken what I wanted."

She stood frozen, her body trembling with an emotion he was afraid to try to name. The sounds of the trainees talking, sparring, and laughing faded to nothing more than a dull buzz in his ears. As he and Grace stood unmoving in a bizarre tableau, and the seconds ticked by one after another, underscoring her silence—her utter silence—he felt hope turn to ash inside him.

He should have expected no better. He'd been a fool to hope. Grace was the descendant of a goddess. She deserved better than a broken warrior.

She deserved better than him.

He let his hands fall from her face and began to turn away, but she caught his hands in her own and stopped him. "What is it that you want?" She sounded breathless as though she'd been running. But had she been running toward or away from him?

"I want to see you shoot those arrows," he replied, the vice grip that had been squeezing his lungs loosening a fraction of its hold. "I want world peace, freedom from tyranny, and a very large piece of pecan pie."

He leaned down until his face was only inches from hers. "I want you."

And then, because the need was too great, and to kiss her would have been to take her, right there in front of the gods and everyone, he stepped back a pace and unsheathed his daggers. "You mentioned a challenge?"

Grace lifted her chin and took a long, deep breath. Then she slowly removed an arrow from the quiver hanging on her shoulder. "You're on, my friend. Dinner is definitely going to be on you, but I'll spring for the pecan pie."

She turned and shouted for Sam to clear the area in front of the targets, and then flashed a seductive smile back over her shoulder at Alexios. "You can go first, if you like. Age before beauty and all that." Then she started to laugh. "Although I think you've got me on the beauty front as well."

"You think I've got you," he said slowly. "I like the sound of that."

Sam, Michelle, and the dozen trainees lined up in rows on either side of the target area, loudly calling out their favorites and bets for the challenge.

Grace smiled and shook her head at them. "Hey, a little more respect here. Loser's buying you yahoos dinner."

She raised her elegant wooden bow and fitted the arrow exactly where she wanted it in a graceful motion that was second nature to her, the bow a natural extension of her arm. Her breasts rose with the motion, straining against the fabric of her shirt, and his mouth went dry again, but this time for an entirely different reason.

He bowed toward the trainees and then to Grace. "After you, my lady."

She leaned toward him a little, opening those lush lips, and he instinctively bent closer to hear. "There's something you should know about me, Alexios. I choose my targets very carefully, and I never, ever miss when I aim," she said, her voice little more than a whisper. "And now I'm aiming at you."

With that she whirled to face the target, pulled back her bowstring, and let the arrow fly. True to her word, the point struck dead center in the bull's-eye of the large straw target that stood twenty yards directly opposite her.

A cheer went up from their audience, and the man who'd had the effrontery to touch her earlier whistled. "Yeah, Grace! That'll show him."

Alexios bared his teeth in a fierce approximation of a smile and lifted one of his daggers over his shoulder, judged the distance to the target next to Grace's, and then threw it with exacting precision. The dagger struck right in the heart of the red circle.

Another cheer went up, and he heard Michelle's British voice rising above the others, "Twenty pounds on Grace!"

"Let's make it more interesting, shall we?" Grace said, another arrow already in her hand. "Five more each, and we'll shoot simultaneously. Whoever has the best array at the finish will be declared the winner."

Words didn't seem like enough. He threw back his head and laughed, sheer joy rising through his limbs, bubbling in his veins, and clearing out the cobwebs in his soul. She had courage as well as the grace that bore her name—a fitting match to a warrior, in every way possible. "As you like, my lady. Be warned, though. I plan to eat a very large dinner. I hope your pockets are full of cash."

With that, he took aim and threw dagger after dagger into the heart of his target. The challenge wasn't the target; it was to keep from being distracted by the way his entire being strained toward Grace.

But he'd trained for centuries to succeed in spite of any distraction, no matter how intense. He threw the daggers, one by one, and his aim was true with each. After he'd released all six of his daggers, he smiled with satisfaction at the way they clustered so tightly in the bull's-eye. Nothing with a thickness greater than the tip of his smallest finger would have been able to fit between any of them.

He'd won. She'd buy dinner, and then he would have her for dessert.

He turned toward her, the satisfaction of victory fighting with the tiniest sliver of regret that she would be disappointed. But nothing remotely like disappointment showed on her face. Instead, bright triumph glittered in her gaze and smile.

He shot a glance at her target. Five arrows stood in a circle in the center of her own bull's-eye, their feathered fletching still quivering with the force of impact.

"Five?" he said, frowning. "But—"

"I have one more." She fitted her sixth and final arrow to her bow, then, staring directly at Alexios the whole time and never once turning her gaze to the target, she let the arrow fly. The thunk of arrow on target was followed by a brief hush and then the sound of a dozen sharply drawn breaths.

Still staring at Alexios, a smile twitching at the edges of her lips, Grace slung her bow over her shoulder again. A resounding cheer made it impossible for him to hear what she was saying, though her lips were moving.

He had to know. He spun around to see her target, but it was unchanged. Five arrows stood tightly together, the work of an expert archer. Puzzled, he glanced at his own target and realization dawned. *His* was the one that had changed. Dead center, nestled in the midst of his six daggers, her final arrow stood proudly in feathered triumph.

He bowed. "I must concede defeat and offer forfeit."

"Well, you do owe us all dinner now." She was glorious in her triumph, color high and eyes sparkling. It took a more than heroic measure to force himself not to jump on her and carry her off like some ancient spoils of war. Yet it had been she who claimed victory. The thought of himself as a conqueror's loot made him laugh out loud again.

"I will buy the dinner. And after dinner . . ." He let the unfinished statement hang there in the air between them like a promise. Like a wish. After dinner, he and Grace would see who would triumph in their personal challenge. He let the heat of it show on his face, and she trembled just a little.

Later, he would tease her, touch her, and taste her until she trembled like a seabird caught in a gale.

"Dinner and much more," he promised. As the crowd came rushing up to congratulate Grace, he moved toward the target to reclaim his daggers, allowing himself to think thoughts long banished of silken limbs and heated passion. She was a conqueror, his Grace.

But tonight he would conquer her.

Chapter 14

Later that evening

Grace's skin felt hypersensitive, as though her nerve endings had been scraped raw and repositioned for maximum stimulation. She was antsy, tense; her breath caught in anticipation of something so momentous she couldn't quite comprehend it. It was an emptiness that needed filling; it was an ache that needed tending.

It was a *wanting* so deep and powerful that she couldn't stretch her mind around the contours of it.

She stood at the edge of the parapet, staring at the sea, trying to focus her mind on the mission. On her orders. On the very real concern that she hadn't heard from Quinn or Jack.

Or the meeting with the Fae in two days.

But there was no room for any of it in her mind; the space was filled with Alexios. His laughter—so rare, but she'd heard the low, rich tones of it a couple of times during dinner. The kindness in his eyes when she'd seen him sneaking scraps to Sam's dog upon their return. The breadth of his shoulders in his elegant but simple shirt; the fabric so starkly white against the deep tan of his forearms and throat. The line of his neck as it curved into that sculpted jaw.

The deep, deep blue of his eyes.

She heard the tapping of ridiculously high heels and smiled as Michelle approached.

"Do we need to have that chat about the birds and the bees?" Michelle leaned against the edge of the wall and smiled innocently up at Grace. "I popped by the store and picked you up some condoms," she continued, dropping into an exaggerated whisper. "Not really sure they even knew about such a thing in his day. Don't want you having any unexpected Atlantean bundles of joy."

A tendril of wistfulness crawled through Grace at the unexpected thought of carrying Alexios's child, but the unfamiliar emotion was quickly followed by shock. "What are you talking about?"

"I saw the way you two were looking at each other," Michelle said patiently. "*Everybody* saw the way you two were looking at each other. Better to be prepared, I'm only saying, before he sweeps you off to Atlantis or the closest bedroom, whichever comes first."

Grace wrapped her arms around her chest, huddling forward into the wind. "I know," she finally admitted. "Don't you think I know? But the timing is terrible. And he has so many issues—he's been through so much—I don't think I'm enough. I don't think I could ever be enough to help him get through it."

She glanced farther down the parapet, to where Sam and Alexios were discussing something with great animation. Knowing guys, it was either the end of the world or hockey scores.

"Do you think they have hockey in Atlantis?"

Michelle blinked and looked at Grace as if she were nuts. Good call. "Hockey. In Atlantis. You really expect me to believe you're thinking about hockey?"

Grace changed the subject, suddenly realizing the four of them were alone. "Where did everyone else go? Off to bed so soon?"

"They're off to check out the local nightlife. You never even heard them leave, did you?" Michelle shook her head. "Lost in happy lustful fantasies, no doubt."

"Actually—" Grace broke off whatever she'd been about to say. Stupid. Girly. Having conversations about her *feelings*. Next she'd be hanging posters of kittens and rainbows in her office.

"It's okay, you know," Michelle said gently. "It's okay to feel. Okay to want an emotional connection with something other than your bow."

"I don't have time or room for it. If I let down my guard, if I start to care . . . and then he doesn't . . . I can't, Michelle. I want to, but I don't know how." She took a deep breath, squared her shoulders. "I can't let my brother down by becoming distracted from the mission, anyway. He *died*. Every day that I go on living, if I'm not working to win the battle, I'm failing him."

"Oh, honey," Michelle said, putting a hand on Grace's arm. "Do you really think Robbie would want this for you? This unhappy, lonely life? I knew your brother, remember? He was so full of life and joy, and you meant the world to him. If you want to dedicate your life to vengeance, perhaps consider that what he would want isn't this grim existence of battles and blood and death. Maybe he'd want you to find love."

Love? Was it even possible? How could a human fall in love with a man certain to outlive her for hundreds of years? Were Atlanteans immortal? She didn't even know. The thought of growing old and wrinkled while Alexios remained with her out of loyalty and obligation, though he was still as virile and vibrant as the day they'd met . . . well, it turned her stomach. She wasn't particularly vain, except about her hair that she really should cut. She couldn't even remember the last time she'd worn lipstick, for Pete's sake.

But to grow old and feeble while he stayed young. No. She couldn't stand the thought of it.

"It's impossible. He's too old for me" managed to make its way out from her frozen vocal cords.

"Maybe. But these Atlanteans are magical, Grace," Michelle said. "Perhaps there's a way around that, too. But we're putting the cart far ahead of the poor horse. You don't even know if you'd want to grow old with the man. Shouldn't you give yourself the chance to find out?"

A burst of convivial laughter startled her, and she glanced down to see Sam giving Alexios a friendly punch on the arm. Men. A good dinner, a few beers, and some war stories, and they were buddies for life.

Why couldn't it be that easy between men and women?

"Maybe it should be. Easier," she told Michelle. "Maybe I should quit worrying about what might happen eighty years from now and focus on now. On tonight. On whether sex can ever be as great as it's cracked up to be."

Michelle's smile was a little wistful around the edges. "It can be, when your heart is involved. Or, let's be honest, sometimes even when it's not." She laughed. "But I have a feeling you're going to find out. Just relax and be open to the experience, promise me? I can tell you care about this man, and—"

A loud scraping noise sounded through the chill, dark air, cutting off whatever Michelle had been about to say and putting them into instant alert. Grace instinctively sought out Alexios, but he was nothing but a blur in the air coming toward her, and then he was next to her, daggers out, crowding against her, pushing her away from the edge.

"Move away from my right arm," she snapped, needing

space to draw her knife. "I knew I shouldn't have left my gun and bow in the room."

"It was dinner, Grace," Sam said, moving in front of Michelle, holding his Glock at the ready in a two-handed Weaver stance. "Who takes a gun to dinner in a tourist town?"

"Who but you, you mean? Funny man." She reached into her pants pockets and through the openings cut in the bottoms of the pockets to the silver-bladed knife strapped to her right thigh and the wooden stake strapped to her left. "Alexios, can you see what it is?"

"It's trouble. Move. Now. There are too many, Sam, and I don't want the women—"

"To hell with that," Grace cut him off. "Michelle, you should—"

"Already on it," Michelle said cheerfully, stepping out of her shoes. "Bet you didn't know Louboutin made a pair of stilettos like this." She scooped up her shoes and pressed something on the insides of each with her thumbs. Four-inch blades snapped out of the heels, glittering with deadly silvery light.

"Good thing those damn rookies are gone," Sam drawled, cool as the ice floating in a Georgia mint julep. "They'd just get in the way. Shifters or vamps?"

"Both, maybe, but definitely shifters. At least ten on this side alone," Alexios said, glaring at Grace. "I know you're a good fighter, but you don't have your bow, and I don't want you caught up close and deadly with a few hundred pounds of shifter. Get the hells out of here and take Michelle and her little toys with you."

"When hell freezes over is when I'll run away like a little girl and leave you to face those attackers alone," Grace said, glaring right back at him.

Alexios growled a threat, but it came out in jumbled-up English and Atlantean, and then it was too late, anyway, too late, because the first wave of them came over the walls, fangs and claws bared. Panthers. They were panthers, but they weren't all in full panther form but an obscene hybrid of panther and human, and just when he had time to wonder how big cats had climbed a thirty-foot stone wall, the first one hit him hard.

Alexios went down, smashed onto his back, but his dagger was swinging up, all of his power behind it, and it drove into the panther's stomach and ripped a path through its entrails, drenching Alexios in guts and blood and rank stench. He heard shots—the Glock firing round after round; thank Poseidon for Sam.

Alexios shoved the panther off him and rolled. In seconds, he was up and going after the next one, scanning for Grace. She'd been backed into a corner by a huge black panther that was snarling and batting at her but not yet ready to brave Grace's long silver knife.

Everything in Alexios pushed at him, hard, to turn to mist, go to Grace, and fly with her clear off the roof to safety, only then coming back to rejoin the fight. But if he did, if he left Michelle and Sam and they died, any feeling Grace might have for him would die with them.

He stayed. He fought.

Sam continued to fire his gun to deadly effect, and now Michelle had a gun, too. Sam must have had a backup. Two more of the panthers, these a tawny reddish brown, leapt in tandem for Alexios's head while another came in low and hot toward his legs.

"I am not in the mood to have my nuts bit off by a panther," Alexios shouted. He leapt up to meet the two coming by air, but he transformed during his leap so that the panthers passed harmlessly through his mist form and crashed into their companion on the ground. Sam and Michelle fired shots steadily, and first one, then the second, then all three panthers lay dead.

Once again in corporeal form, he landed on the edge of the wall and scanned its rock face and the grounds below for any further attackers. They needed to know what they were dealing with. Now.

All clear, at least on this side of the fort. No time to worry about the other sides, though. He spun around as the snarling and eerie high-pitched screams of panthers filled the air, almost drowning out the worst possible sound in the world: the recruits, all loud laughter and drunken singing, were arriving back at the fort.

Another scream, this one behind him, and Alexios whirled around to find Grace standing over the body of the black panther, calmly pulling her knife out of its throat. Or maybe not so calmly, he realized, as light flashed from the blade when her hand trembled.

"They're going after the rookies," Sam yelled, and Alexios turned again, this time to realize that only five of the panthers lay dead or dying and the rest were flowing down the stairs toward the courtyard in a silent wave of lethal purpose.

The shouting and screaming started before Alexios had made it three paces toward the stairs, and he didn't wait to see if Sam followed before transforming into mist again so he could put himself between the attackers and their woefully inexperienced and unprepared prey.

Alexios soared down the stairs and plunged in between a snarling tangle of shifters and humans, steeling himself to tune out the screams, howls, and shouts—to focus—as he transformed back into his body in a barely sufficient circle of open space.

"Bet you didn't see that coming," he said to a very startled panther as he drove his dagger into the side of its neck, efficiently opening its jugular vein and stepping out of the path of blood spray with the agility of years of experience.

Too many years. Too many battles. Too much blood.

"Alexios! Here!" Sam's shout wrenched him out of his self-indulgent musings, and he whirled around in time to see another of the attackers clamping its powerful jaws down on the back of a human's neck. Alexios lunged for them, but he was too late. With a grisly crunching sound, the cat chomped through flesh and bone and then shook the body as if warning them away.

Another one of the recruits screamed, but Alexios ignored it, heading straight for the cat. The dead human was female, and she looked like . . . Smith. It was Smith. The cheerful one he'd helped earlier.

Alexios's rage built inside him with the power of a raging typhoon, until fury exploded into sound and the noise coming from his throat had more in common with the screams of the cats than it did with any noise a man could make. He dove toward the panther, shouting at it to let her go, stretching full out in a leap that took him over the cat's back. As he rose above its spine, he drove both daggers into the base of its skull, smashing through into its brain.

He collapsed on top of the cat, hands still clenching the hilts of his daggers, and then he wrenched the blades out, scraping past bone. The cat's head flopped back down on the ground. It was dead. He'd killed it. But killing the cat meant nothing.

It wouldn't bring Smith back.

And Grace . . . He shot up off the ground, whirling around to find where Grace was in the fray. Sam stood near the base of the staircase, Glock still at the ready, with the forms of two dead panthers at his feet. One of the recruits knelt by another dead cat over near the wall, the human gripping the hilt of the sword that pierced the cat's chest.

Five of the recruits were down, but three of them were moving and trying to sit up. The other two were ominously still.

But no Grace. No Michelle.

Oh, no. Please, Poseidon, no.

"Where's Grace?" he shouted at Sam. "Where is she? Where's Michelle?"

The man shook his head. "I thought she listened to you and stayed topside, out of trouble."

Alexios shot across the ground, running so fast his feet barely touched the grass. "Grace? Listen to me?"

Sam's face went cold. "Oh, no. Oh, not Grace."

But Alexios was already gone, taking the steps four at a time, racing to discover a truth he wasn't sure he was brave enough to face.

"Please, please, please, please," he chanted as he ran, and when he hit the top of the stairs he skidded to a stop at the sight of three figures huddled by the wall.

She looked up at him, oh, thank the gods. Grace looked up at him, and his world hadn't ended before it had even had a chance to begin. He shot across the space between them so fast he barely had time to register that Michelle seemed to be fine, or that the panther wasn't completely dead, but twitching on the ground next to them. But then he reached Grace and swept her up in to his arms so fast that she let out a startled squeal, but it didn't matter because she was alive, she was alive, and then he was kissing her and devouring her mouth and she was alive and he was never, ever going to let her go again.

She kissed him back for a moment, but then she made a noise that sounded like protest and he loosened his hold on her and lifted his head, finally noticing the pain in her eyes and the tight way she held her body upright.

He lowered her to her feet and, still holding on to her arms—unable to let himself release her completely—he scanned her frantically, looking for a wound. At first he saw nothing, but then the wet darkness along the side of her shirt under her arm caught the light. He touched her gently, and his hand came away warm and wet with her blood.

"No. No, I won't have it. You cannot be injured," he commanded, knowing even as he said the words that it was ridiculous—that *he* was ridiculous—that he couldn't command an injury to un-happen. "Where is Alaric? Where is one of your human healers? How bad is it? Why are you standing? Let me take you to the hospital immediately," he demanded in a confused jumble of words.

"Calm down," she said, her voice shaky but determined. "It's not really that bad. He caught a claw on my side and ripped, but my rib cage blocked him from doing any real damage."

Sam, who'd rushed up behind Alexios, quickly assessed the situation and nodded. "Right. Glad you're okay. I'm off back downstairs to sort things out there. Michelle, can you help?"

Michelle nodded and followed after him after she retrieved her shoes. Alexios noticed she held both shoes in her left hand while still clutching the pistol in her right. "You were very brave," he said to her, acknowledging her courage during the fight.

Michelle shook her head once, her face very grim and pale. "No. I wasn't." Then she headed for the stairs.

"I'll be right down," Grace said. She took a step, but then winced and made a small helpless sound.

"It does hurt a lot more than you'd expect," she said, with an attempt at a smile. "I bet you think I'm being a big baby about a scratch, though, after all the injuries you've suffered."

He gently gathered her back into his arms, needing to hold her, careful not to jar her wounded side. "I would suffer a thousand more deadly wounds than ever I have before in order to spare you this single one, *mi amara*. Where is the hospital? I'm taking you there now."

She shook her head, her sweet-smelling hair brushing the skin of his throat and chin and almost masking the coppery-rust smell of blood. "No, you're not. You need to tell me what happened downstairs. We've got to take care of the recruits, decide what to do about these bodies, and question this one when he shifts back to his human shape."

As if on cue, the panther at their feet snarled and tried to pull himself up from its prone position but then fell heavily back onto its side.

"Is this the one that harmed you?" Alexios fired the question at Grace, but never took his eyes off the panther.

"Yes. But don't hurt it. We need to question him to find out what he knows."

Grace leaned her head on his shoulder for a few seconds and sighed. "Please put me down, Alexios. Really, I just need a bandage. Maybe some peroxide and Neosporin. But first we need to lock this shifter up in one of the cells downstairs while we deal with the rest of them."

But it was as if all the gods of war were pounding their drums inside Alexios's brain. He could hear nothing over the crashing, hammering pulses of rage that demanded he hurt and tear and rend this monster who'd dared to touch Grace.

He carefully released her and pressed a brief, gentle kiss on her lips. She said something, but he couldn't hear it over the drums.

He couldn't hear *anything* over the drums.

The monster had hurt her. It needed to die.

He whipped around, between her and the panther, just in time to see that it had been deceiving them. Masking the extent of its injury. Because now it had its legs underneath it, as it crouched, ready to spring at him.

"Grace, get down," he said, shouting so that she would hear him over the escalating pounding in his head. Then he leapt forward, but this time he didn't bother to draw his daggers. This time he'd kill it with his bare hands.

He launched himself toward the snarling beast, matching feral rage with his own primal fury. He smashed into the cat in midair, escaping its opened jaws by inches and catching it around its thickly furred neck. He twisted in flight, using his forward motion to jerk the lower half of his body around until he was almost straddling the panther, and scissored his legs around its middle.

Together, they slammed down to the concrete, knocking the wind out of both of them, but a split second later the cat was bucking and twisting underneath him. He could see it snarling and distantly hear that it was screaming, but no sound could fully penetrate the percussion of his rage thrumming through his skull, through his spine, through every nerve in his body.

His fists took up the beat, took up the rhythm, and he started pounding on every inch he could reach, beating the shifter with every ounce of his strength behind each punch.

"You. Hurt. My. Woman," he said, reduced to nearly incoherent speech. Grunting, caveman-like utterances. Me Alexios. Her Grace.

Hurt her and die.

His fists pistoned forward, over and over, catching the beat of the drums in his head, and then there was screaming or shouting or someone calling his name, but he couldn't hear it over the drums, couldn't understand it through the beat of the drums, except the sound was different. Silvery and musical and lovely, even while shouting. It was her. It was Grace. And she wanted something . . .

She wanted him to stop.

He blinked and suddenly the sound of her voice—pleading and demanding and *Grace*—cut through the drums, and he looked down at his fists and there was redness and stickiness and the cat lay lifeless underneath him. If he hadn't killed it, he'd come damn close.

Grace grabbed his arm and shouted in his ear. "Alexios, damnit, you stop it right now!"

He fell to the side, rolling and shoving and scrambling to be away from her and away from the cat's bloodied body, but even as he moved, the cat shimmered with the oncoming Change. In seconds, the cat was gone and a man lay in its place, bloodied and broken but still breathing.

Still breathing.

Alexios didn't know whether to be relieved or sorry.

Chapter 15

Grace stared down at the man she'd thought she knew. The man she thought she might be falling in love with, who she'd finally convinced during the day and at dinner to give her a glimpse of the man behind the mask. His true self that lay hidden behind his warrior persona.

But maybe *this* was his true self. Maybe centuries of battle, no matter that it was always on the side of right, was enough to scour any trace of humanity from a man's soul. But was humanity even the right word to use?

Perhaps these Atlanteans started from a baseline that didn't contain any gentler emotions. Maybe there was lust and rage and the cold, steely calculation of battle strategy, but no room for kindness, hope, or love.

Maybe wanting to take a step forward into the future with him meant nothing more than exchanging one battle-field for another. She'd become a warrior before she'd grown into a woman, and now she wondered if she would ever make that metamorphosis. Perhaps it was something missing in her. Maybe her own lack of gentler emotions drew this type of man to her.

She took a step back, as if some long-dormant flight-or-fight response had finally kicked in on the side of flight. She would never run from the monsters, but she could run from this man who might break her heart.

She took another step back and hit something hard. A pair of strong arms steadied her and Sam's voice spoke softly in her ear. "I saw the end of that. He did it for you, Grace. He did it because that damn panther hurt you. He saw your blood, and something inside him busted right past any civilized thought."

She pulled away from him, shaking her head. Disagreement, maybe. Denial.

But Sam spoke again, stronger. "He's a man, Grace, and whether you want to admit it or not there's something between the two of you. His need to protect was burning so fiercely through his belly and brain that he probably couldn't think straight. But it's better this way. At least he got to you before it was too late. Not all of us have been so fortunate."

Grace flinched at the pain rasping in Sam's voice. Something in his past trying to bubble to the surface. She wanted to ask, but took a look at the way his face hardened and thought better of it. She owed him more than to pry into his personal life.

Alexios made a noise—a small, strangled noise—and slowly pushed himself up to stand, bracing himself against the wall with one hand. He winced a little as his bruised and battered hand touched the wall, but then he leaned heavily against it. "I'm sorry," he said, his voice hoarse. "It hurt you—the drums, if only—but it hurt you. So sorry."

His broken speech touched her in a way that any chest-thumping never would have done. But it simply wasn't there, the arrogance or triumph she might've expected had he been the monster she'd been near to thinking him. Her adrenaline-driven terror had drained away, and she saw him, really saw *him* in the moonlight. Clearly, with all of her senses fully charged.

He was a man, and he'd called her his woman. Defending her from the panther who'd been poised to attack her didn't make Alexios a monster. It didn't make him a hero, either, on a pedestal and unattainable.

It simply made him a man who wanted to protect his woman. Even though she wasn't the type to need protecting—in fact, was usually the one doing the protecting—she understood. Accepted. Something inside her, something cold and hard that had huddled alone in the dark for far too long, unfurled a tiny, cautious tendril of warmth.

Holding her wounded side with one hand, she held the other out to him. His eyes changed, widened a little, as if he'd been afraid to hope. But then he came to her and carefully pulled her into his arms, as though she were fragile and he were afraid that she might break with rough handling. He bent his forehead to hers and just rested there for a moment, leaning into her, and she felt an awakening. Finally, perhaps, that metamorphosis.

As though she'd finally come home.

Sam cleared his throat. "Let's get our friend here down to one of the cells and locked up. We've got two dead, Grace."

"No!" The words sliced into her as if digging a dull blade into her wounded side. "No, oh, God. No. Who?"

"That young guy from Texas, they called him Armadillo?"

"Reynolds," she said automatically, though she hadn't had time to know him well. What she did know of him sent pain shooting through her at the realization that she'd never again hear his Texas-is-bigger jokes; never again share a smile with the friendly, kind man who'd been so dedicated to the cause.

But Sam had said *two* dead. "And the other?"

"Smith," he said, his face going dark and hard. "Alexios took care of the one who got her, but it was too late. She . . . well, it was quick, if that's any comfort."

Grace's lungs suddenly couldn't expand. Not Smith. Though it was stupid and ridiculous and Smith's death was in no way about Grace, she couldn't help but remember her last, unkind thoughts about the woman. Just because Smith had been friendly to Alexios.

"She was so young," she cried out, the hot, burning tears sliding down her face. "She couldn't have been more than twenty-five."

Sam cocked his head to the side and stared at her with a curious expression on his face. "Honey," he finally said, his voice gentle. "So are you."

She couldn't respond, couldn't explain. Could only stand there mutely shaking her head back and forth in denial and sorrow.

Sam took a step toward her, but then appeared to think better of it. He shoved his hands in his pockets. "Michelle and I are going to take the injured to see a doctor friend of mine. Just so happens I know a retired army doc who has a little place not too far from here. He said give them a call anytime I need them, so I took him up on it. He and his wife are expecting us. She's some kind of big deal in Florida politics, and I know for a fact they've been to the house of that Vonos son of a bitch. Maybe I can get a little information while our friends are getting patched up."

Grace nodded, trying desperately to think. To focus on what still needed to be done. "He's still unconscious," she said, gesturing toward the fallen panther. "We're going to have to carry him."

"I'll do it," Alexios said. "It's the least I can do." He bent down and scooped the injured man, now fully human, up off the ground.

Sam stopped him with a hand on his arm and a look. "It doesn't have to be only you, son. We may not be from

Atlantis, but we do the best we can, and we're on your side."

Alexios stopped, and a trace of a smile crossed his face, perhaps at being called "son" by a man centuries younger than he. "Trust me, my friend. If I were able to bestow honorary Atlantean citizenship, your name would be very high on my list. You're a magician with that Glock. But this thug's weight is nothing to me. If you'd show me to the cell you think would best hold him, I would appreciate that. And then we need to get you and the wounded to your doctor friend's place."

Grace started walking, proud that she could stand mostly upright, despite the jagged tear still seeping blood from her side. "Okay, let's do this."

With that, she headed down the stairs in front of them, her heart in her throat as she saw how many of her people were wounded—and how badly. Michelle knelt on the ground near Smith, weeping. Shame tasted like bile in Grace's mouth as she realized she'd never even known Smith's first name.

She trudged over to Michelle, but stopped when she reached Reynolds's broken and bloody body. His neck tilted his head at an unnatural angle to his shoulders, and his arms and legs sprawled like a discarded child's toy. She knelt down next to him and gently, so gently, moved his shoulders and limbs and repositioned his head so that it lined up with his body. Although it was an observation she'd made before, it surprised her again how very heavy it was, a dead body. Or perhaps the weight was some extra burden that death conveyed when the lightness and buoyancy of the soul fled for what she still believed to be heaven.

A place she would never see. She could never expunge the stains on her soul. Her tears dripped steadily down her face, falling on the dead man's shirt, until Michelle knelt down beside her and gathered Grace into her arms for a hug.

"I know," Michelle said brokenly. "I know. They didn't know enough to face this—"

Epiphany struck. Grace pulled away from the offered comfort and climbed slowly and painfully to her feet, trying not to grimace or actually shout the word *ouch* like an idiot. "That's it. That's what has been biting at the back of my lizard brain. How did they know?"

Michelle looked up, tilting her head. "How did they know? They didn't—"

"No. Not the recruits. How did the shifters know to come after us? We've done everything possible to make everybody believe we're actors and battle reenactors. We even spent a day last week putting fliers up all over town for our debut performance in two months. Why would they come after us?"

Alexios and Sam walked out of the cell block just then, minus their prisoner. Sam had his dog on a leash. Blue. She'd forgotten all about him.

"Where was he?"

"I'd shut him in my room while we were at dinner and hadn't let him out yet," Sam said. "He damn near tore my room apart, probably trying to get out here when he heard those cats."

Blue started baying, a deep bass boom of a bark, and straining at his leash to get away from Sam and explore.

"Blue. Down." Sam rapped out the command and the dog instantly sat, then lay down at Sam's feet.

"I'm glad he's okay," Grace said, a tiny thread of relief winding its way through the crushing sorrow. "And I know it doesn't make sense to be so happy about a dog when humans are dead, but there it is. Nothing tonight makes sense. I was just asking how they knew we were here."

"That's a damned good question," Sam said. "Somebody knows something they shouldn't, or somebody talked."

Alexios lifted his shoulders and let them fall in apparent nonchalance, but the expression on his face promised a slow and painful death to whoever had betrayed them. "There are always traitors in war. We find them. We deal with them."

Michelle scrubbed tears from her face. "Perhaps it was a coincidence."

"I don't believe in coincidence," Grace and Alexios replied simultaneously. They shared a glance filled with understanding and something more.

Implacable determination, maybe.

"I set a guard," Sam said. "Donaldson is watching over the prisoner, but we've got him locked in real tight. Neither man nor panther can get out of that stone cell. One thing those Spaniards were good at was building a fort."

Grace nodded. "Okay then. You need to get going."

She moved forward, helping Sam and Michelle escort the injured through the door built into the portcullis and out of the fort to the two Jeeps. Alexios brought up the rear, hands on his daggers and eyes constantly scanning the area for further threat.

Once everyone was loaded in the vehicles, Sam pulled her aside. "We're going to need to do something about Smith and Reynolds, and I'm thinking we don't want to bring any of this to the attention of the police just yet."

"It would probably horrify you to know this, Sam, but it never even occurred to me to bring the police into this. We need to figure something out, though, because we need to notify their families. We can't just cover this up and leave them wondering forever what happened." Grace felt the weight of command pushing down on her, driving her further and further into a black pit of self-justification and moral ambiguity. Perhaps death was already nudging at her.

Perhaps her soul, too, had flown away, even though her body didn't know it yet.

"I'll take care of it," he said. "I know some people who know some people. A man named Tiny will be in charge."

"What does he look like?"

"Oh, trust me. You'll know him."

He hugged her fiercely and unexpectedly, releasing her with a muttered apology and curse at his own foolishness when she winced from the pressure on her injured side. Then he told Blue to jump up into the Jeep, and Sam climbed into the driver's seat and turned the key. Behind him, Michelle started the ignition of the second Jeep. Sam nodded at Grace, turned on his headlights, and started out onto the street.

As Michelle slowly pulled forward, Grace slapped her hand on the driver's side door. Michelle braked and looked a question at her.

"Be careful," Grace said, trying to force words past the boulder suddenly caught in her throat. "You and Jeeps and trips to doctors—I don't know. It's a weird déjà vu climbing up my spine, leaving chills clear down to my backside."

Michelle patted the very deadly-looking Glock on the seat next to her. "We'll be fine. I'll call you as soon as we have news. You get that scratch looked at, do you hear me?"

Grace nodded, glad she hadn't let on to Michelle that it was more than a scratch. Her friend never would have left, and Grace needed everyone to be gone.

The second wave of attackers could be on its way.

~~~~~

Every nerve in Alexios's body was on fire with his urgency to get Grace back into the fort and out of the open. Not knowing who or what was behind the attack was eating at him, and every attempt he'd made to reach out to Alaric on the shared Atlantean mental pathway met with a vast emptiness. It was unfortunate that human technology like cell phones wouldn't travel through the portal or succumb to the magic that allowed them to transform themselves and any weapons made of Atlantean metal to mist. He rather liked the idea of dialing 911. At least someone was always available to answer *that* call.

Grace waved Michelle off, and he gave her almost two entire seconds to watch them drive away before he was across the parking lot, gently grasping her arm on her uninjured side, and herding her back into the fort.

"They must have known," she said. "They must have known that we were training here. But there are two distinct patterns of attacks, and this one doesn't fit either."

"I agree," he said grimly, pulling the heavy wooden door shut and barring it. "We're clearly not drug lords or a criminal gang, that they would be so open."

"And they made no attempt to stage this attack as a gas leak or other so-called 'accidental' disaster," she said, bending forward a little and clutching her side more tightly.

"That's it." He lifted her into his arms, ignoring her protests. "You need to be cleaned up and bandaged now, and since I'm the only one here to do it, you're going to have to bear with my limited first-aid skills."

"I can manage." But her sharply indrawn breath gave the lie to her words. "Well, maybe you could help me a little," she admitted, leaning her against his chest. "But we should wait until Sam's friends get here."

He strode down the corridor with her in his arms, making sure not to slow down as he passed the entrance to the courtyard. She didn't need to see the grisly sight again in order to have it burned into her mind. He should know. He had many such scenes burned into his own.

"Kitchen," she said. "We keep the first-aid kit in the kitchen."

He made a sharp left toward the space Grace's crew had set up as a temporary kitchen. Sam had told him earlier about how much work it had taken to refit the space so that it was usable but still complied with historical society regulations. Basically, there was a temporary shell fitted into the room that would be removed when the 'theater troupe' vacated the premises.

There was almost no way such a thing would have been allowed before. BV, as Sam called it. Before Vamps. But since the vampires hated the fort and its anti-vampire history, they cared nothing for activities that might damage the historical site.

He gently lowered Grace to sit on the sturdy wooden table and started to peel her blood-soaked shirt up from the hem. She caught his hands in hers and stopped him. "I can do that," she said, her voice husky.

"I know you can do it. But I'm going to do it. You're pale, and your skin is cold and a little clammy. You're probably going into shock, and I can't reach Alaric. You won't let me take you to see the doctor or to the hospital, so unless I throw you over my shoulder and drag you out of here, which seems counterproductive, you're going to let me help you." He hadn't meant to make a speech, and from the surprised expression on her face, she hadn't expected one. But, by Poseidon's balls, he was going to take care of her. Right now.

"I wasn't careful enough, or watchful enough, or wary enough. You got hurt and it was my fault. So I am, by all the gods, going to see how bad it is." By the time he finished speaking, his jaw was clenched so tightly that it ached.

Grace narrowed her eyes and lifted her chin, defiance in every line of her pale, strained face. But then, because she was Grace, she did the unexpected. She laughed and raised her arms, wincing a little as she did. "There are so many things wrong with what you just said that I don't have the energy to even begin to deal with it," she said. "So how about you just help me out of this shirt and let's get the scratch cleaned up?"

Alexios unsheathed one of his daggers and shook his

head. "Put your arms down. I don't want to hurt you any more by wrestling this T-shirt over your head. It's not like you're ever going to want to wear it again."

As she slowly lowered her arms, grimacing with the pain from her side, he pulled the bottom of her shirt a little ways out from her body and sliced the fabric right up the middle and then pulled the two sides apart, exposing the best and worst things he'd seen all night. Her lovely breasts, curved in white lace, and an ugly gouge that ran a jagged eight inches or so down her side.

The drums tried to open their persistent percussion in his skull again, but he pushed them away. Slammed an internal door on the berserker rage. He had no time to lose control. He had to clench his hands into fists for a moment, though, to stop them from trembling. A few inches' difference in where those claws had landed, and Grace wouldn't be sitting on the table in front of him.

She'd be lying on the cold, hard ground of the courtyard with the other two who had lost their lives for no good reason at all this night.

"It's clotted. That's good. If it were deeper, it would still be bleeding. We just need to keep this cleaned up and bandaged," he finally managed to say with some measure of calm.

"At least I don't need rabies shots," she said, attempting a smile. "*The New England Journal of Medicine* ran a report of a study where it was definitively proved that shifters cannot carry rabies."

He turned to the sink, yanking drawers open and pulling out clean dishtowels. Then he ran the water until it was hot, and wet two of the towels, leaving the others dry for the moment.

"*The New England Journal of Medicine*? Is that required reading, then, for rebel commanders? Take a deep breath. This is going to sting a little bit." He placed the hot, wet towel against her wound and held it in place.

She gasped but didn't pull away from him. "Oh, you know. Medical journals, *Shifter Monthly*, *Vampire Quarterly*, all the usual."

He raised an eyebrow, sure that she was teasing him. Almost sure. Her strained smile gave nothing away, though. He gently wiped her side, trying to catch all of the bright red mixed blood and water that ran freely from the heated cloth. Then he threw that cloth away and warmed a second. "You hold this one in place," he told her, putting her hands over the cloth. "I need to go do a quick patrol and make sure there aren't any more of them, and check on Donaldson and our prisoner."

"If they come, you yell for me," she said fiercely. "This scratch won't stop me. Promise."

He looked her in the eyes and promised. Then he headed for the armory, so he could load up. He'd feel a lot better with a sword in his hand and a couple of the humans' guns at the ready. Whatever resource it took to protect her, Atlantean or human, he would use. If there were more attackers coming, they would all die. But he'd kill them all and die in the doing of it before he'd ever call for Grace to help.

He'd never before felt such a complete lack of guilt at breaking a promise.

Chapter 16

Grace waited until the sound of his footsteps had faded before she released the moan she'd been holding in for what felt like hours. She gingerly scooted down and off the table, holding the wet towel to her side, afraid to actually look at the damage. She'd managed to keep her eyes on Alexios the entire time he was cleaning her side, almost mesmerized by the combination of fury and concern in his expression. The ferocious warrior treating her with such care and gentleness that she'd nearly cried from the tenderness of it.

But now she needed to man up. Woman up? Whatever. It was time to be brave and look at the damage. She'd been clawed before, but something about her heritage helped her to heal a little faster. A little better. So her skin remained relatively scar free. But this time the injury burned like somebody had taken a blowtorch to her side, and she had a feeling it was bad.

At the sink, she ran the hot water again and finally pulled the cloth away from the wound, wincing a little when the edges of her skin tried to stick to the fabric. Oh, damn. It *was* bad. No, bad was an understatement.

Just a scratch, she'd told Michelle. But a scratch deep enough that his claws had hooked on her ribs, scraping bone, on their way down her right side. Jagged enough that the skin would never heal properly. She'd have her first scar, all right.

And it was going to be a doozy. Great. Just when she finally had somebody she wanted to see her naked.

She laughed at her oh-holy-bat-shit-inappropriate flash of vanity and the laugh came out shaky and oddly high-pitched. The sound of someone verging on hysterics. There was no way she'd give in to that.

Focus.

She lifted her left arm to reach for the first-aid kit on the shelf, then fumbled with the catch and opened the lid. Maybe she didn't have to worry about rabies, but infection was always an issue. She pulled out a jumbo-sized box of Neosporin and opened it to get to the tube inside. Squeezing a hefty-sized dollop of the ointment onto her fingers, she took a deep breath and held it in her lungs, and then smoothed the ointment over the jagged but now clean edges of the wound.

In spite of the chill air, sweat broke out on her face from the pain of even that gentle pressure, and the room went swirly for a minute. She grabbed the edge of the counter and hung on until the dizziness passed. Some commander. Trying to faint from a little scratch.

She dropped the tube back in the first-aid kit and then washed her hands. Her sodden shirt was suddenly too clammy and nasty, and she couldn't bear to feel it touching her skin. She pulled the remains of it off her shoulders and arms and then wadded it up and threw it in the wastebasket with the used and bloody towels. For a moment, she stared, entranced at the sight. The vivid scarlet of the bloody cloth lay in stark relief against the white plastic garbage bag.

Blood in the trash can. *Her* blood in the trash can. It seemed wrong. Blood was life, and life didn't belong in the garbage. Bodies didn't belong in the courtyard, broken and destroyed.

How had she thought she could handle this? She was no commander. Sam should be in charge. *Alexios* should be in charge, except he would have to leave them soon. Go back to Atlantis. Leave them. Abandon her.

She'd be alone again. Alone always.

A sound in the corridor snapped her out of her miserable bout of self-pity. What right did she have to whine about loneliness when her failure had left two people dead on the ground?

Suddenly, she realized she was standing, unarmed and half nude, in the middle of the kitchen, like a damned target. She pressed a catch on the bottom of the first-aid kit and a drawer—one of Quinn's special hidden compartments—slid open, displaying a sleek and deadly handgun. It was only a .22, but it could do some damage up close. She whirled around and crouched behind the edge of the table, propping her arms on its wooden top to aim the gun at the doorway.

"It's Alexios," he called out before he reached the doorway. "All clear, but we've got company."

She stood up, lowering the gun but not fully relaxing. "What kind of company? How many of them? Do we need to call P Ops in on this, after all?"

He stopped, framed in the doorway so the light from the corridor turned his hair to a golden halo of fire. "Don't shoot," he said, nodding at the gun in her hand. "And I'm sorry I wasn't more clear. It's the good guys this time. Somebody named Tiny. He said Sam sent him."

Her shoulders slumped with relief, and she placed the gun down on the table, careful to put the safety back on. "Are you sure it's him?"

"Well, he knew enough about Sam to make it pretty

clear he was telling the truth. Not to mention that it seems exactly like Sam to have a friend named Tiny who's probably six and a half feet tall and weighs well over three hundred pounds."

"Are they—what are they—" Suddenly she remembered that she was still standing in the middle of the kitchen wearing nothing but her bra and a coat of Neosporin on the top half of her body. "Maybe you could help me with bandages?"

He walked toward her and his gaze dropped to the newly cleansed tear in her side. His face hardened, and when he looked up again, his eyes had turned completely black, except for those tiny blue-green flames in the exact centers of his pupils.

The air between them suddenly crackled with unreleased tension and sharp-edged, urgent emotion. But then he sighed, and the pressure in the air eased.

"I think you're trying to hurt me, here," he said ruefully. "I finally managed to get your shirt off, and it's only so I can bandage you up."

She appreciated his attempt to lighten the mood, and she might even have fallen for his casual banter if it hadn't been for the way his lips tightened and the muscle at the edge of his jaw clenched.

"Bad timing. Story of my life." She pasted a smile on her face, but it didn't seem to convince him.

He turned toward the counter and began rummaging in the first-aid kit, yanking things out with barely suppressed violence and slamming them down on the table while continually keeping up the stream of muttering just far enough under his breath that she couldn't quite make it out. Finally, he held up a plastic-wrapped roll of new bandages and a pair of scissors.

"Success at last," she said. But when he turned around, there were two of him, and both of them were holding bandages and scissors. Strange. Then little black dots started swirling around the edge of her vision, and she realized what was happening just before her knees buckled.

"Going down," she warned him, but he was way ahead of her. He caught her and gently sat her on the table again but stood so close that she was leaning forward in the circle of his arms, resting her head on his rock-hard shoulder. Wondering how it was that the steel bands of muscle he apparently wore under his skin could feel so comforting. So comfortable.

So much like someplace she never wanted to leave.

He patted her back and murmured lovely things that she couldn't understand, smoothing her hair back from her face and kissing her forehead and her temple. "Shh, *mi amara*, shh. You're weak from blood loss and the crash after the adrenaline rush. It happens after every battle, no matter how big and strong the warrior, so before you even get started, you can stop berating yourself for weakness."

She raised her head and looked into his eyes—those exotically strange and seductively beautiful eyes. "What do you mean? You said it to me before. *Mi amara*. What does it mean? You're going to have to teach me Atlantean, you know."

He stared into her eyes for several seconds, unmoving, before apparently coming to some decision. She watched his face as it changed, but she didn't know how to read the topography of emotion on the map of his face.

She didn't even know what to hope for. All she knew was that he felt like coming home, and it terrified her. She pulled back a little, and he instantly released her.

"I think we shall have Atlantean language practice another day," he said, offering up a small smile. "But for now, we're going to bandage your side, get you dressed, and get you into bed with some water and hot tea."

He retrieved the package of bandages that he'd dropped on the floor when she'd almost fainted and ripped it open, then returned to the sink and washed his hands. Carefully, but with a sureness born of long practice, he unwrapped a sterile pad and covered her wound. She held the pad in place while he unspooled the roll of bandaging and then wrapped it around and around her waist and ribs until she felt like an extra in a mummy movie. Finally, he stopped wrapping and fastened the bandage with a tiny metal clip from the package.

She let out a sigh, relieved that it was over. "I'm not afraid of the sight of blood or anything, but I do prefer not to be looking at my own," she admitted.

He tossed all the packaging in the trash and washed his hands again. "I need to find you a shirt. I'd give you mine, but it's in worse shape than yours was, I think."

"In the pantry cabinet," she said, indicating the far corner. "There's a pile of spare sweatshirts."

He crossed to the cabinet and retrieved a bright red shirt with the words EAT AT JOE'S splashed in white across the front. She shook her head, trembling with delayed reaction. "No! No, I mean, not red and white. Please."

His eyebrows drew together for a moment, but then he glanced at the trash can and his forehead smoothed out. "Of course." He tossed the red shirt back in the cabinet and pulled out a black shirt and quickly shed his own filthy shirt and pulled it on, then grabbed another shirt. It looked about two sizes too large for Grace, but it wasn't like she cared about fit. All that mattered was that it had no red or white.

No scarlet.

She started shaking in earnest, and he quickly helped her into the shirt, helping her hold her arms up like she was a child, then pulling the shirt over her head and lifting her hair up and out from where it was trapped in the soft fleece.

Suddenly Grace knew she had to tell him. Had to let him know that she was hanging on by her fingernails, clinging to the face of the cliff with nothing beneath her to catch her fall.

Nothing but him.

She wanted—needed—to let go and, for once in ten long years of her life, discover whether anybody would be there to catch her. Whether *he* would be there to catch her.

"Alexios," she began, but a loud, deep voice boomed through the corridor like thunder trapped in a waterspout, cutting her off.

"Incoming friendly."

Grace tilted her head. "Tiny?"

Alexios nodded, looking amused. "Tiny."

She noticed, however, that amusement wasn't enough to keep caution at bay. He turned to face the doorway, subtly blocking Grace so that an intruder wouldn't have a direct line of fire to her. She noticed it, but for once she was too tired to fight it. Maybe it was blood loss, maybe it was the shock of nearly dumping her emotions out on the table where they could be crushed, but she didn't have the energy to argue with Alexios about who had the bigger . . . weapon.

The man who filled the doorway a moment later was one of the biggest men she'd ever seen. She had an instant impression of dark hair, dark eyes, and a mountain of blue jeans and flannel shirt. The top of his head brushed the top of the doorway, and his shoulders were so broad he had to turn a little sideways to come into the room.

"Are you a shifter?" She blurted out the question and then felt like a total idiot when he did a double take. "I'm sorry, it's none of my business. If Sam trusts you, that's good enough for me."

The man—Tiny—laughed, and it was a wonderful, rolling rumble of a laugh. It was a laugh like Santa Claus or a favorite grandfather should have.

"He better trust me. After what he did for me, I'd follow him into hell to give him a drink of ice water."

Curiosity burned through her for a moment, but it, like her need to prove her toughness to Alexios, faded away in light of the utter physical exhaustion sweeping through her.

"Grace, meet Tiny. Tiny, meet Grace Havilland, the commander of this group," Alexios said formally.

She waved a hand, brushing off the introduction. "Commander of what's left of this group," she corrected, unshed tears clogging her throat again. "We were hit hard tonight."

Tiny nodded, and his bearded face went from amiable to deadly. "Sam told us what happened. We've been trying to keep an eye out for shifter attacks, given what's been going on across the country, and the fact that the top bloodsucker himself puts his head on coffin pillows not too far from here."

"Vonos," Alexios said.

Tiny nodded again. "Vonos. And no, little lady, I'm not a shifter. Big enough to be a bear, though, aren't I?" He laughed that wonderful laugh of his again.

"I'm sorry. I didn't—I just—I'm sorry," she repeated. "You're not seeing me at my best."

"Well, from what Sam said about you, you're good people. He said you took on a panther all by yourself with nothing but a bitty knife. Took it down, too. That's nothing to sneeze at." Tiny's radio crackled from its place on his belt and he held up a hand to them while he answered it. Grace couldn't catch everything, but she did hear the all-clear given from the man on the other end.

Tiny signed off and returned his radio to his belt, his face somber again. "Doesn't look like we're going to get another wave tonight. We've cleaned up your fallen attackers, and there won't be any sign of a battle by morning."

Grace leaned forward and grabbed Alexios's hand for support. "What about my people? There were two, a man and a woman—" She had to stop for a moment and try to breathe before she could force the words out. "What did you . . . where are they—"

"Per Sam's orders, those two had a car accident tonight

when they were out enjoying the sights of St. Augustine with the other tourists," Tiny said gently. "They need to get back to their families, and this is the best way."

Grace nodded, then leaned forward until her forehead rested on the back of Alexios's shoulder.

"Thank you for everything," Alexios said, his voice a rumbling vibration against her forehead. "Will you stay?"

"We're not going anywhere until Sam gets back and lets us know what he needs. I'm going to make a big pot of coffee if you don't mind. Needed to get here in kind of a rush and didn't have time to stop anywhere."

Grace lifted her head, which suddenly seemed to weigh a thousand pounds in an eerie echo of her thoughts earlier. "Of course. Please make yourself at home with anything we have. Thank you so much for everything."

Alexios turned and scooped her up off the table, ignoring her feeble protests. Whatever burst of adrenaline had burned through her during the battle, it was long gone, and exhaustion, blood loss, and bone-deep sorrow had all taken a toll on her last reserves of energy.

"You have my thanks, as well," Alexios said to Tiny. "I will get Grace settled so that she can rest, and then I'll join you on patrol."

The big man nodded and moved aside so that they could leave the room. "There are plenty of us to handle the patrol, but I know about needing to make sure yourself. If you want to get some rest first, though, I'll stand watch for you. We'll check in on your man and your prisoner, too."

Alexios repeated his thanks and headed down the corridor, carrying Grace as if she weighed nothing. It was a new sensation for her, this feeling of being protected. Cherished.

It frightened her how much she didn't hate it.

Chapter 17

Alexios strode toward Grace's quarters, cradling her in his arms. Her face was starkly white against her dark hair; probably too much blood loss. He should have insisted she go to the doctor with Sam. He seemed to lose far too many arguments with her.

Which proved that emotion and good judgment were incompatible.

"Grace, we need to talk," he began, but an annoying buzzing noise sounded from the vicinity of her waist.

"Please put me down. I need to get my phone out of my pocket. It's probably Sam."

He nodded and carefully lowered her feet to the ground so she could access her telephone. She leaned against him, though, and he enjoyed the feel of it far too much. That she might need him filled him with a rush of warmth more like hearth and home than like the flash fire of hunger and need he'd felt for her while sparring.

Of the two, this was by far the more dangerous.

She spoke into the telephone briefly, mostly questions that didn't give him much of an idea of what the other party was saying. Then she snapped her phone closed and shoved it back in her pocket.

"It was Sam," she said, running a hand through her hair. "Things are good. Not good, but better. You know what I mean. The doctor is taking care of everyone and said none of the wounds are critical enough to necessitate going to the hospital. Also, the doctor seems to be like Tiny, in that he'd do anything for Sam. In other words, there's no mention of having to report the attack to the police or P Ops."

"Sam's a good man. It makes sense that he would earn this respect and trust," Alexios said, nudging her toward the open doorway to her room only a few paces beyond. "And now that you've heard from him, you need to rest."

She shook her head, stubborn. "No. I should help you. I should patrol—at least take a shift. I'm supposed to be in charge here. I can't fall down on the job." But as she stepped forward, she stumbled, as if her body's reserves were deliberately mocking her words.

"Even leaders must rest when injuries demand it. Trust me, acting like you're indestructible is never a good option. Exhaustion and injury only lead to careless mistakes." He gently pushed a strand of hair away from her face and tucked it behind her ear, marveling at the delicacy of the curve of her ear and jaw. Such fragile elegance in one so fierce.

"Rest tonight, and you can lead again tomorrow," he said firmly.

She opened her mouth but then closed it again without voicing the arguments that were obviously trembling on the tip of her tongue. She stumbled again, and he tightened his arm around her shoulders and steered her toward her bed. She slumped down onto it and sat, hunched over, a study in desolation and despair.

"I can't do this," she whispered. "I'm a great soldier in

the army, but I'm no good at being the one in charge. People died, and I will always carry that on my conscience."

He knelt down in front of her and took her hands. "As is just and only right. They deserve to remain in your mind and heart forever. They offered themselves up for this fight, knowing the dangers involved. You cannot protect adults from the consequences of their own choices. All you can do is honor their sacrifice with your memories."

She finally looked up at him and her eyes, shimmering with unshed tears, were enormous in her pale, drawn face. The sight sent a wave of pain crashing through something in his chest that had been battened down like a storm-tossed ship.

"I don't even know how to ask this," she said. "And part of me feels I don't deserve it. But . . . will you hold me? Just for a moment?"

"Grace," he said, and the sound of her name was a benediction. "I was going to ask you the same thing."

Carefully, oh so carefully, he sat on the edge of the bed next to her and opened his arms. She came into them with a sigh, nestling her head in the curve where his neck and shoulder met. He felt the gentle warmth of her breath on his throat, and a fierce wave of protectiveness washed through him. He never wanted Grace to have to face this kind of tragedy again. Not tragedy—not pain—and definitely not danger.

He found himself wishing that she were a descendant of Aphrodite, instead of Diana. A beauty content to stay safely out of danger instead of a huntress. But she looked up at him and offered a tremulous smile, and he knew she was both.

And he was lost.

"I'm going to kiss you now," he said, but then he waited, not knowing whether he expected rejection or permission. Not knowing which he feared more.

"I'm going to let you," she whispered, but she didn't.

Didn't passively wait for him to kiss her. Instead, she lifted her face and pressed her lips to his, and the gentle pressure sparked a conflagration inside him.

He wanted to kiss her, claim her, brand her as his own. Every instinct battled common sense and care; reason forced him to act gently—she was injured. Primitive hunger older than mankind—older than Atlantis—roared out its demands. He pulled away a little, winning the battle against his darker side, but she refused to let him go. She moved even closer to him so that she was sitting half on his lap, and she lifted one hand into his hair and pulled his head closer to hers.

"I don't care. I know this is wrong and callous to kiss you like this. To want you like this. When so many were injured—" She stopped and sucked in a shaky breath. "I know it's wrong and weak for me to need you like this, but I do. I could've died tonight, and for the first time in all the years I've faced that final moment, I was afraid."

She stared intently into his eyes, willing him to understand. "I was afraid, because for the first time I had something to lose."

He kissed her again. He could do nothing but kiss her and hold her and touch her. Kiss her even more deeply. Some part of him, some sane, rational part, reminded him to be careful of her injured side. He held her as though she were made of the most fragile Atlantean spun glass, and he kissed her as though to stop kissing her would mean the end of all hope and light and love.

Love. Even as the unfamiliar word flashed across his consciousness, something changed. The world shifted on its axis and the stars somehow fell out of the sky and exploded into the room with them.

Alexios was kissing Grace, and he was falling. Spiraling down into a glowing funnel cloud made of vividly contrasting colors. Darkest green and pale gold, emerald and amber, streaks of black silhouetting the jewel tones composed entirely of light. He was falling into colors, and he suddenly realized a shocking truth. He was falling into Grace's soul.

She made some tiny noise, a moan or a gasp, but he captured it in his mouth, captured a jagged bolt of shadowed amber that he knew, somehow, to be her sorrow and fear.

He instantly understood, though it had never happened to him in all the long years of his life. He was reaching the soul-meld with Grace, and exhilaration mingled with terror and threatened to capsize his sanity.

~~~~~

Grace clung to Alexios with one hand and held tightly to her injured side with the other, as if she could cling to him like ballast and save herself from the raging rapids of her emotions. He kissed her like nobody had ever kissed her. He kissed her as if she *mattered*—as if she meant everything to him—as if his warmth and hunger could redeem the dark, empty spaces inside her.

She pressed closer and closer to him, wanting to feel his heart beating against her own, and the pain of her wounds seemed like a dim memory compared to the heat and hunger searing through every part of her. She was *alive*. She was alive, and she hadn't lost him. That could be enough for now. They could keep the darkness at bay.

But then the heat and the longing changed. Transformed. The metamorphosis she'd wondered about earlier crashed down on her with the force of a goddess's caprice. A spectacular rainbow of colors—the entire spectrum of color—exploded between them and around them and through them. Colors danced and pirouetted through her heart and soul and in the rhythms of the music of their kiss. She tried to pull away from him, dazzled by the light and the color, not understanding but accepting, but he held her tightly as if he couldn't bear to release her.

Suddenly her breath and balance were smashed away,

and she was falling—falling and tumbling and twirling—over and over into the darkness. Into pain, and torture, and fire. She cried out, seeking for an escape, but there was no way out. There was only the falling and the flames.

She smashed into a barrier that was harder than steel but with a peculiar elasticity to it. She knew it couldn't be real. Knew with some rational part of her brain that she still sat on the bed with Alexios.

But if this were her imagination, it had just served her a whopping dose of crazy. Because she was suddenly walking through flames, and Alexios was on the other side. But it wasn't the Alexios she knew. It was an Alexios whose skin was unmarked by any scarring. An Alexios who looked younger. Less grim. Less cynical.

And then he screamed.

Shadowy figures skulked and lurked at the edges of the flames, holding objects she was somehow sure she didn't want to see clearly. She caught flashes of steel and the snap of a whip, and Alexios, chained to a dark and glistening wall, screamed and screamed.

"No!" she shouted. "No, no, no, no. I don't want to see this. This is private; these are the secrets of his soul. I don't want to see his—and I don't want him to see mine. If this is Atlantean magic, make it stop."

As if her words had carried weight with whatever dark power had thrown her into this, she began to rise. Up and away from the flames, up and away from the hideous shapes slashing their whips. Up and away from the phantom of Alexios's torture.

She rose up and up until the darkness began to shimmer with light and color again. These colors were far different from the flames. There was the deep cerulean blue of the ocean on a calm summer's night. There was a fresh, springtime green. Glimmers of a bright sparkling ruby red danced at the edges, offering carefree joy to the palette as if the colors were the heralds of emotion.

But not just the colors appeared to her as she floated upward. Layers of knowing—of *knowledge*—of Alexios's inner being permeated the colors and sank into her soul, as though she were traveling on a journey into his.

Integrity. Loyalty. Honor.

Courage so unshakable that it formed the bedrock of his very existence. This was a man who had offered up everything he had and everything he was for centuries, all in the name of protecting others. He had kept nothing for himself—had wanted nothing for himself.

Until now.

Distantly, she felt him release her, and then the movement as he stood up and backed away. The colors took a few moments to dissipate; it was like living inside of a fireworks display in the sky—as if she herself were the Roman candle. She actually looked down at her chest, to see if lights were exploding inside her, before she shook her head to clear it of the fancy and the remnants of the experience.

She said nothing for a long time. There weren't words.

Finally, from where he'd backed himself clear across the room and against the wall, he spoke. "I bet you're wondering what just happened."

She laughed and was relieved to be able to draw the breath to do it. "Thank you, Captain Understatement."

Relief chased surprise across his face, and then he laughed, too. "I should have known. Always expect the unexpected with you."

"I want to know what just happened," she said, but the exhaustion had intensified tenfold during the experience with Alexios and she could no longer sit upright. She collapsed sideways onto her pillow, with her feet still on the floor. "But maybe I should rest first, because I've got nothing left right now."

He leapt across the room and lifted her feet one by one, removing her boots and then placing her legs on the bed. He drew her blanket up from the foot of the bed and over her and tucked it over her shoulders, then caressed her cheek. "Yes, you must rest and, yes, I will explain the soul-meld to you in the morning. You have the right to know everything but please carry this thought into your sleep: This was not something I did to you. It was a gift that the gods granted to us both."

He bent to kiss her forehead, but she raised her face so that his lips touched hers instead. "I believe you. I *saw* you. That was . . . somehow I was inside your soul, Alexios. The flames . . ."

She couldn't keep her eyes open any longer, though. She gave up the effort, knowing that he would protect her. Knowing that he truly was the man and the hero of her heart's most secret dreams. The secret dreams she hadn't even realized she'd held in the deepest recesses of her soul.

Her eyes drifted shut, and she felt him brushing her hair away from her cheek.

"I fell into those flames myself tonight, *mi amara*," he whispered. "I plunged into the lowest of the nine hells when I saw your blood. Never again, do you hear me? Never again."

She knew she should argue, knew there was something wrong with what he'd said. But her side ached, and the warm darkness of sleep pulled at her.

Tomorrow. She'd figure it out tomorrow.

Alexios stood in the doorway for a very long time, content to watch her sleep. He hadn't expected the soul-meld. Hadn't been prepared for it. But now he found himself fiercely glad that it had occurred. Atlanteans never blindly followed destiny's chosen path. Personal choice was one of the most important tenets of their existence. And yet, somehow, he felt like all his choices had been circling down to center on this one beautiful, courageous human female, ever since the day he had met her.

He would kill anyone who ever again tried to harm her. She was his, and now all that was left to do was to make *her* believe it.

A quiet cough behind him alerted him to Tiny's presence. He was remarkably stealthy for such a big man. Alexios took one last long look at Grace and then headed toward Tiny.

"How is she?"

"She's exhausted, and possibly in shock. But she refused to seek medical attention or even to leave, so rest is the best thing for her right now."

Tiny nodded, grinning. "She's fierce, that one. You're a lucky man."

"I hope she thinks so, too," Alexios said darkly. "Shall we patrol?"

"Coffee first," the big man replied, still grinning. "Hey, if she *doesn't* think so, can I give her my number?"

Alexios glared at him and made a growling noise, deep in his throat, but Tiny just laughed. "Yeah, yeah. Just kidding. Sam already told me how it was between the two of you."

Minutes later, with mugs of coffee in their hands, Alexios and Tiny stood on the parapet looking out at the deserted grounds surrounding the fort.

"I've got a half-dozen men with me, and they're stationed at every possible access point and a couple of the impossible ones." Tiny pointed to a shadow that was just a little darker than the surrounding shadows down near the seawall and another next to the tall shot furnace that had once been used to heat cannonballs. "Those two are mine. We're looking high as well as low, in case these shifters have vampire backup. It'll be dawn soon, though, so at least then we'll only have to worry about attacks coming from one direction."

"Unless the vampires have somehow managed to make contact with the raptor shifters," Alexios said.

Tiny froze, his coffee mug scant inches from his lips.

"Did you say raptor shifters? Are you freaking kidding me?"

"No, I'm definitely not kidding. Although we have not seen eagle, falcon, or hawk shifters in several centuries, that doesn't mean that they don't still exist. If the vampires manage to enthrall a flock of raptor shifters, that gives them an instant airborne army."

"Flock? It's really called a flock?" Tiny gulped down the rest of his coffee and then started laughing. "Don't tell me. Let me guess. We've got possible geese shifters, too."

Alexios just looked at him, puzzled. "No, why would there be geese? That would be ridiculous. Shifters are almost always predatory species."

"Makes sense. Darwinism and all. After all, what could geese do? Throw goose shit at people? Although, come to think of it, that would be pretty nasty."

"I must admit that I often can't understand you humans at all," Alexios said, shaking his head.

For some reason, his comment occasioned a fresh burst of laughter from Tiny. Still shaking his head, Alexios continued walking the circle of the rooftop, constantly scanning for any sign of movement or approach.

He thought of Grace, lying injured on her bed on the floor below, and his fingers tightened around the mug. He needed Alaric.

He needed Alaric here *now*, not off on some hopeless quixotic chase after Quinn. He put the mug on the floor at his feet and then stood up and raised his hands into the air in order to help him call the energy that would power the Atlantean mental pathway between he and Alaric. This type of communication came more easily to some than others; it had never been effortless for him. But then again, he'd never had such need.

Alaric, if you can hear me, answer me now. I have need of you—Grace is injured and needs your healing. Come now.

He slowly lowered his hands, waiting—hoping—for some sign, but there was nothing. Pride gave way to desperate longing, and he added the word he had so rarely used. *Please.*

But still there was nothing. An empty silence instead of a response.

Either Alaric was out of range or he had chosen not to respond. Both options were unacceptable. A perfect storm of helpless rage swept through Alexios, until he had to let it out or explode. He threw back his head and roared out his fury to the stars and the night sea. Grace had been hurt—she could have died—and there had been nothing he could do about it.

He fell to his knees on the hard, cold concrete and let his head drop forward, unknowing and uncaring if Tiny or any of his men were witnesses to his breakdown. The terror of almost losing her drove sharp teeth into his spine and shook him the way the panther had shaken Smith earlier, until he felt he must break apart into splinters, fractured by the fear and pain and rage.

A voice scratched at the edges of his mind, growing more and more insistent. A voice he knew—its familiarity was breaking through the rise of the war drums in his mind. A voice he knew, but it wasn't Alaric.

Are you going to answer me, or am I going to have to come up there and thump your head against a wall? The voice in his head was rich with amusement, but also threaded with concern. *Remember, I can easily kick your ass for you. Hells, my* woman *can kick your ass for you.*

Relief washed through Alexios like a cooling wave over burning sand. It was Bastien. *Thank Poseidon.*

Chapter 18

Alexios watched the sun rising over the horizon and stretched, finally feeling like he could take a deep breath for the first time all night. One of his oldest friends and fellow warriors was on the way, so it didn't matter that the portal still refused to answer his call. Bastien was one of the Seven, and he was bringing Ethan and Kat, both panther shifters and, according to Bastien, far more lethal than any Alexios could have faced the night before.

Ethan is alpha, Bastien had explained. *You'll have to see for yourself what that means, but trust me when I tell you he has nothing to do with these attacks.*

Bastien wasn't much better than Alexios at the use of the Atlantean communication path over long distances, so it had been a very short conversation. But, even now, Bastien, Ethan, and Kat were on the way to St. Augustine from Ethan's home and headquarters near Miami. Bastien has said to give him an hour; the shifters couldn't travel as mist or through water portals.

Alexios hadn't thought to ask Bastien if the portal to Atlantis was cooperating with him. The portal's magic was capricious, and it seemed to open and close according to some rules it never bothered to disclose.

The portal was older than Atlantis and older than any written record of history, so not even the elders, the scroll keepers, or the scholars fully understood how or why it functioned as it did. A thought occurred to him, surprising in its unexpectedness. What if the portal considered itself a protector of Atlantis? There was no question that it was sentient; what if it knew the prince and heir was born and wanted to protect the vulnerable infant?

Perhaps. Of course, as had been true for more than eleven thousand years, there was no way to know. Maybe Keely would be able to use her archaeological skills or her object-reader magic and uncover some of the secrets surrounding the origin of the Seven Isles. But, until then, the portal's magic was just another of the many mysteries Atlanteans grew to accept and abide by.

Tiny called out, and Alexios turned to see the man shaking hands with Grace. Alexios stood, unmoving, warmth spreading through his chest like the unfurling rays of a sea star. Just to be able to watch her, even from a distance, felt like a precious gift.

He would make her his, and soon. He couldn't continue to draw breath if he didn't. But until then, the anticipation was enough. It would have to be enough.

Grace laughed at something Tiny said, and then she glanced up and caught sight of Alexios. Something tangible sizzled through the air between them, as if she'd aimed one of the arrows from her quiver straight at him.

He closed his eyes, shaking his head. Great. Arrows and quivers. Next *he'd* be the one singing "Feelings." She was turning him into some kind of wimp.

Ven would have a field day.

He opened his eyes when he heard her footsteps approaching, and the smile spread across his face in spite of himself. She was so unbelievably beautiful.

His smile faded. So beautiful, and so far out of his league.

She'd showered and changed into a dark green shirt and clean pair of blue jeans. Her hair lay in long damp strands on the shoulders of her leather jacket. It suddenly occurred to him that he'd never seen her in anything but jeans. Not that he was complaining, but he wondered what she'd look like in Atlantean silk.

She tilted her head and smiled up at him, but there was a measure of reserve in her expression. Distance. "That was an interesting smile," she said "Penny for your thoughts?"

"Trust me, they are not worth nearly so much." He lifted a hand to touch her face but she moved, almost imperceptibly, but enough so that she turned away from him and stood staring out at the sunrise. He let his hand fall back down to his side, while his heart sank to the vicinity of his boots.

So. He wasn't the only one who'd decided she was out of his league, perhaps. He shoved his hands into his pockets, ready to walk away.

But injured pride gave way to honesty. He'd seen inside Grace's soul last night, and nowhere had there been arrogance or presumption. Maybe this was just a healthy dose of caution.

"What happens next?" She glanced back at him. "Tiny said Sam was contacting Smith's and Reynolds's families. It was something I should have done myself, but Sam said he has way too much experience at this horrible duty."

Alexios nodded. "He would have. He was a soldier and a leader of men. With that responsibility comes many terrible obligations."

She lifted her chin. "Do you think I'm falling down on mine?"

"No, I do not. I think that Sam is older than you, and so

his presence will likely be more of a comfort to the families. Part of leadership is knowing when to delegate."

She brushed her hair back from her face and sighed. "Maybe that's true. But Sam didn't give me a chance to delegate before he took it on himself. He was trying to protect me, just like you do. *Everybody* does, even though I'm supposed to be the one protecting the men and women under my command. There's something wrong in that."

Before he could think of an argument she would accept, a loud thundering noise to the south caught their attention. Approaching low, at a height that surely must violate human flight regulations, a sleek helicopter zoomed toward them. Alexios immediately put himself between it and Grace, and she shoved him with her left arm.

"That's what I'm talking about," she said, almost shouting to be heard.

Before Alexios could explain why he would never, ever stop protecting her—or else forget explanations and just throw her over his shoulder and start running—Bastien's voice sounded in his head.

Stand down, Goldilocks. It's just us.

Call me Goldilocks again, and you'll find that my boot fits your ass juuuust riiiiiight, he sent back, folding his arms over his chest and grinning.

"It's okay, Grace. The cavalry has arrived."

∼⌒⌒∽

Grace watched the shiny silver-and-red helicopter land expertly on the gentle grassy slope. The logo on the side, a running panther, raced across the top of the words BIG CYPRESS, LTD.

When the engine shut down and she could be heard again, she jerked her head toward the three people climbing out. "Friends of yours?"

He nodded. "Well, the tall one is. Bastien, of Atlantis.

He, too, is one of the Seven of High Prince Conlan's elite guard. I haven't met the others yet."

She suddenly realized she recognized them. Not the Atlantean. The other two. They were the engaged couple she'd seen on the news the other day.

"We need to go down and meet them, Grace. Bastien said Ethan has quite a surprise in store for us." He held his hand out and she clasped his fingers with her own before thinking. It felt somehow exactly the right fit, as though even their hands belonged together.

Dangerous thoughts. She pulled her hand away and pretended not to see the disappointment on his face. "Okay, let's go meet the nice panther shifter," she said brightly, heading for the stairs. If she kept herself so busy she didn't have time to think about what had happened between them the night before, it would be easier to push it out of her mind.

Tiny met them at the bottom of the stairs, and he didn't look happy. "Nobody told me anything about a helicopter. Do you know these people?"

"I'm sorry," Alexios said, stepping forward. "I just found out less than an hour ago, but I should have notified you immediately. These are friends who will be able to interrogate our prisoner more effectively than we can."

Tiny scratched his chin through his beard with a dinner-plate-sized hand. "Oh, I don't know about that. Done asked me a few questions in my day. You could ask Sam about that sometime."

Grace put a conciliatory hand on Tiny's arm. "I'm sure you have, but this is Ethan, an alpha panther shifter. He's going to have methods we couldn't possibly match."

Tiny nodded and patted Grace's hand. "Well, then. That changes everything. Let's go meet these folks."

They walked out and met Bastien, Ethan, and the blond woman from the ranger station, who were walking up to the front entry. Grace noticed that two men, neither looking quite like a tourist, were standing at opposite ends of the parking lot. She wasn't surprised when Tiny gave them each a signal and the men wandered off, probably to circle around the back of the fort.

"Hello, I'm Grace Havilland," she said, stepping forward and holding out her hand. Trying to act like she was in charge again, even though it felt artificial and false.

She knew the Atlantean right away, of course. Even if she hadn't seen Ethan and the woman on television, she would have known which one was from Atlantis. He had the same beautifully sculptured face as Alexios, but where Alexios was golden, this one was dark. Black hair framed incredibly blue eyes, and he was so beautiful she almost didn't notice that he was nearly seven feet tall.

"You must be Bastien," she said, grinning in spite of the circumstances. She turned and beckoned Tiny forward with a gesture. "Tiny, you should meet Bastien. Maybe you two could start a basketball team."

Tiny threw back his head and laughed that wonderful Santa Claus laugh, and Bastien smiled down at Grace. "I had heard that you were as lovely as you are lethal, Lady Grace. I see that the rumors were not wrong."

The lady ranger, tall and lean, with gorgeous tawny gold hair, and dressed in blue jeans and a sweater, walked up and punched Bastien in the arm. "Look, buddy, just because I agreed to marry you doesn't mean you can take me for granted and flirt with other women right under my nose," she said good-naturedly, flashing a smile at Grace to show she wasn't serious. "Kat Fiero, by the way."

Alexios let out a whoop. "Married? Now you're getting married? I had heard you two were serious, but this is amazing." He bowed low to Ranger Fiero, his eyes sparkling with some unholy glee. "Please accept my sincere condolences, Kat."

The other one—Ethan, Grace remembered—shouted

out a laugh. "Finally! Finally, I meet someone with sense." He shook hands with all three of them. "Other than Marie, most Atlanteans don't seem to be big on brains. I can see you're going to be different."

"Marie?" Grace felt like she was a step behind. She'd thought from the excerpt on TV that Ethan and Kat were the ones engaged. "Who's Marie?"

"We'll fill you in on that later, I promise," Alexios said. "Right now, I think the best thing to do is tell them what happened here last night and see what they can get out of our prisoner."

The moment of levity faded, and Bastien nodded. "Ethan can find out."

As Grace led the way back inside the fort, she noticed that Bastien gave Alexios a quick, hard hug. "How have you been, my friend?"

She snuck a glance at Alexios, curious to hear his response. But he caught her looking, because he was staring right at her, his face grim.

"Not good," Alexios said. "Not good at all."

Chapter 19

Grace stiffened her spine and led them through the court-yard to the prisoner's cell. Tiny told her that one of his men had relieved Donaldson, and then he headed off to do whatever it was he did. Sam still hadn't called in yet today, and Tiny was hanging around until he heard otherwise from Sam.

They reached the cell, and Grace nodded to the guard that he could go.

"Good luck. This one's a piece of work," he said, disgusted.

The shifter was yelling obscenities and banging something metal against the walls. The noise was so loud that Grace wasn't sure he'd be able to hear them call out to him.

"Do you want me to unlock the door?" She directed the question to Alexios, not particularly caring if it were proper hierarchy or not. Ethan might be the alpha panther, but Alexios was the one who'd had her back the night before.

Alexios held out one hand for the keys. "I'll do it. You can delegate to me, until your ribs heal up a little."

She smiled a little at the reminder of their earlier conversation, and she handed him the keys. He was right. If the shifter came fast and hard at whoever opened the door, they were better off if it were Alexios, Bastien, or one of the shifters.

"Sometimes it sucks to be the only human in a roomful of superheroes," she said, only half joking.

Kat shot a narrow-eyed glance her way. "Oh, honey. You have no idea how much I agree with that."

Kat didn't elaborate, but Grace noticed that Bastien reached out and briefly touched his fiancée's shoulder. Another story there, probably. Maybe she'd even get to hear it one day.

But not today.

Alexios fitted the key in the lock and looked at Ethan. Bastien and Kat moved back out of the way, as did Grace. Ethan stepped closer to the door and then nodded.

"We're coming in," Alexios shouted. "Back away from the door."

There was a moment of silence, and then the shouting and banging started again, more loudly than ever. Ethan's face hardened, and then he tilted his head back and let loose with a huge roaring sound that Grace had never before heard come from a man's throat.

She knew where she *had* heard it before, though. She'd heard it last night, coming from those panthers.

The silence was immediate, and the noise didn't start up again.

"That's better," Ethan said. Then, his voice growing until it filled the entire corridor, he continued. "I am Ethan, alpha of the Big Cypress pride, and I'm coming in, so you'd better back the hell away from this door."

Ethan nodded again, and Alexios turned the key in the lock and swung the door open.

Grace had to admit the prisoner was nothing like what she expected. He'd been somehow larger and more imposing in her memory. Perhaps because she'd seen the cat first, and the unconscious and battered man after.

Still, the man huddling at the back of the room, snarling and hissing at them even though he was in human form, wasn't exactly a sweet little kitty cat, either.

"I know him," Ethan said. "I can't believe it. He's not part of my pride, but his grandmother is. He mostly hangs out with a bunch of college kids in Miami. He has never hurt anyone before, ever, as far as I know."

Ethan stepped into the room, and the man hurled himself into a corner, cringing and snarling unintelligible sounds. It was as if he'd gone temporarily insane. For some odd reason, he reminded Grace of Renfield from the Dracula movies.

"If he starts eating bugs and calling for his master, I'm so out of here," she muttered.

Alexios and Bastien just looked puzzled, but Kat started laughing. "You are definitely a girl after my own heart," Kat said.

Ethan advanced into the room toward the crazed shifter. "Eddie, what are you doing? You know me. What would your grandmother think about this?"

But there was no spark of reason in Eddie's maddened eyes. Not even a glimmer of recognition on his wildly grimacing face. When Ethan took yet another step forward, Eddie threw himself on the ground clutching his head, and screaming his first coherent words. "No! No closer. You'll kill me. They'll kill me. My head—it's in my head."

Ethan looked a question back toward Alexios and Bastien, but they simply shook their heads. "I gave him a pretty bad beating," Alexios admitted. "He hurt Grace. But, as you can see, the Change healed his injuries."

It was true. The man was still naked, though there was

a neatly folded pile of clothes just inside the door. For a moment, bitterness washed through Grace's mouth like acid. How nice of them to give him warm clothes to wear. After all, it's not like he'd tried to kill her or anything. It's not like his buddies had killed two of her people.

For a moment, she was tempted to retrieve her bow and put them all out of Eddie's misery. But she was supposed to be in charge. She was supposed to have a level head.

So she ought to act like it. "Isn't there some super-duper alpha power thing you can do, Ethan?"

Ethan flashed a grin at her over his shoulder. "Wow. First I have a man who recognizes Bastien's shortcomings, and now I find a beautiful woman who can tell I'm super-duper. This is a good day."

"If you are lucky, my sister will only use her magic to hang you from a tree by your feet, and not any of your other body parts," Bastien said mildly.

Alexios and Ethan both flinched, but then Ethan laughed. "I don't think so, *Brother*. Ask her some time about creating homemade thunderstorms in my bedroom."

"We are so not going there, now or ever," Kat said, grimacing. "And if you boys are done being boys, we have a problem here to deal with."

Ethan held his hands out at his sides and slowly shook his head. "No, we do not have a problem. Eddie isn't going to be a problem at all, are you, Eddie?"

The captive showed no sign of comprehension, but Ethan started toward him anyway. A sound unlike anything Grace had heard before rose in the room, centering on Ethan. No, strike that. It was actually coming *from* Ethan. If someone crossed the purr of a jungle cat with the roar of a motorboat engine, that might describe the sound. It was a low, primal rumbling that somehow managed to insinuate itself into the marrow of Grace's bones. She felt almost light-headed as Ethan continued calling out his alpha dominance to their captive.

Kat shifted restlessly next to Grace, and Grace glanced over to find that the ranger's entire body was straining forward toward the room and Ethan. Kat's eyes had changed, too; the pupils had narrowed and were beginning to look more feline than human. Evidently the alpha's call affected the other shifters in his pride very strongly, whether it was directed at them or not.

Grace's skin tingled from the inside out, and she realized that shifters weren't the only ones affected. Bastien stepped closer to Kat and pulled her into his arms, and Grace noticed that his eyes had gone from clear blue to almost black. A muscle in the Atlantean's jaw clenched, and she wondered if there were some history between Ethan and Bastien that wasn't as rosy as it might appear on the surface.

At the doorway to the cell, Alexios stood sideways, turning his head back and forth, dividing his attention between Ethan and the prisoner on his left and Grace on his right.

Grace stepped forward, almost involuntarily, but Alexios held up his arm to block her from entering the cell. She glanced up at him, but she was still caught in the thrumming rhythm of the alpha's insistent call, and it was as if she suddenly saw him through different eyes.

Through a prism of sensual hedonism.

The drive to take—to mate—burned through her until the feel of her clothes on her body was irritating enough to make her want to tear them off. The bandages itched, and even the silk of her underwear felt heavy and unwanted against her skin.

She stepped into the circle of Alexios's arms and he automatically closed them around her, his eyes widening. "Grace, what—"

"Haven't we talked enough? I'm tired of talking," she said, curving her fingers and running her fingernails down the front of his chest through his shirt. He inhaled sharply and his eyes flashed hot like the eyes of the man who wanted a woman. She needed to be that woman.

She wanted him, too. Now. She lifted her face to him and slowly, seductively, licked her lips. He stared at her mouth, his breath suddenly rasping.

"Grace, I don't know about this. What are you doing—"

"I'd be doing *you*, if you'd shut up and kiss me," she said, not understanding why he wouldn't just take what she was offering. He was a man and he'd claimed her as his woman the night before. All she needed now was for him to get naked.

The thrumming sound built up in her veins and in her nerve endings, swirling through her body and spilling over her skin until she felt it would drive her mad. She pressed her hips closer to Alexios until she felt his erection right where she needed to, except for the layers of fabric between them. She rolled her hips against him, and he groaned, a deep, guttural sound.

She smiled a private little smile and bit his neck exactly at the curve where it met his shoulder, and his body bucked against her and then he lifted her up and off the floor. She immediately wrapped her legs around his waist and held on tight while he turned and practically ran through the courtyard to her quarters. When nobody could see them, he stopped and leaned against the wall, still holding her and breathing hard.

She tried to kiss him but he moved his head to the side. "Poseidon's balls, Grace, what has gotten into you? You wouldn't even hold my hand twenty minutes ago, and now you're ready to fuck me in front of an audience. Not that I mind," he added, his eyes hot. "But I think something must be wrong. This is out of character for you."

Why was he talking? So many words. "I don't need all these words, Alexios. Blah, blah, character, blah. Either you want me or you don't. Make up your mind. Either fuck me, or put me down so I can find somebody who will," she said, just before she licked her way up the side of his neck.

His hands clenched so tightly on her ass that she was sure she was going to have bruises. "Ooh, yeah. Tighter. I think I like it rough. I don't really know what that means, but I might like it," she said, suddenly possessed by a wild urge to giggle. She hadn't giggled since she was twelve years old. She started bouncing up and down on him, rhythmically bumping against his erection right where she needed to feel pressure. "Oh, yeah, that feels good. Let's try it naked."

He looked up at the ceiling and spewed out a stream of Atlantean that sounded like a cross between a prayer and a curse. Then he looked down at her. "If you had any idea what a hero I am being right at this exact moment," he gritted out. "Obviously, something in the alpha's call is affecting you. Is there any reason why a descendant of Diana would be affected by an alpha panther?"

She looked at him for several seconds, considering, and then she started giggling again. "Ooh, kitty cat! Maybe Ethan will want to fuck!"

Her brain felt like it had been marinated in the finest champagne, and the bubbles were frothing their way through her body from head to toes and all the delicious parts in between. She'd never been much for drinking, after what had happened to Robbie, but she'd been drunk once or twice, and it hadn't felt anywhere near this good.

"What was in that coffee?" She giggled again. "That was one heck of a creamer."

Alexios was swearing again, though, and not interested in her coffee questions. It was too bad that he was such a fuddy-duddy, because she was suddenly, desperately interested in what was behind the zipper of his pants.

"Alexios?"

"No," he said from between clenched jaws. "Ethan does not want to fuck. And even if he did, I'd have to rip his heart out. Slowly. Right now we're going to walk far away from the nice kitty and his apparently hallucinogenic alpha call, okay?"

Still carrying her, he headed for the open door and the sunlit courtyard.

"Kitty!" she squealed. "What a funny word! Kitty, kitty, kitty! Ooh, how about pussy? That's a good word, too. My pussy is hot and wet for you. Wanna fuck *now*?"

"Heroic," Alexios snapped. "He. Ro. Ic. Beyond all measure of what a man should ever have to endure. I certainly hope whoever keeps a tally of this kind of thing is seeing how many karmic points I'm racking up here."

A peal of laughter escaped Grace's lips. "Uh-oh. You said rack! Rack means boobs. Do you want to see my boobs?" She squirmed in his arms, trying to raise her shirt, but he wasn't cooperating. She squinted up at him, frustrated and perplexed.

"Why don't you want to see my boobs? All men want to see boobs. Is there something wrong with you? Do Atlanteans not like boobs? Oh, goddess!" She slapped a hand over her mouth and then smacked herself in the forehead, which made her start laughing again. "I'm sorry. You're gay, aren't you? I didn't know. I mean, you kissed me and you said those *things*, but maybe you're bi, like Michelle?"

She leaned closer and peered into his eyes, then lowered her voice to a confidential whisper. "Is this one of your man phases? I could probably set you up with Tiny."

Alexios was grinding his jaws together so fiercely that it was a wonder he didn't shatter his teeth. He put her down, hard, and her feet hit the grass with a thump, which struck her as hysterically funny. She got the giggles again and collapsed down onto the ground and started rolling around in the brittle winter grass. "Hey, I've never done it in grass," she finally managed to say. "Why don't you take your pants off and come down here?"

Before he could say anything, though, another feeling raced through her. A decidedly *un*-fun feeling. She abruptly sat up and unzipped her jacket, then threw it onto the ground. "Too hot," she muttered, suddenly flushed and a little nauseous.

A *lot* nauseous.

"Oopsie," she mumbled, and then she leaned over and was violently sick onto the grass. She kept retching until it felt like everything she'd eaten in the past three days had been purged, and then finally it was over. She pushed up and away from the stinking mess on the ground and, wobbling a little, turned to look for Alexios. He was standing right next to her, holding a wet cloth, and he didn't look good, either.

Guess Atlanteans were sympathy pukers.

She took the cloth and wiped her mouth. "Thank you," she mumbled. "I don't know why I'm suddenly so sick. I felt fine when I woke up other than a little soreness—"

She stopped dead as a look of total incredulity swept across his face.

"Are you kidding?" He took a step back, and then another. "Are you telling me that you don't know what happened in the past ten minutes?"

She started to say of course she knew, but then she realized there was an odd gray fuzziness around her recent memory. Something about the prisoner and Ethan, and champagne bubbles—*in her brain? That couldn't be right*—and then she was here on the ground being sick.

Alexios closed his eyes and ranted under his breath for a full minute. Then he pierced her with a heated stare and folded his arms across his chest. "Nothing? Nothing about begging me to fuck you in the corridor? Nothing about asking me if I'm gay or bisexual—I'm not, by the way, and I damn well deserve a medal for resisting you—and asking if I wanted you to set me up with Tiny?"

She felt the heat rising into her face. He had to be making that up. And yet—Oh. Goddess. The memories started to filter back.

She wanted to be sick again.

Chapter 20

Alexios tried to keep an eye on Grace, after her bouts of craziness and vomiting, but she was making it damn difficult. She wouldn't meet his eye, for one thing, and after she'd come back from washing her face and brushing her teeth, she kept lurking around the corners of rooms as if she couldn't stand for anyone else to see her, either. She was acting humiliated and defeated, and it was starting to piss him off.

Bastien and Kat kept their distance, though. They were having a very intense discussion in low, heated voices, and Alexios figured he was better off not knowing what that was about.

Women.

Although, to be fair, he blamed this one entirely on Ethan. So of course the alpha chose that moment to walk out into the courtyard, a very subdued Eddie trailing behind him. Ethan gestured to Eddie to move to the center of the loose circle the five of them made.

"Tell them," Ethan commanded. "Tell them what you told me."

Eddie mumbled something unintelligible.

"Speak up," Ethan's voice sliced across the distance between himself and the prisoner. "We know about the enthrallment. Tell the rest."

Eddie nodded and started again. "It was Prevacek. Vonos's head guy here in Florida. He runs the mansion. Security, mostly, calls himself a fixer. He's a vamp, but people say he has special powers that most vampires don't. I've never seen none of that myself. Or maybe I have, if this enthrall thing you're telling me is true." He snuck a glance at Grace. "I sure wouldn't have hurt a human on my own part."

She looked supremely unconvinced, but remained silent.

"What about Vonos?" Eddie had all of Alexios's attention. He needed a lead on the Vampire's Bane, and maybe the shifter knew something about it. "Have you seen him? Have you been in his mansion? Tell us what you know."

Eddie's gaze went to Ethan, who gave him the go-ahead gesture with his hand. "It's Prevacek," he repeated. "He's the one who's been ordering the raids. He thought this was a theater group, and it pissed him off—"

His eyes went first to Kat and then to Grace. "Begging your pardon, ma'am."

"Really? You're going to beg my pardon for bad language after you tried to rip my chest open last night?" Grace didn't bother to disguise her hostility.

The man's face flushed a dull brick red. "I'm so sorry for that. We were just supposed to scare you. I don't—I don't remember anything about a fight. Or hurting you. I'm so sorry, ma'am."

"Right," she said, rolling her eyes. "You don't remember anything about—" Her voice trailed off, and she glanced at Alexios then looked back down at the ground.

"Whatever. It doesn't matter. Just tell us what you have to say."

Eddie looked at Ethan again, who nodded. "Well, Prevacek found out that your theater group was operating in the fort after they'd found the proof that vamps had been massacred here by the Spaniards. He was powerful angry. Wanted us to mess you up a little. Well," he said hastily, backing away from Grace, "not you, personally, but your stuff. Your battle reenactor gear or your props or whatever."

"Why would he do that?" Bastien asked. "Why would vampires care about a theater troupe? It's especially ironic, since vampires once performed to great renown in theaters across Europe."

Eddie shrugged. "I don't know. We think it was sort of a symbolic thing, you know? Prevacek planned to offer it up to Vonos like, hey, I'm loyal and all."

"I would suggest," Alexios said, "that we don't bother asking this one about motivations. Vonos is one of the craftiest and most brilliant generals and politicians of vampire kind. He's sure to surround himself with top-notch people, both vampires and human minions. Asking this one to speculate on their motivations is like asking a mouse to tell you what the hawk was thinking."

Tiny, who'd been keeping a lookout on the roof, headed down the stairs, talking into his phone. "Sam's here," he said, his eyes going from Grace to Alexios. Whatever he saw didn't make him happy, if the scowl was anything to judge by.

She nodded. "Thank you, Tiny. Thank you so much. And please thank your men for me. Will you take this . . . Eddie . . . with you outside for a little while, so we can talk?"

Tiny smiled at her, obviously besotted like every other damn man who got anywhere near her. It gave Alexios a cramp in his gut.

Or maybe that was gas.

Certainly couldn't be the way his balls had swollen into melons and then shriveled back into walnuts all in the course of the past hour.

After Tiny left the courtyard with Eddie, Alexios decided the time had come to put it all out on the table. He rounded on Ethan. "What in the nine hells did you do to her?"

"Do to whom, water boy? And you might want to watch that tone with me," Ethan said, narrowing his eyes.

"Alexios, leave it alone," Grace ordered sharply.

"I'll be godsdamned if I will. Whatever he did with that alpha dominance thing affected you badly," he shot back at her. Then, doomed to honesty by some freak of genetics, he shrugged. "Okay, it wasn't all bad, at least for me. But it made you drunk, and then it made you sick. I want to make sure that this can't randomly happen to you anytime you find yourself near an alpha shifter."

"And this is your business because?" Grace left the question hanging in the air, but her voice made the threat plain.

Well, wasn't that just too freaking bad. "Everything you do is my business. Get used to it," he snapped.

Ethan studied Grace for a moment, then turned to Kat, ignoring Grace's sputtered protests. "Is it true? What happened?"

"Are you calling me a liar?" Alexios was very close to the edge of seriously pissed off.

"No, I'm not calling you a liar, you idiot," Ethan snapped. "It's just that Kat is a little more qualified to describe exactly what reaction Grace had."

"I'm standing right here," Grace said, clenching her hands into fists.

"They get like this," Bastien said to her. "Don't take it personally. I'd never survive if I did."

Kat swung her head around to stare at Bastien, her long

tawny hair flying in the sunshine. "What exactly is that supposed to mean?"

"I think you know," Bastien replied calmly. "If I weren't so secure in my manhood, all this shifter ritual and hierarchy and alpha *miertus* might make me feel a little threatened."

Alexios whistled. "Did you really just say 'secure in my manhood'? Oh, boy. Wait till I tell Justice. You will never live that down."

"I don't think you have room to talk," Kat pointed out. " 'Blah, blah, character, blah'?"

Grace flushed a dark red and started to say something, but Kat cut her off. "Shifters have hearing that's far superior to that of humans," she said, not unkindly. "It's true," she said, this time to Ethan. "She was as drunk on the alpha call as cubs at their first Change."

Grace made a strange strangled sound and then blew out a deep breath. "Stop right there," she said carefully. "I am a descendant of Diana. If you think for one moment—"

Alexios was watching Grace, so at first he didn't understand why she stopped speaking in midsentence. Then he followed her startled gaze. Ethan had dropped down and was kneeling, head bowed, facing Grace.

"What in the—"

"The panther was Diana's special animal and consort," Ethan said, raising his head to stare at Grace reverently. "Our pride has been waiting for more than a century to find another descendant of Diana to honor."

"Freaking Poseidon's freaking balls. Here we freaking go again," Alexios muttered. Then he crossed the lawn until he stood between Ethan and Grace, facing the shifter.

"You," he said, pointing at Ethan's fat head. "You are marrying Bastien's sister. You have no right to talk about consorts and honoring with my . . . with Grace. Got it?"

Ethan got a strange look on his face and scrambled to

his feet. "No, no, it's not like that. Strictly an honorary consort kind of thing."

Bastien shook his head as he stepped closer. "No, I don't think my sister is going to go along with the consort concept, honorary or not. I think I might have to kill you. Nothing personal, you understand."

"You can try," Ethan said amiably. "Good luck with that."

Just then, Sam walked into the courtyard with his dog and stopped, staring at the three men. "What in the blazing blue hell is going on around here?"

Alexios was inexplicably glad to see the grumpy old man's face. But Grace needed to feel that she was in charge. *She* should fill Sam in on current events. He turned to ask her to do that, but she was gone.

Kat was gone, too.

Just . . . gone.

Alexios whirled around, frantically scanning the courtyard, but Sam hooked his thumbs in his belt loops, rocked back on his heels, and started laughing. "If you could see the look on your face, boy. She and that lovely ranger woman walked by me a couple of minutes ago. Said something about a pissing match going on out here."

Alexios sighed. He should be used to it by now. As long as he expected the unexpected, he could at least pretend to understand her. "And the injured?"

"Well, we've got two fairly badly wounded who are staying with the doc until their families can come get them, two who are primed and ready to get revenge, and the rest are inside packing up their duffels as fast as they can, so they can get the hell out of here."

Alexios nodded grimly. "My thanks to your doctor friend. It could have been worse."

"Alaric?" Bastien asked.

"Unreachable. Quinn." It was enough of an explanation.

Everybody knew about Alaric and Quinn. A shadow crossed Bastien's face, but he said nothing further.

"It can always be worse," Sam said, answering Alexios's earlier comment. "Anybody gonna fill me in?"

Blue wandered over to Ethan, sniffing curiously, and gave a tentative bark. Ethan looked down at the dog and made a growling sound that rumbled up from his chest, and Blue quickly backed off and hid behind Sam. Sam patted his dog's head and shot a keen glance at Ethan. "Maybe start with the panther."

Alexios made the introductions and then told Sam what they'd learned. Sam listened intently, never once interrupting, until Alexios had finished. Then he nodded.

"Matches up with what my friend the doc said. This Prevacek is a piece of work. Old-school Russian mafia turned vamp. Took a liking to hot weather and moved over here for good in the 1700s. Big, bad, and thoroughly nasty. Has political aspirations, too. Wants to get into the Primus, but doesn't have the buy-in ready. Interesting part is that Vonos is throwing a big ball for the press and the high-society types in a couple of days. Might be something to check out."

"Sounds like Prevacek is running his own game. Either that or he lied to those idiots about why he wanted them to come after our so-called theater group," Alexios said. "I gotta tell you, I hate coincidences. And we are definitely going to find a way to get into that ball."

"I, too, am no fan of coincidences," Bastien said. "However, as you yourself have more than likely realized, this attack does not fit either of the two parallel patterns. You and your 'theater troupe' are neither a fringe group of human society—"

"Unless your acting is really, really bad," Ethan put in.

"Funny man. It's not too late for me to kick your kitty-cat ass," Alexios advised him.

Ethan made a "bring it" gesture, and Bastien sighed.

"Nor, as I was saying, was this an attack made to look like an accident."

"They always like this?" Sam asked Bastien.

"They just met. But there was a little problem with Ethan's alpha call, Grace's response, and something about ancestry and consorts," Bastien explained.

Sam threw up his hands, clearly disgusted. "Stop, already. I can't deal with this on no sleep and not enough coffee. Don't want to know; don't care. So let's say that this Prevacek is offering up a little bit of dead theater troupe to Vonos as some kind of twisted proof of his initiative and loyalty. What's he gonna think when he realizes none of them came back?"

"We could send Eddie in with a story," Bastien said doubtfully.

Ethan and Alexios made simultaneous snorting noises, then glared at each other.

"Eddie hasn't got the brains the gods gave a—oh, hey. Shifter," Alexios said.

"I'd have to agree with that," Ethan said. "He must have some Atlantean DNA in his background."

Sam rolled his eyes. "Enough, already, children. What are we going to do next?"

Chapter 21

Grace walked into the kitchen and introduced Kat to Michelle, still seething about Alexios's high-handedness. The two shook hands, the ranger's blond Amazon height a striking contrast to Michelle's petite darkness.

Michelle hugged Grace. "I'm so glad to see you again. It was a rough night. We've lost all but two of the recruits, too."

"Sam filled me in while you were dropping off your stuff in your room. You may as well go right back and get it, because you're leaving," Grace said. "It's too dangerous here."

"Danger is my middle name," Michelle said. "Actually, I wish danger were my middle name. My actual middle name is horrible beyond the admitting of it. Michelle Danger sounds rather brilliant, doesn't it?"

"You realize you people are all crazy, don't you?" Kat said, not really phrasing it as a question. "Do you have any hot tea?"

"Crazy like a fox," Grace said.

"Panthers eat foxes," Kat pointed out.

"Really? That's disgusting," Michelle said, making a face. "Bushy tail and all? And yes, we have tea. Real tea, not that nasty tea bag stuff."

"Thanks. And no, we don't really eat foxes," Kat said, rolling her eyes. "I'm more of a cheeseburger-and-fries kind of gal. But I don't think you can talk, considering you Brits invented that barbaric sport you call riding to the hounds. I'd love just once to jump into the middle of that as a panther. Scare a few stuffy old men, wouldn't I?"

"Maybe we could talk about what we're going to do now and leave refighting the Revolutionary War for later," Grace said. "Only two recruits left, and I need to get both of them out of here. Boy, won't Quinn and Jack be proud when they get back from wherever they've gone off to?" She clutched her head in her hands and moaned.

"Who cares whether they'll be proud?" Kat shrugged. "You're the woman on the ground, so to speak."

"It was a rhetorical question," Grace said flatly.

"Well, here's one that isn't. What are *you* going to do with the remaining two?"

"I'll be glad to take them wherever you need me to," Michelle told Grace. "I'd rather stay with you, but as long as you have Alexios, I won't worry about you as much.

"Here we go again. Everybody trying to protect me. I'm supposed to be the one who takes care of everyone else," Grace said.

"Hey, these Atlanteans are handy in a fight," Kat said. "Don't underestimate the power of teamwork. We're all better off fighting this fight together, because the bad guys— even the *vampires*—are learning that very lesson."

Alexios showed up in the kitchen doorway, looking a little sheepish around the edges. "I'm sorry about that."

Part of her wanted to make an issue of demanding a long apology on the spot, in front of witnesses, but mostly she just didn't want to hear it. Because every time he did something kind and gracious, or something protective and cherishing, it made it harder and harder for her to contemplate life after he left.

"No worries," she finally said. "Michelle has offered to take our last two recruits off to another training area. Any ideas?"

"Yes, in fact. Brennan is in Yellowstone with a friend of mine. They're setting up a joint command—Pack and human. I think that would be an excellent place for them."

Kat looked up. "Pack? Are you talking about wolves? Because I've got to tell you, I'm not a fan. It seems like the shifters who most consistently take the vampires' side are wolves."

"Perhaps. But Lucas is a friend and very definitely on our side. Sam already has one of Tiny's men lined up to go with them to Yellowstone, though. Michelle doesn't need to go. However, I agree she needs to be somewhere safe, and Bastien and Ethan have a proposition for her."

Michelle took a long sip of her tea, then carefully placed the mug on the table and folded her hands in front of her. "I do happen to be sitting right here. Perhaps someone could ask Michelle directly if they have a proposition for Michelle. After all, my name *is* Michelle Danger."

Alexios looked puzzled. "I thought your name was Michelle Nichols."

Grace couldn't help herself. She burst out laughing.

Sam crowded into the kitchen behind Alexios. "What's funny? Also, and far more important, do you have any coffee made?"

Grace tilted her head toward the fresh pot on the counter. "Help yourself. What's going on?"

Sam took a moment to pour himself a mug of coffee before he leaned a hip against the counter and responded. "We think Vonos is planning something big, possibly something that's going to happen at this fancy-schmancy ball of his."

He filled her in on what they'd learned after she and Kat had left the courtyard. "So, turns out this ball is day after tomorrow."

Alexios and Grace exchanged a long look. "Interesting timing," she said.

"Well, you know what they say about the Fae," he replied. "They never lie, but they never tell the truth."

Bastien appeared and ducked his head under the doorway so he could fit his tall form into the room, which was rapidly becoming crowded. "Who never tells the truth?"

Alexios sketched out the details of Rhys na Garanwyn and his proposed meeting the following evening.

Bastien whistled, long and low. "The elves? I must admit I did not see that coming. I wonder what catastrophic thinking is driving this on the part of the Seelie Court."

"High House, Seelie Court," Alexios reminded him. "That's never good."

"My mum met an elf once," Michelle mused. "Very nearly left my dad over him. Can't trust those Fae buggers."

Grace leaned forward and brushed the curls back from Michelle's ear. "Nope. Not pointy. Too bad. Would have explained a lot. Anyway, you can't trust them, but you can't offend them, either," Grace said. "They usually don't bother with us, since we live our lives so far beneath their exalted presence for them to notice us. And when they do, well—" She shook her head. "It's never good."

Alexios casually crossed the room until he was standing next to Grace. Her pulse reacted to his presence like a trip-hammer, but she tried to portray nonchalant indifference. More and more fuzzy memories of how she'd acted under the influence of the alpha call kept coming back, and the humiliation factor was off the charts. She felt like she could never face him again, but he kept seeking her out.

Beg a man to fuck you in public, and that kind of thing is going to happen, said the dark, gleeful voice in her mind. Grace told the voice to shut the hell up.

Michelle looked up at Bastien, who towered over the room. "I understand you have an offer for me."

"Yes, we do. We'd like to set up a three-way alliance at Big Cyprus, with human, Atlantean, and shifter members all at the table. From what Grace and Alexios tell us, you would be a perfect choice to spearhead the effort. I understand you have no pressing need to return to London?"

Michelle looked down at the table for a moment, twisting her hands together. Then she smiled at Bastien. "Actually, I don't have any need to return to London, pressing or otherwise, and I think I would be perfect for that position. How lovely of you to offer it to me."

Kat was nodding. "It's vital that we find out how panthers are being enthralled. The shifters have always been immune to this type of mind control, but something new is going on. Something deadly for all of us. The sooner we can work together in a coordinated effort, the better."

"It's settled, then," Michelle said. "Now, if you'll all excuse us, Grace and I need a moment alone to say good-bye."

Everyone filed out of the kitchen. Alexios hesitated for a moment, then bent and pressed a kiss to the top of Grace's head. "I'll be right outside," he said.

She nodded, unable to respond, and watched him leave the room. Finally, she smiled at Michelle, ready to say good-bye.

"All right, spill it," Michelle said. "What happened between you two while I was gone?"

Grace hesitated for less than a minute, then she gave in and told Michelle all of it: Leaning on his strength after the battle. The intensity of the soul-meld. What had happened when she'd been intoxicated by the power of the alpha call.

Her face was burning hot enough to melt copper by the time she finished. Michelle stared at Grace, her eyes wide and lips twitching.

"If you laugh at me," Grace threatened, not quite knowing what the "or else" would be.

Michelle nodded, then put her head down on her arms on the table and burst into peals of laughter. "Oh, dear. I would have given enormous amounts of money to have seen that. Serious, reserved Grace humping her Atlantean in the hallway." That set her off again, and she laughed until she was breathless.

"It's so wonderful to have a best friend I can confide in," Grace said through her teeth.

"Oh, honey, don't get—"

"My knickers in a twist, right. Easy for you to say. You weren't babbling on and on about kitties and boobs and fucking." It was Grace's turn to put her head down on the table. "How am I ever going to face him again?"

Michelle reached over and smacked Grace's arm. "You really are an idiot, aren't you? Are you kidding? The way that man looks at you? It was probably his wildest fantasy come true that you were saying those things and acting like that. He's some kind of hero for not having a go at you right there on the spot."

Grace reluctantly laughed. "That's pretty much exactly what he said. 'He. Ro. Ic.' "

"And so he was," Michelle said. "But tonight you'll be alone together, and he doesn't have to be. All he has to be is a man, and you certainly deserve him."

"But he's going to leave me."

"You don't know that. And even if he does, who cares? Live for today for once."

"But what if—"

"No," Michelle said firmly. "No 'what if.' Only do it. Take something for yourself for once. Take a chance. Shave your legs."

Grace grinned. "Okay, maybe just this once."

~~~⚬~~~

Grace stretched, slowly waking from a long nap. The room was dark, so the 8:00 glowing on her clock told her that she'd slept clear through the day and into the evening. She'd been exhausted and weak, and her injury had been hurting, so, for the first time in the past decade, she'd handed over all control to others and simply gone to bed.

Before he'd left, Ethan had made a call and told them a truck would be there soon to load up everything from the armory and take it to Big Cypress for safekeeping. Tiny and Sam had figured out a plan to deconstruct all of the temporary improvements that the "theater troupe" had made to the fort, so that it would be left pristine, with no damage whatsoever to the historical structure.

The blood had merely soaked into the grass, after all, and any that stained the concrete was simply carrying on a long-standing tradition for this fort.

After multiple good-byes, Michelle had climbed into the passenger seat of the helicopter as if she'd been riding in them all of her life instead of being a "chopper virgin," as she'd confided just before embarking. She'd have a great time; Michelle always did. If only she could teach Grace the secret of not taking the world, the war, and herself so seriously.

If only.

And Alexios . . . well, he'd been everywhere. Watching over her. Making sure she wasn't overtiring herself. Catching her off guard, sometimes, with those flashes of heat in his eyes that told her he was remembering the things she'd said and done that morning.

For the first time, though, she didn't feel embarrassed. Instead, she stretched again, luxuriously, in her warm sheets and allowed herself to feel . . . anticipation.

Delicious, tingling anticipation.

Her nipples peaked just from the thought of him and her body grew warm, readying itself for him. She had the desire and the motivation. She even had the bed and the readiness.

All she needed was to find her Atlantean.

Her Atlantean. She wondered where the possessive pronoun had come from, but allowed herself to enjoy it. Cherish it as one would cherish a jewel lovingly loaned by a true friend. It would have to be returned, eventually, but until then . . .

Her Atlantean. If only it could be true.

No. No time for wistfulness or denial now. She threw the blanket back and, still dressed, pulled on her shoes and jacket and went to find Alexios.

Chapter 22

Alexios soared over the ruffled lace of the cresting waves and enjoyed the utter freedom of flying as a sparkling shimmer of mist higher and higher into the night sky. Away from responsibility and duty. Away from all of the humans who needed him—and the one human who didn't.

The Warrior's Creed, burned into his brain through constant recitation as a youngling at the academy, marched in exacting precision through his mind.

We will wait. And watch. And protect.
 And serve as first warning on the eve of humanity's destruction.
 Then, and only then, Atlantis will rise.
 For we are the Warriors of Poseidon, and the mark of the Trident we bear serves as witness to our sacred duty to safeguard mankind.

It was a duty Alexios held sacred. But for all of his life, Alexios had waited and watched and protected. He was tired of waiting. Tired of watching.

He had finally found the one woman he truly wanted to protect.

Would it matter?

Frustrated with himself, Alexios dove toward the surface of the water and returned to his body just in time to slice through the top of the wave. The water was icy; the shock of it left him breathless. He rolled over and over in the water, its cold embrace cooling the burning need that had been building and building in him since that morning.

Grace. Seeing her wild side, even though it was artificially induced, had triggered something in him that he couldn't stop. Couldn't repress. Couldn't deny.

He wanted to bring that side of her to the surface again. Wanted to see the playful, happy, and carefree Grace. She'd lived the past ten years of her life crushed under the weight of the oath of vengeance she'd sworn to her dead brother.

He wanted to show her that life could be different. *Better.* But of all the men she'd ever known, he was probably the most singularly unqualified for the task.

What did he know of happiness? He knew camaraderie. He knew the satisfaction of a battle well fought. But happiness? He'd thought all possibility of it gone forever after what he'd endured as a prisoner.

But then came Grace, offering grace. Offering warmth and light and a chance at home. The only question he needed to ask himself was a simple one. Why was he still here, wasting time in this frigid water, when he could be with her?

He struck out for the surface and the shore, eager to get back to her. Sam, Tiny, and the rest of the men were standing guard all night. Sam had specifically told Alexios that he had no need to take a shift.

"I think you and Grace have things to work out," Sam had said. Yet another conquest who'd fallen hard for a woman who was completely unaware of her own beauty and generosity of spirit.

Once at the surface, Alexios folded his hands together, lifted his face to the stars, and offered up a heartfelt plea. "I don't have any fancy light tricks or priestly magic, Poseidon. But I do have an earnest desire to move forward with my life. Please accept that I'm now ending the vows of celibacy I took during the purification rituals. If there were truly any dark desires left in me from that horrible time, they would have shown themselves when Grace was vulnerable this morning. Instead, I showed what I still maintain to have been damn near heroic qualities."

He started laughing, suddenly feeling more buoyant than the waves themselves. "I've never wanted to be a hero before now. I'm guessing that the desire means something in and of itself. The answer is in me, grasshopper," he said, grinning like a fool.

And suddenly he knew. A kind of peace washed through him. Peace and anticipation—neither were emotions he'd experienced for so many long, long years.

Unwilling to take the time even to return to shore and retrieve his clothes, Alexios soared up through the air in his mist form and arrowed his way over to the fort and down the corridor to Grace's room. He transformed as he landed gently on his feet, scanning the room. She wasn't there.

Which was probably a good thing, considering he'd just shown up in her room stark naked.

"Well, that's one way to make an entrance," she said from behind him, her voice full of warmth and laughter, and he snatched the blanket from her bed to cover himself.

Then he turned around to face his future.

❧～～❧

Grace was a little dazed from the sheer glory of walking into her room and finding a perfect Atlantean backside mooning her. When he turned around, clutching her plaid blanket to his middle, she tried not to laugh. Fought really hard against it.

Lost the fight.

She laughed so hard tears came to her eyes. "You know, I had a really rocking seduction scene planned, but this works, too."

He smiled sheepishly at first, but the smile faded as something hot and predatory moved into his eyes. "Seduction? Rocking seduction? Oh, Grace, I am most definitely at your disposal tonight."

"I can see that. I can see a lot," she said, still laughing a little, but mostly trying not to hyperventilate at the sight of all that muscled chest, shoulders, and arms. Naked. Those long, muscled legs. Also naked.

Her heart started racing, and she hoped the jacked-up Atlantean senses didn't include hearing heartbeats. "Quite a lot," she continued. "Wandering around naked, were you? Wonder what Tiny thought of that?"

He took a step toward her. Stalking her. "Undoubtedly he would have reacted as you are doing now, but I did not travel in a form that could be seen."

"And your clothes?"

"I left them on the beach. You, yourself, are wearing far too many." He took another step toward her. "Perhaps you would care to remove that jacket."

Laughter and breath both whooshed out of her as she realized he was really here. They were really going to do this. Act on the attraction that had been building between them for so long.

"Stop thinking so hard," he said. "This is a simple choice, Grace. Either ask me to leave or remove your clothes. All of your clothes. We are going to resolve this between us, once and for all, and outside of the sparring ring." He flashed a wicked smile at her that sent her pulse racing. "And I hate tennis."

She reacted to his challenge with one of her own, pushing the door shut behind her, then turning to push a chair in front of it. There were no locks on any of the doors here. She'd never needed or wanted one before now.

Suddenly he was behind her, crowding her. Startled, she fell forward a little, bent over the chair, and caught herself with the flat of her hands on the wooden door, then winced as the gash in her side ached from the movement. As was typical of her, her body had begun the healing process in record time while she slept, but it had been a very bad wound. It was still bad. Just because it was sealed shut instead of gaping open, the matter of maybe a week's healing in anyone else, didn't mean that it didn't still hurt.

He pressed against her so closely that the heat of his body was touching her, leaning into her, all along her back from shoulders to feet.

She didn't feel any blanket, either.

Her breath sped up, but she didn't try to get away. Simply turned her head and gazed at him over her shoulder. "Not that I don't appreciate the gesture, but this is a little tough on my side."

Instantly he was pulling her back, gently lifting her, swearing—at himself, she guessed—under his breath. "I am so sorry, *mi amara*. I am a fool. Of course my timing is horrendous. You are injured, and—"

She leaned into his hard, hot chest and shut him up the best way she could think of—she kissed him. His lips were firm and yet soft. Warm. His mouth tasted like spice and heat, and she wanted more and more. She threaded the fingers of her left hand through that glorious mass of his hair and pulled his head down farther so even his breath became part of her.

"Yes," she said, finally releasing his lips, pleased to discover that she wasn't the only one breathing hard. "I was injured, but I'm much better now. I have pretty good healing abilities. I was coming to get you, you know."

He released her and she sank down on her bed. He stepped back as if touching her burned him. "I can only apologize again, *mi amara*. I wasn't thinking, only lusting like a black-hearted . . ." His litany of apologies and self-recrimination trailed off as he seemed to finally remember that he was standing there buck naked.

She let her gaze travel from his head down to his very enticing chest, down to his flat abdomen and the silky-looking trail of hair that arrowed down to his . . . oh. My. The man was *built*. And if his truly impressive erection was any indication, he really, *really* wanted her. She took a deep breath and then, very deliberately, licked her lips while staring at his penis.

Subtle, she was not.

His erection jerked forward, hopefully in response to her provocation, because she had absolutely no practice or experience at being seductive, so she was totally winging it.

"You are trying to kill me, aren't you?" He forced the words out from between clenched teeth. "I am trying to be a gentleman. Heroic again, even. But by all the gods, I think you expect too much of me."

She stood up, ignoring the fact that he backed away even farther, and made her own heroic attempt—to keep her eyes on his *face*. "But you miss the point. Nobody is asking you to be heroic this time." She blushed a little, remembering her actions earlier. "This is just me, Alexios. No strange reaction to an alpha call, no Fae magic, just me.

Just me, wanting you. What if we were to take it easy? Be gentle? Can't we at least try?"

She swallowed past the lump in her throat, humiliatingly aware that her last plaintive question had sounded almost like begging. She looked down at the floor, sure that this moment was one of the most difficult she'd ever lived through. It was far easier to be brave when it was only her *life* on the line.

But this was her heart and her pride.

He took a step closer and began unbuttoning her shirt, leaning down to press a kiss to her forehead, then her chin, then to the pale skin of her chest that he uncovered with each released button.

"Gentle," he murmured between kisses. "I think I can do gentle."

Alexios heard himself tell Grace that he could be gentle, even while everything in him claimed it a lie. How could he be gentle when he wanted nothing more than to throw her back on the bed and slam into her body until he was so deep inside her that his cock touched her womb? How could he be gentle, when he needed to bind her arms and legs and touch her and bite her and leave the marks of his nails and mouth and teeth all over her?

He wanted, no, *needed* to claim her. To brand her. To make her his, indisputably and forever. And there was nothing gentle in any of that.

As if she were in the room with them, he heard phantom laughter. Anubisa's laughter. "And so I win," this phantom born of the hells of memory whispered. "I have conquered you, body and soul, and nothing is left of you that isn't twisted, broken, and wrong."

His fingers shook as he opened the buttons of Grace's shirt, and then he froze, unable to continue. What if the vampire goddess had been prophesying instead of simply uttering more of her vile threats, when she'd spoken those word to him all those years ago? What if Alexios truly were twisted, broken, and wrong?

Shaking his head in denial and despair, he began to back away from Grace. Lovely, brave Grace, who deserved more. He looked up, finally forcing himself to meet her gaze so he could tell her.

"Grace, I cannot—"

"Stop thinking so hard," she advised, smiling as she cast his own words back at him. Then her smile faded. "After what happened here—after our people died . . . I need you, Alexios. I need your warmth so I can feel alive again. I'm willing to take a risk that I've never taken before and admit that I have feelings for you."

She put her palms on his chest and drew in a shuddering breath, then moved closer to him. "I know you're going to leave, that you have to go back to Atlantis and do your important warrior stuff, and save the world or whatever. I know you'll live forever, and I'm just mortal. It's the whole thing I always wondered about when I was a kid—what the heck was Lois Lane thinking? But for now—just for tonight—I really need for you to be with me."

Something in the hard lines of his face softened as he gazed down at her, and a smile quirked at the edges of his lips. "I think I can take a break from 'saving the world or whatever' to be with you."

He closed his eyes for a moment and then held his hand out, palm up, toward Grace. In the exact center lay one of his daggers. "In return, I ask you a favor. If something should go wrong—if I should endanger you in any way—you must promise that you will use this on me."

Her mouth fell open. "Are you kidding me? You want me to promise to, what? Stab you? Wow, Alexios, that's really setting the mood."

He placed the dagger on the bedside table and then turned back to her, grasping one side of her still half-buttoned blouse in each hand. "You want me to set the mood?" His predatory grin glittered in the lamplight. "Watch this."

With that, he yanked, and the shirt tore open, buttons flying through the air. He knelt in front of her, and being so very careful of her bandaged side, he lifted her breasts in his hands and buried his face between them. She stroked his silky hair and tried not to hyperventilate, but then he moved his head and caught one of her nipples with his mouth and sucked hard, right through the lace of her bra, and her knees went weak. He caught her butt in his big hands and held her in place while he licked and sucked that nipple until she was panting, then switched to the other side and gave her other breast the same treatment.

A kind of gasping moan escaped her throat and he looked up at her, flashing that dangerous smile. "How's that mood setting going?" His nimble fingers were suddenly at the front of her jeans, unbuttoning and unzipping them, and he was pulling her pants and underwear down her legs before she could breathe or protest or start cheering. When the jeans were a puddle at her feet, she lifted a leg to step out of them, but he grasped her left calf in one hand and her right thigh in the other, lifted her left leg over his shoulder and put his mouth on her.

She shrieked a little, then stuffed her fist in her mouth so she didn't make any other embarrassing noises that might bring Tiny and his men running, but then she had to say something, had to stop him, surely she should be doing something to pleasure him . . . oh. Goddess.

"Alexios," she moaned. "Please, don't . . . we . . . I want to please you."

He lifted his head and stared up at her, and his eyes were hot with hunger and powerful need. "You are pleasing me. I want to lick you and taste you and suck your honey into my mouth until you scream while you come. I am very pleased."

Then he bent his head to her again and swiped a hot lick

of his tongue directly across her core and licked the hard nub of her clit into his mouth and started to suck it the way he'd sucked her nipple. This time she couldn't stop the scream, even with her hand pressed against her mouth, and then she gave up entirely when he put his finger inside her and drove it in and out, first one, then two fingers, in and out rhythmically while he sucked on her, and the world exploded when she came so hard the edges of her vision went fuzzy.

She collapsed forward a little but he was inhumanly quick and caught her, gently, oh so gently, and made sure she didn't hurt herself, didn't jar her still-healing side. He lifted her onto the bed so carefully, as if she were fragile or delicate or anything but a warrior.

A woman, perhaps. The metamorphosis irrevocably complete.

She sighed with the sheer sated pleasure of it and held her arms out to him when he hesitated. "I'm cold without you," she said. "Please. I still need you. I think I need you inside me more than I need to breathe. Please, Alexios. Don't leave me alone, yet again. Please."

Alexios stared down at her, at this woman who was the center of his soul, of his life, and was humbled. "Never. You never have to say 'please' to me," he said roughly. "I am yours to command and will be until the end of my years."

A strangely sad smile crossed her face, and he lowered himself carefully onto the bed next to her, careful not to jostle her injured side. "Tell me. Tell me what else I can do to please you."

She lowered her lashes, that entrancing blush sweeping across her cheeks again. "I'd rather you told me what I could do to please you. I'm not all that great at this. I mean, of course I've done it before, but it wasn't—I mean—oh, I sound like an idiot."

He clasped his hands together under his head and forced

himself to say nothing while hot rage seared through him. It was ridiculous. It was incomprehensible. Of course she had known other lovers.

And yet the thought of her with another man sent a crushing primal fury swamping through his brain.

"Alexios? Did I say something wrong?"

Her voice was hesitant, and for an instant she reminded him of a shy young dolphin he'd played with as a child. Coming closer, then backing away. Wanting to make contact, but somehow afraid. Grace was like that, and yet she'd gathered all her courage to reach out to him and he was wasting time on useless jealousy.

"I am sorry, *mi amara*. I just felt an emotion heretofore unknown to me through all the years of my existence," he said, grinning ruefully. "Not that this is a particularly good time for me to remind you of our age difference."

"Well, you're only as old as you feel, or so they say. Most days, that makes me around five hundred years old. So I guess I'm really too old for you," she said, shyly returning his smile.

He laughed and then dared to touch her again, tracing the line of her jaw with his fingertip. She shivered and goose bumps rose on her lovely skin. He pulled the thick blankets over them both and something in her face relaxed a little.

"I'm not exactly used to lying around naked with men," she admitted. "I guess I'm a little nervous."

Alexios felt the rage try to build in his nerve endings again. "I have a confession to make, and I am not proud of it. The emotion to which I was referring is jealousy, and it would be much easier for me if you would save any talk of other men until I'm not lying next to you with your taste on my lips."

The hot blush rose in her cheeks again, but she nodded. "Okay, I get it. It's a little hard for me, too, if I start thinking about how many women you've been with over the course of all those centuries. Speaking of which, we need to have the safe-sex talk." She blushed even harder.

"I can neither catch nor transmit any human illness, and pregnancy is not a concern unless a warrior has made a petition to Poseidon for permission," he gently assured her.

"Oh. Well. That's good. I, um, well, now that we have that out of the way, can we go back to the kissing?" She rolled onto her side facing him and grinned, and he was glad to see her shyness fading and his Grace return. She leaned forward and pressed a kiss to his lips, and he opened his mouth to her, delighting when her tongue hesitantly swept inside to claim his mouth.

But the heat of her touch drove the hunger, and hunger drove need, until his cock, which had softened a little while they talked, pulsed urgently with the demand that he be inside her. Inside her hot wetness. Plunging in and out of her in the same rhythm his fingers had earlier known in her body. Fucking her until she came, hard, clamping around his cock.

He changed the kiss, deepened it, drove his own tongue into her mouth. Angled his head to take even more, raised onto his side, and gently pushed her onto her back so that her body was open to him and he was free to explore it with his hand while he kissed her.

He cupped each of her breasts and rubbed his thumb back and forth against each hardened nipple, still kissing her, still catching her tiny moans in his mouth. Then his hand moved lower, to her silky belly, and he splayed his fingers there, where his child would grow if he had petitioned Poseidon for such a gift.

The thought was oddly appealing, and that in itself was a little frightening. Never before had he even considered the idea of fathering a child. But the combination of making love to Grace and, perhaps, seeing Prince Aidan was working on him subconsciously. But just then Grace lifted her hand to his back and gently ran the tips of her short nails down his skin, sending shivers through him. His thoughts shifted from wistful longing to an urgent, driving hunger, and he needed to have her.

He needed to have her now.

Grace wanted him to stop thinking. Now. He'd been toying with her long enough, and really, a girl could only take so much. She let her hand drop to that lovely, perfect butt of his and she squeezed. He jerked against her, and she finally, finally moved her hand to the one place she knew would jolt him into action. She ran her fingers down the length of his penis and then closed her hand around it, and he bucked against her and moaned so hard it nearly made her let go.

Nearly.

"I need you now," she said, and then she pulled him over her, all that lovely, long, lean muscle in his legs moving him exactly to where she needed him, nestled in between her own legs, his arms propping him up so that he didn't rest his weight on her.

Still treating her as if she were fragile, then.

"What if I want you to lose control?" she asked huskily. "What if I want to make you crazy?"

He stared into her eyes, his own going almost completely black, except for that blue-green flame in the center.

"Also, what does *mi amara* mean? And why do your eyes get that blue-green flame in the middle?" she blurted out.

He blinked, then dropped his forehead to hers and sighed, then laughed a little. "Always the unexpected with you, *mi amara*. My beloved."

It was her turn to blink. "Oh. Really?" Her lungs tightened and suddenly it was hard to breathe. "I'm your beloved?"

"Let me demonstrate," he whispered, that evil grin back on his beautiful, fallen-angel face. Then he positioned himself so that the head of his penis was pushing directly at her center and, with one quick, hard thrust, he drove so far into her that she gasped and arched up against him.

"Mine, *mi amara*," he said, his face suddenly harshly somber. "You are my beloved, and you are mine, and I will never, ever, let you be harmed again."

He started thrusting, slowly and steadily, so that every word was punctuated by the sound and feel of their flesh meeting. His penis was so large, and she was so out of practice, that she felt a wonderful, horrible stretching that shivered on the precipice between ultimate pleasure and an edge of pain. When he drove into her, his chest brushed against the tips of her breasts, and the sensation was almost unbearable in its exquisite sensitivity. She felt the orgasm building, building, swirling through her nerves and veins and skin until she thought she might die if he didn't make her come soon.

"Please," she said again, shamelessly, not caring that she was begging. "Please."

He began to thrust harder and faster, his jaw clenched against some inner struggle, and then he shifted his weight to one arm and put his other hand between them and touched, then rubbed her exactly where she needed to feel him touching her. The pressure combined with the force of his body driving into her, and she called out his name, and then she screamed as she fell into the sun.

Alexios felt every sensation as Grace's body tightened around his own, as she arched into him, meeting his every thrust with her own passion. When she exploded, her entire body shuddered in wave after wave as she clamped around his cock so hard that his own release burst out of him, and he needed to catch himself on his arms so that he wouldn't fall forward onto her, crushing her.

He captured her lips with his own and kissed her, swallowing her cries with his mouth, and then she convulsed around him yet again and he soared through mundane reality and into the very fabric of being, and he knew—and was both exalted and terrified by the knowledge—that it was the soul-meld.

Finally complete, finally whole, the darkness of his soul yearned toward her light and the two collided in a shock wave of volcanic proportions, enough to sink Atlantis beneath the sea yet again, enough to lift Alexios from the deepest trench of loneliness and despair.

She was *here* and she was *his* and he would never, ever let her go.

He fell onto his side, pulling her with him, and wrapped his arms and legs around her, his cock still inside her, and he rode the wave of sensation—the purest, most beautiful cloud of hope and light and . . . dare he even think it?

Love.

As he rode the avalanche of light and sound that was the symphony of two souls finding their destiny, he opened his heart and mind and soul and filled them with her light. Filled them with her beauty.

Finally, *finally* knew love.

He would *never* let her go.

It was hours or eons later, time another irrelevancy in the universe they'd built between the two of them, and he felt her body slowly relax as she loosened her grip on his shoulders and her trembling finally slowed and stopped.

"Alexios?" she murmured sleepily, and he kissed her hair and her forehead and her lovely, elegant nose.

"Yes, *mi amara*?"

"Is it always like that for you?"

He laughed, startled as always by the way her mind worked. Then he kissed her gently on the lips. "No, my love, my beautiful Grace. It has never, ever been like that for me before. But it always will be from now on," he promised.

"Oh," she mumbled. "I'm not sure I can take it."

He laughed and drew the blankets around her, and then

he held her, content to feel the beating of her heart, for a very long time after she fell asleep.

"Always," he whispered, a promise and a vow. Then he carefully slipped from her arms so that he didn't disturb her when he left to go join the patrol.

He wasn't about to let his guard down now. Not when he had so very much to protect.

Chapter 23

Grace woke, climbing slowly up out of a delicious dream, and immediately turned to find Alexios. But she was alone. Instantly, all of her old fears swamped her with their cold, dank forebodings.

Why would he stay? What could she be to him, after all, but a blip on the long centuries of his life? Maybe the soul-meld had frightened him, and he'd decided to back off.

Maybe—but then she heard footsteps and relief and something deeper and sharper cut into her with an almost physical pain. How had she gotten to the place where his absence caused her such pain?

How would she stand it when he was gone?

But now wasn't the time. For now, she would take Michelle's advice and live in the moment. For all the years that he was gone she would have this treasure trove of memories to horde and cherish.

Alexios came through her doorway, holding mugs of

coffee and looking like a man who had been well pleasured the night before. He was all rumpled, sleepy-eyed male satisfaction as he surveyed her from head to toe. She let the blanket fall from one bare shoulder and glanced up at him from beneath her lashes, trying on an unfamiliar seductiveness.

His eyes went hot as his gaze went straight for the bared expanse of skin, and she shrugged her shoulders a little so the blanket fell even further, exposing a precarious amount of her breasts. He smiled, but his knuckles on the mugs turned white.

"If you're trying to make sure I don't let you out of bed today, you're doing a very good job," he said, his voice husky.

"Who, me?" she said, batting her eyelashes at him. Then she raised her arms and stretched, and the blanket fell into a puddle at her waist. Alexios kicked the door shut behind him, put the mugs down on the table, splashing coffee everywhere, and headed straight for her with an expression like a stalking lion.

She grinned and held her arms out to him, but he sat next to her on the bed, caught her hands in his and pinned them to her sides, pushing her gently back onto the pillows.

"Your breasts are so beautiful," he said, staring at them so intently that heat flushed through the skin of her chest and up to her face. "I can't look at them without needing to touch them and taste them."

And then he proceeded to do just that, drawing her nipple into his mouth and gently sucking on it, the pressure just enough to make her moan with frustrated longing as her hips bucked restlessly underneath the blanket.

Then, still holding her hands, he released her breast and lay his head on her chest, right over her heart. The tenderness of the gesture took her breath away for a second, and her heart stuttered and skipped a beat or two.

"I could listen to your heartbeat forever, do you realize that?" he asked her, his voice a quiet rumble, his breath warm against her skin.

"Forever is a long time," she said, suddenly chilled by the impossibility of his statement. "I'm cold. May I have the blanket, please?"

He sat up instantly, tucking the blanket up and around her shoulders, a look of concern on his beautiful face. She tentatively lifted her hand to touch the scarred left side, hesitant at first. Afraid she'd offend him. He flinched a little, but then held still under her touch.

"Is it so repulsive to you? My face?" He lowered his eyelids, but not before she'd seen the flash of pain darken his eyes to a stormy green.

The words themselves took a moment longer to penetrate, perhaps because they were so much the opposite of what she'd been thinking. "Are you—what? How can you even ask me that? You are the most beautiful man I've ever seen in my life, and a flaw only makes beauty more poignant."

She leaned forward and pressed a gentle kiss on his scarred face, and he seemed to stop breathing. "Did you know that some master artisans purposely put a flaw in their art so that God will not be offended by perfection?"

He laughed, and the sound was bitter. "That's a pretty story, but the analogy rings false. There is a huge difference between an artist deliberately pulling a thread in a tapestry and Anubisa calling Hellfire to burn my face."

His muscles tensed, and she could tell he was on the verge of pulling away from her. It was a constant dance between them, pushing and pulling, moving apart and coming together. A strange waltz between two hopeful but almost unwilling participants.

"Tell me about it. What is Hellfire?" The question was blunt, but she didn't know any other way to ask it. She sat up in bed, pulling the blankets around her.

"It's exactly what it sounds like. It's fire channeled from

the lowest of the nine hells, and Anubisa, as goddess of Chaos and Night, is mistress over it. She can channel it to her purpose or for her unholy pleasure."

He shrugged and then jumped up to pace the floor. "Evidently one day ruining my face happened to be her pleasure."

Grace didn't even know she was crying until she tasted the hot tears as they ran down her face and touched her lips. She scrubbed at her face but never took her eyes off him. "How could you stand it? How could you be so incredibly brave as to survive?"

He whirled around and glared at her. "Don't you mean to ask why I was such a coward that I didn't take my own life to escape? I tried. Believe me, I tried. But there was always someone there watching me. Keeping me from inflicting any pain on myself." He stopped pacing and laughed bitterly. "Evidently only *they* were allowed to cause me pain."

The memory of the flames from her vision—the whips and torture—burned through her mind like a brand. She shook her head back and forth, denying the vision. Denying his words.

"No, that's not what I meant to ask at all. I know you're not a coward. I've seen your amazing courage. It was much braver to survive that horror than to take the easy way out." She hung her head, ashamed to look at him. "Trust me, I know. And my reasons for wanting to take that final way out are pathetically unimportant compared to what you endured."

She watched as his boots walked into her field of vision. But he didn't touch her. Simply stood there for a long moment. Then he finally spoke, and ice and pain mingled in his voice. "Strange, then, that we found each other. That I finally found the one reason—the one *person*—who could save me from an eternity of wanting to take that final step, and she wants nothing more permanent of me than a brief moment of physical comfort. Believe me, the torture of that knowledge is more than anything Anubisa and her minions could have done to me."

Before she could recover from her shock at his words, he was gone, the door slamming shut behind him.

She sat in the bed, stunned, clutching the sheets to her chest as the enormity of what he had said sank in. He thought *she* was the one not wanting any permanent commitments with him. He thought *she* was the one who only wanted a physical relationship.

She threw off the blankets and jumped up to get dressed. This was one misconception she was going to clear up immediately. She had given herself to him, finally daring to take a risk, body, heart, and soul. She wasn't going to back down now, even if she had to beat some sense into an Atlantean warrior.

~~~

Alexios stormed through the fort, almost wishing that someone would attack. He needed someone to hit. Maybe Tiny would be up for a little sparring.

But then he heard it. Her voice, behind him. And she didn't sound happy.

"Alexios, slow down right now or I'm going to get my bow." Her sharp command rang through the stone corridor, and he found his steps slowing in spite of himself.

He turned, folding his arms across his chest, and glared at her as she approached. Trying not to feel his heart thumping painfully. Trying not to notice how unbelievably beautiful she was with sleep-tousled hair and the rosy pink flush of anger riding high in her cheekbones.

"Oh, save it, buster," she snapped. "You can't go from having your mouth on my boob one minute to storming off the next."

He blinked, taken aback. Sometimes he forgot how direct women could be in this century.

"I'd have to agree with that one, partner," Tiny said

from somewhere behind Alexios, adding a layer of joy to his day. "Sorry about overhearing, by the way. I was just on my way out for some breakfast. I can bring you some back, if you like, Alexios. You must be hungry after patrolling with us all night. Oh, and you, too, Grace, of course," he added hastily.

The flush in Grace's cheeks burned even hotter, but she responded politely enough. "Thank you, Tiny, but Alexios and I are going out to breakfast by ourselves."

"We are?"

She jammed her hands on her hips and gave him back a glare as good as any he'd ever given. "Yes. We are. If you don't have any more stupid objections or stupid opinions, like your stupid idea that I'm stupid enough to want you only for a stupid roll in the sack."

By the third "stupid," he was grinning. "I'm guessing what you're really trying to say is that I'm stupid."

She narrowed her eyes. "Bingo. Got it in one."

Alexios glanced behind him, but Tiny was gone. Smart man. "So. Breakfast. You and me," he repeated. Stupidly, in fact. The realization made him laugh.

She marched up to him and grabbed a fistful of his shirt and yanked him down toward her. "I don't do that," she said, slowly and carefully. "I need for you to hear and understand me. I don't let people in, and I don't open my heart up. So when I do, I don't expect to be treated like I'm only using you as some kind of boy toy. Got it? I care about you. You mean something important to me."

"Boy toy?" His mind raced with the implications and pure, primal male satisfaction warmed every inch of him. "But what if I want you to use me like that?"

She made a strange growling noise in her throat that reminded him of the panther shifter who'd claimed that she should be his consort. But before he had time to even think about being jealous, she put her hands on his face, pulled his head down to hers, and kissed him, hard.

"My beloved, remember? You don't get to call me that and then back away from me."

It finally sank in. She was demanding that he stay with her. That he not run away. She wasn't trying to escape. She wasn't telling him "thanks, it's been fun." She wanted him. She wanted to keep *him*.

He caught her around the waist, carefully putting his hands underneath the bottom edge of her healing injury, and lifted her as high as he could without bumping her head on the stone ceiling of the corridor. Then he slowly and carefully lowered her until her face was level with his, and he kissed her.

"Perhaps I should not jump to conclusions based on faulty evidence," he admitted. "However, I am having a hard time believing that I'm good enough for you."

"I think," she said, between kisses, "you should let me spend the next twenty or fifty years convincing you." But he noticed a quick shadow crossed her face as she said it, and he tucked it away to ask her about later.

Much later.

"Breakfast, then?"

"Breakfast," she said, smiling.

Chapter 24

Daytona Beach, Vonos's mansion

"The humans call a room like this a panic room," Prevacek observed, gesturing to the stark gray walls and steel-reinforced doors of the five-hundred-square-foot room.

Vonos ignored him, or at least gave the appearance of ignoring him. Prevacek did an excellent job as second-in-command in the Florida region. He was top-notch at security, as well. But he had an unfortunate habit of talking too much.

Vonos scanned the room in question, then nodded in satisfaction. The renovations had proceeded quickly, after a visit to the contractor's wife had convinced the recalcitrant human that an estimate of completion date did not mean that the work would be finished two weeks *after* that date.

Or even one week.

Or even one day.

He smiled, reminiscing about that visit. The woman had

been singularly unattractive, her tanned and leathery skin almost too thick for his fangs to penetrate.

Almost.

He'd only drained a mere fraction of her blood before her husband "saw the light," as it were, and moved every one of his crews, available or not, onto Vonos's renovation project.

He wasn't an evil man, Vonos mused. Simply one who preferred *order* and organization in all things.

"Of course, we needed a room where no sunlight could possibly enter. Those double default doors were brilliant," the general rattled on, his Russian accent thickening as it usually did in times of stress, until he sounded almost like a caricature of himself. Not that any ancient Russian mafioso didn't sound like caricature, given what Hollywood had done to them.

Addendum. Prevacek talked too much *and* he was a suck-up. Vonos could never fully trust a man who was either, let alone both. But that worked out fine for him, as he never intended to trust anyone. He had done so before and been betrayed, just like so many others had been betrayed.

Drakos. The name burned through his mind as if the sunlight had managed to find the inner recesses of his skull.

"Explain this to me. This theater troupe." He drummed his fingernails on the slate desktop. He'd ordered the furniture from Pottery Barn, simply because the irony of it amused him. "Why exactly would you order an unscheduled attack, potentially destroying months of my careful planning, merely to go after a group of amateur actors, may I ask?"

"They were flaunting their disrespect, Primator," Prevacek said, bowing low. "They were using the fort as a venue, even after we made it clear that the anti-vampire history of the fort was horrific to us."

"And you didn't think that this open display of aggression might provoke closer attention to our experiments with shifter enthrallment than I either wanted or needed at this stage?"

Prevacek flung himself forward, prostrating himself on the dark gray carpet. Carpet Barn. It fascinated Vonos how the humans had a "barn" for every need, when they were little better than farm animals themselves.

"Please accept my profuse apologies, my lord," Prevacek all but wept. "I will never do anything but exactly what you order, again."

Vonos silently considered the advantages and disadvantages of simply ripping the vampire's throat out and then burning his bones. It would be messy, true, but he had people for that. He wasn't sure the blood would come out of the new carpet, though, and really, he had no time or patience for a new installation before the ball.

"Oh, get up and get out. Don't ever do something like this again, do you hear me? Especially considering that the ball is coming up so quickly. We have many important guests arriving, and I want very much to impress them."

Prevacek shot up off the carpet, not knowing how close he'd been to the true death. "Oh, no, never, my lord, never," he babbled. "I mean, yes, my lord, of course."

As Prevacek scurried out of the room and Vonos returned to his paperwork, another thought occurred to him. "Stop. What happened? What did the panthers report?"

Prevacek froze, his hand on the door handle, and then slowly turned back around to face Vonos. "That's somewhat of a problem. They haven't checked in yet."

Chapter 25

St. Augustine, the beach

Grace tried to absorb the fact that she was walking along a beach, in the daylight, hand in hand with an Atlantean warrior who claimed to love her.

It wasn't working.

First, the day itself was only a brief respite in her duty. Alaric was due to arrive back at the fort to meet them that evening, but whether he would or not was anybody's guess. Apparently there was something between he and Quinn so powerfully compelling that he would literally fly to her side whenever she was in danger, whether she called for his help or not. Alexios wouldn't say much about it, but she didn't want to pry into her commander's life—love life?—anyway.

Whether or not Alaric managed to return, though, she and Alexios had a date with the Fae that couldn't be broken. Her thoughts turned to Rhys na Garanwyn, and her fingers tightened in Alexios's as she missed a step, stumbling on the sunlit white sand.

He shot a questioning glance her way, but she shook her head. They'd been over and over this at breakfast, speaking quietly in a booth in the back corner of the IHOP on the highway.

Alexios apparently had a fondness for all-you-can-eat pancake days.

Their waitress, however, had been cheerful through it all. Grace had figured she would have been ready to kick them out after his fifth helping or so, but the grandmotherly woman just smiled and shook her head and said something about her sons, the football players, and their appetites.

That was when Grace had noticed Alexios handing the woman some folded dollar bills and smiling, just before he asked for a sixth helping, more bacon, and more syrup. A shriek and the sound of dishes falling had been Grace's first clue that Alexios wasn't exactly up on American currency.

The woman had come running through the restaurant back to their table, holding the bills out in front of her. "Oh, honey, you made a big mistake," she said, laughing boisterously. "These aren't one-dollar bills, these are hundred-dollar bills. You gave me a thousand dollars!"

Grace had been impressed with the woman's honesty, especially when she'd tried to give the money back to Alexios, but he'd simply sat there looking slightly puzzled. "Is it not the custom here to render payment for good service?"

He'd directed the question at Grace, so she answered for the flustered waitress. "Yes, it is the custom, but the amount you gave her is about one hundred times the cost of your breakfast, so it's quite out of the range of the normal tip."

Alexios had flashed a smile so dazzling that half the women in the restaurant practically swooned. "Well, her service was quite out of the range of normal, as well. This amount is exactly what I wish her to have. However, we should go now."

He had taken one final sip of his coffee, wiped his

mouth on his napkin, and then stood up and held his hand out to Grace. "We have much to discuss."

She'd just stared at him for a moment, then sighed and shook her head. "Ah, yes, the royal decree." She stood up and retrieved the check that the waitress had left them earlier, and then patted the woman on the arm. "He wants you to have it, with our thanks for your excellent service and your patience while he ate you out of a month's supply of pancakes."

The waitress had stared from the money in her hand, to Alexios, and then back at Grace, who nodded encouragingly. Then the poor woman had thrown her arms around Alexios and hugged him, saying something about a grandchild who needed braces.

Alexios had looked absolutely terrified and so Grace, laughing, had extricated him from the situation and gone to the cashier to pay the check. The waitress had marched right up to her, snatched the check out of Grace's hand, and declared that there was no way they were paying for pancakes—it was on her. By this time, the entire restaurant had been listening in, so a cheer had gone up from everyone. Alexios, though clearly startled, had handled it with aplomb, turning toward the woman and bowing deeply. As they'd left the restaurant, Grace had heard the excited chattering about visiting royalty, and she'd started laughing again.

"I can't take you anywhere," she'd told Alexios, but he'd grinned that sexy grin at her and kissed her right there in front of the IHOP, officially making it one of her favorite restaurants on the planet.

Now they were walking on the beach, working off some of the thousands of carb calories, hopefully, and she kept sneaking glances at him, just to be sure he wasn't a figment of her imagination who was about to disappear any minute.

"What are you thinking?" He didn't so much ask questions as issue demands, she'd discovered, even though he'd quite sternly explained that he was not of the royal Atlantean house, but only one of Prince Conlan's elite guard.

She grinned. He sure had the attitude for royalty.

He stopped walking and pulled her into his arms again, lifting her feet clear up out of the sand. They couldn't walk more than a dozen paces without him touching her, holding her, or kissing her, she'd noticed.

Not that she was complaining.

"Tell me. Now."

"Okay, that's taking the demanding thing a little far," she pointed out. "Don't forget I can still skewer you with one of my arrows at a hundred yards. Just because I'm putty in your hands in bed—"

He kissed her, effectively making her forget where she'd been going with that thought. "Putty in my hands? I like it. Let's go back to bed now." He kissed a path down the side of her neck and suddenly her breath was a little ragged.

"No, we can't. We need to plan what we're going to do tonight, and anyway, Tiny and his men are still there. Also, my side hurts a little," she admitted. "I guess I'm not superwoman after all. I'm healing fast but I still may have . . . exerted myself too much."

Remorse swept over his face. "It is my fault. I pushed you when you should have been resting. I knew I wasn't fit for—"

"Stop. Right now," she ordered him. "I wanted you. I wanted exactly what we did together. I still want you now, but I think a little rest first will make me a more active participant next time."

She tried to project calm assurance but the betraying hot flush climbed into her cheeks. Just not used to discussing sex in broad daylight. Okay, not used to discussing sex at all. She blushed again as the elderly couple walking toward them smiled knowingly.

But once the couple had moved on, she'd kissed Alexios, putting all the feeling she wasn't quite ready to express into it. When she stepped back, she wasn't the only one whose breathing was ragged. She cast about for a topic of conversation that didn't involve sex or kissing.

"So, tell me about Atlantis."

They started walking again, threading their way through driftwood shaped in fantastical patterns that had washed up on the shore.

"What do you want to know?" He ran a hand down her arm, smiling like a little boy on Christmas morning, and she smiled back at him, caught up in his obvious joy.

"Everything! But let's start simple. Where do you live? How long have you been one of the prince's guard—the Seven, you called it? What is that tattoo you have on your arm? Where, exactly, is Atlantis? How is it that none of our oceanographers or submarines have found it? Are you ever planning to rise?" She finally stopped for air and realized he was laughing quietly. "What?"

"You call that starting simple?" He shook his head. "Okay, let's see what I can do with that. I live in the warrior's wing of the palace, although I have a home ready for me to move into should I so choose. It has been simpler to stay in the palace, although that will not always be the case." He cast a long, measuring glance at her, and she shivered, hugging the hope to her chest that he might be picturing her in his house someday.

"I have trained to be a warrior in the royal guard since I was a youngling, and I was honored to be selected to serve in Prince Conlan's elite guard almost right out of the academy. He broke tradition a little and chose guards based on the potential he saw in us, rather than on long years of dedicated service."

"Makes for a very loyal team," Grace said, thinking back to her first meeting with Quinn, and how the commander had given so much responsibility to a teenager. Grace had walked away from the meeting knowing she would do anything for Quinn, and she still felt that way.

"The tattoo is Poseidon's mark and he honors us with it when we have successfully completed our training to be a Warrior of Poseidon. Poseidon's Trident bisects the circle representing all the peoples of the world. The triangle is a symbol of the pyramid of knowledge. All of Poseidon's warriors bear this mark as testimony to our oath to serve Poseidon and protect humanity."

"Is it something you can share?"

He glanced at her, clearly startled. "Is what something I can share?"

"The oath. I'd like to hear it, if it's not too private."

He stopped, still holding her hand, and considered that for a minute. "You know, I've never been asked that. I don't see any reason why I couldn't share it with you; we first swear the oath in front of our academy mates, trainers, and a wide audience of family and friends. Plus, of course, you know about Atlantis itself, which is a far greater secret than the words of an ancient oath."

She tilted her head and said nothing, waiting for him to decide, loath to push him but really, really wanting to hear it.

He took a deep breath and, releasing her hand, stood at what she thought of as a kind of parade rest. "We will wait. And watch. And protect. And serve as first warning on the eve of humanity's destruction. Then, and only then, Atlantis will rise. For we are the Warriors of Poseidon, and the mark of the Trident we bear serves as witness to our sacred duty to safeguard mankind."

When he finished, it was as if the words hung, sacred and pure, in the salty sea air between them. Grace finally remembered to breathe, and she took his hand again. "Thank you. For sharing that with me, and for all of your years of living that promise."

He slowly shook his head. "Expect the unexpected," he murmured. "You know, I think this is the first time any human has thanked me like that."

She smiled even as the chill raced down her neck at the words "any human." Just when she felt closer to him than ever, he said something that highlighted the vast gulf between them.

Live in the present, she berated herself. You can worry later.

~~~∾

Alexios couldn't believe he was blathering on about anything and everything, but the reward of Grace's lovely smile seemed to be a prize worth doing almost anything for. The sunlight on her hair made it glow, and as they walked along the beach, he could almost forget about war and battles and scheming vampire primators with evil plans. He could almost forget about the danger Grace would be in if he couldn't convince her to leave before that evening's meeting with the Fae.

"There's something . . . I really need to know," she ventured after they'd been walking in silence for nearly ten minutes. "About your long lives and, well, you said the prince had married a human woman." Her lovely cheeks turned pink. "What will happen when she ages and he doesn't?"

He considered how much to tell her of what he knew and what was simply speculation, but finally decided that he wouldn't put barriers around trust. He either believed in her or he didn't, and the realization that he trusted her with his life itself forced him to stop and pull her into his arms, yet again.

When he could finally manage to lift his head from her long, drugging kisses, he was so hard he wanted to throw her down right there on the sand and strip her bare.

Her side. Hurting. Right.

He laughed, and she raised an eyebrow at him.

"Nothing. I just seem to revert to a sort of caveman, pre-language thinking style around you," he said, smiling like a besotted fool.

Of course, he was starting to feel like a besotted fool, which meant that if an attack came at them now, he would be worthless. He deliberately put his hands under his jacket and on the hilts of his daggers and moved a step away from her and started walking, this time back in the direction of the car.

"The aging thing?" she prompted.

"Right. The aging thing." He searched for the words. Decided on the simplest. "We don't know. The truth is that living in Atlantis causes the longevity, and it always has. In fact, it was part of the cause of the ancient jealousies and attempts to conquer the Seven Isles. Something in our drinking water, which all comes from magically sourced wells, is apparently the cause."

"Really? Like a real-life fountain of youth?" She looked skeptical, and he didn't exactly blame her. Magic wasn't easy to explain.

"The elders, who now have to worry about these things for the first time in millennia, are predicting that human life spans will extend to several times normal and continue to expand as long as the humans reside in Atlantis," he said, shrugging. "The histories bear out that at least some of this is true, but a great deal of it is a leap of faith on Riley's part, and of course Erin and Keely, now."

"Keely?"

He smiled and described some of the interesting pairings that had occurred over the course of the past year, after more than eleven thousand years of belief that Atlantean-human mating was forbidden.

"Poseidon gave his blessing," he concluded. "Told Riley she'd make a great mother for the heir, so it was hard for anybody to argue with that, although I guess there are factions that would like to try."

Grace nodded. "Some people hate change, especially to sacred traditions. When the Catholic Church decided to stop saying Mass in Latin, you would have thought that

Satan had woken up and decided to eat the pope for breakfast, according to my aunt."

"I don't know very much about your Christian faith, although I am willing to learn, if you would agree to learn about my beliefs," he said, his steps slowing as he realized the enormity of what he was proposing.

Apparently she realized it, too. She slowed to a stop and turned to face him, her lovely dark eyes huge. "I would be honored to learn about your beliefs, Alexios. But that's a pretty large leap of faith. I have to tell you that the idea of growing old and frail and . . . and *wrinkled* . . . while you stay like *this*"—she waved a hand at him—"well, it's pretty tough for me to wrap my mind around."

Then she bit her lip and turned away from him. "Not that you asked me to grow old, or not old, with you anyway. Just, you know, hypothetically."

"Hypothetically," he repeated, drawing her into his arms until she stood with her back pressed to his chest, both of them facing the ocean. It would be easier not to see her face if she refused. "Hypothetically I would like to ask you to grow old or not old with me for the rest of my life."

She gasped but he didn't allow her to speak before he continued. "However, not so hypothetically, all my caveman brain can think and feel around you is 'mine, mine, mine.' So it is possible that I'm never going to let you escape, whatever your answer."

She said nothing, just leaned against him, silent, for nearly an eternity. Finally, she spoke, and her words, though typical Grace, blunt and lacking in poetry, were like bells in his ears. "I wasn't going anywhere for the next century or so, anyway."

He had no choice, then. He had to kiss her again. Which he proceeded to do, thoroughly, until the evil contraption in her pocket started its buzzing noise again.

Grace smiled up at him, her lips swollen from his kisses,

as she answered the phone. As she listened, the smile faded from her face, and her expression darkened. When she finally closed the phone, he already knew it was bad.

"That was Jack. They were caught in a trap. Prevacek set it. Quinn got hurt, and it was bad. Alaric arrived just after Quinn went down, and he pretty much went completely insane, killing everyone in sight, including a couple of civilians who just happened to be out in the swamp trying to poach gators, evidently. Jack said it was worse than anything he's ever seen," she said, her voice grim. "Alexios, Alaric nearly killed Jack, too."

Chapter 26

Back at the fort, late afternoon

Grace pushed the uneaten sandwich away from her, too sick with worry and dread to eat. Alaric was due to return any minute, if he still planned to come at all. Alexios had assured her that Alaric would be there to assist in the meeting with the Fae, but the Alaric that he knew and the Alaric Jack had told Grace about could almost have been two different men. Whatever was going on between him and Quinn, or whatever else the cause might be, Alaric had turned from a somewhat scary ally to a potential enemy.

Jack had said that Alaric had healed Quinn and then Jack, and Alaric had been apologetic about injuring the tiger shifter, but it sounded like a matter of "too little, too late" to Grace.

Alexios had refused to allow her to tell Tiny any of it, citing the need for Atlantean secrets to remain so, and she had stared at him in disbelief and voiced her heated disagreement with the plan.

"Are you kidding me? Tiny and his men are our first

line of defense if your crazy priest has gone over the edge," she'd argued.

But he'd shaken his head. "You have no idea of the scope of Alaric's powers. Imagine if I unleashed my full strength and skills against these humans." He'd waited until she'd nodded, reluctantly seeing his point. But then he'd gone on. "Now add in the most powerful Atlantean magic in the history of the Seven Isles. Tiny and his men would be brutally killed if they tried to oppose Alaric, and they deserve better."

It had been the end of the discussion. Telling Tiny that he was free to leave, because she and Alexios were themselves getting ready to go, and letting him see her toss her duffel bags in the Jeep had been the only way to convince the big man that it was okay to leave her alone and unguarded, except for Alexios.

"You take care of yourself, little gal," he'd said.

She'd thanked him and stood on her tiptoes to press a kiss to his cheek and then watched with some amusement as his face had flushed red under his beard. Alexios had been somewhat less sanguine about it, but managed to refrain from challenging Tiny to a duel or something equally archaic.

It would be a lot to get used to, spending her life with a four-hundred-year-old warrior. If she ever had the opportunity, that was. For now, all she could focus on was the meeting with the Fae. She cleared her dishes and then went back to the more important task at hand: oiling her bow and sharpening the steel and silver tips of her arrows.

"Diana, guide my hand, should I need to use your bow," she whispered and for an instant almost believed she saw the play of moonlight on the feathered fletching of her arrows.

Just for an instant.

~⌒~⌒

Grace heard his footsteps. Heard him stop in the doorway. Felt the intensity of his gaze before she even raised her head. She pretended she hadn't, though. Hadn't heard him. Hadn't felt him.

Didn't want him.

She busied herself with polishing the edge of her gleaming bow again, as if she couldn't already almost see her reflection in the wood. Maybe he would go away for a while, and she could take time to process. To deliberate on the new information and decide what to do with it.

Fountain of youth. Stay in Atlantis or grow old.

Stay with him for the rest of his life—with a man who baldly admitted he might not be able to let her go. What kind of control over her own life and destiny would she have to surrender in order to enter his world?

Was it worth it? Could it ever be worth it, no matter what her heart was telling her? Had good sex—okay, *great* sex—made her think love when the real *L* word in her mind should be lust?

Alexios cleared his throat. "Deep thoughts or avoidance?" he asked, the tone of his voice low and grim. "Are you having second thoughts so soon?"

Grace finally looked up at him. "More like third or fourth thoughts," she admitted. "This . . . whatever this is between us, it's too intense. Too . . . big. I worry that it could swallow me whole. Drown me."

He nodded and offered up a tight smile. "I see. But you are a world-class swimmer, are you not? So drowning is not such a big concern."

"If only that were true. But I'm not—I don't know how to be part of a relationship. I've always thought it would be too confining. I don't need a man to tell me what to do." She closed her eyes and blew out a sigh. "I'm not explaining this very well."

Suddenly, he was standing behind her and drawing her back into his arms. "You're explaining it perfectly," he said, after dropping a kiss on the top of her head. "But, Grace, with all due respect to your concerns, can you imagine any man trying to tell *you* what to do?"

He started laughing and she had to smile. He had a point. Better yet, he'd made the point, and he sounded pretty darn happy about it.

He twirled her around on the bar-stool-style seat and caught the sides of her face in his hands. "Grace, do you think that I could ever be happy with a meek woman who was content to stay home and bake Atlantean spice cookies?"

She shrugged. "I don't know. I just don't know you well enough. Also, what are Atlantean spice cookies? Are they good?"

He tilted his head, closed his eyes, and sighed, then he gave her a rueful smile. "They are, actually, excellent. My favorite. Maybe you could still be a tough warrior *and* learn to bake them?"

She laughed and lightly punched his arm. "Nice. Very nice. How about *you* still be a warrior and learn to bake them?"

"How about we both learn to make them and I can lick spices off your naked body?" he said, flashing that wicked grin.

Then he bent his head to kiss her and she sank into the heat of it, the lovely welcoming warmth that felt like home and soon changed to something sharper. Longing became hunger; hunger became need. She lifted her hand to his face, but he yanked his head back and caught her wrist in his hand. The muscles in his shoulders tightened under her other hand, and his eyes darkened to black in seconds.

"What is this?" he demanded, shaking her wrist a little. "You let them mark you?" His voice had dropped so low it came out as a snarl.

She glanced at her wrist and instantly understood. "Ah. The Fae mark." He was still clutching her wrist, hard, and she jerked it free. "It wasn't like I actually *wanted* him to do it," she snapped. "Quit acting like a Neanderthal."

He put his hands on her thighs and pushed them apart, then walked between them, pressing her back and down until she was leaning back on her elbows on the table behind her. With one sweep of his arm, he pushed her bow and arrows to the side, flinching when his skin touched the bow.

"What in the nine hells—"

"The bow deeded to a descendant of Diana protects itself," she said flatly. "As can I, which you'd better remember if you try to take this any further. You're not going to like what I do next."

He blinked, as if waking from a trance or enthrallment, and looked down at where she half lay, half sat on the table. Shaking his head back and forth, he dropped his forehead until it rested on her chest for an instant, then rose and gently helped her to sit and then stand up from the stool. "Please, *mi amara*, please accept my apologies for my behavior. I saw the Fae mark and the drums started pounding in my head again. I fear I am unworthy of you if I cannot even control my anger and jealousy over such a thing. I will leave you to your work."

Grace caught his arm as he turned to leave, and the look he gave her was heartbreaking in its mingled hope and remorse. "No. Don't go. I want you to stay. I want . . ."

"You want?" He moved closer, so close, and stared down at her, his eyes once again deep, deep blue. "Tell me what you want," he said, his breath warm against her skin.

"I want you," she admitted. "Only you."

The smile began with his eyes and took over his entire face. "I want you, too. Gently this time." He glanced down at her wounded side. "Gently."

He lifted her into his arms and carried her to her room, murmuring thanks to any gods who would listen for this gift beyond price.

Grace watched him as he removed his clothes, and then her own. She watched him as he lay down beside her, his hands touching and stroking every inch of her skin. The sight of his large, scarred hands—warrior hands—on her skin was oddly erotic, and added to the gentle wash of heat and desire flooding through her.

Gently, he'd said. And so they were: Gentle with her wounded side, though it was healing rapidly. Gentle with each other. Gentle with fragile emotions newly awakened and overwhelming emotions newly unmasked.

She rose above him and watched as he caught her hair and brought it to his mouth, first inhaling deeply as if memorizing the scent of her and then releasing her hair to raise his head and kiss her. He lay still beneath her, his muscles trembling with the self-control he was exerting to be passive. To let her take the lead.

Lead, she did. She lowered himself onto him, her softness surrounding his hardness, and gasped at the feel of him inside her. Slowly, but catching and following some internal rhythm, she lifted her hips over and over, then sank back down against him, taking him into her. Taking him all. Reveling in the feel of control.

Until control broke and she had to take, to plunder. To rise and fall with the tides, with the waves of passion, cresting with the heat and power. He arched his body into hers, thrusting up, giving and taking and giving more until she felt her body tightening around his and she made sure she was looking into his eyes as the world exploded around them.

A long time later, when she could finally move, she realized that he'd pulled the blanket around her shoulders and covered them. "Not bad for 'gently,'" she murmured, smiling against the warmth of his chest.

His arms tightened around her for a moment. "Not bad?

Is that all? I'll have to try harder next time," he said, amusement in his tone.

But then reality intruded, slicing into the space between them like a blade. "Alexios? We have to get up. Alaric may be here anytime now, and we need to prepare for the meeting with the Fae."

He lay still and silent for several seconds then finally sighed. "You're right. What does it mean that, for the first time in centuries, I would be glad to forfeit duty and relinquish honor for another hour in your bed?"

She started to laugh. "It means we have a lot in common."

~~~

Alexios paced back and forth across the parapet, continually trying to reach Alaric, but the mental pathway was blackly silent. Either the priest would come or he wouldn't. There was nothing Alexios could do to influence the outcome. The sun was beginning to set over the little town, which meant that the time for the meeting with Rhys na Garanwyn was drawing near.

Grace was blocking him out, avoiding his eyes when he tried to talk to her and compulsively sharpening her arrowheads. Her contented smile had changed to harrow-eyed denial when he'd suggested she stay behind. She didn't want to discuss options, and she had flatly refused to allow him to meet with the Fae alone. Other than forcibly restraining her, he could find no way to keep her from that meeting. And, given that the elf prince had specifically come to Grace, Alexios couldn't be sure that leaving her out of this meeting would not be a grave insult. The Fae were tricky when it came to things like that, and Alexios was a warrior, not an ambassador. The delicate niceties of politics and negotiation were beyond him.

He felt the icy wind first, its temperature far below the

winter sea breeze. When he swung around, Alaric was standing behind him, his dark clothing ripped and blood-spattered, and his eyes wild.

"Bad day?" Alexios asked mildly.

Alaric clenched his hands into fists at his sides, a faint blue-green light pulsing in an eerie halo around his skin, but then the meaning of Alexios's words seemed to sink in, and he almost imperceptibly relaxed.

"You could say that." The priest's eyes were sunken deep into his head and he looked almost worse than the crazed panther shifter Alexios had trapped in a cell. Eddie. Which struck him as a ridiculous name for someone who turned into a lethal predator, but nobody had appointed Alexios as head guy in charge of names.

And now, even his brain was rambling.

"Do you need a break? Are you going to be up to this meeting? The Fae—"

Alaric snarled, and the power sizzling through the air ramped up a notch. "I don't need you to tell me about the Fae, youngling," he snapped.

Alexios held up his hands. "Sure, I'm not arguing with you. Don't want to end up a dark splotch on the cement. But watch the youngling stuff—I'm only a hundred or so years younger than you."

Alaric made that hideous snarling noise again, but this time his gaze had shifted, and his eyes had gone a flat silver. Alaric was in pure predatory mode, and Alexios was suddenly, hideously sure that he knew why.

"Grace," he said, her name a prayer on his lips. "Please tell me you're not threatening Alaric in any way."

"I'm pointing my bow right at him, but it's more of a precaution than a threat," she replied. "You might want to back down, priest. I am a descendant of Diana and my goddess hunted your sea god in her day."

For one horrible moment, Alexios was sure that Alaric

was going to attack. Bow or not, Grace could have no real defense against him. So Alexios moved a little until he was blocking the priest's view of her.

"Here's the thing, Alaric. You are my friend, and I owe you a huge debt of gratitude that I will never, ever be able to repay," he said, working hard to keep his voice calm and level. Trying to tame the savage beast that Alaric had somehow transformed into. "But I will not let you hurt my woman, so you're going to have to go through me to get to her. Do you really want to do that?"

Alaric slowly, oh so slowly, turned, tilting his head as if he were hearing Alexios's words from a long, long distance away. "No. No, I do not want to kill you or your woman," he finally said and, although the word "kill" was disturbing, Alexios kept his calm face on and nodded.

"Okay, then. Grace, can you please put your bow down so we can all play nice? We need to figure out our plan for the Fae and Vonos, and there's not much need to discuss battle strategy if we're just going to kill each other and save them the bother."

Suddenly Alaric's face changed, contorting into a fierce grimace. "Injured. Bloody."

Alexios nodded. "Jack called us and told us about Quinn. I'm so sorry. Is she okay?"

Alaric shook his head, his matted hair flying. "No. Not Quinn. Grace. Need to heal her. Now."

Grace, who'd been walking up to join them, stopped short and mutinously shook her head. "No way is he touching me," she said quietly, clearly thinking that only Alexios could hear her.

He could have told her not to bother.

"Yes way," Alaric said, with a strange, flat intonation. "Now."

Before Alexios or Grace could even move, Alaric leapt forward and caught her waist in his hands. Silvery blue light shot out from his fingertips and swirled around Grace like the bandages Alexios had wrapped her with, but far more helpful. Grace cried out, once, and then fell silent. Alexios tried to go to her but the healing light also served as a barrier and kept him away.

It was over in seconds, and Alaric stumbled back from Grace and then ran to the edge of the roof and leapt off. "Back soon," he called out, and then he turned to mist and was gone.

Alexios jumped to Grace's side and lifted her up from where she'd fallen on her ass on the ground. Her eyes held a curious mixture of fury and startled awe. "It doesn't even hurt anymore," she whispered. She unzipped her jacket with trembling hands and then pulled the edge of her shirt up and yanked the bandaging down from her wound.

From where her wound had been.

Now only clear, pale, and unmarked skin showed where the shifter's claws had gouged her side. There wasn't even a trace of a scar.

She turned her face up to his, eyes wide. "Why did he . . . I don't understand. But I can't believe he's a monster when he went out of his way to do this."

Alexios nodded, gently removing the bandaging. When he was done, she lowered her shirt and closed her jacket, shivering in the chill air of sunset. "Why?" she repeated.

"Maybe penance," Alexios answered.

"Twenty minutes or so until we should leave for the meeting," Grace reminded him, as if he needed to be reminded. "If he's not here by then, we'll have to leave without him. The last thing I need is for a Seelie Court prince to be angry with me."

"We'll give him as much time as we can," Alexios said. "We don't want Poseidon's anointed priest angry with us, either."

Grace laughed, though the sound of it was shaky. "Talk about being caught between a rock and a hard place."

"Indeed," Alaric said from behind them. "I would hesitate to ask which one you consider me to be."

He was cleaned up and dressed in pristine clothes, though Alexios didn't know how he'd accomplished it in such a short span of time.

"So now we go?" Alaric asked.

Grace tightened her grip on her bow. "So now we go."

Alexios followed them down the stairs, saying nothing, realizing that there was absolutely nothing about this situation that he liked, and—worse—there wasn't a damn thing he could do about it.

Chapter 27

Grace looked around the beach where she'd first met Rhys na Garanwyn the week before and tried to ignore the chilling premonition shaking down her spine as simply a nasty case of déjà freaking vu. Tried to stop obsessively watching Alaric as he strode back and forth over the shell-speckled sand.

At the beach with a big, bad, and not so ugly? Check.

Seriously out of her league? Check.

But then Alexios touched her arm and all she could think was what a difference a week made. Then, she'd been alone and contemplating that final step. Sinking under the waves, never to surface. Finally to be able to rest, to release the burden of vengeance she'd taken up all those years ago.

Now, she was taking hesitant, baby steps into a future filled with light, warmth, and love. The last thing she wanted to do was risk her life yet again.

Not now.

And yet, here she found herself, between the proverbial rock and hard place she'd mentioned before.

Alexios bent down to whisper in her ear. "Don't forget that I am a Warrior of Poseidon and channel the power of water. And do you remember what it is that can vanquish rock?"

She grinned. "Water can. But we don't exactly have a couple of thousand years for erosion to do its magic if Rhys decides to turn us into bunny rabbits."

"I think I might have something to say about that," Alaric said dryly from the shadows.

"You're not the only one," Alexios said. He moved and she saw that he held his daggers. The Atlantean metal shone in the moonlight like shards of diamonds, as beautiful as it was deadly in his hands. She'd never known such a fierce warrior, yet somehow had never felt as safe as when she was in his presence.

It made no sense, but then again, neither did love. And she only had to look into his eyes or at his beautiful, scarred face to know that she'd already crossed over the line into love. The force of the realization literally knocked her back on her heels, and she stumbled.

Suddenly, some quality of the light changed, as if the moon herself blinked in surprise or Grace's ancestress Diana rode her silver charger to the hunt across its surface. Alaric hissed in a breath, and Alexios moved away from Grace's right side so she could easily use her bow if needed. She smiled her thanks, but then focused on the shadows between the shadows, knowing that was where the next move would come from.

And of course it did. Rhys na Garanwyn appeared in a clearing between clumps of sea grass and briefly stood there, almost posing, and then stepped onto the beach.

Shockingly, Alaric yawned. It took Grace a moment to recognize the sound, since it was so unexpected. The highest Fae royalty except for the Seelie Court king and queen themselves made a command appearance, and the priest yawned?

When the Fae laughed, she realized that Alaric's yawn had been a kind of posing, too.

"Ah, Alaric, you old fraud. Still playing at celibacy and other unnatural pursuits?" Rhys tilted his head, and his long fall of silver hair shimmered in the moonlight.

"Ah, Rhys, you old faery," Alaric responded, all the boredom in the universe heavy in his voice. "Still need a haircut?"

It was so unexpected that Grace laughed before she could stop herself, then she slapped a hand to her mouth, horrified and expecting to be turned into a frog or tree or sea turtle at any moment.

Alexios casually put an arm around her shoulder. "Nice to meet you, Lord Garanwyn. I am Alexios, one of High Prince Conlan's elite guard and Warrior of Poseidon. I understand you've already met my Grace."

Grace realized instantly what Alexios was doing: claiming her as his own so that to kill her or harm her in any way would be to possibly provoke an international incident. Something the Fae always tried very hard to avoid.

Of course the elf realized it, too. He bared his teeth in what might have been meant as a smile. "Of course. Any descendant of Diana is a possible consort of mine."

Alexios sighed heavily and muttered something that sounded like "here we freaking go again," but she shot a warning glance at him and luckily he didn't rise to the Fae's bait.

"And here is my brother," Rhys continued smoothly, gesturing to the beach behind them. Grace knew better than to fall for that trick, so she just grinned at him.

But then Alexios glanced over his shoulder and his body tensed. She slowly turned and found herself facing a mirror image of Rhys; dark where he was fair, cold and haughty where Rhys at least attempted the impression of seductive warmth.

"She is hardly worth the effort," the newcomer said, flicking a contemptuous glance up and down Grace's body. "These humans are dreadfully ugly, aren't they?"

Grace shrugged. She had no argument with the comment; compared to any of the Fae, she probably looked like a squat toad. Their ethereal beauty was far beyond any human ability to achieve.

"This is my brother, Kal'andel," Rhys said, and Kal'andel stalked forward, his black hair swinging out behind him. Together they were an art exhibit, the two Fae. Light and its photonegative, almost. But both had the cruel, calculating gaze of Fae royalty. That, at least, she had no trouble spotting.

Alaric subtly backed away until he and Alexios were flanking Grace, who didn't appreciate the implication that she was not tough enough to handle them, but she wasn't about to rock that particular boat.

"We're here. What do you want?" Alaric was so blunt as to be rude, and she had a feeling he'd done it on purpose.

"We would like to offer a birth gift to the newborn Atlantean prince," Rhys said.

His brother made a hissing sound. "No, we would not. This one is entirely on you, brother. I have no interest in pandering to these water dwellers or their kind."

"A view that is shortsighted at the very least, Kal'andel," Rhys said, his voice tightening just a fraction.

Evidently this was not a new argument for the brothers, but Grace really didn't want to get caught in the middle of Fae sibling rivalry. "Maybe we could get to the alliance part," she suggested.

Kal'andel leaned forward and, raising his head, actually sniffed the air. Grace had to resist the urge to check her deodorant.

"She doesn't smell human," he said, a faint look of surprise on his perfect, glowing features. "And she dares to interrupt her betters."

"She's human," Alexios replied. "She doesn't have any betters. And quit sniffing her. Can we get to the point already?"

Kal'andel snarled at Alexios, baring teeth that looked kind of sharp. Rhys smoothly took up the conversational thread, preempting whatever his brother had been about to do or say. "We would offer alliance, Atlanteans. Whatever ill-conceived plan the vampires are up to, it bodes ill for the rest of us. None but you have the strength to be anything like allies to us. We offer knowledge, battle skills, and strategy, in return for the secure knowledge of your alliance and commensurate efforts."

Alaric looked, for one brief, terrible moment, as if he would throw their offer in their face. Grace even had time to wonder how bad she would smell as a frog. But of course Alaric time didn't equal human time anyway. Almost before she could register the emotions flashing across his face, he was bowing to Rhys na Garanwyn and his brother, albeit somewhat sardonically. "I will return to Atlantis to discuss your request with Prince Conlan and his brother, the King's Vengeance."

Rhys bowed in return, although it was more of a nod, and then suddenly Grace and Alexios were alone on the beach with Rhys. Alaric and the dark Fae had both disappeared, seemingly into thin air.

"Should we worry about him?"

Alexios understood her immediately. "No, he's fine. He sent me a message on the Atlantean mental pathway that he's returning to Atlantis immediately to meet with the high prince and Ven."

"But you're still here," Grace said to Rhys. "Which means you must want something else."

"Actually, I have something to offer you. I understand

there is a gem you desire, a yellow diamond known as the Vampire's Bane," he said.

"How did you know about that?" Alexios demanded.

"We will waste much time if you persist on trying to discover the source of all of my knowledge. Suffice it to say that I know."

Alexios started to say something else, but Grace put a hand on his arm. "I hate to admit it, but he's right. The Fae never reveal their sources, like some sort of twisted journalists. But he knows what he knows, and it would help us to know it, too."

Alexios bared his teeth at Rhys na Garanwyn, but subsided. "Okay, tell us what you know."

Rhys raised a single, silken eyebrow, and Grace had to bite her lip to keep from laughing again. She would bet that the Fae was not used to being ordered around in such a manner.

"Vonos is having a ball tomorrow night. He has invited every person of any worth to him, both political and material, in the state. We need to be at that ball," Rhys said. "If you will come to Silverglen with me tonight, you will be able to rest in peace and safety, and then tomorrow we can prepare our strategy."

Grace was shaking her head before the end of the sentence was out of his mouth. "No. I won't go to the Fae lands. I know what happens to mere humans who get trapped in Silverglen. I don't want to suddenly wake up and find out I've lost eighty years of my life."

"I can protect you, Grace," Alexios said. "It might be a good idea to find out what he wants."

She shook her head. "No. I'm sorry, I don't mean to offer insult or be difficult. But my grandmother told me enough of the Fae that I have what I consider to be a healthy fear of spending any time in Silverglen."

"Fine," the Fae said, clearly annoyed. "I give my word you will not be harmed."

"One thing is really not clear to me," Alexios said slowly. "Why do you want to help us?"

"Other than the obvious—that it will be a good way to show faith as we begin a possible alliance?"

"Yeah, other than that," Alexios drawled.

"The vampire has something he took from me centuries ago, and I mean to have it back," Rhys said, an eerie golden light shining in his eyes.

"Okay, then," Grace said brightly, her senses warning her that something big, bad, and dangerous was near and not putting it past Rhys to have set them up in a trap. "If it's yours, you should certainly have it. If we can help, just let us know. Need to go now. Meet you later, 'kay?"

Rhys sadly shook his head. "No, I'm afraid I really must insist that you stay here and remain safe."

And then, before Grace or Alexios could move, he waved a hand and the inhumanly beautiful sound of Fae flutes sounded all around them.

Alexios pulled Grace into his arms just before she fell. "Damn it, I knew we should never trust the Fae," he said, his words slurring.

Grace couldn't even form the words to agree before the world went black. The last thing she saw was Rhys na Garanwyn's treacherous, laughing face.

Chapter 28

Alexios woke first, and thanked Poseidon that Grace lay in his arms, clearly sleeping and not dead. He stared around him at the eerie quality of the light that played along the walls of whatever strange room they'd been imprisoned in. It was gold one moment and an emerald green the next, as if they lay behind a flashing light post. He tightened his arms around Grace, silently vowing to himself never, ever to let her go within ten miles of any danger again, but she stirred and then opened those beautiful eyes and stared up at him.

"Where are we?" she asked, as instant awareness flashed into her eyes. "Rhys? What did he do to us?"

"We got elfed, *mi amara*," Alexios said, trying to remain calm and strong for her. Trying not to worry that he'd never be able to release her from an elven prison. "I'm not sure how to get out of here, yet, but I do know that we will."

She bit her lip. "How long have we been here? We weren't Rip van Winkled, too, were we?"

"What?"

"Did they steal time? Are we in the future now?"

"No, I don't think so. The Fae magic cannot glamour the Atlantean sense of time, and I feel no wrongness about the present," he said.

"Well, this is normally not a good idea unless you're dead, but let's head toward the light," she said, pointing at the distant edge of the space where they lay, which was considerably brighter.

He nodded, unable to find a flaw in the idea, then kissed her and stood up. He felt surprisingly well rested, considering that the Fae must have poisoned or magicked him in some way.

The light source was further away than it looked, and they had to cross through what looked like a river of light to get to it. Taking her hand, he nodded to Grace that they should enter together. Other than a strange rippling sensation, he felt no different on the other side.

But one glance at Grace showed him that they *were* different. She was staring at him with similar, openmouthed shock. Their clothing had changed, entirely. Grace was now clad in a long gown of shimmering turquoise, which glowed like a jewel against her honey-gold skin. Her hair was piled on top of her head in some fancy arrangement, and the diamonds at her ears and throat were certainly huge enough to gain them entry to a very posh party.

"You are beautiful," he said, awestruck. The subtle touch of cosmetics, when added to the overall effect, turned her into a goddess and he felt like an unworthy supplicant. It wasn't a feeling he much liked, and he reached up to loosen his tie.

His *tie*?

"You're not bad yourself," she teased, and he looked down to see that he wore the formal dress that the humans called a tuxedo. He noticed that his hair was pulled tightly back from his face and tied, too.

"Well, I don't think you'll see me in one of these again," he began, but then she gasped, cutting him off.

"Alexios! Your face!" Her own had gone dead white, and he raised his hands to his face, afraid suddenly that he would find that the right side—the only whole side—of his face had been scarred, too.

But instead the feeling underneath his fingertips was so unfamiliar that he couldn't quite comprehend it. "What—"

"The scars," she said. "They're gone."

Still walking, they suddenly stepped through a curtain of shimmering light and found themselves on yet another beach. Only this time the beach was a private stretch of sand in front of a true monstrosity of a mansion.

It could only be one place.

"Vonos's house," Grace said, a sneer on that lovely face. "Welcome to McMonstrosity."

"It's just a glamour," Rhys na Garanwyn said, appearing before them from thin air, as he apparently loved to do. "The scars. I'm sorry, but I have no magic to heal Hellfire."

What surprised Alexios the most was that the Fae appeared truly regretful, almost like someone who didn't have a slimy guttersnake for a soul.

Almost.

He went for his daggers, but grasped empty air and a fistful of fabric.

"Ah, yes," the Fae said. "Your weapons would have been inappropriate for a human reporter at a fancy dress ball, don't you think?" He pointed to a gray silk bag lying on the sand at their feet. "However, you will find everything you need in there."

Grace carefully managed to crouch down in her gown and heels so she could examine the contents of the bag. "My bow and full quiver and your daggers and sword," she reported tersely.

"And what exactly in the nine hells makes you think

that we would help you, after that stunt you pulled last night?" Alexios demanded.

"I believe you will help me because in return I will help you. I can get us into that house, and I doubt you could manage that without my glamour. Certainly the security team will have been warned to be on the lookout for Atlanteans, and your description is somewhat unique."

"Why me?" Alexios wasn't moving another step until he had the answer to the question that had been digging at him since he'd first talked to Lucas. "Why are the Fae interested in me, particularly?"

Rhys shrugged. "What makes you think we are? My lovely Grace could have just as easily brought only Alaric or another of your kind."

"And that wasn't an answer, although anybody not familiar with the Fae's truth without honesty techniques might have accepted it as such," Alexios said. "So I'll ask again. Why me?"

Grace put a hand on his arm. "Alexios, is this really the time? We're starting to attract attention, and—"

"I need to know, Grace. So?" He directed a challenging stare at the Fae lord, who would either respond or not. At least he knew that Alexios was on to him.

Rhys stared right back at him, and a lesser man would have dropped it. Good thing Alexios had never considered himself to be "lesser" at anything.

"We are interested in you," the Fae finally admitted. "You withstood the not-so-tender ministrations of Anubisa's hideous acolytes for two long years and emerged sane. We believe your experiences may prove . . . beneficial to know."

"You planning to get yourself imprisoned and tortured by the Apostates of Algolagnia?" Alexios bit off the words as the rage swelled up inside him. "Figure to use me as an experimental eel?"

"Eel? Really?" Grace smiled up at him, clearly trying to defuse the tension. "Not 'guinea pig'?"

Both men stared at her. "Humans," Rhys finally said, "are disgusting."

Alexios caught himself nodding and quickly scowled. "I'm thinking you don't have room to talk. What obscene tortures have you performed over your lifetime?"

"Okay. Enough. I'm going in now, with or without you," Grace said, pasting a brilliant and horrible fake smile on her face. "You can continue your pissing contest out here or help me find this diamond and learn what we can about Vonos's plans."

Then, never looking back to see whether he and Rhys were following her or not, Grace picked her way across the beach in those ridiculous shoes toward the mansion. Alexios sighed and started after her. After a few paces, Rhys fell into step beside him.

"You're in for a very interesting future with that one," the elf said, staring straight ahead at Grace's very lovely backside.

"Yes, I am," he said. "Now you were talking about security, and my 'unique description' before we got sidetracked?"

"Yes. If you can move past my unfortunate abduction of you so we can work together, our mission will have a much better chance of success."

As much as Alexios wished it different, he couldn't argue with the Fae's logic. And he needed the Vampire's Bane far too much to let a snit over their sleeping arrangements interfere with this chance to find it.

He gestured toward the house. "Lead on."

~~~~

Grace walked into the mansion with her head high and her heart in her throat. She'd never been so terrified in her life, and it didn't help that Rhys had been forced to conceal their weapons in a planter just inside the enormous wooden front doors. His glamour had held long enough for him to smuggle them in, and then the plant seemed to take over, acting as a coconspirator, brushing its thick, leafy fronds down and around the bag until even Grace, who knew it was there, couldn't see it.

"Just in case," she whispered, hoping they'd be able to reach the weapons if they needed them.

"Wonder what Sam would say?" Alexios said, grinning. "Nervous as a one-veined redneck in a roomful of blood-suckers?"

She laughed in spite of her jacked-up anxiety, and a few vampires near the door looked up and offered pleasant smiles. "Great, just great," she whispered. "Now they've noticed me."

"You're a reporter, remember," Rhys murmured, startling her. She'd almost forgotten the Fae's presence. "You're supposed to be noticed. Now go ask them some interview questions, so they don't wonder why you're not doing your job."

She rolled her eyes. "I'm a reporter, huh? The first reporter with no press pass, no notebook, and no tape recorder, but wearing diamonds that would buy and sell this house a couple of times over. Nice job helping me fit in, Sherlock."

Rhys waved a hand, and her necklace turned into a press pass and suddenly a small notebook and pen were in her left hand. "Now go investigate," he said from between clenched teeth.

"Fine," she snapped.

Alexios looked a question at her and she nodded. She was fine. She would be fine.

She hoped she would be fine.

He vanished into the crowd, his unscarred face and tied-back hair attracting little to no attention. Vampires were preternaturally beautiful, too, if scary pale. So the only one who would attract notice would be Grace Havilland, country mouse and human. Luckily, there were plenty of humans at this shindig. Hard to hide from a roomful of vamps when you were the only one with a pulse.

She sighed, ready to play Nancy Drew, and then she began threading her way through the crowd, asking a question here, making a comment there, and generally trying to look as much like a nosy, intrusive reporter as possible.

∼∼∼∞

Alexios had only two worries: one, that he would be too far away to protect Grace if danger came, and two, that he wouldn't find the Vampire's Bane before Rhys's glamour wore off and Vonos realized who he was. The last thing Alexios needed was for Anubisa to come after him again.

The pain in his hands finally alerted him that he'd clenched his fists together so tightly that they were aching. He forced himself to relax and, smiling and nodding at one and all, began searching for a doorway, alcove, or other possible entrance to a treasure room.

The usual rich folk and hangers-on were at this party, but not until Alexios turned a corner behind the dessert table did he meet a real thug.

"You tell me why you're trespassing back here, no?" The Russian accent, the thug-like expression. Prevacek.

"I got lost on the way to the bathroom, man," Alexios confided quietly. "Have had to pee forever but this old woman with orange hair didn't want to let me get away. Peter Parker, reporter. *Orlando Sun Times.*" He stuck out his hand with a friendly grin and hoped the old Russian mobster had never watched Spidey movies.

"Yes, yes, do not bother me now," the vamp muttered, lurking in front of a plain wooden door. "Am very busy and important. You move along."

"Yeah, sure. Bathroom?"

Prevacek pointed off toward the back of the hall. "That way. You go now."

As Alexios moved off, he saw a sleek, well-fed-looking human approach Prevacek. Instead of pushing him away as he'd done with Alexios, though, Prevacek pasted a smile full of teeth on his face and, looking quickly in both directions, pulled the human through the door, shutting it firmly behind him.

A touch at his elbow nearly had Alexios whirling around to attack, but Grace's voice murmured in his ear. "Ease down, big boy. What did you find?"

"Found Prevacek, but he was awfully eager to get rid of me. He found somebody he liked more, though—a human man who reeked of money."

Her brows drew together in a frown. "Was that monkey-looking guy Prevacek? Because that was Snyder, the real estate mogul who took over from Fuller, who went through that door with him."

"So the plot thickens," Rhys said, appearing from nowhere, again. "This Fuller had a nasty habit of chopping down forests to create parking lots and shopping malls. He was on our list, and now that he's dead, Snyder will be watched. Especially now that he's shown up here in very nasty company."

"You have a list?" Alexios wanted to hear this. "Who else is on it?"

"Well, the lovely Grace could be on it, naked, if she'd ever regain her sanity and dump you," the Fae said so smoothly it made Alexios a little nauseous.

He shot a glance at Grace and was pleased to see she was having the same reaction.

"You want me, naked, on the same list that had slime-ball Carson Fuller on it?"

Alexios grinned at the sound of the acid in her tone, but they didn't have time for this. "Focus, you two. Garanwyn, I'll kick your ass for you later. For now, we need to find that treasure room."

"It's almost certainly in the central panic room the architect designed, but we'll have to get through double default doors to get to it," Rhys said.

"And you know this how?"

"The architect and I had a little chat." The Fae grinned, a wicked leer on his face.

"I just bet you did," Grace said, rolling her eyes. "Was she a blonde or brunette?"

"Redhead," the Fae said. "A lovely, natural redhead, which is so rare these days—"

"Focus," Grace growled at him. "Why do I find it so interesting that Vonos is coming out of the door clear over there across the room from where his goon disappeared to with the real estate guy?"

"Plausible deniability?" Alexios suggested. "He's out here in plain sight while somebody else eats the guests?"

Rhys murmured something under his breath that sounded like a chant or an incantation, then nodded his head toward the door that was opening again. Prevacek and Fuller walked out, and both looked unreasonably smug. They started walking toward where Alexios and the others stood, but for some reason swerved and avoided them, never seeming to notice them.

"Another glamour," Alexios guessed, and the Fae smiled.

"Let's try door number one," Grace suggested, and they followed her to the door and then slipped inside.

"Bingo," Grace said, looking around with wide eyes. "This guy has got some money."

The door in front of them was shaped like a giant porthole, round and with bolts all around. And it was made of some transparent material that showed them another door just like it, but made of steel, behind it.

"Money and security," Alexios added grimly. "How are we going to get through this?"

Rhys simply waved his hands and chanted something, and the first door gently swung open.

"That's handy," Alexios said.

"Yes, but the extent of what I can do. This inner door is solid, fortified steel, with anti-Fae spells worked into the metal. I am hopeless against—"

The soft snick of lock tumblers falling into place interrupted the elf's words and he looked around, stunned to see that Alexios had opened the second door.

"It's a water trick," Alexios said smugly.

Grace just rolled her eyes. "Enough, boys; can't we all just get along?" She took a step into the inner room and whistled, beckoning to them to follow her in. "This is absolutely unbelievable! Vonos must have been collecting treasure forever."

"This is unbelievable," she repeated softly. "Look at that!" She pointed to a pyramid-shaped pile of golden objects that looked like it had been raided from an emperor's tomb.

"This isn't bad, either," Rhys said dryly, resting a hand on a chest heaped with glittering gems. Rubies, emeralds, sapphires, and diamonds filled the chest and overflowed onto the floor around it.

"If the diamond is in there, we're in trouble," she said. "How can we ever go through all of that? Not to mention I can't exactly smuggle the whole chest out in my bra."

Rhys swept his icy gaze over her and then smiled slowly. "I think you might be missing that item of clothing."

She gasped and looked down at the halter bodice of her dress, only to realize he was right.

"I think I will have your pointy ears on a platter if you mention Grace's undergarments again, elf," Alexios said, lifting a gold-handled, gem-encrusted dagger and pointing it at Rhys.

Grace rolled her eyes. "Seriously? We're in the middle of a treasure trove like nobody has ever seen outside of El Dorado, and you're going to fight about my bra? We need to get moving before Vonos gets back, because there's no way he'd leave all of this unprotected for long. He's no idiot."

"Thank you," a cold, dry voice said from behind them. "So didn't it occur to you that I'd have security? I've been watching your fumbling expedition from the beginning, curious as to what you were after."

"Oh, we're just lost on the way to the men's room," Rhys said, looking supremely unconcerned.

"That's good," Vonos replied. "I don't think a full bladder will bother you when you're dead."

Chapter 29

Grace was suddenly wishing she'd taken the time to make one final phone call to Michelle. And to Aunt Bonnie, though she hadn't seen her in years. To anybody, really. Just to say hi, how are you doing, sorry, I'm not going to be in touch much after I die an incredibly painful and permanent *death* this morning.

Yeah. Somehow that would have made her feel just a skinch better.

"Why?" The Primator stared at each of them in turn, obviously trying to use his vamp mojo on them, but he wasn't having any luck.

"We wanted to get a chance to ooh and aahhhh, that's all," she offered, since her two companions in crime were remaining woefully silent.

Alexios kicked a pedestal and it smashed to the ground, the sound shockingly loud in the walled-in room. "So, Primator Vonos, I hear you've been holding out." He stalked toward a tall pedestal at the center of the room that had been hidden by the fallen one. Then he pointed at the fist-sized square yellow diamond resting on a cushion. "If you'd told Anubisa about this one, there's no way she'd have let you keep your grubby hands on it, is there?"

For a split second, Vonos looked almost terrified. Then he composed his expression and laughed. "What does one such as you know of the most exalted goddess of Chaos and Night?"

Alexios turned toward Rhys. "Hit it, Your Highness."

Rhys nodded, and instantly Alexios's face returned to normal, the glamour gone.

Vonos stumbled back a step. "No. No, it's a trick. You cannot be Alexios from Atlantis."

"And yet, here I am," Alexios said, stalking closer to the diamond. "This baby belongs to me, too. Or at least it belongs to Atlantis, and I'm going to take it home now. So you have two choices. You can get out of my way, or I can use it on you."

"Did you think we'd let you get away with that?" The cheesiest Russian accent Grace had ever heard was still menacing when it came equipped with a very lethal-looking rifle.

And the rifle was pointed right at Alexios's head.

Prevacek stepped into the room. "You called, Master?"

Grace rolled her eyes. "I can't escape the Renfields this week, can I? Was it something I did? Some karmic payback biting me in the ass?"

Alexios started laughing, and the sound of his voice carried something warm from him directly into her heart. She figured it was time she told him something important.

"If I don't get the chance to say this again, I love you," she called out.

"I know," he said smugly, chuckling to himself.

"How touching," Vonos sneered.

"Oh, please. That's so Han Solo," she muttered, ignoring the vampire.

"I love you, too," Alexios said. "But can we hold the rest of that thought until I get us out of here?"

"How about until *we* get us out of here?" Grace fired back.

Rhys threw his hands into the air. "Excuse me? Is anyone forgetting the high prince, High House, Seelie Court, standing right here?"

"The what?" Vonos all but shrieked.

"Let me kill them now, my lord," Prevacek begged.

"Nooo, no. I will present all three of them as a gift for the goddess," Vonos said, all but rubbing his hands together with glee.

Suddenly, all the bravado currently inflating Grace's lungs vanished like a puff of imaginary smoke. Anubisa was coming. They were all screwed.

～～

Alexios didn't dare make a move when the Russian had that gun trained very carefully right on the middle of Grace's forehead. But he knew that seeing Anubisa again might be the end of his sanity. Now was the time for the risky move.

"Why didn't you tell her?" he called out.

Vonos slowly opened his eyes; he'd been "communing" with the goddess, probably. Alexios could only hope he'd gotten a busy signal.

"Trying to move up the ladder, bloodsucker? Enthrall some shifters here, wipe out a theater troupe there, and take over the god spot yourself?"

Vonos's eyes flared red, but he didn't answer. Alexios hadn't found the right button to push, yet. So he'd try again. "I'm just curious. Is the Vampire's Bane going to be part of the gift? Or will we be the 'please don't kill me for withholding' gift, and the Bane is the real gift? What about re-gifting? Is she really a fan?"

"I'd advise you to shut up," Vonos snarled. "The goddess is on her way to us now."

"There's no time for this, Alexios," Grace said.

Rhys simply nodded, but somehow Alexios knew that both of them were telling him to spearhead a charge to escape. Two vamps, one gun, three of them. He didn't like the odds, because all he could think about was the terrifying picture of Grace lying dead from a gunshot wound.

"I don't think . . ." he began.

"Don't think so much," she yelled. Then her hand whipped out and she grabbed a golden dish off the pedestal nearest her and whipped it at Prevacek's head. The Russian ducked, but the gun went off, shattering another pedestal inches from Grace.

Vonos realized what was going on just a fraction of a second too late to beat Alexios to the Bane, and his clawed hand closed around air as Alexios ducked and rolled, coming up on the other side of the pedestal with the Bane clutched in his fist.

"Use it now!" Rhys shouted from across the room. The Fae was tucking something silver and oddly shaped into his jacket, but Alexios couldn't get a good look at it.

"Now is a good idea," Grace said, crouching next to him, and Alexios lifted the diamond and called out "For Atlantis!" and aimed it in the general direction of Vonos and Prevacek.

For an instant, nothing happened. Then a powerful beam of yellow light burst forth from the diamond, rimming Vonos with light so that he looked like a skeleton caught in a flood lamp. Then he simply exploded right where he stood, screaming the most unearthly sound Alexios had ever heard.

"Where was Prevacek? Did we get him?" Grace asked, but he didn't know.

"I didn't see him. Rhys?" But the Fae was gone as if he'd never been there, and Alexios and Grace stood alone in a cell with a deadly diamond, while Anubisa was on her way.

"Out! Now!" He grabbed Grace's arm and they dashed out of the room, leaping over the scorch marks that were all that was left of Vonos.

They ran, dashing through the crowded great room of the mansion, shoving politicians and vamps alike out of their way, the diamond burning a hole in Alexios's pocket, calling out to him to use it, to destroy every vamp in the house. But it wasn't time, it wasn't even necessarily right; there were actually some vamps who were living in harmony with humans.

At least a few.

And he wasn't going to be judge and jury on those who hadn't murdered, plotted, and schemed.

It was enough for now that they had had retrieved the Bane for Atlantis. Another jewel in the Trident. Another step toward Atlantis rising.

But then Alexios heard the voice he'd prayed to Poseidon to never again hear in his lifetime. It was Anubisa, and she was screaming.

May the gods save them all.

Chapter 30

Grace's steps slowed as though she were trapped in molasses or cement or simply caught in the gaze of a vampire goddess who could squish her like a bug, thus bringing her full circle in a distinctly unpleasant way from her original meeting with Rhys na Garanwyn, the lousy rat who'd deserted them.

Everyone in the room started screaming and shouting and cowering at the sight of the goddess. Anubisa shone with a terrible, hideous beauty, but evidently she didn't much like Grace's dress, because with one negligent flick of her wrist, she sent Grace smashing into the front door. Hard.

Possibly all-my-ribs-are-broken hard. So Grace started praying, also hard. To Diana, who'd had reason in ages past to want to kick a little vamp goddess ass, or so Grace had heard. But her prayers were silent and her body was crumpled, so Anubisa dismissed her as nothing to worry about.

Grace only hoped to live to prove her wrong.

Satisfied, the goddess turned toward Alexios and beckoned him forward with one finger. "Oh, how lovely," she purred. "One of my own coming back to me. We will have such fun together this time, and I'll know better than to ever let you go."

"I don't think so!" The Russian was nearly guttural in his rage, and as he limped into view, pointing a pistol directly at Alexios's heart, Grace could tell why. Evidently he hadn't escaped the Bane altogether whole. The entire left side of his body and head was simply gone, leaving a charred mess of twisted flesh on what was left of him. The sight was hideous; a burned manikin limping along on one remaining leg. Grace felt like she was going to be sick from the smell of burnt flesh, and the sight of his half-incinerated head was pushing her farther over the edge.

Anubisa turned toward the horrible meat puppet and shuddered delicately. She was so beautiful that she probably even ripped the wings off flies delicately. Bitch. But a flash of heat and power trailed across Grace's crumpled legs just then, so she instantly released her rage and redoubled her prayers to Diana.

"What are you?" Anubisa asked, her voice filled with crumbling bones and rotted death.

"I am Prevacek, and I worked too hard for that tyrant for too long to give up the jewel," he blubbered out of the remaining side of his mouth.

Anubisa almost casually knocked him to the floor and he lay there, snorting and howling, but he didn't stand up again. He still had his gun aimed at Alexios's head, though.

Another flash of heat shot through Grace, and she cautiously, ever so slowly, straightened her legs and arms, rolling slowly and carefully toward the planter that was only about a foot away from where Anubisa had so considerately tossed her.

Toward her bow and the arrow that she would aim so exactly. The arrow that never, ever missed. Carefully, oh so carefully, she lifted an arm high enough to retrieve her bow and an arrow—luck was with her, or Diana was, and she drew a silver-tipped arrow on the first try—and she carefully fitted it into her bow, not even daring to breathe.

But evidently even the stealthiest movements of humans were no match for the hearing of goddesses. Anubisa swung around to face Grace, smiling that hideous smile, with her fangs fully extended and her eyes brightly, vividly scarlet.

"Oh, lovely," she said, clapping her hands. "A choice. I am delighted to have a game to play with your human whore, Alexios. Did you tell her how you begged me to hurt you?"

Grace heard a growl coming from her own throat, and she aimed the arrow directly at Anubisa's lying, nasty, torturing face. "I will kill you, you filthy bitch," she said clearly. "I will make sure you never, ever hurt an Atlantean again."

Anubisa, clearly insane, clapped her hands again and pealed out a joyful laugh. Everyone in the room tried to clap their hands over their ears, because the sound of her laugh caused eardrums to pierce and brain aneurysms to burst randomly throughout the crowd. The screams and cries seemed to make Anubisa even happier.

"A choice," Anubisa repeated. "You can save Alexios, your true love, with that arrow, or you can shoot me with it. But let's make it interesting. I know how noble you humans like to pretend to be."

She cast her glittering gaze out over the crowd and then squealed with such unholy glee that several people fell to the floor, unconscious or dead, from the sound. "I know! If you choose to shoot this miserable burned husk of vampire to save Alexios, I will murder every human in this room. But if you choose to shoot at me, I will simply order

Alexios's death and let the humans live. There! Isn't that fun?"

Grace said nothing, just calculated the time it would take her to reach for a second arrow. Before she could decide, the bag behind her, carrying her arrows and Alexios's gear, burst into flames.

"No cheating," Anubisa said, giggling wildly, like a demented child.

Grace turned toward Alexios in despair and locked gazes with him, hoping he could read everything she felt for him in that one last glance. It was a choice, but it wasn't a choice. There was no option. The lives of dozens of innocent humans or Alexios's life, freely given as the warrior he was.

He nodded, and she knew that he understood. That he was encouraging her to make the worst choice in the world. The one choice she would never be able to live with, instead of the choice that neither of them would be able to live with.

Anubisa started to say something else, but in one smooth motion, Grace drew back her bowstring and shot the vamp goddess directly in the heart. Expecting nothing. A puff of smoke, maybe, as Anubisa destroyed her arrow mid-flight.

Instead, the unthinkable happened. The arrow hit home.

The arrow *hit home*.

Anubisa started shrieking as smoke poured out of her chest and she yanked at the arrow, trying to get it out. Grace yanked herself out of her shock to leap up with some idea of running to Alexios, but a single gunshot stopped her in mid-step. Tears poured down her cheeks; she was afraid to look.

"It's okay, *mi amara*. The old man has a few moves left in him."

She whipped her head up to see Alexios, gun in hand,

standing over the body of Prevacek. Anubisa still writhed and screamed on the floor, smoke roiling out of her.

Grace decided it was time to make a dash for it. She jerked her head toward the door and Alexios shot down the hall toward her, both of them nearly to the door when a thunderclap of force boomed through the hall and forced them, almost against their wills, to stop and see what had happened.

Behind her, almost too faintly to be seen, a silvery female form fired arrow after arrow from her own phantom bow into the vampire goddess, who was screaming and shouting vile curses.

"It's Diana," Grace whispered, and for an instant, the silvery goddess seemed to meet her eyes. But then Anubisa screamed and the moment was broken. Grace and Alexios ran out of the building and into the moonlight, followed by a river of people escaping the titanic struggle between goddesses going on inside. Another thunderclap boomed through the air, and then the mansion shook and imploded, collapsing into itself, hopefully burying Anubisa for all time.

"It's too much to hope for," Alexios said in response to her unspoken wish.

"I know, but so were you," she said, throwing her arms around him and knowing she would never, ever let him go. "So were you."

They stood together for a long time, well after the sun had set and the moon rode high in the night sky, watching the pile of rubble for signs of disturbance. The firefighters, police, and EMTs had come and mostly gone, although there would be flashing lights and investigators around long into the night and in the days to come. She and Alexios had even answered a few questions, professing a complete lack of knowledge about the cause of the explosion.

After all, it's not like they could tell the police that a clash between the vampire goddess and the moon goddess had blown up Primator Vonos's mansion. Even P Ops would have had a tough time with that one.

"Should we go?" Alexios finally asked.

"Go where?" she replied, dull with exhaustion. "Home? I don't even have a home."

He pulled her into his arms and kissed her. "Your home is with me. I think it's time you see Atlantis."

"I think not," whispered a voice that shimmered with light and rang with the music of a thousand symphonies. "Rather it is time that my descendant met her ancestress."

Grace froze, then slowly pulled away from Alexios and turned. A woman stood between them and the sea, her feet in the water and her hair whipping in the cool sea breeze.

But, on taking a second look, Grace quickly realized that this was no woman, but the goddess. Power sparkled around her, crackling and sparkling in the long, waving strands of her hair, and the silver gleam of the moon itself shone from her eyes.

Grace dropped to her knees. "My lady."

Diana, for it must be she, laughed and the sea tides crashed on the shore and splashed a fine mist on Grace at the sound. She dared to look up only to find Diana untouched and completely dry in the center of the swirling waves.

"You have served me well, my daughter," Diana said. "You have earned a rest and are welcome to visit our allies under the waves. But beware: I will not stand for you to pledge yourself to Poseidon. I am a jealous goddess."

"How about if she pledges herself to me?" Alexios asked. "As I do to her?"

Grace gasped and yanked at his arm to get him to kneel beside her before Diana crushed him for his daring, but the goddess only laughed again.

"Yes, you have pledged yourself to her, have you not? And a worthy companion you are," Diana said. "Shall I gift you the removal of those scars. I wonder?"

Grace gasped again, but then stood up, not wanting to be on her knees for this discussion. Alexios looked into her eyes. "What do you say, Grace? Would I be more appealing to you without the scars?"

She smiled and then raised up on her toes to press a kiss on his scarred face. "It's not possible. I will love you no matter what happens to your face."

He caught her hands in his and gazed intently down at her. "And so you understand why your concern about aging and wrinkles is so unimportant. I will love you until the last waters fade from the oceans of this world."

"That is lovely and poetic beyond the telling of it, but I must away to other matters. Decide now," Diana commanded, and this time her voice held tsunamis and crashing destruction and the weight of ages. A goddess was a goddess, no matter how appealing. Grace made a mental note to never forget that.

"I think I'll stay the way I am, if I might ask another boon, my lady," Alexios said. "Will you offer your blessing on our union? I will promise to learn more of you, so that Grace and I may raise our children to know you."

Grace was speechless at Alexios's daring, but Diana merely tilted her head to one side, as if considering. Finally, she smiled. "I accept your request and bless your union, now and until the moon no longer crosses the sky. You will name your daughter Penarddun."

Grace felt like she was choking on the boulder that somehow had gotten lodged in her throat. "What? I mean, thank you, my lady, for your blessing. I will attempt to live up to it."

Alexios's mouth had fallen open but he snapped it shut, staring at Diana. "What daughter? We're going to have a daughter?"

Diana gestured gracefully at the moon. "In about nine turns of the moon, if I remember these things correctly. You shall name her Penarddun, and she shall be blessed by the huntress moon."

"Pregnant? Are you saying I'm pregnant?" Grace put her hands on her entirely flat stomach. "But . . . I . . . why Penarddun?" she asked stupidly, settling on the least important question of the hundreds whirling around in her mind.

"A showdown between the gods is coming. Yet another Doom of the Gods, as the wheel of the world progresses inexorably onward." Diana's face grew grim. "The ancient prophecy foretold that only a child who has blood from all races in his veins will save the world from the folly of the gods. Penarddun is to be part of that prophecy coming true, as shall the young prince, Aidan."

"But—"

"Enough!" Diana raised her hands into the air and the moonlight bathed her in a whirling vortex of spinning, shimmering light. "This is all I can tell you for now. Go to Atlantis. Meet your new family. We will talk again, my daughter."

And then she was gone. Grace and Alexios just stared into the air, at the empty space where she'd been, for a long while until Grace realized she was going to have to face him sometime.

"So," she began, at the same time he said, "So.

They laughed, and then Alexios put his hand on her abdomen, a look of wonder on his face. "My child? You are truly to bear my child?"

She nodded slowly. "So it appears, although I'm probably going to need a pregnancy test or two before I believe it. Modern medicine meets ancient prophecy, oh, my."

"Penarddun?" he said doubtfully. "It's a lovely name, but—"

"Penny," she said firmly. "We'll name her Penarddun, no way I'm disagreeing with a goddess who happens to be my ancestress, but we'll call her Penny."

He smiled, and it was like the dawn sunshine breaking over the waves. "Penny. I like it. Only fitting since you and she will always be my fortune."

They kissed, standing on the beach where a goddess had just foretold their future, for a very long time. Then he raised his head and sketched a gesture in the air. A shimmering oval began to form, and Grace caught her breath.

"Shall we take the diamond home where it belongs, *mi amara*?"

She wrapped her arms around her warrior—her love—and nodded. "Home, Alexios. Wherever you are will always be my home."

He kissed her again and then, together, they stepped through the portal and into Atlantis. As they passed through the magical doorway, she was certain that she heard her brother's voice, and she stumbled from the shock of it.

"Well done, baby sister. *Now* you live. For me, for yourself, and for your baby. Well done."

If there were tears in her eyes when she first stepped foot on Atlantis, she thought it was only fitting. Now. Now she would live, with love, light, and laughter.

Alexios smiled down at her, and together they and their unborn daughter took the first step into their future.

Turn the page for
a special preview of the next book
in the Warriors of Poseidon series

ATLANTIS REDEEMED

By Alyssa Day

Coming soon from Berkley Sensation!

Rome, 202 B.C.

Brennan fell against the stone wall of the tavern, laughing uproariously. "Another round for the house!" He fumbled in his pouch for a fistful of gold coins and tossed them on the serving wench's tray. Her dark eyes widened until he could see white all the way around her irises.

"But this is far too much," she protested, her gaze darting furtively toward the fat innkeeper. "He will cheat you, you know," she whispered.

He took the tray out of her hands and dropped it on a table, uncaring that the mugs and coins flew in all directions, then pulled her close in a drunken embrace. The generosity of ample breasts, overflowing the bodice of her gown, distracted him from his pursuit of ale for a moment. Her right nipple was barely covered by dingy lace, and he experimented with tightening his embrace to see if it would pop out entirely.

Sadly, his brilliant ploy didn't work. He inhaled a deep breath of the roasted meat and ale scent of the tavern and immediately wished he hadn't, as his head started spinning.

"So, my lovely one, is there some place more private we might go and I can give you a chance to earn even more of that gold?" He grabbed a fistful of her lovely round arse and squeezed, grinning.

But her face wore an expression of utter confusion. "I'm sorry, I don't know any foreign language," she said, almost cringing as if he would beat her for her failure. She sidled away from him and scrambled for the scattered coins, slapping the hands of greedy bar patrons trying to help themselves to either coins or free mugs of ale.

Brennan blinked, befuddled, but then he realized he must have been speaking in Atlantean, which he had a tendency to fall back on in times of stress or extreme drunkenness.

He spoke Atlantean a lot these days.

He felt the rumble coming up from his belly and managed to considerately turn his head to avoid belching in her face. "An—Another place? Private?" he managed, this time in her native tongue instead of his.

"Oh!" Her face cleared as she understood instantly. He probably was not the first, or even the tenth, of her customers to seek out a dark and private place with the buxom wench during the past several days. The thought momentarily sent a shudder of distaste through him, but as he released her and downed the bottom half of his mug of ale any misgivings vanished in a sea of effervescent intoxication.

Catching his hand, she dragged him through the cheering crowd of revelers, all raising a toast to their benefactor. He bowed sloppily, nearly tripping over the unfamiliar sandals, but the determined woman, almost certainly more enchanted with the contents of his pouch than with him, righted him with a steadying arm and herded him toward a doorway in the back of the tavern.

"Give her a good one, Brennan," one of his most regular drinking buddies, a Centurion called Sergius, called. "She likes it if you squeeze her tits while you tup her."

Brennan stumbled again, a disquieting sense of wrongness pervading his sodden mind. Why was he here? He was one of Poseidon's finest, finally called to service in the sea god's chosen elite, and he was rotting out his brains and his gut with second-rate women and third-rate ale.

The wench shoved the wooden door shut behind him and grabbed his cock through the heavy folds of his toga, and his doubts disappeared in a spike of lust.

"Now let's be seeing what coin you have for a poor innocent girl," she cooed, leering at him with pursed lips and with narrowed eyes that had not seen innocent in years. Then she squeezed his cock again, harder.

He roared out a great whooping noise and grasped her melon-sized tits with both hands. "Now that's the idea," he said. "Why don't you lift that skirt and let me see what you've got under there?"

As he bent his head to hers, the wench's eyes widened again and then went blank, almost fish-eyed, as they glazed over and then closed. Her head fell back and her plump body went limp, oversetting his already precarious balance so they both went crashing to the filthy floor. Some remnant of courtesy stirred Brennan to flip them as they went down so he landed on the bottom of the heap, cushioning her unconscious body from the fall.

"Well. I never had exactly *that* effect on a woman before," he muttered, staring around himself in befuddlement.

"AND SO YOU STILL HAVE NOT," a voice thundered through the room. Brennan's free hand automatically went to his dagger, but he found only an empty sheath.

"YOU THINK TO DRAW YOUR WEAPON AGAINST ME?" The voice continued, and now it sounded somewhat annoyed. Brennan's head tried to clear but the sheer quantity of ale he'd consumed during the day thwarted any attempt at mental acuity.

"I am a Warrior of Poseidon," he declared, but even to himself he had to admit the claim feeble, considering his present circumstances.

"YOU ARE MY WARRIOR, YES, THOUGH I WOULD BE MOCKED AMONGST ALL OF THE OTHER GODS WERE THIS TRUTH TO BECOME KNOWN."

Oh, *miertus*. This was one tsunami of an ale-induced hallucination, if Brennan suddenly thought he was hearing the sea god himself. He struggled with the limp weight of the wench, trying to move her to one side so he could rise and at least face this . . . whatever this was . . . on his feet.

A flash of silvery blue light shot through the dark room, and suddenly the woman was gone—vanished as if she'd never been there. Brennan leapt to his feet and whirled around and around, nearly falling down again as vertigo overtook him.

"What? Where did she—"

"THE WOMAN HAD NO PLACE IN OUR DISCUSSION. SHE IS NOW AT HOME IN HER BED, ALONE FOR A CHANGE," came the dry response.

"But why are you here—" Brennan belatedly realized that he was in no way showing appropriate deference to the sea god and dropped heavily to his knees. "My lord, accept my profuse apologies. Do you have need of me?"

"WHAT SAD EXAMPLE OF GODHOOD WOULD HAVE NEED OF SUCH AS YOU?" the voice thundered. "YOU HAVE TRIED MY PATIENCE WITH YOUR CONSTANT DRUNKEN DEBAUCHERY AND EXCESS. HADES HIMSELF, RULER OF THE NINE HELLS, ASKED ME TO GIFT YOU TO HIM."

"Hades?" Brennan struggled to follow the sea god's logic. His knees hurt from dropping to the stone floor and his head was thumping from the booming sound of Poseidon's voice. In fact, he was feeling quite sorry for himself and not a little beleaguered by his severe misfortune. "What would Hades want with me?"

"PRECISELY. A MATTER OF A SENATOR'S DAUGHTER, PERHAPS? BUT THE KNOWLEDGE THAT YOU HAVE FALLEN SO FAR, DRIVEN BY YOUR LUSTS AND EMOTIONS, THAT THE GOD OF THE UNDERWORLD WOULD DESIRE YOUR PRESENCE, SADDENS ME GREATLY."

"But—"

"SILENCE! BE ADVISED THAT I AM NOT A GOD TO ENDURE SADNESS. EVER. I AM NOW AT AN END OF MY PATIENCE. NOW THAT YOUR EMOTIONS AND HUNGERS HAVE DRIVEN YOU INTO THE ABYSS, I WILL REMOVE ALL SUCH FROM YOUR LIFE FOR ALL ETERNITY."

Brennan shifted on the floor, daring to raise his head and search yet again, but the sea god had only manifested his voice. "Not to be impertinent, but when you say eternity—"

Lightning and thunder crashed through the room, the percussive force smashing Brennan, facedown, into the ale-soaked stone.

"DARE QUESTION ME AND YOU WILL SPEND ETERNITY CLEANING THAT FILTH WITH YOUR TONGUE."

Brennan nodded, not daring to say another word, as the hot, slow trickle of blood from his battered head spread under the side of his face. Eternity. Silence. Got it.

"I CURSE YOU THUS: FOR ALL ETERNITY, UNTIL SUCH TIME AS YOU MEET YOUR ONE TRUE MATE, YOU WILL FEEL NO EMOTION. NEITHER SADNESS NOR JOY; NEITHER RAGE NOR DELIGHT."

Thunder crashed through the room again, and Brennan belatedly wondered why no one from the tavern had come back to investigate the storm taking place in their store-room before the sea god continued.

"WHEN YOU DO MEET HER, YOU WILL EXPERI-ENCE A RESURGENCE OF ALL OF THE EMOTIONS YOU HAVE REPRESSED OVER THE YEARS AND CENTURIES AND EVEN MILLENNIA."

Poseidon laughed, and his laughter contained all the sound and fury of storms at sea and civilization-destroying tidal waves.

"IF THAT ALONE IS NOT ENOUGH TO DESTROY YOU, YOU WILL ALSO BE CURSED TO FORGET YOUR MATE WHENEVER SHE IS OUT OF YOUR SIGHT. ONLY WHEN SHE IS DEAD—HER HEART STOPPED AND HER SOUL FLOWN—WILL YOUR EMOTIONS RETURN TO YOU, THUS ALLOWING YOU UNTIL THE END OF YOUR DAYS TO REPENT BRINGING DISHONOR UPON THE NAME OF THE WARRIORS OF POSEIDON."

Brennan, robbed of any coherent response as the enor-mity of Poseidon's curse sank in, just lay on the floor, stinking of blood and ale, still too drunk to comprehend the full extent of what was happening to him.

With a final crack of thunder, the sea god disappeared with a booming admonition. "REMEMBER."

The peculiar feeling of heaviness that always accompa-nied great power disappeared, and Brennan's ears popped with a sizzling burst of pain as they adjusted to its absence. Warmth pooled in his ear canals, and he wondered what had burst in his head and whether the healers would be able to repair what Poseidon himself had wrought.

Dragging himself up off the ground, slowly and cau-tiously lest Poseidon reappear and smite him, Brennan patted his chest and arms, reassuring himself that he was still whole. Once he found that he had sustained no bodily injury, he laughed in relief.

Except . . . he did not.

He did not laugh, and he did not feel relief. He felt precisely nothing, save for a vast, bleak emptiness in the wasteland of his soul where—just moments ago—his emotions had resided.

What Brennan did not know then was that he would not laugh again for more than two thousand years.

GLOSSARY OF TERMS

Aknasha—empath; one who can feel the emotions of others and, usually, send her own emotions into the minds and hearts of others, as well. There have been no *aknasha'an* in the recorded history of Atlantis for more than ten thousand years.

Atlanteans—a race separate from humans, descended directly from a mating between Poseidon and one of the Nereids, whose name is lost in time. Atlanteans inherited some of the gifts of their ancestors: the ability to control all elements except fire—especially water; the ability to transform to mist and travel in that manner; and superhuman strength and agility. Ancient scrolls hint at other powers, as well, but these are either lost to the passage of time or dormant in present-day Atlanteans.

Atlantis—the Seven Isles of Atlantis were driven beneath the sea during a mighty cataclysm of earthquakes and volcanic activity that shifted the tectonic plates of the Earth more than eleven thousand years ago. The ruling prince of the largest isle, also called Atlantis, ascends to serve as high king to all seven isles, though each are ruled by the lords of the individual isle's ruling house.

Blood pride—a master vampire's created vampires.

Landwalkers—Atlantean term for humans.

Miertus—Atlantean slang for excrement.

The Seven—the elite guard of the high prince or king of Atlantis. Many of the rulers of the other six isles have formed their own guard of seven in imitation of this tradition.

Shape-shifters—a species who started off as humans, but were cursed to transform into animals each full moon. Many shape-shifters can control the change during other times of the month, but newly initiated shape-shifters cannot. Shape-shifters have superhuman strength and speed and can live for more than three hundred years, if not injured or killed. They have a long-standing blood feud against the vampires, but old alliances and enemies are shifting.

Thought-mining—the Atlantean ability, long lost, to sift through another's mind and memories to gather information.

Vampires—an ancient race descended from the incestuous mating of the god Chaos and his daughter, Anubisa, goddess of the night. They are voracious for political intrigue and the amassing of power and are extremely long-lived. Vampires have the ability to dematerialize and teleport themselves long distances, but not over large bodies of water.

Warriors of Poseidon—warriors sworn to the service of Poseidon and the protection of humanity. They all bear Poseidon's mark on their bodies.